LETHAL
CODE

BY THOMAS WAITE

Lethal Code
Terminal Value

LETHAL CODE

THOMAS WAITE

47NORTH

This is a work of fiction. Names, characters, organizations, places, events, and incidents are either products of the author's imagination or are used fictitiously.

Text copyright © 2014 Thomas Waite
All rights reserved.

No part of this book may be reproduced, or stored in a retrieval system, or transmitted in any form or by any means, electronic, mechanical, photocopying, recording, or otherwise, without express written permission of the publisher.

"For You" by Bruce Springsteen. Copyright © 1972 Bruce Springsteen, renewed © 2000 Bruce Springsteen (ASCAP). Reprinted by permission. International copyright secured. All rights reserved.

Published by 47North, Seattle

www.apub.com

Amazon, the Amazon logo, and 47North are trademarks of Amazon.com, Inc., or its affiliates.

ISBN-13: 9781477825051
ISBN-10: 1477825053

Cover design by Stewart Williams

Library of Congress Control Number: 2014936918

Printed in the United States of America

FIC
WAITE

In 2012, FORMER CIA DIRECTOR AND
DEFENSE SECRETARY LEON PANETTA GAVE A
STARTLING SPEECH ABOUT U.S.
VULNERABILITY TO CYBER WARFARE:

"The collective result of these kinds of attacks could be a cyber Pearl Harbor; an attack that would cause physical destruction and the loss of life. In fact, it would paralyze and shock the nation and create a new, profound sense of vulnerability . . .

"Before September 11, 2001, the warning signs were there. We weren't organized. We weren't ready and we suffered terribly for that lack of attention. We cannot let that happen again. This is a pre-9/11 moment."

To the men and women who work tirelessly in anonymity defending the citizens of the U.S. against cyber attacks every day.

AUTHOR'S NOTE

While *Lethal Code* is a work of fiction, most of the technologies, cyber attack vulnerabilities, and cyber war scenarios contained in this novel are based on facts. As much as I would like readers to find this novel to be a gripping, entertaining thriller, I also hope it will illuminate the very real dangers our nation now faces.

CHAPTER 1

LANA ELKINS WATCHED HER daughter, Emma, sweep into the kitchen so quickly that she was immediately suspicious. More so when her fourteen-year-old positioned herself behind the cooking island, which could hide whatever skimpy outfit she'd just put on for school.

Lana waved her to the side. "Come on, let me see."

Emma's dark eyes flared as she moved begrudgingly into view.

"That's just over the top," Lana said, shaking her head at the gauzy mauve miniskirt. "You can't possibly sit and be decent in that."

"Yes, I can," Emma insisted, helping herself to a frozen waffle that Lana had toasted for her.

With her long black hair, fair skin, and freckles sprinkled delightfully across her nose, Emma bore a sharp likeness to her attractive mother. But the girl's getup worried Lana, who knew that some boys would stop at little if they thought they'd been lured.

The daily battle over Emma's outfits was getting tiresome. Lana had often wished a wholesome adult male were around to share the responsibility of child rearing, especially with Emma starting to experiment with alcohol. But the man who'd fathered Emma was neither wholesome nor present, having fled for good as Emma entered toddlerhood, which might have been for the—

Lana's thoughts were silenced by the lights turning dark in the kitchen. So did the matching sconces in the hallway a few feet away. A sunny September morning, but all the bulbs turned cold in a blink.

She looked around, listening to the refrigerator shut down. It sounded like a strangely human groan. The whole house seemed to settle at once, as if the power had drained not only from lamps and stove and radio but also from the concrete foundation itself.

She glanced at her watch: 7:40. In five minutes she was planning to drive Emma to school in suburban D.C.

"What's happening?" asked Emma as she stared at the blank readout on the espresso machine, a forkful of waffle frozen in the air.

"I'm not sure." Lana stepped to the bay window in the living room. Her neighbor, a pale-haired gent in his seventies, was peering up and down the street while wearing an aqua blue bathrobe, as if to spy a light in someone else's house. The weather looked clear, headed for another hot day, but Lana recalled no warnings about thunderstorms. "Could be a blackout from all the air conditioners," she thought aloud.

Pulling out her smartphone, she tapped a quick text to ask a few of her cybersecurity firm colleagues if the outage was affecting them. Strangely, her phone wouldn't transmit, despite being fully charged. With a sigh, she called up the browser to check the Web for news.

No service? Lana knew their phones should work. At the very least, she should be able to get online.

Emma, a famously fast texter, worked her own phone, and then looked across the living room with a "fix it" plea in her eyes.

"Everything's shut down," said Lana as she tried—and failed—to resend her text.

"What's happened?" Emma demanded.

"I'm not sure."

Lana pulled out her satphone, which connected directly to communication satellites, bypassing any earthbound blackout. That phone had service, so she feverishly tried other Internet service providers in the farther reaches of the country. None was available.

Emma drifted close to her side as distant sirens came alive in a chilling chorus. No blackout had ever shut off power to the whole country or knocked out ground-based communications so thoroughly. Those two startling facts kindled Lana's deepest fear: that a massive cyberattack had targeted the nation's grid, a conclusion based on all she had learned during her decade as a cyberspy at the National Security Agency—and in the years since she'd started her own security firm, CyberFortress. As far as the power and communications were concerned, the U.S. had just turned into one big blank. And if that were true, the next stage, which could come quickly, might be bedlam.

She grabbed her bag and fished out her key fob. "I don't think there's going to be school today. I need you to stay home until I find out for sure what's going on. Do *not* go out or open any windows. You'll just let the hot air in."

In any potential disaster, Lana knew you wanted to keep the house as airtight as possible for reasons far more frightening than hot air, but she spared Emma those fears.

"I don't want to stay home," Emma complained. "If there's no school, I'm hanging out with my friends."

"Listen to me, please." Lana stepped closer to her daughter. "First of all, there may be school. Just let me find out. But if there isn't, there could be problems today. Things should be fine, but if the power is off all around the area, people might start doing stupid things."

"What stupid things?" Worry softened Emma's voice, bringing out the child in the adolescent.

"I don't know," Lana said. "Hopefully nobody will do anything stupid. But I don't want you wandering the streets if this turns into an emergency. So stay inside and keep the doors locked. I'll come back and get you if this is just a local problem."

Fat chance, Lana added, but only to herself: Those sirens were growing louder.

She hurried into the garage, lifted the heavy door by hand, then headed directly for CyberFortress in her Prius. Her company had ample emergency power; hopefully, she'd get some answers there.

A lot of other people must have decided to seek greener pastures as well, because traffic was even heavier than usual.

Lana inched toward a railroad overpass, stunned when she failed to find a single radio station after scanning the dial. All she heard were those sirens. The radio's silence was yet another bad sign.

A shadow fell over her, and she realized she was under the trestle.

More stop-and-go eased her back into the bright sunlight. She found herself drumming the steering wheel.

Still moving slowly, she came to a stop on a slight rise about two hundred feet beyond the crossing. Seconds later, a horrendous screech of train brakes turned her attention to her rearview mirror. An Amtrak Acela Express was heading straight toward a Norfolk Southern locomotive with a long line of freight cars, including fuel and ammonia tankers.

Lana strangled the steering wheel when the two trains collided thunderously. The Amtrak slid toward the railing. The steel bent like licorice. Astounded, Lana watched the engine car tumble slowly over the edge of the concrete overpass. Passenger cars twisted off the rails one by one, flattening automobiles and SUVs across all four lanes.

She could no longer avoid acknowledging her worst suspicions, because they had just become tragically clear: *The grid's down. After all our warnings.*

Much of the work she did every day—often involving developing counterespionage measures against Chinese hackers—was meant to avert this very crisis: not just losing the grid, but all the devastation its loss would entail. It was unfolding before her very eyes.

The crushed nose of the Norfolk Southern locomotive pointed toward the ongoing tragedy, as if it were content to merely peer into the abyss. But not for long: The engine car broke through the demolished railing and also began to fall.

Lana saw a mother with an infant race out from under the engine car's shadow. But a man tangled in a seat belt made it only halfway out of his big pickup before he was crushed to death.

Boom-boom. Boom-boom. Boom-boom.

Cars on both trains slammed down from the elevated tracks in a perversely syncopated series of terrifying crashes.

Lana heard a lone scream, horrific and piercing—followed quickly by scores of others.

Then the explosions began.

CHAPTER 2

A TANKER CAR, FILLED with ethanol, blew up with such force that shock waves shook the Prius as if it were made of lint. As the flash widened—engulfing the vehicles closest to the tracks—Lana looked ahead, frantic to get moving. But nothing in front of her budged. She turned back and saw boiling flames, several hundred feet away, heading toward her and gobbling up cars. Then she witnessed a series of violent explosions as their fuel tanks blew up, adding to the pandemonium.

She opened the door to run when two things happened at once: The outside air hit her like a huge broiler oven, forcing her back inside, and the blue Yukon in front of her started to speed away.

She drove as close to the big SUV as she dared, wishing she could see past its high profile but grateful to be moving at all—and acutely aware of the explosions that were chasing her.

Another quick glance in her rearview showed that fireballs were now reaching where she had been idling only moments ago—and they were *still* mushrooming outward.

"Don't stop!" she screamed when the Yukon's brake lights came on, but the driver must have been tail gating as closely as possible, just like Lana, because the red lights blinked off a half second later.

Too fearful to look back, she continued to ride that bumper as tightly as she could, feeling the temperature in the car rise. Sweat dripped down her brow and burned her eyes, and she smelled smoke. But when she did look back, she saw that she'd widened the gap between herself and the burgeoning hell storm.

In Lana's side-view mirror, flames shot from the tops of mature cherry trees that had turned into tinder during the long hot summer. Cinders rose into the air, fiery seeds spreading the conflagration to a nearby park.

Up ahead, she spotted the first intersection after the overpass. She had driven through it countless times, but this morning it looked scary and surreal. The stoplight was dark, but somehow traffic just kept moving forward, which seemed like a miracle: that drivers—no doubt panicky themselves—were letting the cars in the most immediate danger pass through the intersection.

But it wasn't a miracle. It was heroism. Young adults in satiny blue robes had linked arms and stationed themselves in front of the cross traffic on both sides of the four-way to keep the passage open for those escaping the disaster. A bus, the same bright blue color as the robes, had pulled up on a curb, CAPITOL BAPTIST CHURCH CHOIR painted on its side.

Lana filled with gratitude, not just for herself, but for the people in even greater peril behind her. Those kids out there were lifesavers of the first order.

She also spotted dozens of people running *toward* the flames and ongoing explosions, some carrying first aid kits, others bottled water; many bore nothing more than their considerable courage.

7

Lana wanted to join them, but not with cars still behind her trying to flee the deadly train wreck.

After driving about a mile she spied a place to pull over. She rushed to her trunk and pulled out her running gear, which she typically kept stored away till lunchtime. In less than two minutes she changed into her cross-trainers, running shorts, and a sleeveless top, leaving her heels, hose, and blouse strewn on the passenger seat.

She raced off to see what she could do. She had no special training, though she might be able to administer CPR, having taken two classes when Emma was an infant. Mostly, she was able-bodied and thought she could, at the very least, help the injured away from the smoke and flames.

But the open intersection where the young choir members had saved the lives of so many motorists had turned into gridlock. A couple of hundred yards beyond it, the fire still burned the cars and bodies trapped in the hungriest flames. The park near the tall cherry trees was also fully aflame; dark plumes rose from the plastic playground gear and soccer field stands.

A whole new set of sirens rent the air, but she could not see fire trucks, ambulances, or police cars; access had been cut off by the chockablock cars, most of them now abandoned. People were running off, arms full of belongings.

The sirens grew so loud that Lana might not have noticed a young woman's cries for help if the teen hadn't been waving her arms frantically; the satiny blue fabric caught Lana's eye. A choir member, she realized. The girl looked just two or three years older than Emma. She was clearly distraught, huddling over a supine figure.

Lana hurried to her, finding the young woman cradling the head of a man wearing an identical robe. He was bleeding from his leg and hands. But his eyes were open, and he was conscious enough to notice her.

Crouching, Lana asked the girl how badly he was hurt.

"Real bad," she said. "I've got to get him out of here, but I need help getting him up."

"Maybe we shouldn't. What happened to him?"

"We had to stop those cars," the girl said, "but some of them wouldn't, so we made them stop by forming a chain, but they kept bumping us, and then one of them hit Shawn pretty hard and then just ran him over and took off. Then a bunch of other cars started coming through. I barely got him out of the way. They would have killed him," she added in disbelief.

Lana looked around. No help anywhere. "All right, let's move him, if you think he can walk. I've got a car."

"Shawn." The girl leaned close to him. "We're going to try to get you out of here."

Smoke swept over them. He looked around, clearly worried. So was Lana. The fire was creeping closer.

"What's your name?" Lana asked the young woman.

"Tanesa."

"Okay, Tanesa, you take one arm and I'll take the other. And let's be careful of his hands."

Shawn was lean, thankfully, but Lana and Tanesa still struggled to help him up. Once standing, though, he was able to put all his weight on his left foot. That's when Lana noticed that he was missing his right shoe and that his anklebone was sticking out of that foot.

"How close is your car?" Shawn asked in a shaky voice.

"Not far." Not true, but Lana wanted to give him hope.

She kept lying as he hopped along between them, an arm over each of their shoulders. Smoke billowed past them every few seconds. All of them coughed, Shawn most painfully of all; every movement made him grimace.

But Lana peppered him with lots of question, doing all she could to keep him from falling into shock. She learned that their prize-winning choir had just returned from a tour of rural churches in the Carolinas. He was an alto, Tanesa a soprano. Lana was already thinking of nominating them for community service awards, holding a fund-raiser—doing something to recognize their extraordinary courage.

After what seemed an interminable hike, the car appeared. But it was agony for the young man to get his right leg in the Prius. He pleaded with her to let him leave it out while she drove. That was inviting the foot's complete ruin, but all Lana had to do was shake her head and, with a mighty howl, he used both hands to yank his leg into the car. More than his ankle had been broken, she saw now. It looked like the bones in his lower leg had also been snapped.

Lana rushed him to the nearest trauma center, Bethesda's Suburban Hospital. Cars were already backing up.

"Tanesa, can you drive?"

"I've got my permit."

"It's an automatic. You take over. Inch along when you can. I'm going to get some help."

Lana saw right away that the hospital had power, but it was from generators, she learned from an orderly; all electronic communications were down.

The orderly grabbed a gurney and followed her to the car. Tanesa rushed from the driver's seat to Shawn's side. With another grievous howl, the young man got his leg out and was wheeled away. Tanesa called back to Lana, thanking her profusely.

"I'll see you later," Lana yelled. "Promise."

She had just paused for a breath when a cop rushed up and asked her to move the Prius, pronto.

In the scant minutes they'd been there, a massive lineup of cars had formed in back of them.

Lana pulled away, her thoughts turning to Emma immediately. "She's all right," she tried to assure herself. And when that didn't work, Lana tried reasoning: The derailment and explosions were about a mile from their house. That was uncomfortably close, but the trains had fallen on the Bethesda side of the tracks, which meant the first responders would have accessed the disaster from Kressinger, where she and Emma lived. She figured the first line of defense for the firefighters should keep the blaze from spreading into her neighborhood. As long as Emma stayed put, she should be all right. That might be assuming too much, Lana realized at once. What she wouldn't have given for a smartphone that worked. She tried her cell again anyway. No luck.

Driving home might take hours. CyberFortress, on the other hand, was just on the other side of Bethesda, and the company had emergency power.

That put Lana back on her original course to the bland-looking office park where she'd based her firm's headquarters. The entrance bore no sign, no fancy logo toying with the "CF" that was the shorthand everyone used in intracompany communications.

She found about fifty employees, about a fifth of her workforce. She wasn't surprised. Thankfully, they included Jeff Jensen, the crisply attired VP who handled internal security. He was running antivirus software of his own design on the company's network, which he'd delinked from the Internet. That was in case a worm on the Web had set off a contagion that might lapse only long enough to deliver a second blow—in emulation of terrorists who set off a bomb to lure rescuers to a far more lethal strike.

The power came from generators that Lana had built into the system. You don't work in the field of cybersecurity without having redundancy engineered into your power source.

"It smacks of a huge cyberattack," Jensen said, looking up to acknowledge her.

Lana nodded, glancing down long enough to see Shawn's blood on her leg and a small red smear on her sleeveless shirt. It had never occurred to her to change—a perk of owning the shop. Jensen, on the other hand, was in one of his dark blue suits. He didn't change colors often—the kind of guy who would always love a uniform, even one of his own making. He was a tightly wound thirty-seven-year-old Annapolis grad and veteran Navy cryptographer who had served in Afghanistan and Iraq.

"Why do you think it's a cyberattack?" she asked him.

"I can't access any DoD networks." The Department of Defense had three primary communication systems that escalated in security. But Jensen generally had few problems accessing the first two—as did far less benevolent hackers.

"Are you saying DoD is down?" Lana asked.

"Like a dead dog," Jensen responded. "And we're getting reports of some bad stuff in the District. Your friends at NSA could probably tell us a lot."

His eyes practically pushed Lana back out the door. Since she started CyberFortress, Lana's firm had done critical contract work on governmental counter-cyberterror. In each instance, she and her colleagues at the NSA had concluded that the U.S. was the single most vulnerable nation in the world to cyberattack because it was the most Internet-dependent of all countries, while having few effective defenses to fend off cyberwarriors, including the ones who might live down the block. CF's warnings—contained in a series of reports classified "top secret"—had been received with much approval by Congress and the White House, but little had actually been done to bolster the defense of the country's most critical communication systems.

Lana told Jensen and several other top staffers who had gathered near her about the Amtrak and Norfolk Southern collision, including a quick summary of the heroics of the Baptist choir. "Has anyone heard anything about that train wreck?" she asked those assembled. "Emma's home alone."

Phillip, a stylishly attired computer nerd, as odd as that sounded, said he had just driven by the edge of the suburb and had seen no evidence of the fire on the Kressinger side of the rail line.

"If Emma's home, she's in about as safe a place as you can find around here now," Jensen said.

"So what are you hearing anecdotally?" Lana asked, wondering how much worse the news could be.

"Sheila came in from the District this morning. Tell her," Jensen said to his younger aide, a Princeton Ph.D. who had bristled at times to find herself working for the Navy vet. ("Grow up, girl," Lana had told her. Jeff had earned his stripes, even if he had the overbearing personality of a career-driven technocrat.)

Sheila rested her hip on the side of a desk and nodded at Lana. "There was a bad subway collision near the Federal Triangle stop." Close to the White House. "I saw huge amounts of smoke coming up into the street, and people were staggering up the stairs. But the first responders couldn't even get close because the stoplights were out and there was no getting through all the jammed-up cars."

"Let's get you over to NSA," Jensen said. "We'll keep our eyes on things in Kressinger. Emma's probably more worried about you."

• • •

Emma wasn't worried about her mom. Emma wasn't worried about herself, or anything, except maybe suffering a boring day alone at home.

Seconds after her mom's car turned the corner, Emma had run over to Payton's house to hook up with her classmate for a morning of heavy petting and hickeys.

"Stop doing that," Emma finally said, pointing to her upper neck. "My mom's gonna freak out."

"Okay, okay," Payton replied, nodding numbly.

He returned to simply kissing Emma, at least for a few seconds. Then he started right back up again.

"Get *off* me." She shoved him away, stood, smoothed down her striped skirt, and announced that she was leaving.

It was only as she stepped outside that she saw the smoke. Most of the sky had turned black. And the sirens were wailing left and right.

Emma pulled out her phone to check for messages, but of course it didn't work.

Now she was scared. On instinct, she started running for home. And that's when she got her first whiff of ammonia. It burned her lungs and eyes and nose, and stopped her short. The second whiff dropped her to her knees. The third doubled her over.

Emma keeled to the sidewalk, coughing convulsively.

• • •

Fort Meade sounded like a sanctuary as Lana dodged pockets of traffic in Bethesda before jumping on the Beltway. She found relatively few cars on the famed thoroughfare, but the warning light for her gas tank came on. A single expletive slipped past her lips; even in a Prius, that red light was unnerving. It sent stress straight to her shoulder blades, where she carried it like a Sherpa. She hadn't seen a single open gas station. She also knew that if she found one, the line would be so long that she'd end up having to push the Prius to the pump.

She thought she had enough range to make it to the Army base, barring the unforeseen, though the morning was filling with the unexpected. Far more important, in the next few minutes she spotted commercial airliners heading toward both

Reagan International and BWI, the Baltimore airport, which meant that if this was, indeed, a cyberattack, the aggressors had spared civilian airlines. Those big jets were fatally dependent on the Internet for information vital to safe flight. Their presence in the skies suggested that the attackers had a base level of civility and were not completely insane, though colliding trains and horrific fires proved hollow consolation. While airliners were landing, only fighter jets were taking off.

Kinetic war is not going to help, she said to herself as an F-15 streaked across the skyline. "Kinetic" was the designation that cybersecurity experts used for traditional warfare.

With great relief she pulled up to Fort Meade's broad entrance, knowing that she would at least make it to the NSA. The guard stations resembled a big drive-through bank with a series of slots for mobile customers. The 9/11-sharpened procedures at the massive base were thorough but efficient, and within minutes she drove toward the arena-size parking lot that surrounded three sides of the agency's enormous black building, one of more than fifty structures that made up the intelligence complex. All of it was secured by heavily armed guards, electrical fences, antitank barriers, and a full panoply of security cameras and motion detectors. That was what you could see. Copper hidden inside the walls and one-way windows kept electromagnetic signals from the prying eyes—and instruments—of the outside world. A white structure that resembled a sheet cake sat atop the largest building, the one to which Lana was headed.

She gave thought to throwing on her skirt and top in the car, but as soon as she shut off the Prius, the unrelenting summer heat started baking her.

The moment she entered NSA headquarters, security staff escorted her up to Deputy Director Robert Holmes's office. His stout assistant, Donna Warnes, greeted her with a welcoming smile, an unspoken acknowledgment of Lana's key role in vacuuming up a particularly nasty bug that had attacked the agency's counterintelligence files three months ago. The bug wasn't the only thing that had been nasty. She'd had to butt heads with several in-house forensic stars to get the job done—territorial disputes in the cybersphere—but she'd prevailed and had received a commendation from Holmes himself.

Donna led Lana into her boss's large conference room, where he'd gathered five members of his top team at the end of a long table. Lana wasn't the only one in mufti; Ronald Wilkes, who oversaw much of the agency's liaison with congressional intelligence committees, was still in his tennis whites, which matched the color of his hair.

His blue eyes were all over her, moving from the blood on her long legs to the dabs on her cheeks, making the most of any excuse to gaze at her. He'd told her several times that he thought she was beautiful, loved her "jet black hair," "great cheekbones," "bee-stung lips." Lana considered it fortunate for the country that his work for NSA was more creative than his comments about her body.

Holmes, always the old-school gentleman, gave no obvious notice of Lana's gritty appearance. Unlike so many power brokers in Washington, the deputy director assumed the best about the people he surrounded himself with. If Lana Elkins had smoke smudges on her arms and blood on her leg and face, then she had her reasons. He confirmed his confidence in her in the next few seconds with an offhanded acknowledgment of her unusual condition.

"I think our trusted consultant here has already been fighting the good fight. Donna, please bring her water, coffee, and a damp cloth."

"It was bad out in Kressinger," Lana said. She explained what had happened to the Amtrak and freight trains.

"We heard about that," Holmes said. "Rail switches and signals have stopped working everywhere."

"Do you know if the fire has spread into Kressinger? I'm worried about my daughter."

"No, but an ammonia tanker exploded, and they're trying to evacuate everyone within about a mile of the track," Holmes replied.

"Jesus, that might include us."

"They're letting people know. Is your daughter inside your house, windows closed?"

"Yes," Lana said, with only a little confidence regarding Emma's whereabouts.

"She should be okay, then. And if you're too close, they'll evacuate her," Holmes added. "I wish our response to every crisis in the country was unfolding that smoothly. What else do you know about the overall situation at this point? Have you been at CF?"

"Yes. I understand the Web is down, and Jeff Jensen said the military networks have failed."

"That is correct. *We're* getting our information piecemeal, and it's worse over at DoD." He shook his head. "Go ahead, tell her," Holmes said to Joshua Tenon, a more immediate contemporary of Lana's.

Tenon tugged nervously on a salt-and-pepper beard that hid his recessed chin and gave her a quick nod. "The Eastern and Western Interconnects are down." The two big grids that covered the U.S. "Texas is down, too." The Lone Star State had its own grid. "So all of the U.S. has lost power, along with parts of Canada and northern Mexico."

That made sense to Lana: The power links among the North American nations did not have a strict respect for borders.

Donna set coffee, water, and a facecloth on the table for her. Lana wiped away the blood on her leg. Holmes pointed to her cheek, and she cleaned that off, too, as Tenon went on:

"China cut itself off from the rest of the world immediately, and has suffered very little damage, if any. All of their electric and rail systems have switched to non-networked control systems, and they're using backup radio."

In the parlance of the spy trade, China had "pulled up the drawbridge." China could do that because it was a far less open society than the U.S. Moreover, from a cybersecurity standpoint, it was notably ahead of much of the world, so it *could* cut itself off from the Web.

"But what's interesting," Tenon said, "is that China might not have even been targeted. Russia, Europe, Asia, Australia, South America, Africa, and the Middle East are hardly affected at all, compared to us."

Lana nodded. "And I saw commercial aircraft."

"That's right," Tenon replied. "That unwritten rule has not been violated."

"What about banks?" she asked. Another unwritten rule. The U.S., for instance, never launched a cyberattack on Iraqi banks during its wars, though the U.S. had the capacity to ruin that country's financial system.

"There's no sign yet that the banking community is subject to a direct attack. Of course, they can't operate without the Web."

"But we're not seeing the wholesale destruction of bank records?" *Let's cut to the chase*, she thought.

"No, but again, we should add a big 'yet' to any assessment of that nature," Tenon replied.

Holmes leaned forward. "But there's plenty of bad news, because a lot of other systems have failed. We have train wrecks in more than fifty locations, including downtown Chicago and Los Angeles, pipeline explosions in Michigan and Wisconsin, and there are reports of chemical plants in New Jersey releasing massive amounts of chlorine." Another deadly gas. "We've got miners stuck underground, and people stuck in elevators." He shook his head. "And without power, evacuation is a nightmare in most of those places. There's more." Holmes nodded at Teresa McGivern, a veteran NSA analyst. "Show Lana what we're seeing on our own network."

McGivern, spry and nearing retirement, clicked the keyboard on her computer, and a flat screen came alive on the wall across from Lana. A huge fire bloomed as orange as a California poppy field.

"That's a gas pipeline right outside Atlanta," McGivern said. "It could turn into a firestorm, and it's definitely heading toward my hometown." The analyst lent a trace of her Southern roots to her voice. "And this"—she clicked her computer keys—"is the Miami harbor. Those are cruise ships, though you'd never know by looking."

No, you wouldn't, thought Lana. She'd used that terminal on her honeymoon, and now it was burning down, just like her marriage had when Emma was two years old and Lana finally realized that she had more than one toddler in the house. Three massive vessels were on fire, sending up smoke plumes the size of skyscrapers.

"We suspect that logic bombs were placed in the ships' computer systems to overload the electrical circuits." Logic bombs could lie in wait in a computer network until signaled. Then, after overloading electrical circuits, for instance, a logic bomb could erase all data that might make its presence known or even traceable.

"Were the ships full?" Lana asked.

"To capacity. And all the sprinklers and smoke alarms were disabled." McGivern spoke without emotion. She'd been at NSA for decades and had seen a world of horrors. But Lana's insides were twisting tight as hawsers.

"This is another pipeline explosion," McGivern said. "It's near Denver, but as you can see, it's already moving through national

SIMMS LIBRARY ALBUQUERQUE ACADEMY

forest land. It's possible that it will turn into the state's biggest wildfire ever, because heavy winds are expected for the next week and there's not a drop of rain on the horizon."

"Do we know how many fatalities we've got nationwide?" Lana asked Holmes, knowing he would be slated to make any comments about that sensitive issue. The extent of casualties was not in Lana's purview, narrowly speaking, but after looking at pipeline explosions and those incinerated cruise ships, she had to ask.

"Minimally, just this morning? Tens of thousands would be a conservative guess," Holmes replied. "That's what we're releasing to the media, the few who actually made it to our door to get answers. But in truth? We could easily be looking at more than a hundred thousand fatalities. This makes 9/11 look like a piker's picnic." Holmes cleared his throat, and his gaze took in each of them. "We're at war."

Hearing that from a man as serious as Holmes sent a chill straight to Lana's core. For the first time in her life, real war had overtaken most of her country. Not with bombs or bullets or missiles, but with software written by anonymous hands and delivered in stealth and silence. Cowards with codes. She couldn't wait to lock on to them in the cybersphere.

Whoever the hell they are.

"What galls me most," Holmes said, as if reading her mind, "is that we don't even know who's attacking us." He pointed to the screen. "But we're sure seeing what they're capable of." He glanced at his watch. "It's been two hours, and our homeland has already suffered more overall damage than in all its previous wars combined."

What was notable, Lana thought, was that neither Holmes nor anyone else at the table was rushing to speculate about the perpetrators of the attack, though numerous suspects came immediately to her mind and, undoubtedly, to theirs as well.

"It's going to get worse," Tenon added with another nervous tug on his beard.

That wasn't news in nearby Washington, D.C. Smoke was already drifting over the White House.

CHAPTER 3

RUHI MANCUR DIDN'T SEE the smoke rising above the city, much less the plumes drifting over the Capitol. Not yet, anyway. His eyes were on a smooth footpath that meandered alongside the slowly flowing Potomac River, his favorite part of the morning's eight-mile run.

He heard sirens, but that wasn't unusual in Washington. Neither was it unusual for him to ignore them. When he hit the trails, he paid little attention to anything but the American pop of his immigrant youth. His parents had brought him to D.C. from Riyadh, Saudi Arabia, when he was seven, and he loved listening to his iPod. Right now it was filling his head with the exuberance of Cindy Lauper's "Girls Just Want to Have Fun." He never tired of her anthem, always recalling her crazy dresses and hair, and the brightly colored bangles and bodices that made her look like an exotic tropical species with a rich plumage all her own. Living under the House of Saud, he'd never seen anything remotely like Lauper, that's for sure. For him, the pop star had always personified the irrepressibly relaxed wonder of America.

But right now her music helped him ignore the world as he put his body through its rigors. He was a broad-shouldered veteran of fourteen marathons, and Lauper had made many of those miles bearable. So even on a bad day, the frenetic interference of the nation's capital was a poor opponent of Ruhi's amply armed iPod. And a brisk Monday-morning run was an altogether marvelous way to start his week, before going to work at the Natural Resources Defense Council, NRDC. He liked to think that the organization got some "mileage" out of the irony that he hailed from a country in which oil accounted for ninety-five percent of its exports and seventy percent of its profits. Very much the lapsed Saudi.

But as Ruhi headed back to Georgetown, the sirens and alarms grew uncomfortably loud and vastly more numerous until they bled over one another and forced him to recognize that they were going off all at once. It was like cell phones in a crisis, which, from all appearances—a rush of ambulances, fire trucks, police cars—was taking place.

That's when he paused and emerged from his endorphin fog. Traffic lights were not working—and they hadn't been since he'd turned from the river. He'd been darting across streets on automatic pilot. But now he recognized a change in the city's pulse. Cars were doing a fair amount of darting as well, slowing down and then blowing through dark intersections. Their scurrying reminded him of the city's rats when headlights lit them up. But admittedly, he wasn't a big fan of the country's automobile culture, which was strike two against him as an expat Saudi, because his countrymen had long adored American muscle cars.

Moreover, he spied an urgency in the drivers' faces that made him wary of sprinting across any more streets. Better to dodge and feint and take nothing for granted. As an urban runner— fleet-footed, but calm in demeanor—he was accustomed to the mindless quirks of motorists, but the gunning of engines and screeching of brakes was all out of proportion to the simple power outage that he observed. In short, he sensed a palpable panic beyond the measure of ordinary turmoil.

Everywhere he looked—cars, cabs, pedestrians—people appeared on edge. *Nothing* had power. No cheery welcome or open signs blazed in shop windows. And there was no Internet, either, to judge by the frustrated reactions of people staring dumbfounded at their suddenly not-so-smart phones.

Ruhi had left his at home, as he generally did for his daily run.

He turned down M Street, one of Georgetown's main thoroughfares, and headed home, passing a Starbucks where the green-apron brigade was busy apologizing profusely as it ushered customers out the door—*sans* java.

Not far from his apartment, Ruhi ran right past the location of Alexander Graham Bell's first switching office more than one hundred years ago. That irony did not elude him, either.

As he bounded up the granite steps of an old, distinguished townhouse, long ago converted into a tony fourplex, he had to step aside for Candace Anders. She'd moved into one of the upstairs units last month—and shot right to the top of Ruhi's list of desirable neighbors. That was saying a lot about Candace's blond, ponytailed appeal, because Ruhi's leafy street had lots of eye candy of the female persuasion.

"Do you know what's going on?" Ruhi asked Candace, as casually as if they had shared much more than passing nods on those steps.

"It's definitely a power outage," she said, which, of course, added little to what Ruhi already knew.

But he had gleaned a fair amount about Candace from the Web, once he learned that she was a recent hire of her conservative Indiana congressman. That made her one of "them," in Ruhi's world: a climate-change denier and tool of Big Oil and Big Coal.

It was hard not to peg them quickly when you were the director of research for the NRDC. Ruhi knew the congressional roll call as well as the sergeants-at-arms of the House and Senate.

Before he could riff on power outages and the nation's insatiable appetite for energy, Candace went on:

"It may actually be a lot more than a glitch in the grid. Somebody running by said the blackout is all across the country."

"Really?" That stunned Ruhi. It would be a first, according to everything he had read about power outages in his adopted country, which was voluminous. "A *total* blackout?"

"That's what I heard—" She sounded like she'd cut herself off.

"What?" he asked.

"Well, there was a rumor flying around the Capitol that a cyberattack had been launched by jihadists."

"Oh, no," he groaned. As a dark-skinned Middle Easterner who had endured his share of open hostility in his adopted country after 9/11, he was mindful of what that rumor could mean.

"It's not confirmed."

"But it was the first one to come up, I'll bet," he replied.

She didn't disagree.

He hoped to God his countrymen hadn't done anything now. They'd had a notorious role in the attacks on the World Trade Center and Pentagon. The last thing he wanted to hear was that more religious zealots had claimed the mantle of Mohammed to serve their own earthly needs. He just wished he could convey his harsh judgment of extremists to a dark-suited guy in a Lincoln Navigator who was giving him the stink eye as he drove by.

He and Candace paused at the top of the steps to look down the street. Neither said a word for several seconds. He wanted to see if she'd continue the discussion. In truth, he figured Candace probably held deep suspicions about Muslims, even lapsed ones like him. That was strike three, in the view of most Saudis.

A man in a pinstripe suit swore loudly as he hurried past them, working his phone with both thumbs. Then he looked around and declared, "Nothing's working," before jamming the device into his pocket.

"I can't get online, either," Candace said. She looked at Ruhi expectantly. "You?"

"I don't have it with me."

"That's a first for this town. I'm not saying it's jihadists, but it does smack of a cyberattack."

"What makes you say that?" It hadn't occurred to Ruhi, but the possibility sure grabbed his attention. He knew plenty about energy consumption and distribution in the U.S., and if this was, indeed, a nationwide problem, cyberattack made grim sense.

"I guess it could be a Martian invasion," she said, "but short of aliens, nothing else explains it."

"Bombs would. A tightly coordinated widespread attack might."

"We'd know about the attacks," she replied. "We'd have instant reports, instead of an instant loss of power."

"If that's the case, we're in serious trouble," he replied. "This could go on and on. Do you know about 'just-in-time delivery'?"

She shook her head.

"It's a wonkish kind of thing."

Happy to have her attention, he explained that the U.S. was highly dependent on centralized power plants that replaced broken parts—even the most vital ones—on the so-called just-in-time delivery principle.

"It's just the opposite of 'in stock,'" he went on. "It means that if a cyberattack on a power plant forces a big turbine to spin so fast that it tears itself apart, it could take six months before anybody can build the replacement and put it in place. You can thank deregulation for that." *Starting with your boss*, he almost added.

Candace shook her head and lifted her eyebrows, which Ruhi found an endearing way to disagree with him. In fact, it made him wish that he'd left out the jab about deregulation.

"If it is a cyberattack," she said, "we'd better start thinking about China. Or blowback for our cyberattacks on Iran. I wouldn't be the least bit surprised if they'd decided to retaliate massively and anonymously."

He was surprised to hear those words coming from a staffer for a congressman who'd supported every war the U.S. had engaged in for the past four decades.

"Have you had a chance to tell your boss that?" he asked mischievously.

"No! I like my job."

She smiled, and it occurred to him that he might be cultivating a source on a conservative congressman's staff.

Or she's cultivating you.

Jarred from their conversation by a boisterous crowd of about fifteen young men—late teens, early twenties—racing around the corner. They spotted him immediately and yelled "raghead."

Oh, shit. That's also when he spotted huge funnels of smoke rising into the sky from the heart of the nation's capital.

"What's going—"

Ruhi interrupted Candace by taking her arm and hurrying her to the door of the converted townhouse. Locked, of course.

The young men were stampeding now, perhaps spurred by his own rush to get inside. He looked back and found them only two townhouses away, fury contorting their faces. They had closed the gap to within a hundred feet. He heard Candace swear under her breath as he fidgeted with his key. He looked again.

Fifty feet.

He knew he was going to get severely beaten, at best. He didn't even want to consider what might happen to an ingénue from the drought-stricken cornfields of the Midwest who was audacious enough to consort with a "raghead."

Twenty-five feet.

He managed to work the key into the old lock, but it was catching on something.

"Come *on!*" she whispered.

He *hated* that lock. He jiggled it frantically . . .

Ten feet.

. . . and the lock slid open.

She rushed inside. He followed a breath behind, slamming the door and locking it just as the thick wood thundered from pounding fists and boots. Unseen hands grabbed the handle and tried to force it open. He thought he heard a gunshot.

"My place," she shouted. "Upstairs."

They raced past Ruhi's first-level apartment and up the broad stairs that rose from the grand old entryway. He heard the door rattling behind them and looked back as an elderly neighbor stepped out of her downstairs apartment.

"Go back inside," Ruhi stopped to yell. He gestured wildly at the front door. "And lock up!"

"What?" she said, slowly inserting her hearing aid.

A loud crash turned their attention to the front door. The mob had split the top part right down the middle. Two gunshots plowed into the handle and lock. Ruhi was sure about the shots this time, but the door still didn't give.

A face appeared in the opening. Ruhi felt like the easiest target in all of D.C. The guy's gaze followed Candace rounding the top of the stairs. Ruhi was glad the man wasn't the shooter.

"Go back inside," Ruhi screamed at the older woman as he resumed his sprint up the stairs. But she had figured out the threat on her own and was hobbling into her apartment.

Ruhi was sure he was dead if the mob broke down the door. This was much more anger than the worst animosity that he had experienced after 9/11. And the guy who had his face in the opening had glimpsed where he was headed.

"This way," Candace yelled as he reached the top of the stairs.

He ran into her apartment. She threw a bolt lock into place in less than a second. Then she raced to what looked like a jewelry box and pulled out a 9-millimeter Beretta, matte black and wholly menacing. While he watched, she popped the clip, checked the load, and jammed it back in. Then she shocked him further by pulling two spare clips from the "jewelry" box.

"Over here," she said, setting up behind an antique oak armoire.

She was rapidly turning Ruhi's gallant notions of rescuing her on their head. He couldn't have been more grateful. Guns? He wasn't raised with guns. But he was fortunate, he realized, to have ended up next to a farm girl who appeared more than competent with semiautomatic weaponry. Maybe that's what they did on dates out there in farm country—went shooting. *Who knows?* Rural America could have been Pluto, as far as he was concerned.

"The first time someone touches that door," Candace vowed, "I'm putting a bullet through the top of it. They do it again, I'm lowering my aim. These babies penetrate."

She reminded him of those Korean grocers in Los Angeles, back in the '92 riots, who had saved their stores by fighting off mobs of looters with carbines. Ruhi had been a kid, but he remembered the video like it was yesterday.

"I thought you just got here from Indiana," he said. She looked and sounded like she'd been running a crew where times were tough and gunplay plentiful. Which, as it turned out, was true:

"From Indiana via guard duty at the embassy in Kabul."

"No kidding?"

She nodded, but her eyes were on the door because someone was smashing the hallway fire extinguisher through the top panel, and gunshots plowed into the lock. But you needed more than a couple of bullets to knock out a strong bolt.

As soon as the red canister reappeared, she fired, as promised, into the lintel. But a half second later, someone bashed an even bigger hole with the extinguisher, and a hand came through the opening, searching blindly for the handle. They heard hellacious shouting and swearing in the hallway and pounding on the door.

Candace shook her head and rested her shooting hand on the edge of the armoire.

What?

Ruhi was sure she'd lost her nerve. He reached for the gun, figuring one of them needed to pull the trigger.

"No!" Candace snapped.

"Sorry." He backed off.

"Stop," she yelled toward the door, "or I'll shoot *you.*"

The threat didn't discourage the guy—or he failed to hear her amid the pandemonium. He tried the handle, and then groped blindly for the lock. A second later, he found it.

Candace squinted and fired twice. The first bullet grazed his arm; the second tore through the back of his hand and buried itself in a thick horizontal board in the middle of the door.

The guy's screams and profanities filled the room. He tried to jerk his arm out of the opening, catching his sleeve on a jagged edge of shattered panel long enough for Ruhi and Candace to get a good look at the wound. It was a couple of inches below his wrist. Then his hand disappeared and they heard the mob thundering down the stairs, shouts and threats receding as they raced away.

Candace immediately rushed to the side of the door, holding her pistol in both hands with the muzzle pointed to the ceiling.

She wheeled and aimed through the opening. Ruhi braced himself for the worst. She held her fire.

"You're not going out there, are you?" he asked.

Candace shook her head. "Not right now." She never moved her eyes from the opening when she spoke. Her soft countenance had vanished, replaced by a rigid, determined look. Now Ruhi had no difficulty imaging her performing guard duty in Kabul. Or leading a platoon in Afghanistan's notorious Korangel Valley, for that matter.

Who is she?

"Is there any way I can help?" he asked.

She shook her head. "But I can't spend the night in this place. Look at that."

Candace nodded at the ruined door. Blood splatters darkened the area near the handle. Big drips spotted the hardwood floor.

"You're more than welcome to stay in my place."

She gave Ruhi a skeptical look that he had seen on the faces of other women.

"I don't mean *that*," he protested. "I'll sleep on my couch."

"I'll consider it," she replied.

But she was still staring at the hallway, as if she didn't believe it was actually empty.

• • •

"Get off me," Emma mumbled. "Get *off* me."

It felt like Payton's mouth was pressing down on her—again. On the sidewalk! And there were sirens, but when she opened her eyes it wasn't Payton at all. It was blurry, but she was pretty sure an African American guy was giving her mouth-to-mouth resuscitation. Except he wasn't using his lips, not directly. He had some plastic thing over them.

Whoa. What's going on?

"What are you doing?" she managed as the plastic thingy fell away.

"You're going to be all right, young lady." Now the guy was picking her up and moving quickly with her in his arms.

All right?

That's when the pain returned—with a vengeance. Her eyes and the insides of her nose and mouth felt burned. So did her lungs.

Just as she took inventory of her agony, she was flopped onto a gurney with folding legs and shoved like a pizza into the oven of the ambulance.

A sweaty white guy dripped on her as he placed an oxygen mask over her mouth and nose, and offered the same solace as the African American: "You're going to be all right." Drip-drip. Except he added, "Hang in there."

Hang in there? Emma's thoughts were a muddle, but *Hang in there?* Didn't that really mean that you might *not* hang in there? You might frickin' die?

She didn't want to die, but passing out right about now would be really nice because her throat and nose and eyes hurt like *hell*.

Emma glanced to her left and saw that she wasn't the only injured one in the ambulance. Sitting strapped onto a jump seat was a skateboarder from her homeroom. He was holding his arm, which was bent kind of funny, and looked like he was in grievous pain. He'd wrapped his other arm around his board, as if worried that one of the paramedics would make off with it. His good hand held a phone. He tried it, shook his head, then turned his gaze to Emma. His eyes skipped down her body quickly, growing big as Dunkin' Donuts.

Why? she wondered.

Tentatively, she reached down and found her short skirt hiked up to her hips.

Oh, no. My panties.

And not just any underpants; that was the really embarrassing part. She'd been in such a rush that she'd worn some funky old ones she'd found under the corner of the bed: *Dora the Explorer.* They were a joke. A joke! Last Christmas her mom had given them to her as a stocking stuffer.

The humiliation. The *scandal.* Dora the Explorer underwear—in *high school!* Emma could have screamed, but it hurt too much. She tried to wriggle her skirt down. Couldn't manage it. But a female EMT, whom she hadn't noticed, leaned into view and gave her hem a businesslike tug. The guy from homeroom looked away.

Wait, he had his cell phone out. Did he take a . . . picture?

Phones aren't working, remember, she told herself, giving herself a moment's reprieve. But then she wondered: Maybe the phones don't work. Maybe the Net doesn't. But the camera? That's an "internal function," as her mother would put it.

Oh, God. Oh, God. Oh, God.

She glanced at him. He was looking at her once more, but her face this time. And he was pretty damn cute.

• • •

Lana bolted from the massive NSA building and ran to her car, desperate to get home to check on Emma. Deputy Director Holmes had made sure that she was given a fuel allotment at the Fort Meade pumps, now powered by generators.

That put Lana back on surface streets within fifteen minutes, where traffic had lightened considerably. People had either fled their homes and businesses, or hunkered down for the duration—whatever that might turn out to be. Horrifyingly enough, Holmes had said that widespread power outages could, in reality, persist for *months.*

The nationwide blackout was scarcely four hours old, and even as she had conferred with Holmes and the others, disaster reports arrived from two Gulf Coast ports where supertankers, fully loaded with oil, had collided. And a container ship bound for China had crashed into the north pilings of the Golden Gate Bridge. The destruction had been well planned.

Panic had gripped the nation so quickly that it astounded her. All morning, reports were filtering in of widespread looting in more than a dozen metropolitan areas, including Washington itself, and in suburban towns with staid reputations. Gripping fear clearly knew few borders or socioeconomic barriers. And there was no way for the president, a consummate communicator, to speak to the American people: another first.

Besides, what could *he say?* Lana wondered as she sped onto the Beltway.

With a kinetic attack, Congress would be rushing to declare war, granting the commander in chief the right to bomb, invade, and absolutely level opponents who had inflicted even a tenth as much damage to the country. One hundredth as much: Look at 9/11. But with physical weapons—missiles, bombs, bullets—you knew who had attacked even as the weaponry took its toll. That hadn't always been true—especially with terrorism—but in the twenty-first century it had been all but impossible for a country to escape responsibility for wide-scale violence directed against its enemies. Fighting a cyberwar, though, was like trying to tackle fog. There was nothing to hold on to, or even see. Nothing you could pound to rubble.

Lana made good time but passed so many fires that she felt certain the attackers had planned to maximize the visual impact of their otherwise invisible electronic firepower. The rising columns of smoke looked like the iconic photographs of Baghdad during the U.S. invasion.

The first Bethesda exit was still several miles away, but she saw thick black clouds filling the sky from the Amtrak–Norfolk Southern crash. Then, as she neared the beleaguered town, she caught grim glimpses of almost a mile of freight and passenger cars burning.

She planned to take an exit ramp one town past Bethesda, if she could, and loop around to her house. But she came to a crawl quickly as flaggers in orange vests directed all four lanes of traffic into one. It was the first semblance of traffic control that she'd seen since the church choir had held back cars near the train collision. She thought those kids should receive a presidential commendation of some sort, or at least front-page attention in the *Post.*

Lana didn't know why she'd been squeezed into a single lane until she moved close enough to see that the ones to her right had been turned into a staging area. Bodies, neatly bagged in black plastic and lined up next to one another, were loaded into troop transport trucks—even as more of the dead were off-loaded from smaller Army vehicles.

Exits were blocked for another three miles. Then she spent forty-five teeth-grinding minutes navigating bottlenecked traffic; drivers, she guessed, who had plans similar to her own.

As she neared her house, the radio suddenly came alive. She thought, *Oh, thank God!* believing the outage was over—*finally*— and the attack withdrawn. But the invaders—that's how she thought of them, even if they couldn't be seen—had taken over the airwaves. A monotonic computer voice delivered a message:

"We are communicating to the American people directly. Not to your leaders. You are under attack. Count your blessings that we are not using bombs. We are more humane than your leaders. We are using your own technology to make your lives difficult . . ."

Difficult? Try deadly, asshole.

"We demand that the American people tell their leaders to remove U.S. military forces from its seven hundred and fifty foreign bases. Send home all your ships, tanks, fighter jets, bombers, and service people. Remove all your missiles. Stop all your invasions. Stop all your cyberattacks on foreign powers.

"This is your only hope, Americans. If your country does not return its forces to its own borders, we will burn you to the ground. Look around. Do not doubt our ability to turn you to ash. Look at what we are doing to you today."

The message began to run again. It was on an NPR station, clearly powered up for this sole purpose. Lana figured the attackers had long ago inserted a "trapdoor," software that allowed them to take control of the airwaves today.

On the third listening, she found only two noteworthy usages in the text: "blessings," used idiomatically in "Count your blessings," and the threat to burn the country to the ground, which suggested that the attackers' aims did not include a complete conflagration—yet.

"Blessings," she thought, certainly could be used by a secular entity, but more likely hailed from a religious person.

Or people who want to make it sound like it came from the mouth of a believer.

North Korea? she asked herself. The message had the crazy menace of the "Supreme Leader," or whatever antic title the latest one had taken. And the North Koreans had been busy building a cyberarsenal—and using it: On July 4, 2009—*Happy Birthday, America*—Unit 121, reputedly North Korea's slickest cyberattack team, with upward of a thousand warriors, had hacked into classified information on more than 1,350 hazardous chemical sites in the U.S. Some of those sites contained chlorine, a gas used to devastating effect in World War I.

That's right—the chlorine in New Jersey. Deputy Director Holmes had told them that there were already releases of the deadly gas from chemical plants in the Garden State.

But after she made that unnerving connection, she reminded

herself that releases of chlorine gas hardly nailed down the North Koreans as the culprits. There were numerous cyberwarriors in scores of countries—*including our own,* she reminded herself—capable of launching a new and very different world war.

Still, if you walk like a duck and quack like a duck, you're a goddamn duck, and North Korea had already attacked the U.S., so it was not difficult to imagine that country doing it again. Moreover, Lana could not help but suspect the Stalinist state because of its underlying message in 2009: *The great America is vulnerable to the mighty North Korea.*

The subtext was not a complete exaggeration: To pull off its 2009 coup, Unit 121 had turned 166,000 computers into robots, or "botnets," as they were called in the trade. The very word made Lana shake her head. Basically, it meant that the North Koreans transformed vast numbers of computers into zombies that carried out their commands.

Most people, including Lana, had experienced inexplicable slowdowns in the functioning of their desktops or laptops. Sometimes that was because a hacker had hijacked some of the devices' power. It was agonizing to accept that today's attack might have harnessed much of the country's own computer power—and then turned it on itself. Roughly speaking, she thought it was like putting a pistol into someone's hand, pointing it at his head, then using his own strength to pull the trigger.

The North Koreans had surely sharpened their cyberwarfare skills since the end of the century's first decade. Could they pull off an attack of today's magnitude? She looked at the smoky skies and knew the answer was a terrifying "maybe."

Those were her thoughts as she pulled into her driveway. Without pausing, she pressed the automatic garage-door opener, and then tossed it onto the passenger seat in disgust.

She ran to the front door, finding it unlocked, which infuriated her: *When is Emma going to learn to lock up around here?*

"Emma?" she shouted, once inside. "I'm home."

No response. She charged from room to room, stricken with fear when she saw that her daughter had left the house.

After double-checking, she raced outside, looking up and down the block.

It's a ghost town.

She hurried back to her car, planning to drive over to check with Amy Burton, one of Emma's closest friends. If her daughter wasn't there, then she would troll the streets. *And then what?* The police stations and hospitals, much as she didn't want to allow for those darker possibilities.

As she closed the car door, the old gent from across the street—the guy she'd seen in his bathrobe a few hours ago—came rushing out of his house, fully dressed this time and waving his arms.

She jumped out of the car, realizing, as he hurried up with his eyes on her blood-smeared top, that she still hadn't changed. He panted loudly, bending forward to hold his thighs for support.

Her first thought, admittedly uncharitable, was *Please don't die before you tell me what happened to Emma.*

"She collapsed," he gasped, sounding as if he might fall over as well. "Your girl, over there." He pointed to the sidewalk down the street. She looked, but there was no sign of Emma. "I mean when the ammonia cloud passed over us."

"What?" Then Lana remembered Holmes mentioning the crashed ammonia tanker and the evacuation order for within a mile of the tracks.

"But—but," her neighbor sputtered, "they were warning everyone to get inside and were right there with an ambulance. Really, I didn't even have time to get their attention." His breathing had calmed. Lana's chest, though, felt as tense as barrel staves.

"Was she okay?"

"I know she was alive. The cloud passed over us quickly, and they administered mouth-to-mouth. I could see from my window."

"Do you know where they took her?"

He shrugged. "Maybe Suburban? They have a trauma center."

"I was just there this morning, about eight thirty," Lana said, opening her car door.

"This was later, closer to ten o'clock. They gave a lot of warnings. I don't know how your girl missed them."

"I've got to get going."

He shooed her off. "I'll have her in my prayers."

As soon as she cranked the ignition, the radio started replaying "A Message to America," or whatever inanity they were calling it. She swore cathartically as she switched off the dial.

It was impossible to find a parking spot within five blocks of Suburban. Lana grabbed her bag, strapped it across her chest, and took off running. As she neared the hospital entrance, she felt faint from all her rushing around, and remembered that she hadn't eaten since this morning.

She forced herself to walk and pulled an energy bar from her bag, all but inhaling half of it before deciding that she'd better save the rest. It was not like they had a big supply of food at home.

When she saw people waiting eight deep at the hospital's information desk, she pulled out her NSA laminate to try to look official, despite her worn appearance, and walked the corridors on her own.

No one stopped her. Every hospital employee was clearly in triage mode, and every hallway was crowded with beds and gurneys, IV stands and chairs—and suffering patients.

She came across Tanesa and Shawn up on the second floor. His leg was in a cast that extended from midthigh down to his toes, the plaster already blazoned with a couple of green Sharpie "get well" greetings. An odd bit of normalcy for such a bizarre and distressing day.

"You're back!" Tanesa exclaimed with a wide smile. "You really made it back here." She hugged Lana. "He's doing okay," she volunteered, nodding at Shawn. "They said his bones had clean breaks." She nudged him. "Do you remember—"

"Sure," he interrupted, beaming at Lana. "You got me here before the big line formed." He reached out with both of his bandaged hands, and she hugged him, too.

"I'm glad to hear you're feeling better," Lana said, "but my daughter was exposed to ammonia from an overturned tanker car and might be here."

"Upstairs," Tanesa said, taking her hand. The girl turned to Shawn. "I'm going to show her where they took the ammonia people."

"Yes, go," Shawn said, looking concerned.

Tanesa rushed Lana toward the stairs. "They're not running the public elevators. Saving power."

"Smart."

"I heard they brought in a dozen people who'd breathed in some of that stuff," Tanesa said.

"Were they okay?"

"Don't you worry," Tanesa said as they stepped from the stairwell. "They're amazing in this place."

The third floor was less crowded than the first two levels. Lana spotted Emma almost immediately in a room with three other patients.

"How are you?" she asked as she rushed to her daughter's side.

Emma's eyes glistened with salve, and she spoke so softly that Lana had to lean close to her lips. "Sore throat. Gave me painkillers. Not supposed to talk."

Lana held her girl's face in her hands, marveling over finding her alive and intact. She wanted to claw apart the people who had done this to her kid.

Tanesa leaned in and said, "I'm going to leave you two."

"Not before I introduce you," Lana said, regaining her composure. After the formality, Lana told Emma how Tanesa and her friends had saved her life and the lives of many other drivers.

"Wow," Emma mouthed.

"I'm going to run back down to Shawn," Tanesa said, "and let you two have some space."

"Thanks so much for your help," Lana said to the young woman.

"Back atcha," Tanesa volleyed, heading out the door.

Lana stayed by Emma's bedside, providing sips of water all day. When the girl fell asleep at about four, she raced over to CyberFortress, but Jeff Jensen and the others had no news; even their contacts remained in the dark.

That night Lana slept in Emma's room, and didn't awake till almost seven a.m. A stocky nurse checked on Emma and the other patients, as he had during the night.

"She's doing well," he whispered to Lana; Emma was still sleeping. "She was very lucky," he went on. "Paramedics literally saw her fall down and were right there. She might not be doing so great if they hadn't been."

Lana nodded, gripped once more by a raw anger that she'd never before known. The term "mama bear" took on a whole new meaning for her.

She asked about the protocol for ammonia inhalation victims.

"We're going to release her in a little bit. She should take liquids, nothing solid, until the burns heal. Her burns aren't bad, but they're internal, so food would definitely make her uncomfortable. We're guessing she'll be feeling a lot better in a few days."

"Is there a doc I can talk to?"

The nurse shook his head. "I'm sorry, but you would not believe what we're dealing with. Your girl has a head cold compared to what we're seeing down in trauma."

About ten minutes after he left, Emma awakened. As Lana helped her daughter climb out of bed to use the bathroom, her phone rang. For what had been such a common occurrence, it sounded extraordinary, almost miraculous.

She got Emma settled quickly and answered it. Donna Warnes from Holmes's office was calling. Power had returned across the country exactly twenty-four hours—to the second—after the grid went down. The deputy director of NSA wanted Lana to come to Fort Meade as soon as possible.

Then Donna delivered the big news: Congress would be convening within the hour. There was talk of declaring war. But there was a huge obstacle: With the country bleeding, burning—and with thousands dead and thousands more dying—no one, not even America's finest military minds, knew where to point the guns.

CHAPTER 4

LANA HELPED EMMA THROUGH the crowded, noisy hospital lobby, eager to get her daughter home and safely settled so she could head out to Fort Meade as soon as possible.

The child was a little woozy from painkillers, and Lana had to hold her close as they started down a sidewalk that bordered a packed parking lot. She explained that their car was a few blocks away.

The high heat hadn't hit yet, but the sun still felt uncomfortably warm until they found the shade of maples a few minutes later. With cool air on her damp skin, it seemed surreal to Lana that such horrors could have struck on a bright, beautiful, and seemingly normal summer day.

Emma, on the other hand, appeared only dimly aware of her surroundings.

Just as well, her mother thought, considering what they were about to drive past on the way home.

She helped Emma into the passenger seat and hurried around the car, eager for the A/C but annoyed by the initial blast of broiling air that had been heating up under the hood.

She had to remind Emma to put on her seat belt. The girl nodded but still looked a little out of it. When she fumbled with the device, Lana helped her. Typically, Emma would have minded anything she perceived as meddling, but she leaned back and closed her eyes.

"That's a good idea. Take a nap."

But as soon as Lana pulled away, Emma stirred.

Within minutes, smoke heralded the grisly train collision and raging fires. Then, to make matters worse, a troop transport truck turned onto the road right in front of them. Lana had a bad feeling about that, quickly confirmed when the vehicle braked, stopping all traffic behind it.

Out of the corner of her eye, she watched Emma stiffen when a soldier lowered the tailgate, offering a view of body bags stacked several feet high. Men and women loaded nine more victims aboard.

"What happened here?" Emma asked, mostly mouthing the words.

Lana kept it brief and as appropriate as possible, a challenge with a massive train wreck and nationwide devastation. She reminded Emma of what Tanesa and her friends had done to save her mom's life and the lives of so many others. The girl nodded solemnly as the soldier closed the gate of the troop transport truck and it pulled away.

But Lana quickly realized that it was like finding yourself stuck behind a school bus, because every block or so the truck stopped again. Instead of opening its door to boisterous children, though, the vehicle idled as the soldier lowered the tailgate so rescue workers could load more body bags. There was no way to get around them—and no mystery about the victims in the smaller bags or where they came from: Passenger train cars still burned in the distance.

As the troop transport pulled away again, Lana thought of Congress convening in the midst of this mayhem to consider a declaration of war. She wondered if the country was required by law to identify the enemy before such an act could be passed. It was such a basic question, yet in all of U.S. history, she doubted that it had ever come up. Why would it have? But that question, more than any other, had to be hanging over every discussion at the Capitol today. Congress would never declare war if it had to leave a big blank space where the name of the enemy should be. It would be hard to imagine a more blatant display of powerlessness.

A large part of her mandate at NSA would be trying to determine the aggressor. She'd handled cyberforensics on many other cases for the agency, including the North Korean breach in '09 and the mostly hapless attempts by Iran to strike back at ongoing U.S. sabotage of its nuclear ambitions.

Much as she loved her daughter, Lana wanted to help her country respond to the crushing toll of the invisible invasion. She'd arranged for a friend to come over and take care of Emma.

The radio came alive with a man's dulcet tones, not the monotonic computer voice that had delivered the heavy-handed propaganda she had heard earlier. It sounded like NPR had managed to get itself back into broadcast mode in remarkable fashion.

"I once lived in your country. It was in Detroit, not so long ago . . ."

A foreigner, she figured, though his accent was light. Probably commiserating with America in its time of greatest need. She remembered similar expressions of sympathy after 9/11, and made no effort to search for another station. She found his easy emphasis soothing, and thought he could be narrating a children's book; but then she realized that he was telling the most terrifying tale she'd ever heard:

". . . all your military power cannot protect you now. It will only leave you cold and dead. That is because our cyberwarriors have leveled the playing field of war, and they have done it for the cost of one of your attack helicopters.

"I am not exaggerating, America. Look at what we have done with so little. We have killed more than fifty thousand of you in twenty-four hours, almost as many as all the U.S. soldiers who died in the Vietnam War, and that lasted eleven years. It will be weeks before you can confirm that number, but we are confident of its accuracy because we calculated the impact of every action we took."

Lana was torn between wanting—*needing*—to listen, and exposing Emma to such a horrific recounting of those murderous hours, most of which the girl had spent sedated in the hospital. With a quick shake of her head, she reached to turn off the radio, but Emma put out her hand to stop her. Lana relented.

"They were terrible deaths. You do not even know the many ways your fellow Americans died. But we do. Again, that was because we planned so carefully and for so long. Thousands are still dying. This morning and tomorrow morning and for many mornings to come, they will wake up to chemical contamination that will last years.

"We warned your leaders about our plans. They never told you. We announced to them that we would shut you down for a full day . . ."

"That's a bald-faced lie!" Lana said to Emma.

The girl didn't respond, even with a nod. She leaned closer to listen.

"They thought we were bluffing. We even told them exactly when it would happen. They still didn't tell you. So from now on we will speak directly to you. We now have the means to do so, and if we are blocked, we have other ways to communicate to large numbers of you. We want to talk to you directly because we do not trust your leaders. You should not, either. They are deceitful, and their intransigence is killing you. Not us.

"We have made our requests clear. America must withdraw all its troops and military hardware to its borders and abandon all its foreign bases . . ."

More of that bullshit, Lana thought.

". . . That is all we ask. That is a very simple way to have peace. But your leaders refuse to take even such a small step.

"So this is what we are going to do next. Without further announcement, we will shut you down for good. We won't say when. It could be tomorrow or the next day, or next week, but it will happen soon. We promise."

The troop transport truck stopped again. Lana braked. She glanced at Emma, whose eyes were pinned to the soldier lowering the tailgate again. Just as Lana was about to ask Emma if she was okay, her daughter glanced at her. Lana took her hand. Emma didn't resist. It was the most intimate moment that they'd shared in months. Lana didn't dare spoil it with words—but someone else did:

"Next time we will attack everything. We will include your banks and passenger jets, which we spared during the twenty-four-hour demonstration that we just completed. The three-plane collision on the runway in Chicago that cost the lives of more than six hundred passengers and crew was not planned by us. That was pilot panic. But next time your planes will drop from the skies. We promise.

"We also left your banks alone, even though we have easy access to your records. Only minutes ago, we drained all the assets from your president's accounts. We did this to demonstrate how thoroughly we have taken over your country. His net worth is now nothing. That is how much his efforts to protect Americans are worth to you. Next time we will destroy all your banking records.

"Next time, millions of you will die . . ."

Incredibly, even vowing wholesale killing did not ruffle the man's voice. But Lana did not want Emma to hear any more of this. She used the on/off switch on the steering wheel, knowing that she could catch the rest of the statement later.

"No!" Emma gasped. She grabbed the dial on the dash and turned the radio back on.

"At your weakest, when you are starving and desperately dependent on world aid organizations for the most basic foodstuffs, we will unleash a final surprise.

"Your leaders have left you entirely defenseless. They told you that you were strong. They told you that you were the most powerful nation on earth. They told you that you were safe. They told you lies.

"You are weak and defeated. For the price of one helicopter, we have brought you to your knees. We are like the Iraqis who used software that cost twenty-six dollars to spy on your Predator drones. Your big guns, nuclear bombs, and powerful armadas belong in museums. Your leaders, past and present, belong in prison for crimes against humanity.

"In purely functional terms, you are no longer a nation.

"Now we will slaughter you."

The radio went silent, and the digital readout for the station disappeared.

When Lana lifted her eyes higher, she saw that the troop transport truck was fully loaded. The soldier closed the tailgate, and the vehicle pulled away. When it turned at the next corner to enter a broad boulevard, Lana drove straight ahead.

She looked at Emma. Her daughter's jaw was set. The girl was crying. Lana took her hand once more.

"I'm a victim of terrorists," Emma croaked. "I'm fourteen years old, and they did this to me." She pointed to her throat.

Lana nodded. "And a lot worse to others."

Emma returned her mother's nod with one of her own, then glanced at the burning train cars. She gripped her mother's hand hard. Lana felt the child's fear and grief, and then her anger.

Emma was, after all, Lana Elkins's daughter.

CHAPTER 5

LAST NIGHT HAD BEEN harrowing for Ruhi and Candace. It didn't start off that way, at least after the Afghan War vet had cleared out the last of the mob that had tried to break down her door and shoot its way into her room. She'd also found a couple of drunken teenage boys lingering in the lobby. They ran off the instant she waved them out of the building with her gun.

Candace had accepted Ruhi's offer of his apartment, packing up her belongings quickly; her greatly damaged door wouldn't keep out anyone. But before he could even wonder whether his appeal extended beyond a convenient couch, she told him not to get any big ideas.

"I just don't want to be traveling anywhere right now."

He watched her secure his apartment by checking the closets and even under his bed, nodding approvingly when she saw that the first-floor windows were a good eight feet off the ground—a benefit of an old building. Then the two of them moved a heavy bureau from his bedroom to the front door, which they backed up with a gorgeous silk heirloom couch that had been shipped to him all the way from Riyadh. It pained Ruhi to think of it getting shot up. *But better it than me*, he said to himself quickly.

When he made a stab at gallantry by saying, "Of course, I'll take the couch and you can have the privacy of my bedroom," she shook her head.

"No. I'm the first line of defense. Unless you're holding out on me and have extensive firearms training for close-quarters combat. Otherwise, I should be on the couch. Besides," she added with a winning smile, "I'm a light sleeper. Remember that."

Not that sleep was on the horizon anytime soon.

The neighborhood remained calm for about another hour. Then gunshots erupted down the street. The burst ended quickly, but shots continued to startle them sporadically well into the evening. Never right in front of the old townhome, but close enough to make them wary of errant bullets—and grateful for the brick exterior.

As twilight thickened, they used no emergency lights or candles, keeping the apartment dark and watching through the blinds. They observed crowds of mostly young men moving down the street, weaving in and around parked cars, smashing windows and stealing everything within reach.

By midnight, the heat in the apartment grew stifling. Without power, they had no air movement. Ruhi improvised fans from the lid of a cardboard box, but that was the best he could come up with. He suggested opening a window. "We're right here. No one's going to get in." But "Homeland Security," as he'd privately dubbed Candace, wouldn't hear of it.

By twelve thirty, though, even she couldn't take the steaming conditions. They opened the window in his dark living room and raised the shade, then dragged a plush love seat over to it. She rested her gun in her lap as soon as she sat down, pointing to an orange glow in the night sky. The fire looked about a mile or two away.

"At least it's not the Capitol now," she said. "That looks like it's over by the Cultural Center." Georgetown. Distant gunfire erupted a second later.

"I thought Americans were supposed to pull together at times like this," Ruhi said as he walked back to the bathroom, returning moments later with two damp, cool washcloths. "Look at 9/11," he added, handing one of them to her and claiming the other half of the love seat.

She thanked him and wiped her face. "We still had power on 9/11. People weren't sitting around in the dark, or trying to take advantage of it. They weren't directly affected."

"Where were you back then?" he asked.

"Ninth grade in good old Bloomington, Indiana, already thinking about going to IU to be a social worker."

"You're kidding. Sorry, Candace, but you just don't strike me as a caseworker, counselor type of woman."

"I wasn't for long, because 9/11 changed all that. I was so angry I started thinking right away about joining the military. I started ROTC a few years later at IU, and then it was off to basic training and 'Hello, Afghanistan.'" She smiled. He loved the way it lit up her whole face, even in the dim light. "Where were you?"

"University of Vermont," he replied. "Environmental studies. 9/11 didn't have that kind of impact on me."

She wiped her neck with the wet cloth, always keeping an eye on the open window when she talked. "I never could get how people weren't stunned by those attacks. But for a lot of them—I guess you, too—it wasn't such a big deal."

"I'm not saying that," he responded quickly. "It's just that I might have seen it differently, being born in Saudi Arabia. That kind of anger toward the U.S. didn't surprise me."

"I didn't know you were born there."

"Why would you?" he asked.

"I guess no reason," she said.

"Thirty-four years ago, right in Riyadh."

"So did you think 9/11 was justified? What they did?"

"Absolutely not." He felt like he was being grilled by the customs officer who "welcomed" him back to the U.S. the last time he'd visited Riyadh and several other major cities in the Middle East and South Asia. "Are you kidding? And it was painful to find out that a bunch of Saudis carried out the attacks. So, no, I didn't think anything justified it. But it was a huge mistake for U.S. intelligence to have missed all the static out there. And then the country made a mistake of historical proportions by invading Iraq."

"What about Afghanistan?"

Talk about being put on the spot. Ruhi opted for honesty: "That didn't work out so well, either."

She took a deep breath. He sensed she was about to explode, but she breathed out slowly and surprised him, saying, "No, it didn't. Sometimes I can't even stand to think about the buddies I lost over there, or the ones still in Walter Reed." She looked at him. "Were you angry at the U.S.?"

"No—do I look like an angry guy to you?" He watched her closely as she turned back to the window. Her feet were up on the sill. He didn't mind her questions. In fact, he was flattered, because he thought there was a good chance she was asking them to figure out whether they could possibly be compatible. He didn't have a political litmus test for a potential mate. Life was too short for that.

Candace shook her head, but kept her eyes trained on the street. "No, I'd have to say that you don't seem like an angry guy to me. I was around a lot of them in the service, so I know what they're like. Not much fun. I have a simple policy about angry guys: Avoid them."

He let the silence settle between them. And then their eyes met. *Kiss her*, he thought at once. The stillness held for another second. He was about to lean forward when she looked away. He almost groaned, then reminded himself that she'd at least shown interest in his background and his thoughts about her country. He still had trouble thinking of it as his nation, despite his citizenship.

Candace sat on the edge of the love seat, scanning the street. "So who do you think did it? As long as we really can rule out aliens." Deadpan with that last comment.

Ruhi lifted his feet to the windowsill and leaned back. "I know the grid end of things, and I've read some articles about cyberwarfare, stuff in the *Post* and *Times*, but that's about it. I'm sure you know a whole lot more about it than I do."

He was going to have wait to find out if she actually did because right then—and directly outside his door—they heard what sounded like a dozen young men pounding up the stairs, opening fire seconds later on the second floor.

Candace was already down behind the love seat. Ruhi joined her right away.

"Four weapons," she whispered. "Handguns."

"You can really tell?"

"Of course."

"Sounds like they're back for blood," he said, realizing that those words had never before crossed his lips, not with any seriousness, anyway.

Candace scrambled over to the couch, keeping her head below the top of the bureau, listening carefully. Ruhi crawled up beside her, arriving just as a gunshot went off close by. It sounded like it could have come from right outside his door. He wondered if the guys out there had stopped long enough to read the names on the mailboxes—and if they were worldly enough to know that Mancur could belong to the "raghead."

"Being this close is not a good idea," she said softly. "We'd better back up."

He followed her behind a breakfast bar that set off the kitchen from the larger living area. More footsteps issued from the stairs.

"Do you think they're still going up?" he asked.

She shook her head.

"I hope Mrs. Miranda doesn't come out of her apartment," Ruhi said, nodding toward the wall that he shared with his elderly neighbor.

"Does she leave her hearing aids in at night?"

"I have no idea. She likes to wander out when she hears things. I think she's lonely."

"Oh, Christ," Candace said, "that's scary. If I hear them taking down her door, I'm going to have to be able to get out there." She nodded at the furniture blocking his door.

And do what? Probably more of what Ruhi had seen up in her apartment.

"Let me know if there's anything I can do," he said, feeling wholly ineffective.

"Just stay down," she replied, "till I say different."

"I can handle that. What do we do if they try to burn the place down?" It didn't seem like a remote possibility, given the orange glow in the night sky.

"That would be the biggest mistake any of them would ever make." As if by reflex, Candace checked her load.

Even now she didn't appear anxious. Calculating, yes. Alert, absolutely. But not at all fidgety, while he thought he had enough nerves for a roomful of insomniacs. His jumpiness had him flinching when they heard loud crashing noises on the stairs.

"Sounds like your furniture is dying," Ruhi said.

"It's not actually mine," she replied. "Mine's not showing up for a few weeks. I had to ship it from Indiana. It's the landlord's. He said he was happy to loan it to a vet. I'll bet that's the last time that happens. I hope he's covered."

Me, too, thought Ruhi, *or the rent's going up*. The guy was tighter than a tourniquet.

The distinct sound of breaking glass quickly followed.

"The mirror," Candace said calmly.

Then footfalls came heavily down the stairs. In seconds, the two of them heard pounding on Mrs. Miranda's door.

"Don't open it," Ruhi and Candace both implored quietly at the same time.

"Is she always there?" Candace asked right away. "Does she have family she might be staying with because of the outage?"

"I haven't seen anyone since her husband died last year."

The pounding on Mrs. Miranda's door ceased. But Ruhi flinched again when the thugs beat on his door.

"Open up."

"Yell 'Go away,'" Candace whispered. "They hear a woman, it's going to get worse."

"Go away," Ruhi shouted, deepening his voice and glad he sounded as American as the next guy.

"Open up or we're coming in, you fucking raghead."

"Tell them you're not some 'fucking raghead' and that you're armed and you'll shoot."

Ruhi did as directed.

Three bullets blasted through the door in response. The last sounded duller than the first two and must have hit the dresser. He wished they'd put the back of the bureau to the door—and hoped his couch had been spared.

Candace aimed and fired twice, but high, as she had initially in her apartment.

"I don't want to hit anyone right now," she said to him. "It'll just escalate if I do. I'm hoping they'll go look for low-hanging fruit and leave the building. I can't imagine they want a real firefight."

They didn't, evidently. They moved on without another shot. But from then on, all through the night, either Ruhi or Candace kept watch in two-hour shifts. She always kept the gun, even when she napped a foot away on the couch, assuring him that she was never more than a blink from battle.

By morning the streets of Georgetown were quiet and largely empty. When they gazed out the window together, both bleary-eyed, they saw only rubbish, and a burn barrel halfway down the block sending up dark plumes that joined other smoke drifting over the District.

But as far as they could see, there were few signs of devastating destruction. And no bodies.

Ruhi provided a breakfast of dry cereal and tepid milk. He'd kept the refrigerator closed since yesterday morning.

Both of them were ruing the absence of coffee when the electricity returned, startling them with sudden light from above and air-conditioner racket.

"Get that java jumping," Candace urged without missing a beat. "I'm going to shower, if that's okay with you."

"Of course."

She took her gun and locked the door. Ruhi ground the beans and put on the water.

He was examining the bullet holes in the top half of his front door when he thought to put his kitchen radio on. Nothing. All the stations were still off the air.

Candace stepped out in a fresh change of clothes. Wet hair. No makeup. Ruhi thought she looked fabulous.

"I've got to get over to the Capitol," she said. "But I'll be back tonight, if that's okay."

"Sure, but wouldn't you be safer somewhere else? They're hunting for you."

"Not just me, Ruhi, and I can't leave you high and dry." She helped herself to half a cup of the brew. "I don't want to," she added in a soft voice that he hadn't heard till now.

"Then stay, by all means," Ruhi said, doing his best not to

overwhelm her by sounding too ebullient. He dug around in a kitchen drawer and handed her a spare key.

"Thanks."

They started moving the couch away from the door when a smooth, comforting voice came on the radio:

"I used to live in your country. It was in Detroit, not so long ago . . ."

They both walked across the living room, listening closely. In moments, they turned to each other in alarm.

• • •

Emma was not pleased. Sure, she understood that her mother needed to go fight the war on terror, or something like that. But the power was back on, so how bad could it be? But that's not what really pissed her off. She was actually feeling pretty good about her mom, even holding her hand in the car. That was kind of nice. But all those warm feelings ended a few minutes ago when Lana said that Mrs. Johansson was coming over to take care of her.

"I'm too old for a babysitter," Emma seethed, even though it hurt her throat to argue. If it hadn't been so painful, she would have made an even louder case. That's how irate she felt when she heard that Johansson the Jabberer was coming over to make sure Emma got her meds on time.

"She's not really a babysitter," Lana said. "She's more like a care-giver."

"I don't care what you call her, she's a babysitter!"

Oh, that hurt her throat. Emma gripped her neck, making sure her mother noticed how much she was sacrificing to make her point.

But it was true. Plus, Johansson hogged all the fun food. Potato chips, ice cream, you name it. All of it disappeared when Johansson came around. Gone. *Poof.*

"You're on meds, darling," Lana said, "so stop fretting and stay ahead of the pain. I can't leave you home alone. You've got your phone, so get in touch with your friends. I'm sure they'd love to hear from you, and there's some service now."

Of course, if her dad hadn't disappeared on them, she wouldn't have to put up with "caregivers" at all. She forced herself, as she had many times before, to stop thinking about him. She already had plenty of pain with her throat, which felt like it was on fire. Argh. And here came Johansson, moving slowly up the front walk.

Her mom rushed out to greet Mrs. Johansson, gave Emma a quick hug, then hurried back out to her car.

Can't get away fast enough, can you, Mom? Sure makes a girl feel loved.

But Emma knew she was being unfair—to her mom. Johansson was another story.

Emma hand-signaled Mrs. J immediately that she was going back to her room.

"Don't lock the door," her mom's "friend" said. "You have your medicine to take." Pronounced med-a-*sin*. It curdled Emma's ears just to hear her say the word.

At least Emma had the phone. That was a relief. She checked her messages and could have screamed. Really and truly, raw throat or not. Skateboarder Boy must have gotten her number from someone, because he'd sent her a text, and there she was with all her Dora the Explorer glory on full display. His message SUCKED: C ME OR EVERYBODY WILL C U.

Emma didn't know which was worse: the indignity of wearing those joke panties that weren't so funny anymore, or lying like a slab of meat on a gurney with her skirt up over her hips. She wished it had been over her head.

She groaned and beat the bed with her first. She just knew that he'd already sent it all over the Internet. "Asshole!"

"Don't talk like that," Mrs. J said, standing over her shoulder with a glass of water and the pill bottle.

Emma looked up, then hid the phone against her chest. Too late.

"Are you sexting a boy? Give me that."

Mrs. J put aside the pills and water and made an aggressive grab for the phone. Sedated or not, Emma rolled away, kicking wildly. Johansson wasn't so easily daunted, though, and tried to shove Emma's legs out of the way.

"I'm telling," Emma tried to yell. *She hit me, Mom. She did. Hard.*

"You go right ahead. I want to hear what your mother has to say about all this."

And Johansson kept coming, grabbing her arms. Geez, that hurt. And she was yelling, "Give me that phone. Give it to me!"

Now Emma panicked. Johansson had to have at least a hundred pounds on her, and she was coming in fast. Emma kicked frantically.

Uh-oh. She caught the babysitter right in the belly.

Mrs. J keeled, but got both feet under her. She staggered toward the door, groaning.

Emma felt horrible. She hadn't kicked anyone since she was really little. But as soon as Mrs. J moved into the hallway, Emma eased the door shut and locked it.

She was actually relieved when Mrs. J had enough breath to say, "You are an evil child."

"I'm sorry," Emma whispered, her voice almost gone.

Johansson rattled the handle. The lock held. Emma listened to Mrs. J plod away, and then threw herself on the bed, feeling miserable. She looked at the photo of her and her panties and felt even worse. But then she studied it closely. It was really kind of flattering, wasn't it? Her face looked great, not like she was in pain, more like she'd found inner bliss. Like a saint. St. Emma.

It might have been shock that she was seeing on her face, but Emma didn't care. *I look great. And you can't really see anything.*

As for wearing little-girl underwear to high school, she'd play it cool, be ironic: *Yeah, I wear them all the time. "Dora the Explorer" panties? Don't you get it?*

So . . . maybe it wouldn't be so bad if Skateboarder Boy posted the photo.

She texted him back: I'M CALLING YOUR BLUFF. DO WHAT YOU GOTTA DO. BUT I'LL C U ANYWAY.

• • •

Lana put on her headset and rang Jeff Jensen, her VP at Cyber-Fortress, before she backed out of her garage. After he'd checked the company's computer system, he'd texted her saying they needed to talk.

"I'm here," Lana said when he picked up the line she had reserved for only her calls to him.

"I found APTs."

Nothing like posting the headline right away, Lana thought. APTs were "advanced persistent threats," virulent bugs generally Chinese in origin. "How bad?" She drove impatiently through the outskirts of Bethesda.

"Bad. They'd set up shop some time ago, though. We're talking at least a few months."

"And we're just finding them?" Lana sounded annoyed—for good reason: She was.

"These are very slick," Jensen replied.

"What were they going after?" She spoke about the APTs as if they possessed volition of their own. Easy to see why: They were canny enough to extract data and leave. Sweet—if you weren't being pillaged.

"I don't know what they wanted, and I don't think we ever will. For all we know, most might have already returned to the mother ship. But if I had to hazard a guess, I'd say Defense Department secrets. The takeaway here is that they came well before the attack on the grid."

"So you're pulling the weeds?" she asked him, meaning extracting the APTs.

"I've started on it."

"Use as much of the workforce as you need. We want them out of there ASAP." Not telling him anything he didn't know, but adding urgency to whatever sense of purpose he might already have felt.

Lana was now making great time on the Beltway, which at this point in her life had become more familiar to her than her own backyard.

"This puts us in company with Cisco and lots of others," Jeff said, perhaps to contextualize the violation of the system whose security was his domain.

Lana agreed. Cisco was just one of the many marquee names of western technology companies that had been targeted by Chinese hackers. In one of their biggest coups they stole Cisco's innovative router, a device that forwarded packets of data to parts of a network system.

"Their fingerprints are showing up everywhere," Jeff said, "so they were bound to target us sooner or later."

"The point is they *have* fingerprints."

Which had also been found on defense contractor Lockheed Martin's own highly classified government work. The Chinese had even been brazen enough to copy information right off the Secretary of Commerce's laptop when he was in Beijing. That attack had been dubbed "Titan Rain." More like a monsoon when it was over, because the data from the secretary's laptop was used to gain access to Commerce Department computers, which proved vital to the exfiltration of upward of twenty *trillion* bytes of data from the Pentagon's unclassified network.

"So let me know if those prints show up at NSA or anywhere else," Jeff said.

"You're covered," she told him. "Now go play exterminator with those bugs."

Twenty minutes after she hung up—while charging across the vast NSA parking lot—she received a furious call from Irene Johansson vowing that she would never, "under any circumstances," watch Emma again. Then she informed Lana that her daughter had kicked her in the stomach after she'd caught her sexting "filthy pictures."

"What?" Lana exclaimed, still rushing toward the monolithic headquarters, struck almost numb by the fact that she was having to deal with this kind of total crap while the fate of the country was up for grabs. She tried desperately to think of a way to ameliorate the situation between the two antagonists. She knew Emma was unhappy about having Mrs. Johansson at the house, but kicking? And *sexting*?

"Yes, both," Irene bellowed. "She kicked me because I caught her red-handed with her dirty little pictures on the phone. I *saw* them."

"Of her?"

"Yes, she had her dress pulled all the way up. She was showing off her undies. The Dora the Explorer ones. I've seen them under her bed for months."

At least she wasn't naked. But "sexting" a picture of herself in Dora the Explorer underpants? Unless there was something super-kinky going on that Lana simply couldn't fathom, that didn't make any sense. Dora the Explorer and sexting sounded like an oxymoron—not that she wanted Emma having her panty pictures on the Web.

"So is she still in her bedroom?"

"I don't know. I'm at home."

"Oh, please, don't do this to us, Irene," Lana said as she paused before undergoing newly fortified security at the agency entrance.

"Good-bye," Irene said. "You have raised a bad girl."

Lana stared at her phone, shaking her head, then speed-dialed Emma. "Are you all right?" she asked immediately.

"Yes, but—"

"Stop! Don't say another word. Can I possibly trust you to take your medicine on time and stay home with the doors locked?"

"Of course, Mom," Emma said in a hoarse voice. "Why would you think—"

"Because you're in this mess because you didn't do that yesterday."

"Oh. Right. Yes."

"Do it. Stay ahead of the pain. I'll be home as soon as I can. I love you. Now good-bye."

Lana handed over her phone, briefcase with laptop—everything—to hard-eyed security agents. After undergoing an intense screening, she headed up to Deputy Director Holmes's office.

Donna Warnes, his efficient executive assistant, directed her to a Sensitive Compartmented Information Facility. SCIFs—pronounced "skiffs"—were large secure rooms that prevented all electronic surveillance while eliminating the threat of any data leakage.

But before entering, Lana had to check her laptop and personal items with blank-faced security personnel. She also had to be "read in" by an official who announced that the world would crash down around her shoulders if she ever breathed a word of what she was about to learn.

"Do you understand?" he asked her.

"Got it."

But it wasn't over. "Sign this," he ordered, handing her a form that acknowledged that she had been fully briefed and understood the strict nature of the security demands.

It wasn't Lana's first time in a SCIF, not by a long shot. But each time she entered one she was taken aback by the absence of windows and the appearance of utter impregnability that came from being encased in masonry. The room also came equipped with motion detectors in the corners of the ceiling to catch anyone entering the facility during off-hours.

Lana took a seat about halfway around a large conference table. Holmes thanked her somberly for coming, adding, "We've just started reviewing the damage. We have our internal communications up, so after a quick look at the toll, we'll turn our attention to our list of suspects, which I trust you'll help us with."

"I heard the 'commentary.'" She made air quotes with her intonation. "Any accuracy to the claim of fifty thousand dead?"

Holmes nodded, raking his white hair. "It might even be worse, but we're not confirming anything right now. A huge problem at the moment is the wide-scale looting and rioting. It's taking place in more than a hundred cities and suburban areas. That number could be greater, too, but our reporting is still terribly hampered. The social upheaval is exactly what the enemy was planning on, we think. By putting the power back on, and then threatening to cut it off any second without warning, they set off waves of panic. The Army and National Guard are deployed virtually everywhere."

Holmes used a remote to bring a large flat screen to life against the solid white wall. "So let's look at all the suspects now—nations, rogue players, terrorists, and our own domestic enemies."

The screen showed a list of nations along with a multicolored globe. "There's no consensus on a culprit; let me say that at the outset. But if we can winnow the wheat from the chaff at this stage, we can focus our efforts more efficiently."

Holmes was speaking to a full table, including the NSA officials Lana had sat with just yesterday. Ronald Wilkes, last seen by her in his tennis whites, now sported a dark suit that managed to look neatly pressed after his all-nighter at the Capitol; he had been liaising with congressional intelligence committees. With a declaration of war in the offing, Wilkes was probably taking furious heat from senators and congressmen eager for an identifiable enemy to crush.

Joshua Tenon, of the salt-and-pepper beard, sat directly across from her. His expertise on international energy matters had justified his presence at almost every meeting Lana had ever attended at NSA.

Next to Lana, veteran policy analyst Teresa McGivern worked her laptop with one hand, a skill that Lana had never seen executed with such élan. McGivern would not be retiring anytime soon, no matter her plans of little more than thirty hours ago.

The gray-haired McGivern had an assistant, a younger handsome man whose name escaped Lana, much to her chagrin. NSA was not a name tag kind of place.

"I'd like to dispose with the 'red meat' first," Holmes said, a blunt acknowledgment that many pundits and so-called opinion makers would be screaming for retaliation against the country's traditional foes, even if that mind-set harked back to a Cold War era already eclipsed by far more wrenching events.

Just as dangerous, Lana thought, was a reflexive bellicosity toward certain nations in the Middle East.

"If we're in housekeeping mode," McGivern said, "I think it's incumbent upon us to put aside any notions of Chinese responsibility." Tenon moved to speak, but she put up her hand to quiet him. "Yes, I know they drew up the drawbridge right away, but seriously, what else would we expect them to do? If we had that kind of capability over all the computer systems in this country, we would pull the damn drawbridge up, too. We'd do it preemptively to protect ourselves from the fallout. That's all the Chinese did. Furthermore, they're not going to destroy an economy on which they are highly dependent for their own domestic stability, and they're not going to destroy a currency when they own a trillion dollars of it. I can't imagine what the exchange rate is going to be on the U.S. dollar, but the Chinese are going to get clobbered on their dollar holdings. No, they did not cut off their nose to spite their face."

Spoken with the crisp eloquence for which McGivern was long regarded. Her last comment might even have elicited a chuckle or two at any other time. But this was war, declared or not.

"But what about 'GhostNet'?" Lana asked pointedly. "Look at what they were caught doing with that operation."

She respected McGivern, but Canadian intelligence had found that the Chinese had taken over 1,300 computers in the embassies of a number of countries worldwide, including their own and the U.S.'s. What was extraordinary was the engineering that allowed Chinese hackers to remotely turn on cameras and microphones in the hardware of those computers without signaling those actions to the actual users. Then the hackers had the images and sound sent back to servers in China. The targets of GhostNet were offices working with nongovernmental organizations dealing with Tibet.

Lana wasn't through: "The same year—and this is what's so directly relevant—we know that Chinese hackers penetrated the U.S. power grid and left behind tools that could have brought it down."

"Those were cleared out," Tenon said, pulling on his beard. Nervous habit.

"Yes, and maybe newer and more sophisticated versions took their place and then took down the country," Lana volleyed.

"Look at how much China could benefit if we pulled out of the Pacific theater."

"It's a given," McGivern retorted, "that they would have tried to penetrate our grid with better devices, and that they would benefit if we were foolish enough to withdraw from our bases. But it still doesn't explain why they would so profoundly harm their own interests. And let me remind everyone that the penetration of our grid was all about keeping us on the sidelines in their squabble over the Spratlys."

Numerous small islands lay between Vietnam and the Philippines, some of which were claimed by both of those countries and China, as well as other nations. The region of the South China Sea contained the world's fourth-largest natural gas deposits; a critical trade route from the Indian Ocean to the Pacific, through which most of the world's oil was shipped; and also some of the largest stocks of fish left on Earth.

McGivern was stating that the Chinese grid penetrations were a subtle means of blackmailing the U.S. into standing aside as China had its big beef with Vietnam and the Philippines.

"The Chinese even hacked President Obama's campaign material," Ronald Wilkes chimed in, "so maybe taking them off the table isn't such a good idea. Ideology can trump economic concerns."

"Speaking of ideological blindness, just look at North Korea," a grizzled analyst said, at about two o'clock from where Lana sat. "Is it mere coincidence that they hacked those classified hazardous chemical sites, and now we're seeing chlorine releases in New Jersey and Pennsylvania?"

"I sincerely hope it's not the North Koreans," Holmes said to nods around the table. Everyone in the SCIF understood that if the trail led to the North Koreans, a huge kinetic response was all but inevitable. Such an attack would almost certainly result in the

North Koreans unleashing thousands of rockets that they had trained on Seoul, obliterating the city and most of its ten million inhabitants. That, in turn, would surely set off a new Korean war— or a new chapter of the old one, in the view of many Asia experts— no doubt bringing the Chinese back into the conflict. The dominoes clacked almost audibly in the minds of everyone present.

"Let's not disregard China, but let's look at Russia, another traditional . . . rival," Holmes said diplomatically.

"They're perfectly capable of doing this to us," Lana volunteered.

"They certainly are," McGivern echoed.

Russia's FSB, Federal Security Service of the Russian Federation, might even be NSA's equal. The Russians ran what NSA officials conceded was one of the best hacker schools in the world. Its graduates had left their own cybertrail across U.S. intelligence. NSA had hounded the Russian hackers closely—sometimes, alas, only after the horse was out of the barn.

"SIPRNet, anyone?" the young male aide to McGivern asked.

Others, including Lana, groaned at the allusion to Russian penetration of the Secret Internet Protocol Router Network, a U.S. Defense Department and State Department interconnected computer network for classified information. Russian hackers had engineered spyware that was downloaded onto thumb drives, unbeknownst, of course, to their users. Once those drives were inserted into SIPRNet computers, the security of the entire system was greatly compromised. Within hours, the Russians had infected thousands of high-level and supposedly secret U.S. military computers in a number of nations, including Afghanistan and Iraq.

"So we know the Russians have superb abilities," Lana went on, "and we know they try to cover up their hacking any way they can."

She was referring to the country's extensive history of attempting to disguise its hacking by claiming the cyberassaults that originated on its soil were done by "patriotic citizens" who supposedly carried out the highly sophisticated and coordinated attacks on their own. Patent nonsense.

Those "citizens," usually on the payroll of the Russian security agencies, were known to have launched "distributed denial of service attacks," DDoS, on a number of former Soviet-era republics that had proved too feisty for their minders in Moscow. DDoS attacks overloaded servers in those countries, which denied service to their users, or slowed down the services so severely that they became, for all intents and purposes, nonfunctional.

"Who else has the capability to attack us like this?" Holmes asked. "Friend, foe—let's get it all on the table quickly. There can always be a rogue player in an agency friendly to us."

As others responded with a dauntingly long list that included Taiwan, Iran, Australia, South Korea, India, Pakistan, Israel, and several NATO countries, Lana was struck by the underlying assumption of Holmes's question: that the U.S. was so vulnerable to cyberattack that it was necessary to compile a *lengthy* list of suspects, some of which were two-bit players—at best—on the international scene.

But the success of the attack on the U.S. lay unquestionably, in Lana's view, in the criminal lack of the country's preparedness. There were several long-festering reasons for that vulnerability.

For starters, America was far more dependent upon privately owned computer systems than were *any* potential enemies. Those private U.S. networks held extensive control of vital national interests, everything from electric power to banks, pipelines to airlines, even the numerous private contractors that provided critical support services to the Department of Defense.

Washington had long expected those private concerns to protect their systems. Clearly, they had failed. But as former presidential adviser Richard A. Clarke had noted, telling those companies to protect themselves was like telling American corporations at the beginning of the nuclear age to buy their own bombs.

Clarke had long maintained that the political power of those private companies was so great that they routinely blocked the development or implementation of many government regulations that could have protected them—and the country—from a devastating cyberattack, like the one America had just suffered. Short-term profit concerns trumped long-term security demands with numbing regularity.

Most alarming to Lana was the unnerving understanding that even if the military's own networks were secure—and recent history had demolished that delusion—the networks of its contractors had proved unreliable. The complicated case of Edward Snowden spoke clearly to that. The easy mining of those private networks placed an additional—and in her opinion, unwarranted—risk on the nation's defenders.

The U.S. also suffered from an inverse relationship between its computer power and its vulnerability. A developing country, far less dependent on computers and the Internet, could launch a cyberattack on the U.S., knowing that it was risking far less in computer resources than its wealthy target. Ironically enough, that left the poorer country getting much more bang for the buck.

As discussion of both putative allies and known enemies trailed off, Holmes said he wanted to talk about rogue elements.

"The Internet is filled with them," McGivern said. "It's the Waziristan of cyberspace."

Muslim terrorists were mentioned by name, their faces flashing on the same screen that had listed suspect nations earlier. Lana had been in enough of these sessions with Holmes to sense his impatience and know that he wanted to move the discussion along. What surprised her was the direction he took:

"What about our domestic enemies? The Ted Kaczynski Unabomber types?"

That brought James Restess to life. The analyst's portfolio was exclusively U.S. extremists. Lana had heard him once say that as a nation we should all be glad that Kaczynski was born too early to have used the Internet for his madness.

Restess summarized his research, which included an ample number of profiles. He brought up the names of Islamic militants, some of whom were familiar to Lana, along with members of anarcho-primitivist groups espousing survivalist skills and supporting hackers who attacked corporations—oil, coal, gas companies—deemed enemies to environmental causes. But what shocked Lana was when Restess veered toward a much more mainstream suspect: Ruhi Mancur, the director of research at the Natural Resources Defense Council. She didn't know Mancur, but NRDC? Christ, she donated money to them.

"Really?" Tenon said when Mancur's face appeared, sounding as surprised as Lana felt.

"Yes, really," Restess replied. The NSA analyst bore an uncanny physical resemblance to WikiLeaks founder Julian Assange, with whom he otherwise had nothing in common. "Mancur has been advocating increasingly militant positions over there"—meaning the NRDC—"and, I'm glad to say, meeting with considerable resistance from his colleagues. But he has sent his own money to groups engaged in illegal occupations of land slated for the latest pipeline the Canadians want for pumping their tar sands oil down from Alberta. And he's been observed meeting with the more militant factions of the environmental movement. He also has close ties with his Saudi homeland and has traveled extensively in recent years in South Asia and the Middle East."

"How close are those ties?" Holmes asked. "Because what you

just said could apply to thousands of people like him. I'll tell you, if we sweep him on the basis of that, we'll be in big trouble, and we'll deserve it."

"How about an Al Qaeda cousin who's clearly linked to terrorist attacks and to Mancur himself? Ruhi Mancur has traveled extensively in recent years to Saudi Arabia and other Middle Eastern countries, and we have it from reliable sources that he has met on a consistent basis with his worthless cousin."

Restess sounded exercised, to Lana's ears. And he wasn't through yet:

"We've also unearthed emails that Ruhi Mancur sent to al-Awlaki praising the madman for his work."

That left everyone at the table silent.

Holmes cleared his throat. "That does place him in a much stricter category. Bring us up to speed on your investigation."

"Wait just a moment," Wilkes said. "The Saudis would never countenance this kind of attack. U.S. oil imports from the kingdom are about to fall off a cliff."

"I'm sure you're right," Restess said. "But I'm also sure I needn't remind you that militant Islamists in Saudi Arabia have a history of taking actions highly embarrassing to the country's leadership."

"So what steps have *you* taken?" Holmes asked Restess.

"The attorney general has authorized close surveillance, and we expect FISA warrants shortly on fifteen of our domestic suspects, including Mancur." A FISA, or Foreign Intelligence Surveillance Act, warrant permitted searches of the property of anyone in the U.S. linked to foreign spies, terrorists, or threats.

"It's time to do more than surveil," Holmes said decisively. "Let's bring them in for some questioning. The country is in meltdown."

Lana certainly understood the desire to grill Mancur.

Talk about hiding in plain sight.

CHAPTER 6

LANA LEFT NSA HEADQUARTERS with a clear assignment: Join Deputy Director Holmes's team, which was tasked with identifying the unknown enemy.

"Then we're going to crush them," Holmes vowed.

Right now Lana had to rush back to Kressinger to arrange care for Emma. She also needed to find out how Jeff Jensen, her second in command at CyberFortress, was doing with his own battle against those APTs—the viruses that were almost certainly Chinese in origin.

"Yes, Lana," Jeff said, picking up on Lana's direct line.

"How's it going?"

"I've corralled most of the troops, and I think we might have found the last of the viruses. But do you remember the code you wrote just before the first cyberattack?"

"Sure." Tailor-made to stop a Chinese hacker who had singled them out on another matter.

"That might help us," Jeff said, "in setting up our firewalls." Software that Lana had written to analyze the data coming into CF to make sure it was actually welcome.

"I'll encrypt and send it as soon as I get home," Lana told him. "Anything else?"

"No."

"Gotta run."

She speed-dialed Emma to check on her. No answer. That left Lana in a mild panic because of the girl's experiments with alcohol. It petrified Lana to think that Emma might have decided to imbibe while taking pain medication. Her daughter's behavior of late was off the rails, even when judged against the low bar of adolescence.

Kicking Irene in the belly?

Minutes later, she tried again. Still no answer. On the drive, Lana turned on the radio, hearing NPR say that it had regained control of its own airwaves. In a series of "alerts," the network told listeners that it had also become a victim of the cyberattack and was not aligned with the enemy—despite the claim of various nutbars on the extremes of the political spectrum.

The network also snagged her attention with a report about the heroics of the Baptist church choir, which included an interview with its director, three of its members, and a reporter for the *Washington Post*. The woman had just written a front-page story headlined "Courage in Kressinger."

Lana smiled; she'd called the incident to the *Post* reporter's attention.

Otherwise, little good news filled the air.

Lana used the electronic garage-door opener, relishing the device anew, and hurried inside. She found Emma asleep in bed, covers curled tightly around her chin. No bottles of gin or vodka or scotch sat on the nightstand next to the prescription drugs. Lana's worst nightmare vanished at the innocent sight of her daughter sleeping.

The air-conditioning was on, too, and the house had cooled. But what proved deeply unnerving for Lana was knowing that such normalcy could end any second—a possibility that gripped her so intensely she feared she would sicken. The first panic attack of her life had begun.

Her ears rang sharply, and her heart beat so furiously that she gripped her chest and had to sit on the edge of Emma's bed. Slowly, she was able to take deep, deliberate breaths. Perspiration streamed down her face. But her heart rate slowed, and the shrillness in her ears faded.

Lana's sudden unraveling shocked her, even as it eased. Her entire adult life she had been a steadying force for others—for the country. If this could happen to her, she thought, an entire generation of children and young people was going to need intense help to adjust to the intimidating world that had dawned that week.

Thankfully, Emma remained blissfully unaware of her mother's duress.

Calmed, Lana walked out to the kitchen and drank a large glass of water, as if to douse the final embers of distress. With another deep inhalation, she switched on the small screen under a corner cabinet. A CNN anchor was reporting that the "unknown enemy" had released a six-hundred-word statement.

Lana wheeled right back down the hall, scooting past her bedroom to her study, where she powered up her desktop computer. She found the message just as it was posted on an NSA website.

Though the author claimed he was not the same man who had voiced the last "communiqué," he stated in his opening paragraph that he had written the man's words. So it was not surprising that Lana still heard that smooth male voice in her head as she read the following:

"Now that we have given you back your precious electricity, all of you can read my words. And if you read fast, you might even finish my message before you lose power. You should pay close attention, because I promise to give you a jolt or two at the end."

Without thinking, Lana moved back, as if she might be zapped any second by her own computer. But that was absurd, and she knew it. No one could execute such an attack through the Internet, though clearly they could execute much more devastating blows.

Just print it out, she admonished herself. *Before it disappears and he does whatever he's going to do.*

She retrieved the hard copy and resumed reading her screen.

"By now, you must know that we have done great damage to you, more than any of your enemies could ever have dreamed of doing. Do you want to know more about us? I think you do. But I won't tell you too much. I shall not play a cat-and-mouse game, as you Americans like to say . . ."

That's exactly what you're doing.

". . . but I will say that we are never far from you. Just a keystroke. That is all. But that is the great significance of the world we live in now. You send your drones to the Middle East, South America, Asia, Africa, wherever you want. We send out little soldiers wherever we want. Fair is fair. You assassinate. We retaliate. Then you boast that you will kill us. Good luck with that. Isn't that another of your favorite expressions? Or maybe I should say, 'How's that working for you, America?'

"Some of your leaders say America will 'pulverize' us, as if we are rocks you can grind to dust. We are not so easy as rocks. We are working very hard, and we have humbled you. All you can do is shout and shake your fists. That used to be scary. Now that we have democratized the battlefield, that is not so. Battlefield democracy is the only true democracy, and we have achieved it: one man and one computer in a world made 'one' by the Internet.

"That is the magnificence of the moment we are living in. History will record that we have brought fairness to warfare for the first time. That is the real reason you shake your fists, America. You cannot bear fairness because it bodes your end.

"Meantime, you don't even know where to point your trillion-dollar arsenal. For all you know, you should point your guns and missiles at New York City or San Francisco. Your enemy could be staring you right in the face or standing by your side, all the while smiling at your misery. You do not know.

"But you have heard the story of David and Goliath. Christian, Jew, Muslim, we all know about the boy with a sling and five stones. But in our version, there are many Davids. I can assure you that right now your leaders are meeting and pointing their fingers this way, then that, saying, 'Where is David? Where is he?' Here is the answer: David is everywhere. David stands in the shadows defeating Goliath with bytes that you cannot trace.

"Now, do you remember what David of the Old Testament did once he brought Goliath crashing to the ground? He cut off the giant's head. That is what we will do to you. Do not doubt us, America. We will cut off your head and hand it to you.

"So this is your last chance, Goliath. Do not fail the American people again by continuing your ruinous adventures abroad. Do not fail them for fear of shame. As you now know, there are much greater threats to worry about. The ones that come true. Delay, and we will behead you. That is a promise."

The message disappeared, but the screen remained lit.

Lana sat on a stool, reminding herself that all the capability the enemy had displayed had been the subject of her own reports to NSA. The president had read them. The Joint Chiefs of Staff had been given copies. So had the intelligence committees of both houses of Congress. All of those officials had been strongly warned that this day was coming. They had banked—in every sense of that loaded word—on U.S. supremacy in cyberwarfare when it was patently clear that the country's vulnerability had become manifest to friend and foe alike.

Emma walked into Lana's office. "What were you looking at?" she asked.

"A message."

"From work?"

"Yes, exactly. Come here." Lana opened her arms.

For a second, she worried that her daughter would spurn her overture. But Emma let herself be held. She seemed to want to be comforted, and hugged her mother back.

Then the lights dimmed.

They both stiffened. But the power came back on. The screen returned to life. Lana looked to see if the bastard had uploaded another message. Nothing.

But the lights went right off, then came on and off repeatedly. She heard the air conditioner groan from the sudden surges and losses of power.

It lasted for at least sixty seconds before the power stayed on for more than a few seconds. Lana gasped, realizing that she'd been holding her breath.

Then the screen went dark.

At the very moment she squeezed her eyes shut in anguish, the power returned once again, and her screen glowed with these words: "Any time now."

"What's that mean, Mom?"

Lana paused before telling Emma the truth: "It means they really want to hurt us."

Then she offered her daughter the kind of solace that often turns out to be a lie: "But we're going to stop them, Emma. You'll see."

CHAPTER 7

RUHI HAD BEEN APPALLED to see his name—and a photograph lifted from the NRDC website—all over the Internet and news channels. He feared that his big smile would look arrogant and suspicious to a nation suffering from the worst attack in its history.

For the first time since the major renovation of NRDC office, he loathed the glass walls. He'd always appreciated how they allowed the offices to bathe in natural light—and lower the nonprofit's carbon imprint. But now it left him feeling like he was in the proverbial fishbowl.

Sure, a number of colleagues had come by to offer him words of support, but others were clearly hoping to keep their distance and do all they could to avoid being named as a key member of a "fifth column."

That accusation came from an octogenarian pundit on one of the cable networks.

"And what would we expect?" the craggy old beast asked his viewers. "He works for an outfit that has done more to undermine the American way of life than any other group I can think of."

"Really?" Ruhi talked back to the YouTube posting. *More than Al Qaeda? More than the old Soviet Union?*

And there was another "more," Ruhi realized: The creep's video had *more* than 1,110,000 viewers—so far.

"A *Saudi!*" the crepe-skinned hatemonger intoned ominously. "And I'm sure I don't need to remind you of what the Saudis did to us not so long ago."

Hyperbole and invective—cruel and vicious—were clearly the order of the day.

But didn't he and Candace talk about how much Americans pulled together in a time of crisis? *No, that's what you said,* he reminded himself. She pointed out that everyone still had electric power on 9/11. They weren't sitting around in the dark, or trying to use the cover of night to rape and plunder. And they surely weren't worrying that they would be thrust back into riots and the deepest darkness at any moment. *They weren't directly affected.*

How can anyone even think that I would do something like that to America? he wondered as he listened to the pundit's rant online— and the frothing comments of his many fans.

I've lived here since I was nine. They treat me like the biggest saboteur in world history.

Ruhi could have howled in frustration.

Then, around three o'clock, a convenient leak from the Justice Department revealed that he had traveled extensively in the Middle East and South Asia, especially as an adult. He was said to have held numerous meetings with Islamists and other radicals. That led in minutes to rumors that he had trained at an Al Qaeda camp in Tajikistan.

Tajikistan? He knew it was one of the five "Stans" of the old Soviet Union, but Ruhi had to look it up on a map to locate it exactly. And he supposedly had trained there? How could anyone believe that?

Moreover, Ruhi didn't even know how to shoot a gun. And what meetings with radical Muslims? He felt positively allergic to them. He'd talked to energy experts, not people who made a career of chopping off the heads of "infidels" and posting videos of the crimes on YouTube, cheek-to-jowl—in the "cloud"—with the craggy old beast's crazy accusations.

The only questionable actions he ever took overseas were to have a few perfunctory meetings in Pakistan with solar energy experts so he could deduct the travel on his taxes. But Islamists? Radicals?

Give me a break.

But there were no breaks coming his way. Only a tsunami of telephone calls from the *Post, Washington Times, New York Times, Guardian, Telegraph, Mirror, Globe and Mail,* CBS, CNN, FOX, and more than a hundred other news outlets around the world. He'd lost count. Could be two hundred by now. He hadn't even thought that many journalists still had jobs. Wasn't the news business contracting? Not fast enough, was his dismal view this afternoon. He'd had hours of this. How was he supposed to work?

"Defend yourself," a *Washington Times* reporter demanded. "Or can't you do that?"

How am I supposed to defend myself? Or account for every minute of trips I took abroad twelve, fourteen years ago?

"Does this explain your strident opposition to the development of the Alberta oil sands?" a Canadian reporter demanded, as if Ruhi would lay the entire country to waste to stop a single pipeline.

But he knew people who would. He couldn't kid himself about that. The fringe elements of the environmental movement saw climate change as such a threat that they would gladly shut down the U.S. to stop more greenhouse gases from getting pumped into the atmosphere.

But the unknown enemy wasn't even making climate-change demands. *That'll be the day.* Why would they? Mohammed would somehow take care of those earthly concerns. Just like Jesus would turn carbon dioxide back into fossil fuels—à la water into wine—for the fundamentalists in America.

People, including reporters, were going crazy, and he'd had it. He'd endured this crap for most of the day.

He walked out of his office, past a wall of plants growing right there in the building, and bolted out to the street, hoping to catch the Metro that ran past NRDC office—and had been a key factor in building at that location. He suddenly longed for the unencumbered days when he had immersed himself in such purely rational decision making.

There appeared little clear thinking in the air right now, and all the finger-pointing—at him—made Ruhi both highly visible and clearly too vulnerable to stand on a crowded street waiting for light rail. He started walking—fast.

He wore his Ray-Bans as a matter of course, and was pleased to don them today. But with TV screens and the Web filled with photographs of him, the shades didn't feel sufficient to hide his identity, so he snapped up a cheap fedora from an Ethiopian street vendor. But he still caught glances coming his way. No one accosted him, though, so he figured every guy from the Middle East was probably getting the same going-over. He took heart in thinking that even now he might be more anonymous than he feared.

He made it halfway home before a friendly-sounding man yelled, "Hey, Ruhi, are you doing okay?"

Before he could catch himself, he turned. A guy in his early twenties took his picture with a phone and stood five feet away brazenly working his screen, undoubtedly uploading the photo: "Ruhi Mancur in his latest disguise."

He wanted to knock the camera out of the shooter's hand and stomp it, but that would just draw additional attention and dozens of even more damning photos.

That was when Ruhi started running. He would have preferred

to be in his trainers, rather than thick-soled and brilliantly shined brogues; his light running shorts and sleeveless shirt, instead of a Brooks Brothers blazer and chinos. But at least he was moving.

He thought of the old movie *Marathon Man*, and felt like the young, lean Dustin Hoffman trapped by accusations that he could not answer. He longed to escape his grim circumstances and see Candace, to assure her that he wasn't guilty of any complicity in these horrible crimes against America. Surely, she would believe him.

They almost kissed last night. He relived the moment as he ran. It came as they sat on the love seat, when their eyes had locked. It was just after she said that she didn't think he was an angry man, that she'd known those kinds of guys in the service, and they weren't fun. The implication had been so clear: *You, Ruhi, are fun.*

If she'd looked at him a second longer, or shifted a half inch closer, he would have kissed her. He'd wanted to *so* much.

Ruhi didn't care that she worked for a conservative congressman who, given half a chance, would ensure that every last lump of coal in the world was burned. She was appealing. Immensely so, and not just those fine blond locks and shapely legs, or her bright blue eyes. Candace was strong, unabashedly so.

Maybe it was a reaction to his own patriarchal culture, but the very fact that she could take a dangerous situation in hand with such brio impressed him. He found that alluring at a level he'd never before known. He'd always felt sorry for subservient women. His mother was his father's slave. He felt terrible for her. The lack of a wonderfully invigorating give-and-take in a relationship was a complete turnoff for Ruhi.

But Candace was honest, maybe the most honest woman he'd ever met. He wanted to see her. And he also welcomed the prospect of having her armed and by his side. She said she'd come back to his apartment after work because the mob was looking for him, too. She meant the thugs who'd tried to break down her door. He groaned, knowing that she could not have known that in less than twenty-four hours the mob would metastasize to include much of the nation.

If he'd been able to reach her, he would have suggested they meet at a friend's home. But the only number he had for her was the congressman's office, and that line had remained busy all day. How had he failed to get her cell number? Well, there had been a ton of distractions this morning, culminating in that deeply offensive broadcast by the man who threatened to shut down the grid again at any second.

He kept his pace up. His feet burned inside his leather shoes. Sweat soaked his slacks and shirt. He felt the underarms of his blazer dampen, his collar chafe. He slowed to loosen his tie, and then wished he hadn't. A woman yelled, "That's him. That's the guy who did this."

What the . . .

She pointed boldly, indignantly, at him from less than fifteen feet away.

He sprinted down the block, trailed by heavy footsteps. It couldn't be her, could it? He looked back. Nope, not her. A guy was chasing him. Big as a Redskins linebacker, which gave Ruhi more ease than pause: Linebackers weren't built to run distances, and this guy looked winded after a block.

But Ruhi felt like a criminal as he dashed through the sidewalk throngs. He turned the corner of his street and raced the last few hundred feet as if his life depended on it, which he thought might well be the case because, incredibly, his hulking stalker was not that far behind him.

Ruhi scrambled up the steps, where he and Candace had stood side by side just yesterday. The door to his building was open on the strength of a small stool. That was a real blessing because his pursuer was now only about five townhouses away.

Ruhi kicked the stool inside and slammed the door behind him, checking the lock.

He was breathing hard.

His landlord, Jackson Halpen, stood a few feet away with his arms across his chest. They looked huge as hams. Ruhi had never noticed how muscular Jackson was. And his landlord looked pissed. Sounded it, too, snarling when he spoke.

"Hey, Ruhi, what's the big fucking rush?"

Ruhi caught his breath quickly. He had great recovery times. He also had his eyes on the front door and his apartment key in hand.

"I'm not the most popular guy on the block." Trying to make light of his infamy.

"Yeah? You think so? You're not even the most popular guy in this lobby. I saw the way you kicked my little stool. Did you destroy the furniture in that apartment upstairs, too? And the door? I mean, when you weren't busy attacking the whole country with your computer, you slimebag."

"Are you serious?" was all Ruhi could manage in those first few seconds, because he was listening for his stalker.

"And now you kicked my stool like it was nothing. Look at it."

Halpen picked it up and—to Ruhi's way of thinking—held it like a club to point out a crack in the seat that could have been there for the past ten years.

"Did I say you could kick my stuff around?" Halpen shouted. "I sure as shit did not. I might have company coming over to help me clean up this mess. I might *want* the door open for all kinds of reasons."

"Look," Ruhi pleaded, "a guy's been after me all the way here."

"No kidding?" Halpen said with the worst smile, the kind that promised a whole series of unpleasantries. "You're mistaking me for someone who cares, Ruhi *Mancur* from Saudi Arabia."

Halpen said Ruhi's last name like it were an epithet, then unfolded his arms and examined his hands, as if he were taking inventory of his knuckles.

"I had nothing to do with tearing up that furniture or door," Ruhi said rapidly. "There was a mob trying to break down her door. *They* shot at her lock. She shot back. She had to. Then they came back last night and tore the place up. We were barricaded inside my apartment."

As Ruhi talked, he hurried down the hallway. Halpen watched him.

"Just the two of you. Nice young blond girl and *you.*"

Ruhi swore silently, remembering that Halpen was named after the city of his birth: Jackson, Mississippi. He could hardly believe that people would play the race card now. But of course they would. The same racist sentiment had driven someone in the intelligence community to leak the background information on him.

Bam-bam-bam.

"You want to answer that?" Halpen asked with another wicked smile. "I'm sure it's for you. One of your many fans."

Ruhi pulled out his key, acutely aware that Halpen was walking to the lobby door, and that right outside was the man who'd raced after him for several blocks.

"I'm opening it," Halpen yelled. "Hang on. He's right here."

Ruhi was so nervous, so shaken, that he had difficulty slipping the key into the lock.

He threaded it as Halpen worked the one on the front door.

I'm toast, he thought when he saw Halpen's hand moving on the lock. But it took his landlord three attempts to free it because the mechanism proved as nettlesome as it had yesterday afternoon when Ruhi had tried to open it for Candace and himself.

While Halpen swore loudly at the lock, Ruhi opened his door—finally—and darted into his apartment. But unlike last night, he didn't have Candace by his side with her semiautomatic.

Thankfully, the bureau was still near the door. It had two bullet holes in the second drawer, right about the height of Ruhi's heart.

He shoved the dresser into place just as the pounding resumed, this time on *his* door.

He ducked and yelled, "What do you want?"

"I want to talk to you, sand nigger."

"He *really* wants to talk to you, Ruhi," Halpen yelled. "Give him a chance to say his piece. Open the door and hear him out," he added, with no attempt to hide his amusement.

"You got a master key I could use?" the intruder asked Halpen.

"I do, and you'd be welcome to it, except I don't have it with me."

Bam-bam-bam.

Ruhi realized that he'd never stopped sweating, even in his air-conditioned apartment.

He heard more people gathering outside his door. They were shouting. Ruhi thought he heard pushing. He wished like hell he had a gun—two or three of them.

Then he heard what sounded like people falling or getting shoved against the door and walls. Fighting. Halpen was shouting for everyone to get out of his building. His landlord didn't seem to be having such a good time anymore.

A punch landed on someone so hard that the noise carried right into Ruhi's apartment. A man was screaming, "Yeah, fuck him over. Do it. Do it!"

Someone else yelled, "Kick his ass. He's harboring the enemy."

A huge fight broke out. Halpen was yelling for help.

Ruhi hated him but called 911, knowing he could be next. The line was busy, which came as no surprise: Emergency services were a mess.

He wished Candace would show up. Right then gunfire exploded in the lobby.

Holy shit.

Nothing hit his door, much as he could tell. He thought there were three or four shots, but they came so fast he couldn't be sure of that, either.

For several seconds he crouched behind the bureau, worried for Candace's sake. Had she shown up and been taken unawares? But he realized it wasn't Candace when a guy yelled, "You shot him?" and another guy yelled, "Goddamn right I shot his ass, and I'd do it again."

Ruhi didn't hear anything from Halpen. All he heard were men, maybe some women, running off. The lobby was emptying. He tried 911 again. Busy.

He hit "redial" at least fifty times in the next half hour.

When he finally got a response, it wasn't on the phone. It came as a knock on the door, polite after all the pounding.

Candace? It had to be her, but she was so late. "Who's there?" he asked, keeping his head below the dresser.

"Ruhi Mancur?"

A guy? "Who are you?"

"Agent Simmons of the FBI. Unlock your door and step back with your hands up so we can see you clearly when we enter."

"How do I know you're the FBI?" *The FBI! What the hell?*

"Look out your window, but keep your hands up."

"But you're at my door."

"Mr. Mancur, look out your window."

Ruhi scampered across the floor to the love seat where he'd almost kissed Candace last night. Standing, with his hands up, he saw dark-suited men, armed with rifles, spread out around as much of the grounds as he could see.

An agent held up ID, though Ruhi no longer had any doubt about who had come to collect him.

He moved the bureau aside and said, "The door is unlocked. I'll step back. I'm definitely not armed."

"Tell us when you're in position in front of the door with your hands raised."

Ruhi did as directed.

"Is the bureau clear of the door?"

"Yes."

The door exploded open an instant later. Armed men in flak jackets and helmets with clear plastic shields poured into the room.

Ruhi caught a glimpse of Halpen lying on his back in the lobby, eyes open and lifeless.

In the next second, he was forced facedown on the floor.

"You are being held pursuant to guidelines established by federal terrorism statutes, and you are also under arrest as a suspect in the murder of a man identified as Jackson Halpen."

"What? *What*?" Ruhi shouted. He felt blinded by panic.

The agents dragged him to his feet and hauled him out the door.

He looked for Candace even now, but there was no sign of her. Maybe she'd come but was barred from getting close to the building.

Then he asked himself a simple yet disturbing question: How did the FBI know that he had a bureau in front of the door?

CHAPTER 8

AS RUHI MANCUR WAS hauled from his apartment in the heart of Georgetown, even more formidable teams of FBI agents converged on NRDC headquarters in New York City and the NRDC office in Washington.

Agents in the District swept right through the building, as if they knew every detail of the layout. They did. Because Ruhi had been a "subject of interest" for many months, schematics of the NRDC offices had been drawn up. After the grid went down, all the agents assigned to his case—and there were now several dozen—were given copies of the layout to study.

A corps of agents headed directly to Ruhi's office, commandeering the space and overseeing the methodical removal of all the office equipment that he conceivably could have used. That included computer components for NRDC copiers, along with memory chips for every other device that kept records, which included most everything in the building, short of the furniture. They spared the energy-saving thermostats on the walls.

Other agents demanded the surrender of all recording devices from NRDC personnel. That meant, of course, cell phones. When a wiry, bearded, middle-aged man demanded to know why, the curt response was, "National security."

A young, summer-suited man made the mistake of trying to surreptitiously record the raid anyway, perhaps with visions of YouTube fame in mind. Agents grabbed him immediately and forced him against the wall for a pat-down. He was Flex-Cuffed and led away.

"What are you doing? This is an outrage," a younger, fair-skinned woman yelled at the agents.

Coworkers tried to calm her, but she shouted, "I will not be silenced."

Silenced? No. But arrested when she nonsensically tried to block agents from entering a conference room.

Lawyers for the environmental organization pored over the legal documents provided by the FBI team. NRDC's legal staff studied the papers they'd been served, but the best legal minds in the environmental movement were accustomed to fighting civil actions on behalf of air, land, and water—and the people affected in those cases. They appeared to be on less confident ground parsing documents related to the arrest of their director of research. Most of them looked stunned to learn that Mancur had been swept up by the FBI as part of its investigation.

"We're absolutely certain that you'll find everything in order," said the FBI's lead counsel.

"Is this really necessary?" asked his counterpart at NRDC. The woman was in her fifties with sensibly styled short gray hair that matched her equable manner. The latter was considerably at odds with the attitude taken by the junior staffer who would not be silenced, who, in fact, was still shouting as she was dragged out of the building.

After glancing toward the departing uproar, the older woman said, "We are certainly prepared to cooperate with any legitimate investigation."

"That's where we might be at loggerheads," the Bureau lawyer said. "The word 'legitimate' is highly subject to contention. We are not taking any chances. I'm sure you can understand why."

It was not a plea. It was a clear allusion to the cyberattack, from which the country could not possibly recover for many months. The stock market had crashed to record lows, the U.S. dollar was at its lowest ebb in history, and martial law was unlikely to be suspended anytime soon because every day the number of "domestic disturbances" increased, setting abysmal records for what others simply called riots.

"Where have you taken Ruhi?" an NRDC field director asked. He had just burst out of the lavatory to find an office in tumult.

"We are not at liberty to comment," said a hawk-faced FBI agent in his early thirties. He spoke with a smile that appeared plastered to his face. "We can say only that he has been taken into custody for questioning."

"Has he seen a lawyer yet?" demanded NRDC's counsel, who appeared to be tiring quickly of the boilerplate responses she was receiving.

"We can't comment on that, either," the smiling agent replied.

"I didn't ask you," she replied, "I asked him"—training her eyes back on the Bureau's legal talent—"lawyer to lawyer."

"Lawyer to lawyer, I'd have to say that we can't comment on that," her counterpart said.

Up in New York City, the personnel files of the organization were being loaded on to handcarts and trundled out the door to long black vans waiting on West Twentieth Street. At the same time, dozens of computers were carried carefully out of the building by a stream of agents.

Stunned NRDC staffers watched in silence as the office was swiftly stripped of almost all its electronic devices. In New York, it was the group's legal counsel, not a lower-ranking employee, who went ballistic. That happened after the regal-looking lawyer was served with the search warrant by the FBI attorney overseeing the raid. Then she was told by a husky agent to hand over her phone, laptop, and "any other electronic devices."

The woman raised her voice in protest, saying, "Just stop this right now. I mean immediately."

"Please provide the requested devices, ma'am," the agent said evenly, "or we'll have to place you under arrest."

"You do that," she declared. "And I'll see you in court."

"Yes, ma'am, you will."

She smacked the search warrant down on a desk repeatedly. A fellow employee stopped her. She handed over her devices and walked away, visibly shaken.

Deputy Director Holmes sat at his desk receiving a live video stream from both locations on a wide split screen. Witnessing the NRDC's New York lawyer's explosion made him grateful that no news media had been permitted anywhere near either location, and that those recording devices had been confiscated so quickly. Watching a search warrant executed was rarely a joyful experience when it involved a staid establishment like the NRDC, a legal entity that he actually held in high regard. But one's personal feelings could never come into play at times like this, because keeping the nation secure was not for the faint of heart. Then he cringed, thinking that even the strong of heart hadn't fared very well in that mission lately.

Donna Warnes sat by Holmes's side, laptop open so she could take notes. But Holmes said nothing. He watched and listened in silence to the live video streams of the raids. He always worried at times like this that a suicide bomber would suddenly appear. It was not a rational response, and he knew that; but it wasn't a rational world, and he knew that even better.

When it appeared that both search warrants were being executed without incident, he turned back to reviewing the interrogation video of Ruhi Mancur. They had paused it just as the two agents who were grilling Mancur turned their attention from the murder of his landlord to questions about the cyberattack. Mancur had asserted that he'd locked himself in his apartment and remained there during the time that shots were fired in the lobby—when Halpen, apparently, was murdered. Voice stress analysis indicated that Mancur might well be telling the truth.

The voice technology was hardly the final word, but it synced with Holmes's own assessment of Mancur, and with the physical evidence acquired to that point.

The murder weapon, for instance, had not been found, and it was not easy to conceive of how Mancur could have killed Halpen if he'd been locked in his residence until the FBI arrested him. And it was unlikely that he had left, considering the hostility of a mob that from all reports was clamoring to kill *him*.

Possibly, final answers about Halpen's murder would come after forensics scrutinized every square inch of the man's apartment, but the initial search—and it had been thorough—turned up no firearms in Mancur's residence. Neither was a gun found in Candace Anders's apartment upstairs, which Mancur could have had access to, considering the compromised condition of the door.

Agent Anders had rented it as part of her FBI undercover assignment. She had done an outstanding job of insinuating herself into Mancur's life at a most propitious time. And her valiant defense of him—at deadly risk to her own life—would earn her Holmes's nomination for a National Intelligence Distinguished Service Medal, the top honor in the intelligence field.

Holmes could scarcely imagine what it would look like right now if their chief suspect, in the most damaging attack ever endured by the country, had been murdered by a mob. It would have smacked of Jack Ruby rubbing out Lee Harvey Oswald, only much, much worse.

Not on my watch.

Holmes resumed the interrogation video. The two agents were now boring in on Mancur about the cyberattack. The suspect remained as steadfast in denying that crime as he had been about the murder. Well, that certainly was no surprise to Holmes; he had received updates on the questioning, and he knew Mancur hadn't confessed, but he'd wanted to "read" the man himself.

At that moment, Holmes received an encrypted message on his computer that made him moan. It contained an update of the voice stress analysis that was unsettling: In denying the cyberattack, Mancur had registered readings remarkably similar to his answers about the shooting. Ditto for his denial of having ever had any affiliation "whatsoever" with Islamists, including Al Qaeda.

The latest results bothered Holmes deeply. They'd polygraph Mancur, too, but Holmes had a bad feeling that Mancur was a good guy.

He rubbed his forehead so hard that he might have been trying work a genie out of a magic lamp. The effort earned him only a concerned look from Donna, which he did not acknowledge.

And then it got even worse. Another encrypted message said that Mancur came out with similarly consistent results when he confessed, of all things, to cheating on his taxes by phonying meetings with solar energy experts in Pakistan.

Like we care about that crap, Holmes said to himself. *Does he actually think we want to nab him the way Hoover nailed Al Capone?*

Those were the days, when life was simple. Not that Holmes had lived through them himself, but he was sure you could be nostalgic for times you'd never known, because that was exactly how he felt right now.

Could the stakes possibly be higher? They'd arrested a man of Saudi descent, which was getting huge attention around the world, and the suspect was passing voice stress analysis without missing a beat. If he really was innocent, that meant that their best hope of finding a fast means to stop a final and decisive cyberattack was vanishing. Any second now the country might get plunged back into darkness. Holmes had absolutely no doubt that the terrorists would follow up just as they had promised.

Cocky sons of bitches.

They had to be supremely confident that they could deliver their coup de grâce, or they wouldn't be waiting. And he had to grant that they'd earned the right to their sickening self-assurance.

In his estimation, the only reason the enemy hadn't shut down the grid for good was that the anxiety over when that would happen was producing unprecedented social unrest, as well as the means to display the complete demoralization of the United States to the world. From Beijing to Patagonia, from Stockholm to Johannesburg, people were tuning in to video showing Americans in full-scale panic, replete with looting and burning and massive lawbreaking by ordinary citizens. Talk about a propaganda coup. Why would any enemy throw the death switch now? Let her roll. They were probably offering hosannas to whatever deity they worshipped.

Holmes thought the grid would go down for good only when Americans hit rock bottom, leaving his most haunting question unanswered: How much further down the devolutionary scale would the country fall?

He paused the Mancur video and leaned back in his chair. Then he looked at Donna. He had all manner of experts at his command—voice analysts and forensic psychiatrists and cyber-security geniuses, among scores of others—but it was Donna, with her associate of arts degree from some obscure junior college in Arizona, whose opinion he often valued most at times like this.

He didn't even need to ask. She shook her head, saying, "I don't think so."

Not bad, he thought, for not having seen the results of the voice stress analysis.

"Meaning?" He wanted her to be completely clear.

"I don't think he had a hand in it."

NSA chief James Bolls would howl if he ever got a gander at this scene, but Donna had been right much more often than most of the higher-priced talent. She swore that she had developed her "BS detector," as she put it delicately, by raising three daughters, all of whom hit their teens in the 1990s. "If you can decode an adolescent girl's excuses and 'stories,' these guys become a piece of cake" was her explanation for her strange prowess.

"How do you figure the links to terrorists that they found on his laptop?" he asked her.

Links that on the face of it were powerfully persuasive. The cyberforensics squad had already uncovered communication with known Islamist officers in the Pakistan military and with various chieftains in the northwestern region of that country. About the only thing they hadn't found yet were communiqués from the caves of Waziristan, like the burrow that had proved so hospitable to bin Laden at Tora Bora. But given the enormous sophistication of the attacks, Holmes was reasonably sure that they weren't emanating from the medieval reaches of the planet's most infamous redoubt.

"I don't know, Bob." Donna turned informal only when they were alone. "Except maybe he was right when he said the Chinese might try to frame him. Whatever the reason, I think he's telling the truth."

"I don't see any Chinese hand in this attack," Holmes said at last. "I agree with McGivern on that." The gray-haired analyst had agreed to postpone her retirement at his request.

"We're not talking about the attack per se," Donna replied. "We're talking about the Chinese exploiting an anticipated attack by planting evidence, in advance, against its enemies. We know they're opportunists of the first order. You've said so yourself many times, whether it's computers or cars or flat-screen TVs. So let's look at it this way: What if the Chinese saw an attack on the U.S. coming, even just a strong possibility of it, and put the Islamist evidence on Mancur's computer because they wanted him silenced? However they do that stuff."

Holmes had to suppress a smile. Donna had a clear conceptual grasp of cybersecurity, and could handle all manner of office systems, but when it came to the bytes and packets of cyberspying, all she had was her golden gut.

"It's possible," Holmes allowed. "But it's hard for me to accept that the Chinese would have bet on the come, so to speak, and done it with such success."

"Well," she said with a shrug, "they had a strong reason to frame Mancur, even if they didn't launch the attack themselves."

Donna was referring to Mancur's contention that the Chinese were angry with him because of his vehement and outspoken opposition to the pipeline that would carry crude from the Canadian tar sands down to the Gulf Coast. The bulk of the Canadian oil wasn't going to the U.S. but to China, to feed that country's seemingly insatiable thirst for energy. It was now the world's number-one emitter of carbon dioxide.

Donna went on: "The defense secretary himself said publicly that we could be looking at the Pearl Harbor of cyberwar, long before this ever happened. I'll bet there were all kinds of skulduggery going on in the cybersphere."

"This was no Pearl," Holmes said. "This was a lot worse."

But he couldn't quarrel with Donna's larger point: The secretary of defense had been very public about U.S. vulnerability to cyberattack. Holmes knew that all too well, because he had helped craft the statement the secretary delivered when he stepped in front of the cameras to alert the public and Congress. Everyone in the intelligence community had hoped the man's words would provide a strong warning—and great impetus for strengthening American defenses against cyberattacks. In the end, though, Congress had sat on its hands, and the message proved more prophetic than powerful.

It was never pleasant being right about disastrous outcomes, and that had been confirmed, once again, this morning when a gaggle of congressmen called for the defense secretary's dismissal.

"I suppose you could ask the Chinese about it when they stop by," Donna said.

She wasn't kidding. A Chinese delegation was actually heading to the White House to talk directly with the president. The Russians had booked some of his time as well.

The leadership of both countries had raced to assure the administration that they'd had nothing to do with the attack. China and Russia, independent of each other, had also assured the U.S. leadership that they had started investigations of their own to find the perpetrators.

Holmes believed both countries on both counts. Why wouldn't they do all they could to eliminate such a maverick terrorist threat? Russia and China could also become targets of a rogue warrior. And both nations had large stakes in America's welfare. That was especially true of China, which was the single-largest holder of U.S. dollars, and whose own economy, after blazing along for years on the strength of low wages, cheap exports, and currency manipulation, was starting to sputter. The last thing the Chinese wanted was the U.S. in its present, weakened state—or worse, if the plug were pulled for good. They already had lost hundreds of billions with the collapse of the dollar.

Russian willingness to help the U.S. stemmed, first, from not wanting to endure the enmity of the world's foremost military power; even in its greatly weakened state, the U.S. arsenal was not to be trifled with. And second, Holmes knew the Russians did not want to see their ally Iran blamed for the attack; they would undoubtedly make the case for not moving against Iran when they had their meeting in the Oval Office.

Russia's reasons for trying to keep the Iranians out of U.S. crosshairs were geopolitical in nature. The Great Bear and Iran shared a common interest in wanting to limit U.S. influence in Central Asia, and the two had formed a gas exporters' organization to further their individual and mutual interests.

But a lot of U.S. fingers were pointing to Iran, particularly because in recent history it had been identified as the source of Shamoon, a crippling cyberattack on Aramco, the state-owned Saudi oil company that also happened to be the world's most valuable firm. Iran's Shamoon virus erased critical data on seventy-five percent of Aramco's corporate PCs. That was an extraordinary amount of information, including spreadsheets, files, emails, and documents.

To add insult to considerable injury, the data was replaced with an image of a burning American flag, driving home a point widely held in the Middle East—that Saudi Arabia was little more than an American proxy.

The attack on Aramco was "a significant escalation of the cyberthreat," in the defense secretary's words at the time. Holmes was certain of their accuracy because he had also penned them.

Shamoon had been part of an escalating cyberwar between Iran and the U.S. that America had actually started when it launched Stuxnet, the worm that targeted Iranian centrifuges at a nuclear facility—and then squirmed past its target to infect millions of computers worldwide.

The U.S. also took aim at Iran with Flame, a virus that went after the Iranian oil industry. It forced Iran to shut off Internet connections to their Kharg Island oil terminal, through which eighty percent of that country's oil exports flowed. Flame also smacked down Internet service to Iranian oil rigs and the country's oil ministry itself, which wreaked all sorts of havoc pleasing to the U.S.

So the tit-for-tat had taken its toll, especially on the Iranians. But would that have prompted them to launch an all-out attack on the U.S.?

Holmes had no love for the Iranians, but he didn't think they were responsible for the devastation of the past few days. The mullahs running the show in Tehran were too calculating for that, in his view. And those religious leaders knew their country's cyberwarriors were still too inept to avoid leaving identifying clues in their viruses. That was clearly evident in Shamoon, which had been quickly traced to the Persian Gulf power. Even the most fanatical Shiites in Iran had to know that their country would be demolished if a wholesale attack on the U.S. were ever traced to them.

Though Holmes was operationally dubious of agents in situ—preferring intercepted communication from the source—those on the ground in Tehran felt certain that the Iranians "weren't that crazy," as the CIA's most highly prized asset put it.

But that didn't stop the punditocracy from going berserk. Last night, as Holmes tried to relax with a nightcap by watching a late-night Fox broadcast, one of the network's dimmest bulbs started humming an old Beach Boys song.

"Oh, Christ," Holmes mumbled, knowing what was coming.

Sure enough, the anchor, who couldn't find his way out of a hallway with an exit sign at both ends, started reprising John

McCain's take on the classic, "Barbara Ann": "Bomb-bomb-bomb, bomb-bomb-Iran . . ."

What *was it about the drumbeat for war?* Holmes wondered as Donna gathered up her computer and retreated to her office, sensing, as she often did, when her boss needed time to think.

Holmes had earned his stripes, and then some, in Vietnam. There was nothing romantic about that war. It was all mud and blood and gore, and though he kept his political preferences to himself, he loathed, to his very core, the non-vets who called for war, even when they were right. He could never say so publicly, given the string of non-vets for whom he'd served—Clinton, Bush/Cheney, Obama—but that's how he felt. The hell with political correctness.

His phone brightened; Donna was alerting him that two of his top cyberforensic specialists were outside his office. Holmes said to send them in.

He thought of them as twins because they were both dark-haired, mustached, and in their early thirties. They also spent a lot of time with each other outside Fort Meade. Not that Holmes cared. He was glad that people could no longer be blackmailed for their sexual orientation. Made for better national security.

The two stood stiffly in front of his desk, which was par for the course.

"Sit down," he told them.

Jason, the taller one, settled first. He tugged on his lab partner's sleeve, startling Jacob. The shorter man might have been in a daze.

Holmes watched Jacob Rena sit, wondering if he'd fallen asleep on his feet. Nobody was getting much shut-eye with the cyberattacker's Damocles's sword hanging over the nation's head.

"What have you found?" Holmes asked Jason Barnes. With their given names both beginning with *J*, Holmes had often thought it was as if they'd been coordinating their lives since birth. At least Jason was taller and generally more dominant. It helped to keep them separate in Holmes's mind.

Predictably, Jason delivered the news: "We've recovered another cache of emails that Mancur sent to Anwar al-Awlaki," the U.S.-born Muslim cleric who was killed by an American drone attack. "It turns out that Mancur was a big fan of the guy's videos."

Awlaki, a leading Al Qaeda figure in Yemen, had made scores of pro-Islamist videos extolling terrorism against the U.S. And he'd had his macabre successes, most prominently Major Nidal Malik Hasan, the Army psychiatrist at Fort Hood, Texas, who shot and killed thirteen people at the base, wounding thirty-two others. The massacre took place after Hasan exchanged inflammatory emails with the radical cleric.

"Looks like Awlaki really did inspire the biggest killer ever from the grave," Jason added.

"How many emails to Awlaki?" asked Holmes.

"Twenty-three in the latest batch. We're still working on it," Jason replied. "We thought you'd want to know right away."

"I do. What's Mancur saying in his emails?"

"You could safely put them in the category of more fan mail," Jason answered.

"In some of them, to Islamists in Pakistan," Jacob added, "Mancur sounds incensed that a drone killed Awlaki's son."

Abdulrahman al-Awlaki, a U.S. citizen like his father, was sixteen when he was killed with others by a U.S. drone a month after his father died. Like father, like son was the consensus in the intelligence community, but the killing of the kid had raised a ruckus among human rights activists that had yet to settle down. National security, Holmes reminded himself, was not for the faint of heart.

"Do you want this released to the media?" Jason asked, sitting up straight, which made him tower over his lab partner.

Holmes thought Jason was clearly energized by the prospect

of his investigation finding a larger audience. Which immediately placed him in Holmes's mental suspect file, in the event there were ever any leaks from the man's department.

"Let me think about that," Holmes said and dismissed them.

He watched them file out, not the least bit satisfied with their findings. *It was a little too pat, wasn't it?* he asked himself. *Finding more of them?* It made Holmes think that the Chinese might, in fact, be setting up Mancur. It was just like them to manufacture every last bit of possible evidence. The Chinese had a penchant for larding on the "evidence," as if they had little faith in their most straightforward lies. Tossing in al-Awlaki was like throwing in the Islamist kitchen sink.

He brought up the interrogation video and watched it for a few more minutes.

Would prosecutors ever get a jury to convict Mancur? Holmes shook his head. Not if the Donna Warnes of the world were sitting in judgment.

What about you? he asked himself. *Would you vote to convict? Jury's still out.*

• • •

Ruhi forced himself to sit down in his cell. Every horrific photo he'd ever seen of Abu Ghraib came back to him now. Dogs snarling at the faces of bound prisoners, naked men stacked on top of one another like cordwood, and always, *always* that pathetic Army grunt, Lynndie England, standing with a leash around the neck of a Muslim man lying on the floor of a cell block. Ghastly. And that's what he might be in for now. Probably worse. They thought he'd been party to the worst attack on the U.S. ever. They wanted to know whom he'd been working with. What was he supposed to say? The truth? He'd tried telling them the truth. They didn't want to hear the truth. Soon they'd subject him to sleep deprivation, hallucinations, earsplitting rap music 24/7. *Waterboarding.*

Fear made his stomach so tight that he could have been swallowing boulders all afternoon, instead of the bile that even now seeped into his mouth.

At least his story had been consistent. And why wouldn't it be? The truth was simple to keep track of. But the truth wouldn't be good enough. He could tell by the way they questioned him that soon his adopted country would torture him, and he knew—had no doubt— that he wouldn't last two seconds once they put pliers near his fingernails. He'd tell them anything they wanted to hear, for all the good it would do, but then his story would be inconsistent and they'd accuse him of lying. And that would be all the excuse they'd need to use the worst torture on him. That's probably exactly what happened to everyone who found himself in one of these cells, guilty or not.

"Did you commit these acts against America?"

He spoke to himself as he imagined some central figure would in the plot against him. He saw the man not as an American jurist but, bizarrely, as a British officer of the court in a white wig.

Where do I get this crap from? And when will I get to see a lawyer?

Under the terrorism laws, he could vanish into the American version of the old Russian gulag—but with the added, all-American patina of patriotism and *torture.*

Ruhi thought-felt-feared all of this over and over. He lay back on his simple bunk and stared at the ceiling, knowing that somewhere a lens stared back at him from whatever impregnable material kept him incarcerated.

Maybe Candace, too. *Is she watching?*

She'd worked him like a puppet, and he'd bought into her. Oh, God, had he ever. More than that, he'd fallen for her. He thought she was so honest. The most honest woman he'd ever met. He cringed when he remembered saying that to himself. But when the FBI came calling at his apartment, the only way agents could have known that he'd had a bureau in front of his door was if they'd had one of their own right next to him during the terrifying encounters of the previous twenty-four hours. At that very instant he'd known who Candace really was. All her gunplay, bravado, and coolness under fire had come from Quantico as much as Kabul—if her stint at the embassy were even true.

And yet, if she hadn't defended him, he'd be dead. She'd put her own life on the line to save his. That had to mean something, right? Or was he deluding himself once more? Forgetting that protecting him was her duty. *She was paid to do it.*

But wasn't there something between them? He couldn't forget the moment on the love seat when they'd stared into each other's eyes. One second longer, a half inch closer, and they would have kissed. They *would* have.

He closed his eyes now, tried to measure his breath. Sweat trickled down his checks.

Ruhi felt lost, like Josef K. in Kafka's *The Trial.* He'd read it in Honors English at the University of Vermont. What was happening to him was different, but strangely similar. Only it was worse because when he'd read the book, he'd only glimpsed the horror of accusation. And while it had etched itself into his memory, it was nothing compared to this. Now he knew the horror firsthand.

Kafka's book had ended with a knife. Ruhi could feel cold, sharp steel coming for him. Sooner or later it would find his heart, and—worst of all—Ruhi could imagine how he, too, would say, "Like a dog," as his last words. Yes, he would also die like a dog, but only after screaming anything they wanted to hear.

He lay there, eyes closed, thinking, *It's only just begun.*

He had no idea.

• • •

Lana made it into CyberFortress by midafternoon. Jeff Jensen reported that he expected to have CF's systems clean in twenty-four hours.

"Do you think you'll ever be able to confirm that it was the Chinese?"

"I don't know. But I'm not going to rest till I do." It sounded like a vow.

"Make sure you let people get a breather around here. There are lots of personal challenges that everybody's facing, and you're going to be running things for the foreseeable future."

Jensen was a good one to leave in charge while she worked with the team at NSA. The sober-minded Mormon had a like-minded wife who ran their house full-time, with the same efficient friendliness that her husband showed at work.

"All right." She rose from her desk. "I'm going home to spend the evening with Emma. I hope she's okay. I feel like a totally negligent mother."

She'd tried calling and texting Emma, but her daughter wasn't responding, which meant she was either feeling too crummy, which was scary, or so good that she was too busy texting her friends to bother with her mom. That would be irritating—to the extreme.

"Audrey asked Irene Johansson if she'd please go back."

"She did?" Audrey was Jensen's executive assistant. Another Mormon.

"Irene's in her ward." A Mormon administrative district. "She pointed out that it was vital to national security that she help Emma for you."

Jensen spoke with just the lightest hint of irony.

"That's good news, I think," Lana said, wondering how Emma was responding to these machinations. "I'm going to head out."

"Audrey says it's working out just fine with Irene and Emma."

And it was. When Lana walked in the door, Emma was curled up on the couch, meds on the end table. Irene sat next to her in an armchair. The television was on—horrific aerial shots of the huge forest fire near Denver that had started after a pipeline explosion.

"The president's going to be on, Mom," Emma said drowsily.

"When did they announce this?" Lana asked. She'd heard nothing about it, and she'd been listening to NPR until she pulled into the garage.

"Just like a minute ago," Emma said. She slurred her words but seemed to speak with little discomfort.

Lana greeted Irene, mouthing "Thank you" when Emma's eyes returned to the TV.

She shifted the girl's feet and sat down, then placed them on her lap. Emma practically purred. She sure seemed agreeable.

The station switched to the White House Briefing Room, where the president was walking to the lectern. He looked, in a word, shaken, as if he'd been rushed from the Oval Office to make a statement. Maybe they were doing it on such short notice to prevent the cyberterrorists from shutting down his address to the nation. Nonetheless, she thought the president's makeup team could have spruced him up for his first public words since the attack.

"Good evening, my fellow Ameri—"

Right then the power went out and came back on almost immediately. It did that two more times in rapid succession. Then three more times—but slowly. The president looked around, as if lost.

Don't look weak. Don't!

The power came and went three more times quickly, before coming back on for good.

Lana slumped back into the couch when she recognized the pattern. It was the international distress signal: · · · — — — · · ·

SOS. Save Our Ship.

Of state, Lana realized.

Her faced reddened. Her hands curled into fists.

Mocked by a murderous unseen enemy.

The president persevered with his short speech, but not impressively. The great orator, who many had said was a throwback to another era with his magnificent metaphors, uplifting language, and ringing intonations, sounded flat—all fizzed out. He told his "fellow Americans" to stay calm, even as he appeared defeated and bewildered. Then, after a few minutes of speaking—which proved painful to watch—he looked left and right of the lectern, as if bereft of direction, and walked away.

Reporters yelled questions at him. They were boisterous, maybe even outraged. But the president's one good move, in Lana's opinion, was to never turn back to face them. That would have been another mark of indecision. If he looked shaky before his exit, at least he proved resolute in his leave taking. *Small consolation,* she thought.

The Morse code—the SOS—appeared to have rattled him. Lana presumed the president had decoded it in the moment, as she had, or that someone had informed him almost instantaneously. The bald irony of the message itself was unnerving: using the earliest means of telecommunications to scuttle the first few words of a president's address about the most sophisticated attack in world history.

We have you coming and going.

In so many words, that was what the enemy had said, Lana realized.

And maybe that was what had flustered the president most: that the enemy had infiltrated the most critical circuits in the country—the ones that kept the White House at the center of world power.

CHAPTER 9

AGENT CANDACE ANDERS SAT in her office at the FBI's training center in Quantico shaking her head as she watched the president walk out of the Briefing Room.

She felt so discouraged when the phone rang that she could scarcely pick it up. Only a stalwart sense of duty prompted her to answer. A woman said that the deputy director of the NSA, Robert Holmes, wished to speak to her.

Candace sat upright, smoothing the creases in her slacks and shirt, as if she were about to Skype or appear before the Joint Chiefs of Staff. But this was just a call, if anyone could ever say that having one of the most powerful people on earth on the line was "just a call."

"Agent Anders?"

"Yes, this is she."

Holmes identified himself formally, and then asked how she was doing with a genuineness that surprised her.

"I'm fine, Deputy Director Holmes."

"Please, Bob is fine when we're just talking between the two of us."

Just talking? "Yes, sir." She could *not* call him "Bob."

"I wanted to express my deep appreciation for the work you did on the Mancur case."

"Thank you, sir."

"Your great courage has been noted. I cannot think of a single instance in my fifty-plus years of service in the intelligence field where an individual agent's heroism was more important to the country than yours was in the Mancur case."

"That's very kind, sir."

"It may be a lot of things, but it is not kindness, Agent Anders." Perhaps he was taking a cue from her in remaining formal in his manner. "It is an accurate summation of what you did, and while the media are still trying to figure out who did what to whom, your enduring silence is appreciated as well."

"Of course, sir. I wouldn't think—"

"I know you wouldn't, and that's why I want to talk to you about Ruhi Mancur. Just you and me. Face-to-face. What's your schedule look like?"

"When, sir?" She could scarcely imagine any appointment that she wouldn't be expected to cancel to respond affirmatively to the deputy director's request.

"Right now."

"I'm available, sir. Certainly."

"I thought so. I checked with your superiors to make sure that you would be. There's an NSA helicopter waiting on the pad that you can see right outside your window." She stood, as if commanded, and opened the blinds, spotting a Chinook, its rotors already turning. "Let's go for a ride."

Candace hung up, caught her reflection in the dark glass of the window, and considered freshening up—for no more than a second. Surely he knew exactly how much time she would need to make it to the bird.

But she did pause. She couldn't help herself. She thought of her brother, Liam, lying at rest in Arlington Cemetery, one of thirty-three funerals at the national shrine on the day he was buried. He'd been a Marine, fighting in Afghanistan's Helmand Province. Killed by the insurgents in a grim firefight that had also taken the lives of two other jarheads.

That was another reason Candace had gone ROTC at Indiana U. She didn't talk about it much, had never mentioned it to Ruhi Mancur, but the thought of her bloodstained brother never felt more than a breath away.

She wondered what Liam would have thought, seeing his little sister all grown up now, grabbing her shoulder bag to run off and meet with the deputy director of the National Security Agency.

He'd think you're doing good. He'd say, "Go get 'em, girl."

And he'd tell you to wipe that tear away, she said to herself when she felt it rolling down her cheek.

As soon as she stepped from the building, a dark-suited man identified himself and escorted her to the chopper.

Deputy Director Holmes shook her hand when she climbed in.

The copter's long rotors whirled faster. Holmes handed her a headset. She belted in and put on the device, placing the mic in front of her mouth.

Candace had been in helicopters plenty, but never with such widely esteemed company. Other than the two pilots, they were alone, rising quickly into the smoky night.

She had flown into and out of the nation's capital countless times, but she had never crossed its airspace in a chopper maintaining such a leisurely pace. She quickly spotted the Washington Monument, Capitol Dome, White House, and the cheerful glow of D.C.'s commercial districts, which appeared to be coming back to life.

Then she spotted the arson fires that she'd glimpsed on the ground in Georgetown, still burning not more than a mile and a half from the apartment she'd taken at the Bureau's behest. She had already relocated to a building near Dupont Circle.

"There are more fires over there." Holmes pointed out his window. "That's Anacostia," he noted as they began flying in a wide circle high above the city.

The Anacostia blazes had begun within hours of the cyberattack and consumed much of the capital's poorest neighborhood.

"What a mess," she said.

"Yes, it's a mess," he agreed. "And it doesn't much matter about the socioeconomic strata, now, does it."

She knew it wasn't a question. He went on:

"People always like to blame the 'other' when things go wrong. Usually the poor. But what we're seeing across the country is that what we have to fear most are our own worst selves. Our behavior, as a people, has been sorely tested. We have failed."

She wondered if it was really that bad. But the countless tongues of flames offered a brutally blunt answer.

Candace nodded at him, sickened by the panic of her fellow citizens. It made her think the whole country could use boot camp and a year or two in the military.

"But I didn't bring you up here to comment on the loss of American resolve, Agent Anders. I brought you up here to remind you of the war we're fighting now. It's not just against a cowardly enemy, but our people's greatest fears and the war they make on themselves."

He sat forward, weighting his big broad upper body on his forearms, which pressed down on his knees. He looked like the lineman he'd once been at Notre Dame.

"You know Mancur better than anyone in the intelligence services. I need your most honest assessment of him. So what was your first take on him?"

"Smart," she said without hesitation.

"What else?"

"Moderate. I don't mean politically, though I sense he's also moderate that way, too, despite the accusations. I mean emotionally moderate. He reminds me of another person of color who . . ."

She stopped. *You're way overstepping here*, she told herself. He didn't ask for your opinion of the president.

But Holmes wasn't going to let her off easy:

"I need *all* your thoughts, Agent Anders. Please continue."

With a deep breath, she did. "He reminds me, temperamentally, of the president. Both are men who seem to me to have reined themselves in so they don't fulfill any cultural stereotypes."

Holmes stared at her. Candace felt queasy. *But it's true*, she almost blurted.

He waved his hand as if to say, "Go on." So she did:

"Mancur was measured in how he spoke to me. How he treated me."

"Maybe he was hiding something. Maybe he was hiding all this." Holmes glanced down at the fires. He must have directed the pilots to keep the flames in view. It felt tightly choreographed to Candace.

"That is possible," she said. "But that's not what I believe."

"Was he attracted to you? And let me remind you that I expect nothing but honesty."

She acknowledged what he said last with a nod. The light in the bird's cabin was dim, but a small bulb burned brightly—beautifully—on her head, highlighting her blond hair. "I think so."

"You think so? You don't know?" Holmes sat back. "No feeling in your gut?"

His questions flew at her. She knew he wanted directness more than anything, difficult as it was becoming for her.

"Yes, I think he was attracted to me."

"What makes you think so?"

"The way he looked at me. He . . . he wanted to kiss me. I held the moment as long as I dared, but looked away in time."

"In time?"

"I didn't think I should let him."

"You thought he would have, though?"

"Yes, I did."

"Here's a tougher question. And let me say that there's no right or wrong answer, Agent Anders. Only an honest one. Were you attracted to him? Was there any spark that you felt?"

Oh, shit. There was always a right or wrong answer. *Don't kid yourself.*

"You did feel a spark, or you wouldn't have paused," Holmes asserted.

She nodded again "Yes, there was a spark. But I would never, ever compromise an investigation or my standing at the Bureau, or with your agency, by bowing to any kind of personal impulse. I'd never let that get in the way."

Holmes smiled. She felt the fool. But what she'd said was true, painfully so. But what she had not told Holmes was that the spark was a bonfire that warmed her even now.

Holmes spoke to the pilots: "Take us back to Quantico." He turned to her. "Have you seen enough of this?"

"Yes, but we were just talking about Ruhi." She cringed inwardly when she heard herself use his given name, the way it hinted freely at the intimacy that she felt even as she flew high above the city.

But Holmes ignored that, telling Candace that he'd nominated her for the National Intelligence Distinguished Service Medal.

"Really? I mean, thank you, sir. It's not necessary. I was just doing my—"

He waved her quiet. "It is necessary because you did your job superbly. As you did just now."

"I'm sorry, really sorry that I was attracted to him."

"No need to apologize, Agent Anders. Your answer means . . ." He paused, as if perplexed, when she began shaking her head.

"I know. I'm off the case," she said.

"Quite the opposite. You're very much on it, and it may take a turn in the near future that could prove surprising to you. You see, Agent Anders, you only confirmed what I strongly suspected."

"Could I ask what you mean, sir?"

"Yes, and I would have been disappointed if you didn't have the gumption to do so. It would have indicated a sorry lack of curiosity for a professional in our field. But I'm afraid I can't tell you. Not yet. Just don't make any plans that will take you more than an hour from the city by car."

And that's where Holmes left it as they touched back down at Quantico.

• • •

Holmes had ample reasons to suggest that Agent Anders had been attracted to Ruhi Mancur. Close monitoring of the detainee in his sleep had revealed him mumbling "Candace" on several occasions. It was Holmes's long-considered opinion that attraction deep enough to make a man mutter a woman's name in his sleep with such obvious longing was rarely one-sided, at least among the saner members of the species. And Ruhi Mancur, in the deputy director's view, was eminently sane. So much so that Holmes planned to schedule another appointment in the very near future—with the detainee himself.

• • •

In the morning, Lana could barely rouse Emma from a deep sleep. She gave up for the time being and checked on Irene, who was still snoring at seven thirty, which was highly unusual. On the few nights when she had used the guest room, Irene had never awakened later than six a.m.

Well, best to let her sleep, Lana thought. God knows, Emma could drain the energy of a nuclear reactor these days, especially when the girl was feeling grumpy.

But she hadn't been tetchy last night. She'd actually been loving.

Lana got ready for work, and downed a quick cup of coffee before deciding that it was time to make another attempt at waking the girl, to see how she was feeling. Regardless of her condition, though, Emma would not be heading to classes. That was because Kressinger schools were still closed. Education officials still appeared too shaken to open the doors, which Lana found profoundly wrongheaded. If firefighters and cops and other first responders could be on the job, so could district administrators and teachers.

"Emma?"

Lana sat on the bed, running her hand over her daughter's forehead. The girl turned away, saying, "I'm sleeping."

"I'm going to work. Is there anything you need?"

"No, I'm good," she mumbled.

"How's your throat? Can you tell me? Come on, look at me."

Emma faced her. "It *hurts*. It's strep to the tenth power."

"I'm sorry to hear that." Lana wondered if Emma actually knew what "to the tenth power" meant. She hoped so. It would suggest that her math skills were on the upswing. "Do you need a painkiller?"

"Yeah, I do."

"You're sounding a little better."

"But it hurts so bad."

Lana handed her a Tylenol with codeine and a glass of water. "Here you go."

Emma took the glass and swallowed the painkiller. "Thanks," she managed.

"How are things with Irene?" Lana asked.

"She's all right."

"I'm glad that's working out. I need to go into the office. I'll wake her now."

"I just want to sleep." Emma rolled over.

Lana left, treading lightly on the floor. Less lightly when she reached the guest room. She poked her head in, saying, "Irene, are you awake?"

It was, no kidding, like raising the dead. But once Lana saw Irene sitting up, she told the babysitter that she was leaving but could be texted at any time.

• • •

Moments after Lana drove away from her stately abode, Irene trudged heavily into Emma's room and plopped down on the side of the bed.

"You awake?" she asked the girl, who was now lying on her back.

With no response forthcoming, Irene took the pill bottle and emptied out three Tylenol with codeine. She grabbed Emma's glass and tossed them back in a single swallow.

"You are *so* busted," Emma said, opening her eyes fully. "I saw what you did. I saw you do it last night, too."

Irene reddened. "I don't know what you are talking about. You are on drugs. You must be seeing things. Hallucinating."

"Yeah, I sure thought I was seeing something all right. Give me that bottle."

Irene hesitated, and then handed over the prescription bottle. Emma put it in the nightstand drawer.

"Let's go watch cable," she said.

Irene, already leaning to the side, nodded, which may or may not have been the effect of the opiates. Regardless, she smiled, and that did look genuine, if loopy.

Irene trailed Emma into the living room, and the pair assumed their respective positions: Emma stretched out on the couch, Irene flopped onto the recliner.

"You took my pills, so break out the breakfast," Emma said. "I know what you're hiding."

With great effort, Irene pulled out a huge box of Godiva chocolates that she'd stashed under the couch. Though her efforts were clumsy, she managed to pry the top off.

Emma picked out three coconut creams and a couple of dark-chocolate cherries.

"Bon appétit," she said, handing the box back to Irene, who fumbled around for a milk-chocolate caramel.

Emma worked the remote, and they both started munching.

• • •

Lana called in to CyberFortress as she drove by crews still cleaning up immense piles of debris from the train wreck. Body recovery had ended yesterday. Sometime during the night, two large cranes had arrived and were now lifting the smashed freight cars onto a series of extra-wide truck trailers.

Jensen picked up on the second ring. "Do you need me?" she asked.

"They need you more out at Fort Meade than ever, so we'll make do around here. But throw some work our way, while you're over there," Jensen joked.

Truth was, CyberFortress wasn't even waiting on a contract. They were all-hands-on-deck with the Defense Department cyberteams. In times of crisis, there was no more than a photon's width between the private and public sectors, which both the left and right ends of the political spectrum deplored.

At that moment, though, nobody was complaining—at least not loudly.

• • •

Holmes wanted to see Lana immediately. When she arrived at his office, the well-coiffed Donna Warnes took her directly to him. That entailed returning, once more, to the SCIF, the Sensitive Compartmented Information Security room. After gaining entry, Lana saw that the windowless facility was not full of colleagues, as she had expected. Only Holmes.

"Well, this is a first," she said.

"I can't say I've ever found it necessary to do this with you before, but a couple of things have come up. Go ahead, have a seat."

Lana pulled out a chair and settled across from Holmes, who continued almost immediately:

"CyberFortress will be contacted this morning by the Lawyers' League for the Rights of Detainees. Don't ask how I know this. I just do. They're going to try to hire your company to review our work on Mancur's computers. They're dubious, in short, about our having him held."

"We'll turn them down, of course."

Holmes shook his head, shocking her.

"No, don't. Take the work. I want your best to double-check my best. The league knows precisely what they're doing. They know you work for us on a contract basis. They're so sure Mancur is innocent, they're playing the only cards they have, which is to say *all* of them." Holmes paused and looked directly into Lana's eyes. "And they're probably right about Mancur."

"No kidding?"

"No kidding. Voice analysis, polygraphs—we ran him through the lie detector regimen early this morning—everything says so, including this." He patted his flat belly. "So feel free to do the work."

"Is that why you wanted to talk in here?"

"No. I wanted you to know that it's critical to get to the bottom of Mancur's claims that the Chinese framed him in advance of the attack. There are a lot of emails on his computer from Al Qaeda, Islamists in the Pakistan military, even Anwar al-Awlaki."

"Seriously?"

"Yes, and I don't believe any of it. But nobody I can think of, outside of our agencies, has had more 'encounters,' let's say, with Chinese hackers than you have, especially in the past year. Look, we want you and Jensen to check on the work done at NSA, and go as deep as you can. You two will be doing our final vetting of Mancur."

"Vetting? That sounds like you have plans for him." Now she felt they were moving toward the real reason Holmes had felt it would be necessary to meet in the SCIF.

"We want to turn him."

"Into an operative?"

Holmes nodded. "He might bite. He's been absolutely disgraced, completely demonized in this country. If we're 'forced' to release him by a federal court—which under these dire circumstances can be arranged, believe me—he could look like a hero to elements that we're interested in. And not just for this case." He lifted his eyebrows. "I say that because for all we know a lone wolf like Kaczynski, working away in a laboratory that's off the grid, could have done this to us. We just don't know yet.

"But we're certain that Islamists have tried to attack us in the past, and at the very least they're celebrating the fact that somebody out there managed to cripple us. In fact, so many of them are taking credit for the attack that there are quite a few insults getting traded in that crowd," Holmes said with obvious loathing. "So if we can get them to accept Mancur with open arms, that would be a tremendous advantage—if not now, then down the road. That's assuming he'll play ball with us, and then conducts himself in the right way."

"Which would be the wrong way in the view of most of the world."

"That's correct. The civilized portion, in any case. We think he's smart enough to pull it off. We just don't know if he's tough enough."

"To survive?"

"Well, there's that, too," Holmes answered dryly.

"But we have to vet him first," Lana said, nodding. Then she looked at the ceiling, knowing that something in the ceiling was undoubtedly looking at her.

"Yes, and I want to make sure that he's got a computer that won't get him in trouble over there, because he's going to be vetted by them, too, whoever 'they' turn out to be. We have no idea where this thing could take him. And if we're not super careful, they will literally hand him his head and post the video on the Web."

"You can't possibly be optimistic about turning him, Bob. It sounds to me like he'll have a lot of reasons to tell us where to go."

"Plenty. But his only path to redemption will be to do what we suggest. If he survives, then he might turn out to be the greatest hero in American history. He'll certainly rehabilitate the image of Saudis in the American mind-set."

"He'll be a hero in the Federal Witness Protection Program forever."

"That's hardly a hellish existence, Lana. He and his descendants will live well. We'll be able to assure him of that. And if wants to let us change his appearance, no one will ever be able to identify him. He'll know more freedom than most Americans. For one thing, he'll never have to worry about making a living or having the resources to send his children to the best schools in the country. And he'll be protected by the best security service in the world."

"Do you think he'll do it?"

"We're not banking on it, I can tell you that much. He's just one of our approaches right now. We're running more than a hundred major investigations. I'm giving us a one in five chance of turning him. But that's only if you find him clean as the pro-verbial whistle."

"We'll take care of it," Lana told Holmes.

"If you find he's all right, you might be spending time with him, too."

"Really?"

"If he'll work with us, we'll want you prepping him on encryption. He's going to have to be perfect."

"If he's clean, I'll be glad to help. Just tell me something. Was this your plan from the beginning? Is that why you picked him up so fast?"

Holmes shook his head no, which meant more than just "no"—it meant nothing at all.

CHAPTER 10

RUHI WOULD NEVER BE ready. Never in a million years. Not for what he saw coming. A guard, faceless through a narrow slot, ordered him to get ready to move in the next fifteen minutes, "because your vacation is over."

Vacation? He'd just come back from a long polygraph exam. He'd barely had time to catch his breath.

"And just in case you think we're releasing you," the guard went on, "let me promise you that you are not leaving here. You're not even getting lunch today."

Just how was he supposed to "get ready"? He had nothing he *could* do, except gird himself for the worst—torture. What else could it be? So he began to pace, which made him feel like a caged animal.

You are a caged animal, and now you're about to find out just what they can do to a man when they yank him out from behind bars.

He had thought they were going to bring out the long knives this morning, but they'd run him through that endless lie detector test instead. He knew he'd failed. How could he have passed? He'd been so anxious that he never stopped sweating. The needle tracking his emotions must have turned the page into scribbles worthy of a toddler. The exam had run the gamut of his life, but this morning, at least, they were interested only in prying answers out of him—not fingernails.

The polygraph had come on the heels of hours of interrogation last night. They were clearly unhappy with his denials. He'd pleaded with them, and all he got for his efforts were stony faces, the same grim expressions that greeted his every answer on this morning's test.

Torture had to be next. Wasn't that the drill? He thought he'd read that somewhere. Probably in an op-ed piece in the *Post* or *Times*. They start soft, then hammer hard.

They would have to get tough. He sure would, if he were in their position. With the entire country grinding its teeth over the coming collapse of the grid—for good, this time—his warders could ill afford to take a leisurely pace to his undoing.

Son of a bitch.

As much as he hated his cell—barely long enough for a bunk, and so narrow that he could reach out and flatten both hands against the walls—he didn't want to leave it. Not now. And no lunch? Even gruel would be a diversion.

The answer came to him on a wave of dread: *They don't want me vomiting on them.*

Where the hell were his friends? His colleagues at the NRDC? Nobody had been trying to help him. That's what his inquisitors had told him.

"You're a real popular guy," a guard said to Ruhi yesterday.

He figured that all the guards' words were scripted down to the last syllable to make him feel weak, alone, isolated—dependent on his jailers. But here was the rub about Ruhi's friends: He had seen no evidence that the asshole guard was wrong. Zero. Zilch.

Why weren't lawyers banging on the courthouse doors demanding a writ of habeas corpus? Oh, that's *right*, he scolded himself, because detainees don't have constitutional rights anymore. No opportunity to face an accuser—the U.S. government, in this case—by standing up in court to demand to see the evidence against them, until, that is, they'd been sufficiently tortured to tell any lie that would make the agony stop. Then, and only then, did they get to go to court and hear how they had, in effect, indicted themselves.

Maybe the courts weren't even operating anymore.

It doesn't matter. I'm not going to indict myself in this place, he vowed. Though the implications made his legs feel weak, he shook his head and promised himself that he wouldn't turn his life into a sham for the sake of unseen interrogators—the ones who reputedly watched the torture of detainees from a distance.

In seconds, he heard a metallic click from the door. A command came next:

"Hands out."

A waist-high slot slid open. He stuck out his hands. After they were cuffed, a slot by his feet opened, and his ankles were manacled.

"Step away."

He withdrew his hands and took tiny steps back, making sure not to trip.

Someone looked in, although he was sure they had cameras secreted in the cell.

Now a series of clicks signaled that the steel bars in the door were retracting all the way. It happened so quickly that it made him think of man-eating creatures rearing back on their hind legs to spring at him.

Two huge guards in dark blue uniforms walked in. One ran a chain from Ruhi's handcuffs to his ankle manacles, and then drew it tight before locking it in place.

By design, he could move only slowly. By desire, he did not want to leave his cell any faster than necessary, for what could await him but the worst?

Even so, stepping outside did provide some relief. He was chained, but no longer sealed up like an anchovy in a factory ship.

Relief proved both scant and brief.

"Where are we going?" he asked as respectfully as he could.

"The prisoner will not speak unless he is spoken to," said the guard to Ruhi's right. He gripped his bicep hard, with a hand so big that it wrapped all the way around his arm.

The two men led him to an elevator. The buttons on the control panel were not labeled. The doors closed. The elevator dropped so quickly that Ruhi's empty stomach lurched.

When the doors opened, he saw nothing but metal cages lining a corridor. The passageway was scarcely wide enough to accommodate him and the guard in blue, who continued to apply hard pressure to his arm.

The other guard walked ahead, spine straight, shoulders back.

Both of the men moved too quickly for Ruhi's comfort. His ankle manacles chafed with every step as he tried desperately to keep up.

Then he heard a growl. Deep. Throaty.

In moments they were passing a kennel on his left.

It's empty. So whatever it was must be—

"Fuck!" he yelled as a black German shepherd lunged from the shadows and crashed into the cyclone-fence barrier. It was all that stood between Ruhi and the most vicious display of animal fury that he had ever witnessed.

The beast was on its hind legs, snarling and tearing at the kennel—mere inches from him.

The guard forced Ruhi to stop and face the crazed creature, pushing him so close to the steel mesh that Ruhi could smell the dog's gamy breath.

"Meet your cell mate," the guard said.

They choreograph it to make you feel scared, he tried to reassure himself as they moved on.

Farther along, they entered a well-lit corridor with cinder-block walls. But he still heard that dog howling, and then noticed reddish-brown smears on the wall. Stains. Dried blood.

"Did I say that you could look at that?" the man holding his arm asked.

Ruhi shook his head.

The guard squeezed harder. "I asked you a question."

Ruhi's arm was going numb. "No, you didn't say I could look."

"But as long as you're so curious, do you know what we call that shit?"

"No."

"Terrorist graffiti. We use you guys like spray cans. Certain colors explode right out. The reds, and the—"

The guard in front interrupted his colleague by opening a door. Ruhi was led into a room containing a wooden armchair with a spotlight directly above it. Otherwise the room was dark. The chair legs were bolted to the floor.

With a shove, the guard released his arm and forced him onto the seat. Another spotlight beamed a second later—on a tub in the corner of the room. A hose, long wooden board, and sheet lay next to it.

As Ruhi's ankles were released from the manacles, they were bound to the leg of the chair with a thick, Velcro-lined material.

Both guards secured his arms and wrists. That's when Ruhi noticed indentations in the wood for his hands.

The guards cinched each finger as tight as a racing saddle. Ruhi could not flex so much as a knuckle. Only the tips were exposed.

"What are you guys doing?" he asked. "I swear, I've told you everything I know."

• • •

Deputy Director Holmes watched Ruhi Mancur on his large wall monitor. He was intensely interested in seeing the detainee's reactions to the most miserable threats—and nobody was better at issuing them than the guard nicknamed "Tire Iron."

"We don't really think of these as fingers." Tire Iron's voice arose from the screen as he strummed a series of Ruhi's fingernails. "We think of them as memory aids. Sometimes it's a miracle, the shit that comes to mind once we get a firm grip on the situation."

Mancur appeared reasonably composed to Holmes. Not remarkably so, but he wasn't screaming or weeping inconsolably. The deputy director had seen plenty of that in recent years. Mancur also made no stupid attempt to resist or verbally stand up to the staff, which was smart. Holmes had to watch a potential operative under the most abject pressure, particularly when there was so little time to vet him for an assignment that would challenge the most hardened, experienced spy. He wanted to see for himself if Mancur was tough enough to survive, but the deputy director wasn't alone. NSA psychiatrist Dr. Paul Williamson sat to his right, Agent Candace Anders to his left.

All three watched the screen as Tire Iron tried to raise Mancur's stress levels even more:

"Some guys are such nail biters," the guard said to the detainee, "especially after they're in here awhile, that we really have to dig down in there to get a hold of them. You're cool, though."

Holmes watched Mancur swallow. His Adam's apple rode high. Dr. Williamson toyed with the arm of his clear glass frames. In the light, they looked as white as his closely cropped hair. Agent Anders bit her lower lip, a nervous habit that Holmes had noted.

"Any quick thoughts?" Holmes asked Williamson.

"Not yet," the psychiatrist replied. "Let's see how he does in a moment. How far are you going to go with him down there?"

"Depends on how much he can take," Holmes replied. He glanced at Agent Anders. Her eyes were on the screen, where it looked like Mancur was about to speak up.

That drew the psychiatrist's interest. Williamson leaned forward, studying Mancur's stark demeanor intensely. But Tire Iron reached down and cupped the man's privates, and whatever the detainee might have said was silenced. Then the guard smirked at the camera in the ceiling and stage-whispered, "We've got plenty of play with this one. Enough to work with, that's for sure."

He turned back to Mancur, offering a quick squeeze that made him moan. "Some fat guys make it tough as shit to get in there and work around. We find a way, believe me, but we like you lean ones. But those fat guys don't run marathons, do they? Not like you." Tire Iron was chuckling when he added, "I'll bet you wish you could just take off running right now. But here's the thing, Mancur, you are about to begin the longest, hardest marathon of your life. You will never forget it, trust me. And guess what? The whole thing is going to happen right . . . in . . . this . . . room."

He smacked the top of Mancur's head with each of his last four words. Then the guard gave a thumbs-up to the camera. Rap music blasted into the room. Both guards walked out.

Holmes turned to Williamson and Anders, saying simply, "Here we go. Let's see how he does."

"Let's see if he *lasts*," Williamson said, "given the conventions of the trade."

• • •

The psychiatrist was alluding not just to the rap music but to the fact that it signaled that every act they were about to witness, no matter how degrading, would conform to popular ideas of American torture. Those were the images that seethed with an arsenal of memories and misgivings for a man like Mancur, who would have seen the photos of Abu Ghraib and had read accounts of torture, according to the ongoing analyses of his computers. The "practitioners," as the torturers were delicately called by some agents, knew that no surprise could possibly rival the deepest fears already known to a man or woman.

The conventions of the trade? Holmes marveled over the Orwellian world he inhabited. He wondered if Williamson had even noticed the irony when he said those words.

• • •

The acoustics were horrendous. Intentionally so, Ruhi figured. He could scarcely think, with the furious rap ripping apart his ears.

Above him, the spotlight began to flicker. So did the one lighting the tub, where they would no doubt waterboard him before they were done for the day. For seconds he harbored hope of a power outage—*The big one, now!*

The room did go black, but not silent. It stayed completely dark for more than a minute before light from a strobe exploded all around him. His eyelids could just as well have been made of tissue paper, for all the protection they provided.

He tried clenching them shut, and that helped marginally. He would have kept them in that frantic lockdown—if he hadn't heard that growl again.

He looked around, spotting the big black German shepherd lunging at the end of his leash by the door. The beast's eyes, pinned on Ruhi, blazed in the strobe light.

His handler stepped in a second later, locking up behind him. The man wore dark goggles and had to use both hands to restrain the crazed animal, whose carnivorous impulses might have been thrust into overdrive by the assault on its eyes and ears.

To Ruhi's horror, the handler began to feed out the leash inch by inch.

The animal clawed the concrete floor, lunging with all its might. Twice the power of the dog's exertions earned it a foot or more of lead before the grimacing handler regained control. He looked severely tested by the creature, whose jaws worked wildly and were lit in nightmarish, freeze-frame fashion by the unrelenting strobe.

Ruhi struggled to force down a scream. It was almost unbearable to end up in the grip of American torture, but worse to give in so easily.

He squeezed his eyes shut again; the strobe seemed to paralyze his thinking.

The dog's paws landed on his legs like clubs. Ruhi could not avoid its rank breath. He twisted his head to the side as far as he could, only to feel moist heat and spittle on his skin.

Even over the rap blistering his ears, Ruhi heard those teeth snapping, now only an inch away.

• • •

Holmes stepped closer to the monitor, so close he might have been studying the pores in Mancur's face. "Keep the shot tight," he called to a small black speaker.

The screen filled with the side of Mancur's face as he strained to keep his features away from the dog.

"Back the dog off," Holmes ordered.

In two seconds, the creature was pulled off Ruhi.

"Keep backing up," Holmes directed.

The camera lens widened to include the handler and canine retreating to the door.

"No. Stay tight on Mancur." Holmes sounded exasperated.

The camera zoomed in just as the detainee looked up and yelled, "Fuck you!" to the observers he must have guessed were watching him. He could not be heard above the rap, but it was impossible not to read his lips.

Holmes turned to Dr. Williamson and Agent Anders. The deputy director's face was lit up with a smile.

"Did you see that? That's good news."

"If you want defiance," Williamson said, "you just got it, in spades."

Holmes agreed. "I'll let you get going on the microanalysis of his nonverbals. From the time they got off the elevator down there."

"You'll have it," the psychiatrist said. "We had three teams watching him."

"Fine. I'll see you"—Holmes glanced at his watch—"in about three hours, then."

After Williamson left, Holmes turned his attention to Candace Anders, whose lower lip now looked chewed. "Okay, what's your gut check?"

"I'm surprised," she said.

"A little shaken?" Holmes asked.

"Yes," she acknowledged. "I am, sir."

"Because you care for him?"

She nodded. "But I think it would have been hard to take anyway. That was, well, scary."

"Yes, it was. What surprised you?" Holmes asked her.

"He handled it better than I thought he would."

"My thoughts exactly."

"It almost makes me wonder if he was gaming me when we were under attack in his building. And that makes me wonder if he was tough enough to take part in the attack on the country."

Holmes shook his head and froze Mancur's face on screen,

then pointed to it. "Maybe tough enough, but he didn't do it. See that? That's defiance, just like the good doctor said. But it's more than that. It's also rank indignation. He feels profoundly wronged, and that, in my opinion, has put some steel in the young man's spine, probably more than he ever knew he had. That happens to some people at times like this. It's not as common as watching them collapse, but it does happen." Holmes bent his head side to side, relieving the tension that built up in his neck on an almost daily basis. "He's going to need lots of spine. We all are."

The deputy director sat back down, facing Anders. "I think it's time we had that appointment."

"With him?" she asked.

Holmes nodded. "And with you there."

He watched Anders nod and curl her pretty blond hair behind her ear. She was part of the lure that Holmes would use with Mancur, along with offering the man a chance to redeem his decimated reputation—and those of his Saudi countrymen.

But if Holmes was right, nothing would drive Mancur to act more than the defiance and indignation that the deputy director had just witnessed on screen. They could be fuel for a fire that would have to burn hot and bright—if Mancur were to survive the coming days and weeks.

But the first question was whether he would even come on board. Holmes wasn't sure about that, because he had also seen something else on the man's face—resentment. The flip side of indignation.

Deep-seated and ready to explode.

CHAPTER 11

FIVE FLOORS ABOVE RUHI Mancur's smoldering anger, Lana reviewed all the NSA analyses of his computers. Cyber-Fortress had also been hired by the Lawyers' League for the Rights of Detainees, just as Deputy Director Holmes had foretold.

Lana was double-dipping. Both the league and NSA were paying her to do exactly the same work. The ethics felt fuzzy, even though each party knew what she was doing. Both apparently felt confident of their goals.

The league wanted to confirm what it believed was Mancur's innocence. NSA, on the other hand, wanted to know as quickly as possible whether Mancur was part of the cyberattack on the country. If not, then the agency wanted to determine whether his suspicion was correct that the Chinese had framed him opportunistically. NSA also wanted to know if he could possibly make a viable operative.

To avoid even the appearance of war profiteering, Lana was donating all of her fees from the league to the 9/11 Pentagon Survivors' Fund.

So far she hadn't found one scintilla of evidence on Mancur's computers to suggest that Chinese hackers had done anything to implicate him, but that didn't necessarily make him a liar in Lana's opinion, much less a cyberterrorist destined to loom large in the annals of infamy. As she knew all too well, Chinese "finger-prints" could be hard to unearth. And she was troubled by the language that Mancur had supposedly used in communicating with the assassinated al-Awlaki. Awkward, in a word. The language struck her as the locution of a hacker imagining how a Muslim might sound while sidling up to a fellow terrorist in the cybersphere.

She'd also been going back over Mancur's keystroke speed, which could be excavated even now. While his varied, as almost everyone's did, the emails that were verifiably his—to NRDC colleagues, for example—differed markedly from the cadence used with al-Awlaki.

Both the awkward language and keystroke rhythms could be explained by nervousness—if he had been anxious about writing emails to such a notorious cleric. Or it could be that a Chinese hacker had failed to replicate Mancur's style with unerring accuracy.

So far, though, she had not found the characteristic irregularities that she and Jensen had discovered when Asia's most notorious hackers had descended on CyberFortress.

She leaned back in an ergonomically designed chair, pressing her spine and ribs into the webbing that supported her back. Her earbuds were plugged into a full array of devices. After a relaxing breath, she went to work on another series of Mancur's firewalls.

They were not proving especially difficult to penetrate, which Lana considered another factor in his favor, for surely someone who would launch an attack against his adopted country would never attend to his own security so cavalierly. It also didn't fit the terrorist profile—and there were profiles for those maniacs just as there were for serial killers. Ironic, she thought, that the threats posed by the Ted Bundys and Jeffrey Dahmers of the world actually felt quaint compared to the wholesale death delivered by faceless cyberattackers.

Which was no small reason that every advance that Lana made in decoding a computer gave her a thrill. That was true whether she was working on the actual device—up close and personal, as she was now—or working at a great distance, applying her own considerable hacking skills. She simply loved to ferret out someone's darkest secrets. Though she'd be loath to admit it to anyone, she likened herself to a sheriff in the Wild West, holstered up with touch pads and touch screens to bring law and order to an unruly realm.

That's how she saw the Internet—a technological version of the lawless American frontier. Experts like Lana were constantly on the very edge of an ever-changing world, one that sobered her whenever she tried to imagine what it would look like even five years down the road. It struck her as nothing short of extraordinary to consider the accelerating expertise that had taken place in the past five years, even putting aside the cyberattack that had crippled her country.

On a positive note, what came immediately to mind was how social media like Twitter had emerged powerfully enough to help drive cultural and political revolutions. The "Arab Spring" embodied both. And Wi-Fi had completely untethered entire populations. Flash drives, for instance, enabled individuals almost everywhere to keep massive amounts of data in their pockets. Of course, that technology also resulted in the unauthorized releases of highly classified files.

The Chinese had become infamous for employing their own forms of cybershenanigans. Lana was quick to recognize that if China's hackers had tried to frame Mancur with those emails to al-Awlaki and other Islamists, they might well have been motivated more by money than ideology.

In China, as in most technologically advanced countries, it wasn't unheard of for top-end freelance hackers to sell their services to the highest bidder. And which bidders almost always had the deepest pockets? The ones lavished with government largesse—intelligence services.

So in that sense it was also like the Wild West—with official bounties as bright as silver spurs.

But even the most sophisticated hackers screwed up. In millions of lines of computer code, software designers made mistakes, and when hackers found them they often reacted with glee and great malice. But software designers were hardly unique in their fallibility. Hackers made mistakes, too, and it inevitably brought a smile to Lana's face when she realized that she'd tracked one down and come face-to-face with the anonymous assailant in a virtual O.K. Corral.

• • •

Holmes's interrogation chief marched into his office. Colonel Miles Wintrem had, in fact, worked at Abu Ghraib and the Bagram Air Force Base in Afghanistan, two of the most notorious sites for U.S. torture. Colonel Wintrem had lost an eye in the first invasion of Iraq, and the black patch made him look particularly pugnacious. Holmes thought it also lent the colonel a resemblance to the late Moshe Dayan, the gritty Israeli defense minister several decades ago. Holmes wondered how many of his underlings even remembered Dayan.

"Do you want him in an interrogation room?" Colonel Wintrem asked.

Holmes nodded. "But one with a desk and something comfortable for Mancur."

"Comfortable?" the colonel asked, cocking the only eyebrow he had on display.

"Yes. I think he's had quite enough for one day."

Wintrem pivoted sharply and made a crisp exit.

Holmes sensed disapproval. Didn't care.

He turned back to the large screen as the last of Mancur's fingers was unbound from the wooden armrest. The first thing the detainee did was shake out his hand, as if he'd suffered a shock. In a manner of speaking, he had.

Mancur stood on his own power. Not all of them did after they'd been through a round with Tire Iron and the canine corps.

Holmes saw a mix of fear and fury in Mancur's expression. Even as the deputy director took note of that, the younger man expressed open disgust when Tire Iron directed two guards to chain him up once more. The full treatment followed: cuffs on the wrists and ankles, and the encumbering chain that linked them both.

Poor son of a bitch.

Holmes didn't have an ounce of pity for the guilty. *String 'em up and let 'em swing.* But Mancur appeared to be innocent, unless he was a complete psychopath capable of beating the most sophisticated devices ever designed to test a man's honesty. Holmes doubted that. But he knew that Mancur's abuse by his government would likely have stripped the detainee of any lofty illusions about the intelligence services—the world in which he was about to be offered a post.

Yet Holmes had been around long enough to know that it was absolutely necessary for Mancur to have suffered the deepest, most abject fear of what could happen to him, if he was to have even the slimmest hope of surviving as a U.S. operative. The deputy director knew it was optimistic to even think that the Saudi would sign on, given the open resentment he continued to see on the man's face. But if Mancur were to agree to work for the government that had just put him through his miseries, he might well have to draw on visceral hatred of the U.S. to prove himself to the enemy in the near future. Hatred, in those circumstances, could be a real survival tool. Sometimes the only one you had left.

Holmes buzzed Donna Warnes to check if Agent Anders had returned. He had ordered her to take a breather after witnessing Mancur's "testing," the clinical term used for the process that their prisoner had endured.

"She's just walked in," Donna replied formally.

"Tell her we'll be meeting with Mancur momentarily."

• • •

Tire Iron marched Ruhi out to the corridor. Only after starting back to the elevator—and breathing fresh air for the first time in an hour—did he realize that he'd been saturated with the dog's scent when the beast had climbed on top of him and tried to rip off his face. He didn't know if he'd ever be able to stand the sight of another dog. Like many Muslims, even lapsed ones, he'd had no great love of them to begin with.

As he passed the kennel, now on his right, he picked up a strong whiff of the scent again—and braced himself for the beast crashing against the cyclone fence. But the animal was either giving him a pass or busy terrorizing some other poor slob.

As he waited for the elevator, he told Tire Iron that he'd urinated on himself.

"Because you're a pussy," the behemoth responded.

But after taking him up to another floor unmarked on the elevator panel, Tire Iron and the other guard led him into a room with tall, slate-gray lockers. A man entered with a change of clothes, damp facecloth, and towel.

Ruhi's cuffs and manacles were removed, and he was ordered to strip down and clean up. Unchained, but hardly unguarded—all three men surrounded him. Each wielded a Taser. He gave them no cause to use it.

Freshly attired, and feeling much less foul, Ruhi was escorted farther down the hallway by the same two guards who had been with him throughout his ordeal. They led him into another room that was about half the size of the one in which he'd been subjected to the dog. It was also furnished differently. A utilitarian-looking metal desk sat in front of the wall that he faced upon entry. A high-backed leather chair rose behind it, and an armchair squatted to the side.

The guards sat Ruhi directly in front of the desk. Though less cushy than the other two chairs, it was still a step up from where he'd last perched.

The room also, thankfully, contained none of the apparatus for waterboarding that had given Ruhi such pause earlier—and no doubt had provided near-death experiences for other detainees.

At the very least, where he now sat contained the veneer of civilization. But then again, he reminded himself, so had America until the attack.

• • •

Lana's pulse was racing as she worked on Mancur's computers. She'd just found the cyber equivalent of a military feint—a deceptive move designed to throw off an investigator—and batted it down. The success, which felt pivotal, came after two hours of intricate efforts so intense that the time that had passed might have been no more than ten minutes. She'd been lost in the underworld of the cybersphere.

But lost only to time, because she felt certain that she was getting closer to key data. She didn't know that empirically but sensed it much as blood-spatter analysts, after poring through hundreds of photographs and lab results, might find themselves beginning to read the direction and intensity of a fatal blow. For Lana, it was purely intuitive at this point—and wholly gratifying.

She called Jensen. "I need the last code we wrote for our foreign friends," she said elliptically, unwilling to trust phones when the much more sophisticated cybersecurity of the country had been compromised so fatally.

"It's on the way, even as we speak," Jensen said. "Thar she blows." Always a nautical man at heart.

With an even faster "Thanks," Lana hung up and put to work the most advanced tools of her trade bit by bit.

"Or should I say byte by byte?"

She often talked to herself when the trail warmed up. A good sign, and recognizing the sound of her own voice made her smile.

As she neared her quarry, she reminded herself that hackers came up with complex schemes and programs, but nothing in the universe was as molecularly complex as a human's cerebral cortex. And right now, she was putting every bit—"Or should I say byte?"—of hers into action.

She was still smiling.

• • •

Holmes adjusted his tie before entering the interrogation room. He always did that, believing he was according a detainee a degree of dignity by appearing before him as well attired as he would for the president. After what constituted a mock torture session, a man could feel all hugger-mugger. They'd already started to grant him at least a semblance of control when they permitted him to clean up. Now, if Holmes was right about Mancur, the next step to letting him reclaim his manhood would come by giving him a chance to vent. That's why, for the moment, he'd meet alone with him. Well, strictly speaking, the guards would be there, but not Agent Anders.

The overriding truth of the seconds before they brought Mancur into the room was that Holmes had liked what he had seen of him. Ruhi, as he was beginning to think of him, had not broken under pressure.

What Holmes did not expect was how fast Mancur would pounce. As Holmes stepped into the room, Ruhi's guards stood back from the chained detainee.

Mancur took one look at Holmes and yelled, "I don't know who you are, but I know you're a player. You reek of it, and you should know that I'm innocent before you put any goddamn dogs near me again."

Holmes didn't respond immediately, and when he did he surprised not only Mancur but the man's warders.

"Take off his restraints and please leave."

Tire Iron looked aghast. "I would not recommend—"

"I didn't ask for *your* recommendation. I gave you an order."

The guards took off the chain, cuffs, and ankle manacles. Tire Iron left them on the floor and started to walk out.

"Take them with you," Holmes told him. He wasn't about to let a pissed-off guard leave hard objects next to a man whose own anger could not yet be measured. That was passive-aggressiveness on Tire Iron's part, thought the deputy director. He would pay for it, too. In fact, if he wasn't careful, he'd end up pulling guard duty at G-bay, widely scorned as a miserable assignment.

Holmes was hardly unprotected. Security cameras remained on, and highly trained personnel waited only steps away.

"Innocent?" Holmes said when they were alone. "Well, this may surprise you, Mr. Mancur, but I believe you."

"What was this, then?" Ruhi shook his hands as if they were still cuffed. "Some kind of game?" But he had stopped shouting.

Anger, though, was still present in his tense features; and Holmes knew that if words were rocks, he surely would have been stoned with every syllable that had come out of Mancur's mouth.

"No, not a game," Holmes told him. "May I call you Ruhi?"

"May I call you whatever your name is?"

Holmes smiled, almost said *touché*, and nodded. "It's Bob. And please do. Look, Ruhi, this is definitely not a game. We have a proposition we want to run by you."

"We? I don't even know on whose behalf you're speaking, *Bob*."

He is very angry, thought Holmes. *He needs softening*. The deputy director pressed a button.

"What's that for?" Ruhi asked. "Lurch and his sidekick?" He rolled his eyes toward the door.

"Not quite."

Agent Candace Anders entered the room through a side door that most detainees never noticed till it opened, usually to accommodate a team of security personnel. Ruhi appeared surprised, of course, for another reason, but evidently not pleased. He shook his head and looked away. Holmes watched him closely. This was critical. How angry was he at *her*?

"You sure had me fooled," Ruhi said seconds later when he looked back at Anders. "But I guess that's your job."

"So was saving your life, but I would have done it anyway," she replied, working the script like the pro she was.

"Really? And why is that?"

"I think you know why."

144

"The fact that you're saying that in front of him leaves plenty of room to make me wonder."

"I get polygraphed, too," she replied.

Oh, she's good, Holmes thought. *Very good. On a tightrope and balanced perfectly.*

"Okay, I'm alive, thanks to you," Ruhi said. "Now, are you guys going to let me go? I'm guessing not."

"You're going to have to earn your freedom, Ruhi," Holmes said.

"Oh, shit. Here we go again," Ruhi muttered. "You're the good cop. Maybe she is, too. I don't know," he said directly to Candace. "But the way I figure it, Lurch out there is the bad one who's abused me, by any human rights standard, and yet you're telling me that I have to *earn* my freedom?"

"Ruhi, after what you've been through since your detention—"

"Try 'abduction,'" he interrupted.

"Since your apprehension?"

Ruhi waved away the issue in disgust.

"After what *we* put you through, your freedom will never come easily again. But you could have it, if you listen carefully to what I have to say."

For several seconds Holmes didn't think the detainee would listen to him at all. He wouldn't have been surprised, in fact, if Ruhi had covered his ears with his hands.

But the man looked him in the eye and said, "Go ahead. Tell me what I have to do to get out of here."

• • •

Lana pulled into her driveway still thinking about Mancur's emails. She'd left a message for Deputy Director Holmes, letting him know that she was getting very close to puzzling out those messages to Islamists. Bob had been too busy to meet with her or take her call. She wondered what he'd been up to.

She'd been plenty busy finding clear evidence of Chinese fingerprints on the emails that Ruhi allegedly sent to al-Awlaki and other Islamists. Enough data that if she had to give Holmes an answer right away, she would have to say that the detainee looked like an innocent man to her, too. His claim that the Chinese were out to get him for his outspoken opposition to tar sands pipelines was starting to look plausible.

It wasn't as thorough an analysis as Lana would have liked to have performed—and she would go back to work on it from her home office in the next few minutes—but Chinese hackers had definitely sent out several of those awkwardly worded emails, which made them first on her list of suspects for all the others that she hadn't confirmed. Furthermore, she had found nothing to suggest that Mancur had the technical know-how to replicate the highest levels of cyberspying.

She didn't bother parking in the garage, because she planned to drive Irene to the Metro station. Local rail service had been restored this afternoon, a miracle that rivaled, in Lana's view, the rapprochement between her daughter and the girl's babysitter.

Don't use that word. It's "caregiver." "Babysitter" drove Emma nuts. No sense setting her off unnecessarily.

Lana figured Irene would be overjoyed to be relieved a little early. If a florist had been open, she would have brought her flowers for returning to Emma's side; but the flower business was not up and running yet. As national priorities went, it fell somewhere south of rodent tacky pads. The latter were in sharp demand because rats had behaved as if the power outage were the bonanza that thousand of generations of the pesky little beasts had been waiting for.

So Lana did not come bearing flowers, but she had rushed into the understocked commissary at Fort Meade to pick up chocolates for Irene.

Pleased to find her front door properly locked, Lana walked in as Irene—still in her pajamas and bathrobe, weirdly enough—careened across the room as if pushed. She stumbled into the stone hearth hard enough to chip a bone.

What's going on? Was Emma kicking her again? Jesus Christ!

But wait a minute, Lana cautioned herself. *Emma's not doing anything. Emma's right there, sleeping on the couch.*

She looked back at Irene. The caregiver's mouth was moving, but no words were coming out.

Lana rushed to help her, thinking she might have been suffering a stroke. "Are you all right?"

More mouthing. Still no words, though.

Lana helped her to the recliner, where the older woman collapsed. That was when Lana got a good look at Irene's eyes. Each one appeared as dark and small as a pebble at the bottom of a deep well. So tiny, so impenetrable, that Lana looked away, searching the room for a reason that her trusted friend was so . . . discombobulated.

The answer came as soon as she spotted the prescription pill bottle on its side, a handful of Tylenol with codeine lying on an end table.

"Handful" felt like the right word, because it looked like Irene had taken a lot of the opiates.

Maybe Emma had, too.

"Emma!" Lana shook her sleeping daughter when it dawned on her that the girl might have overdosed.

Quickly, Lana dropped to her knees and checked Emma's pulse. She had a strong one. *Thank God!*

"Emma, wake up." She squeezed her daughter's cheeks. Slapped her gently.

Emma's eyes opened slowly.

"Emma!" Lana exclaimed loudly again.

"She's been real sleepy," Irene said.

Lana, growing furious, ignored the warbly voice.

"Emma. Emma, darling, it's me, Mom."

Her daughter opened her eyes. Thankfully, they bore no resemblance to Irene's teensy-weensy black pupils.

"Here, let me try," Irene managed with a slur so thick that her tongue might have been caught in an eggbeater. "She can be a hard one to wake up."

"No!" Lana pointed a finger right into Irene's face. "She's awake. Don't you even come close to her. Just get your stuff and get the hell out of here. You stole her painkillers, didn't you?"

"It's not what it looks like," Irene said, raising her hand as one does to swear an oath, which was what the addled caregiver apparently had in mind. "I swear to God . . ."

Her voice trailed off, as if she'd forgotten what she was swearing to. Then Irene rose, but made it only a few feet before sitting heavily on a coffee table.

"We've had some challenges here," she mumbled, "in case you hadn't noticed. But why would you? You've been gallivanting all over the place." She turned "gallivanting" into a ten-syllable word.

"Your only challenge, Irene, is to get out of here before I have you arrested. Here, sit up," she said to Emma, who allowed her mother to help her.

"Actually, Mom," said Emma, eyeing the tipsy Irene, "I think she's been taking a lot of those pills. You'd better get someone over here for her."

Lana realized that Emma was right. She speed-dialed Jensen, who brought Audrey on for a three-way call.

"I'm sorry," Audrey said. "It sounds like a relapse . . ."

Relapse?

"She's been completely clean for three years. I'll come get her. She'll get help."

By the time Lana got off the phone, she felt more pity than anger toward Irene. The heavy-lidded caregiver had moved to the recliner, where she lay, eyes glazed, mumbling, "Cable, cable," as she worked the remote.

• • •

Ruhi paced in front of Holmes and Agent Anders. He hadn't asked for permission to get up, which the deputy director saw as another healthy sign that the detainee was reclaiming his dignity. Traversing the breadth of the room had been Ruhi's immediate response to hearing that releasing him from government custody would be easy, but getting him out of the crosshairs of his fellow citizens would be much more treacherous.

He stopped pacing and looked directly at Holmes. "Wait a second, *you* put me in those crosshairs. *You* can get me out by announcing that I'm innocent. Case closed."

"We don't think you understand the anger that's out there," Holmes responded. "More than a hundred thousand of your fellow citizens have been killed. And the number of casualties grows higher every day, because emergency services simply can't keep up with the aftermath of the attack. Even as we're sitting here, they're finding more bodies in crashed train cars and burned buildings. People are too scared to get on a plane, and who can blame them when they could start falling out of the sky any second? For all intents and purposes, our country, Ruhi, *our* country, is at a standstill. And everyone knows that our enemy—the one we can't even identify to make a serious declaration of war—has vowed that it will get infinitely worse. So, yes, we could tell them that you're not guilty, but do you really think, given the chaos and anger and disbelief alive in the land, that you'd still be safe?"

Ruhi stared at him. Holmes knew that he'd struck a chord. And he hadn't exaggerated the threats to the Saudi-born man one bit.

"Let me tell you a sad fact, Ruhi. So far, more than a thousand Middle Easterners have been killed on the streets of this country for no reason other than their appearance. We had four strung up on light poles in Dearborn last night. And we don't even have a single fact to link this to Muslim extremists yet. And it's not just men getting killed. Women and children are, too. A mother in a head scarf was one of the three in South Carolina."

What Holmes didn't add was that the thousand dead was just an estimate. But then again, you'd have to be an optimist to think that unleashing that kind of fury wouldn't add to the death toll in the near future. And Holmes was not an optimist. He'd seen too much of the world to fall prey to Pollyannaish appeals.

"Ruhi, I don't want anything to happen to you," Candace said. "I'll be by your side, no matter what you decide. But if you try to go back to your old life right now, it's going to be dicey out there. I can't guarantee that I can save you again."

The unstated part of her comment, as Holmes and Anders both knew, was that she could die trying to save him next time. And if he cared about her, he might want to hear how he could spare both himself and the agent the harrowing dangers of an America none of them now recognized.

Holmes quickly picked up where he'd left off: "There's a lot of blind anger out there, Ruhi. So, yes, we want you to help us. And if you do help us, even if you don't succeed in what we want you to do, you'll always be protected by a grateful government, and so will your descendants. It's really that critical." Holmes paused, not for effect but because as his final words came to him, goose bumps rose on his back: "If you're successful in the assignment that we have for you, it could turn out to be the most important victory ever achieved by a single American. And when all is said and done, you *are* an American. Please don't forget that."

"Did you forget that? From the moment you arrested me?"

"Never. Not for a moment, Ruhi." Holmes paused, then asked, "Are you game? Do you want to hear what we're thinking?"

No answer.

Holmes watched Ruhi's gaze settle on Candace again. They stared intently at each other. The deputy director felt like a voyeur in the presence of naked emotion. He looked away, trying to give them space. He knew right then that Anders felt more deeply for the Saudi than he'd realized. And it seemed clear that Ruhi felt equally strongly about her.

Talk about dicey.

Putting passion into play was a dangerous decision, and Holmes knew that under any other circumstance he'd never countenance such a move. But all the rules of warfare had been broken, and love—or whatever powerful attraction he sensed in the room—was a small violation when weighed against the murderous dictates of hate.

CHAPTER 12

HOLMES TOOK MORE THAN an hour to outline his proposal to Ruhi. Agent Candace Anders sat next to the deputy director the entire time. The large, white-haired man made a persuasive presentation, and as he seemed to be reaching his conclusion, Holmes leaned forward to look Ruhi straight in the eye. It startled Ruhi to realize that no more than ninety minutes ago a large attack dog had loomed even closer, and that the distinguished-looking man talking calmly to him undoubtedly had played a role in generating the excruciating fear that he'd experienced in the bowels of that building.

"I'm not going to pull any punches, Ruhi. What we're asking you to do is dangerous, potentially brutal, and will demand considerable courage. Time is extremely tight. Only this morning I was informed that CIA analysts found evidence of 'trapdoors' in nuclear missiles, nuclear power plants, *and* in nuclear-armed submarines."

"Hold on," Ruhi said. "What's a trapdoor?"

"Bugs that will let whoever hacked the missiles, power plants, and submarines get right back into them whenever they want, maybe even take control of them."

"Nuclear missiles?" Ruhi could scarcely accept that the nation's most powerful weapons were vulnerable to outside programmers. But before the cyberattack, who would have believed unseen and unknown enemies could have been crippled the U.S. so easily? Only the experts who had warned the president repeatedly, but Ruhi knew nothing about those top-secret briefings.

"Yes, nuclear missiles," Holmes replied. "We're dealing with the most extreme elements out there. By inserting those trapdoors, they might as well have announced that they're not taking any prisoners. We need *your* help."

"What am I supposed to do? I'm not a computer expert, clearly, or you wouldn't have to tell me what the hell a trapdoor is. And I'm not exactly buddy-buddy with Al Qaeda, no matter what you think."

"But you do have a cousin who is, and please don't waste our time or yours by trying to deny it."

Ruhi shook his head, because he now knew the real reason he'd had to endure all of this "attention." Ahmed Mancur, bearded, tall, and lean, bore such a physical likeness to bin Laden that it could only have been a badge of honor among the terrorists with whom he'd collaborated. The son of a bitch had trained in Al Qaeda camps in Pakistan's North-West Frontier. And, yes, Ruhi had been in Ahmed's odious presence at times over the past decade. His cousin had an uncanny ability to sneak into family functions in Riyadh, make his worthless pronouncements on the state of Islam and the world, and slip out. To say Ruhi loathed him would be an understatement—and that was before he understood that Ahmed, while never convincing him to join the ranks of jihad, had certainly forced Ruhi into the arms of its sworn enemies.

"Yes, I know about Ahmed," Ruhi allowed. "And I hate his guts."

"We're not fans, either," Holmes replied. "We think he's had a hand in the attacks. I can't tell you why, and it's not important to know the source, but it appears to be true. If you can contact him and basically say, 'Cousin, you were right,' he might find your desire for revenge believable and welcome you to his flock."

"That's a long shot," Ruhi said.

"It is, and we're taking lots of long shots. You're not the only one. But you could be the most critical."

"I'll bet you tell that to all your recruits."

Holmes shook his head. "No, I don't. I am a straight shooter, for better or worse."

Candace was nodding, Ruhi noticed.

Given the threat to the nukes, Ruhi realized that taking time to think about Holmes's proposal was a luxury that no U.S. citizen could afford to take. In truth, his consideration of the mission was driven by concern both for his adopted country and his own self-interest. If he didn't work for Holmes, Ruhi felt that he'd never live safely in America again. Nor would he likely succeed in leaving. But Ruhi also recognized that the U.S. was struggling for its very survival, and that another cyberattack—one that shut down the grid for good—could bury it forever. Worse, if that was even conceivable, it now looked like the next attack could incinerate America with its own nuclear arsenal.

"I'll do it," he said simply.

"Thank you," Holmes said.

"If they're finding trapdoors in nuclear missiles, it makes you wonder what the analysts *haven't* found," Ruhi replied.

Holmes nodded. "We have no time to spare. We feel like our backs are against a brick wall, and that if these crazies aren't found and stopped, they'll bomb us into caves. We'll be living like animals. Some of us," he added with a rueful shake of his head, "already are."

Holmes came around the desk to shake Ruhi's hand. "Welcome aboard," he said gravely.

Candace congratulated him with a handshake of her own, which sent a rousing current up his arm. Even here, even now—even after the extreme duress he'd suffered and the ghastly news that he just heard—he relished her warmth and affection. Her eyes peered into his. She seemed both searching and open, strong yet sensitive.

He didn't believe that she was putting on a show. They'd moved well beyond that. When she'd said, "I get polygraphed, too," she only confirmed what he had come to feel.

"We're going to drive you to the Farm right away," Holmes told him.

Before Ruhi could ask what the devil the Farm was, Holmes explained: "Its official name is the Armed Forces Experimental Training Activity, but everyone in the defense community knows it as the 'Farm.'"

"I've heard of it. It's down near Williamsburg. I think there was even a film with Colin Farrell set there, right?"

"A facsimile thereof, yes. Although the face I remember most from that movie was Al Pacino's. My generation," Holmes added with a smile.

Ruhi felt a spell of light-headedness. He steadied himself against the desk.

"You okay?" Holmes asked.

"I didn't get any lunch today. I think I've been burning up a few too many calories."

"Sorry about that. We'll have lunch ready for you in the vehicle that will take you down there. Look, Ruhi, before I send you two off on this mission I want you to remember, no matter what, that you're damn tough. Probably a lot tougher than you think. I've had veteran CIA agents and hardcore terrorists who couldn't take as much as you did downstairs without falling apart. I want you to remember that if things go bad over there."

"Over there?"

Holmes grinned. "One step at a time."

"We'll begin by taking a few steps this way," Candace said with her inimitable lilt.

She led him through the well-concealed door that she had used to enter the room. It took him into a hidden hallway system, prompting his suspicion that Holmes wanted him completely protected—even from the eyes of men and women with the country's highest security clearances.

Each corridor appeared seamless at a glance; so did an elevator that was also unmarked, except for a narrow vertical line in the wall.

The doors opened to a steel car that dropped many floors.

"How far does it go?" he asked Candace. "We're already way below headquarters."

"I can't say," she replied. "Sorry."

Yet they descended for another fifteen seconds—it felt much longer—before the doors parted and they entered a garage where a man as large as Tire Iron held open a door of a huge SUV. At any other time in his life, Ruhi would have groused about traveling in a monstrosity that could not possibly get more than single-digit mileage. But right now desiring anything less than short-term survival felt like an indulgence, even to the greenest side of him, which was very green, indeed.

"Bulletproof," Candace said, tapping her knuckle against the glass. "Doors, too."

"How long a drive?" he asked.

"With these guys running the show and emergency lights if we need them, maybe ninety minutes. Mere mortals? Much longer."

Ruhi hadn't been outside for two days, and he longed to see daylight. But after driving for several minutes they still hadn't escaped the underground warren of tunnels and parking areas. A few more minutes passed before he saw the sun. He checked his watch, which had been returned to him along with his other possessions. Five o'clock. Plenty of light left.

A lot of smoke, too. He couldn't smell it in the vehicle, but columns of it rose in the distance. It reminded him of so many pictures of devastated Middle Eastern cities that he had seen on television growing up.

"It's happening across the country," Candace said, pointing to a fire in a gated community. "People are angry." She touched the back of his hand, which was resting on the open seat between them.

He looped his fingers through hers, but she withdrew after a reassuring squeeze. Then she glanced at the security detail in the front seat, the men's shoulders so broad that they almost bridged the space above the console.

"Mr. Mancur," the guard in the passenger seat said, "I understand that you did not have lunch today. I've got some stuff we picked up for you. And orange juice and coffee. If you're hungry."

"I'm starving."

The man handed back a bag, along with the drinks. Ruhi found one of his favorite lunches, Asiago cheese bagels with turkey and lettuce. He almost asked how they knew, but then didn't bother. The coffee, as he could have predicted at this point, was also as he preferred it—strong, with a splash of cream.

He offered Candace one of the sandwiches. She declined.

"You eat. When we get to the Farm, we're going to start with small-arms training. Sounds easy, but it's not. You'll need your energy."

"Handguns?"

"Right," she said.

"Doesn't sound too arduous."

But about ninety minutes later he found that it was nerve-wracking. Ruhi was "shot" in the head five times in the first two minutes of training at the facility, which looked much like a real farm with broad pastures, split-rail fencing, dirt two-tracks lined with shade trees, and a huge pond. What it did not look like was a hardcore training ground for a citizen now taking a crash course in becoming a spy.

He was supposed to enter a room with an air gun drawn, ready to shoot. The weapon was an exact replica of a Glock 17. That much he could handle. The challenge came when human figures popped up that he was ordered to "take out." They were taking *him* out until the instructor said it was time for the "step-by-step."

He meant that literally, as it turned out. With Candace sitting up above the unroofed area, the short man showed Ruhi precisely how to scope out the threats upon entry and move his feet efficiently, "So you don't trip."

"I'm not even sure how to shoot or hold this thing," he said, eyeing the air gun.

"Understood, Mancur," the instructor replied, "and we'll have you on the range soon enough, but given our extremely tight schedule, we want you to know the basics of self-defense and combat in close quarters with natural light. The fact that it's getting dark is perfect, but it does make it more difficult to see the 'enemy.'"

Ruhi accepted the reasoning, followed the man's brusque instructions, and burst through a door into another room, this time firing at a figure to his right before pivoting quickly to his left to "kill" another one. The instructor nodded approvingly.

I'm enjoying this. Ruhi recognized that a primitive desire to prevail in combat was stirring the juices of his reptilian brain for the first time.

With each entry that followed, the instructor worked on the "choreography" until he said he was reasonably confident that Ruhi would not shoot his partner in actual combat.

"You have pretty decent hand-eye coordination, from what I can see," the man told him. "Bodes well for the gun range."

That was where they headed as night fell in earnest. Candace was by his side as they piled back into the large SUV.

"So what did you think?" he asked her, with a glance back at the unroofed rooms he'd just "cleared."

"Pretty good. There's hope for you yet," she joked.

The same security team drove them to the gun range. Ruhi figured the men were tasked with keeping them safe and on schedule.

The indoor range was well lit. Life-size paper targets of a man's upper body hung from clips along the entire width of the room.

A new instructor, a woman about Candace's age, with a blond ponytail and clear safety glasses, told him that he was going to get "stripped-down training" on everything from gun safety to shooting to kill.

"First, I want you to point to the target."

"Don't I need a gun?" Ruhi asked. Out of the corner of his eye he saw Candace cringe.

"Not yet. Point to it," the instructor said in a noticeably less restrained voice.

Ruhi pointed.

"Okay, mission accomplished. Now hold your arm right there." It started to feel heavy immediately. Ruhi realized that he was exhausted. "You see the slight bend in your elbow? How it's not locked out?"

Ruhi nodded.

"Helps if you answer verbally, Mancur. Then I don't have to look away from the subject at hand."

"Yes. Got it."

"Okay, now point with your left."

He repeated the exercise, wondering if there was something wrong with his execution, some bad habit that he would have to break.

"Again, you have the same bend in your elbow, correct?"

"Yes, is that—"

"That's good. When I hand you a pistol, which I will do momentarily, I want you to point, keeping your elbows bent in about the same position. That natural bend is important."

She handed him a real Glock 17. He realized why he had drilled with a replica; right away, the actual weapon felt less foreign. Its thumb rest and grip accommodated his fingers so readily that it was as if he'd been born with it in his hand.

"That gun is not loaded. But always check. Always know what you're handling."

She demonstrated how to pop the clip to check the "load," and then slide it back in.

"What's this?" she asked rhetorically as she racked the slide that rode above the barrel. "That's how you get this semiautomatic ready to rock."

Then she showed him how to hold the gun with his right hand and support it with his left. She tapped both elbows. "See?"

Indeed, he did. Those bent elbows looked like the arms' own shock absorbers.

"About seventy percent of your strength in holding your handgun comes from your dominant hand, which in your case is your right. About thirty percent with your left. It's in the support role. You create isometric pressure to steady your aim."

She went on to explain that he should not hunch over to shoot, "unless you're ducking bullets. Otherwise, stay upright, and raise the weapon before your eyes. You don't want your body and arms all moving at once, no matter what garbage you've seen on TV or in the movies."

She took the weapon back from him. "I'm sliding in a full clip. Seventeen rounds. I'm going to hand it over to you like this." She showed him proper handgun handover. "Now I want you to aim at the center of the figure and shoot until you empty the clip.

Take whatever time you feel you need between shots. This is the fastest training program—and you can put quotes around 'training program'—that I've ever been part of, but that doesn't mean you have to fire fast. Just do your best and pay strict attention."

Ruhi turned to the target, trying to remember everything she'd told him.

The sketch of the man's upper body suddenly looked about a mile away. But what really shocked Ruhi was that fourteen of his first seventeen shots hit the target. Only six were definite "kill" shots. The rest just winged the figure. But he figured that hitting an arm or leg with a 9-millimeter round would ruin just about anybody's day.

"That's good shooting for someone who says he's never shot before."

"I haven't, really."

"I didn't mean to imply differently," she said.

Sure you did. You probably think it was at some terrorist training camp.

He shot five full clips. Out of eighty-five rounds, he missed the target entirely only nineteen times. He felt certain that he would have done better if fatigue hadn't made him so shaky. He mentioned that to the instructor.

"Don't console yourself with that excuse, because in real combat you'll be shaky with adrenaline, and that uses up so much of your energy so fast that we'd like you to be able to do this half asleep. That's clearly not on the agenda in your case. But then again, I'm surprised that you can hit the target at all. What sports did you play in high school and college?"

"I'll bet you already know," he said, smiling.

"You mean your high school basketball career?" She smiled for the first time. "Sixteen point five points per game, along with twelve rebounds and six assists. Yes, we know. Like I said, you have good hand-eye."

After she finished with the care and maintenance of the weapon, she told him that he'd be issued his own Glock 17 when he "touched down."

"Where?"

"Not for me to say, Mancur."

He looked at Candace.

"Me, neither," she said. "But it won't be long till you find out. You only have thirty hours of training left before we leave. You're going to need some sleep now."

He and Candace were fed, and he was escorted by the security detail to a private room. Small, but military neat. A new pair of guards took control of the door for the night shift. There were no windows in his room. He could tell by the guards' respectful treatment of him that they thought he was an important asset. That scared him for reasons he couldn't immediately put his finger on.

Though physically and emotionally depleted, he lay in bed wondering if the big cyberattack had come. After all, he was in a super-secret installation that could surely run on generators for the foreseeable future. Were planes falling from the sky? Nuclear missiles launching from underground silos, targeting the great masses of Americans?

He slept fitfully, awakening for good at dawn for a breakfast heavy on protein. Then he was whisked over to a martial arts training center. He had yet to see Candace this morning. The day began with jujitsu and Krav Maga on a thick mat, for which he was grateful.

Krav Maga was borrowed from the Israeli Special Forces. The instructor, a swarthy man who looked as tough as buffalo hide, was openly dubious of the value of trying to teach a "recruit," as he called him, much of anything in such a short time period. After three arduous hours the man's opinion didn't appear to have changed much; he offered Ruhi only a "Good luck" when the session ended.

What did I learn? he wondered. Not much more than how to isolate an opponent's most vulnerable body parts—and to expect to be beaten nearly senseless while he tried to attack eyes, gonads, fingers, or ribs. The instructor had him repeat those moves over and over.

Ruhi was brought into a large office, where Candace waited for him alongside a Middle East intelligence chief who told him that he'd be going to Riyadh. The bullet-headed man looked like he was in his late fifties. He squinted as he talked, as if he'd spent too many years in the desert sun. The lines radiating from the corners of his eyes were deep, dark, and reached almost to his temples.

"You have family in Saudi Arabia, correct?"

Ruhi answered affirmatively, though his faith in the intelligence services would have been shaken to dust if they hadn't already confirmed that fact.

"Here's your cover story. We want you to tell them that you're repatriating to Saudi Arabia. That after your miserable treatment by the U.S., you knew you'd never be accepted by your adopted land again. You must not only feel free to criticize the U.S., you must let your genuine disgust over what you've been through be known.

"Think about it, Mr. Mancur," the bald briefer went on. "Your fellow Muslims have been slaughtered since the cyberattack. Hung from street poles. It's like the Jews after Kristallnacht. Does that mean anything to you?"

He nodded. The Night of Broken Glass. Beatings, burnings, murders, and the arrests of tens of thousands of German Jews— and a mere prelude to the Holocaust that followed.

"Your friends and relatives are going to want to know how you got out of the U.S. 'Weren't you restricted from traveling?' That sort of thing. You'll tell them that you were innocent, that after torture and tests—and please feel free to describe all of that to them—we believed you. Say that we cut a deal with you. That you could go back to your homeland, but only if you kept your criticisms to yourself. No public statements about what you went through. Tell them that we said we'd kill you if you spoke out. Then tell them that you're going to talk publicly anyway about the humiliation and murder of Muslims in the U.S., that you'll tell the whole world what happened to you. Say you don't give a damn about any deal, that you're ready to join the jihad. Show real anger, Ruhi. Use the rage that you had to be feeling back in the basement at Fort Meade. They *must* believe you. Praise the cyber-attackers. Praise jihad. Talk to your cousin."

"So you know about him, too?"

"Of course."

"I doubt the Saudi secret service even knows about Ahmed."

"We're not sure they do," the Middle East expert told him. "We never shared that with them. We're not going to now. We want *you* to get to Ahmed. Not them. The only thing we've shared with the Saudi agents is that we understand that you are heading there and that you agreed not to speak out against the U.S."

"They don't know that I'm playing ball with you, do they?"

"No way. So they might try to shut you up when you start criticizing us. It depends. Our reading of the Saudis right now is that they play to strength, and the U.S. is not strong, so we're hearing more militantly anti-U.S. voices on the street there. But they still might try to muzzle you."

"And if they arrest and torture me?"

"Hang in there. It'll give you a lot of credibility when you get out."

"Thanks! If I get out."

"If it comes to that, you'll get out. But not right away."

"Oh, shit."

"We don't think you're going to have any problems, Ruhi. Not with them. You might have problems with Ahmed. What's your relationship?"

"Not much. Lots of arguments for years now. I didn't even see him the last couple of times I visited my family. He was gone once. Another time he refused to meet with me, which was fine with me. All we ever did was argue."

"Then tell him, however you have to, that the U.S. really is the Great Satan. People love to win arguments, and the longer they've gone on, the sweeter the victory. So tell him everything that happened to you. Show him the dog bite."

"What dog bite?"

"The one that we're going to surgically implant in your thigh."

"Nobody said anything—"

"We don't have time for this. Trust me, Ruhi, we're not siccing a dog on you. But we will painlessly create the bite of a German shepherd. We'll also create burn marks on your genitals from electrodes. You'll want them, Ruhi. I'm telling you, they could be your ticket into that world."

"But it's only one of many investigations. Holmes told me that himself. Why do I have to go—"

"Through all of this? *So you don't die.* And, yes, we have more than a hundred major investigations going on, but this one is the hottest lead we have right now. Your cousin Ahmed is well connected."

"I know. And I also know he's the reason I'm here and why you"—he turned to Candace—"were put into my fourplex."

"I cannot comment on that," the briefer said, "and neither can she."

Ruhi shrugged. Strangely, a growing part of him was glad to be there. It was as if he'd never really lived before. This was blood. This was real. This was life.

Until you die.

"Learn to love Ahmed, Ruhi. He's your cousin, and now we want him to be your brother-in-arms. Everybody loves the prodigal son, especially if he comes back ready for jihad."

"Then what?"

"Then let's see where that takes you. You're a great propaganda coup. We think we'll be seeing you on YouTube very quickly."

"With or without my head?"

His briefer laughed. "With it."

Ruhi was hustled off to two more trainers, a man and woman about his age. The guy, so glassy-eyed that he looked like he hadn't slept in days, reviewed basic means of avoiding detection. Because it included no training outside the tight office in which Ruhi now found himself, he felt that the briefing had questionable value.

Then he was handed over to a lithe young woman, who appeared considerably better rested. She laid an Apple MacBook on a table, finger-combing her short red hair as she spoke.

"Go ahead, open it. Start it up."

It was his own device. He could tell by a telltale scratch on the cover. He was glad to have it back. The arrangement of the desktop on the screen hadn't been changed.

"So what did you do to it? You did something, right?"

"It's not yours," the woman said. "But we're glad you think it is, Ruhi. It's been outfitted with a history that makes it look like you were contacting jihadist websites. The Chinese did you a favor when they framed you. They made it plausible for you to assume this role. Gave you a vital history. It includes the email to al-Awlaki. It even includes email back from him."

"The jihadists will know that I never contacted him."

"No, they won't," she replied. "Al-Awlaki was sloppy with his contacts. He had horrible computer skills. It's one of the reasons he's dead. He's the one guy we could do that to. But he's still important, because he's revered. He was a turncoat American citizen, just like you'll appear."

"He was a fraud," Ruhi said.

"You'll get no arguments here," the woman said, sitting across from him. "Tomorrow, after lunch, you'll be meeting with a cybersecurity expert to review deep encryption so once you're in the Mideast you can stay in contact with Agent Anders and your agent supervisors here. You're booked out of Dulles on a nine p.m. flight to Riyadh."

"That's it? That's all?"

"No. You'll have more gun training in the morning. Plus, more hand-to-hand combat. We're doing what we can," she added. "Time pressures are enormous. Did you sleep okay last night? Do you need a sleep aid?"

"What?" The question startled him.

"A sleeping pill. Sleep's critical. You'll need to absorb a lot tomorrow. Are you too charged up to sleep?"

"No. I've been sleep-deprived for the past couple of days."

She nodded. "If you need anything, let us know."

"Dinner?"

"You'll enjoy it."

"How do you know *that*?"

She smiled.

Why do I even ask?

It was his favorite meal, lamb rogan josh, served to him and Candace in a private room off the Farm's main dining hall.

When they were alone—although Ruhi doubted they were unseen or unheard—he had an unsettling flash of uncertainty about Candace.

"I have to ask you, is your interest in me just to make me part of this insane mission?"

"I can understand why you'd wonder. All I can tell you is that I'm really attracted to you, Ruhi, and I honestly find that confusing. I'm sure that if circumstances were different, less pressing, I would feel much more comfortable with my feelings. But to feel this way while being forced to go out on what could be a hellishly difficult mission?" She shook her head. "It's kind of crazy, I know. We hardly even know each other, but something definitely sparked for me right away. I don't mean to sound immodest, but I saw that in you, too, the night in your apartment when we sat by the window."

"You're not being immodest at all. Of course I felt something. So where does that leave us on the personal side of things during all this?"

"The same place it leaves us on the professional side—just trying to survive. But I should tell you that I'm not a fast mover under any circumstances."

"Meaning?"

"I've never jumped into a relationship with anyone."

Ruhi was pleased to hear her last comment. His upbringing and Muslim faith, no matter how lapsed, still made him uncomfortable with women who flaunted their sexuality or used it too readily. Candace's words didn't strike him as a dodge or a convenient means to keep him at bay. They struck him as the truth.

Dinner ended on that sincere-sounding note. They walked back to the dormitory, escorted by the security team.

Ruhi settled down in his room by himself, wondering if he should have taken a sleep aid. Between his imminent departure and his feelings for Candace, he was as awake as he possibly could be. He lay with his hands on his chest staring into the darkness, head buzzing in the absolute silence of the room.

A moment later—or so it seemed—he awakened to his last day in the States. Maybe ever.

He still called it the "States." Nobody he'd ever met who was native born used that term, but he did. A small part of him had never fully emigrated from Saudi Arabia, and he was reminded of that in little ways.

My last day.

He sat on the edge of the bed, shocked by the tectonic shifts in his life. His work at NRDC, as important as he had deemed it, now paled. But he guessed that any number of his colleagues probably felt the same way after seeing their country descend into mayhem.

A knock on the door startled him.

"I'm up," he called out.

"Good enough, Mr. Mancur. You have fifteen minutes to shower."

His "hosts" had provided a toothbrush, floss, toothpaste, soap, shampoo, conditioner, and a full complement of washcloths and towels. But no razor.

He looked at himself in the mirror. Stubble everywhere. It grew so fast. After only a few days he had the unkempt look of so many jihadists. He understood why his minders would want him bearded, less Westernized. That made sense—but it also itched.

Candace joined him for breakfast. She looked freshly awake and utterly beguiling. If he survived, if she did too, could they possibly make a relationship work? He knew better than to think that there could ever be an easy answer at this point, but he also knew that clinging to that notion could prove to be a critical lifeline.

Breakfast was ample. After a second round of sessions with his firearms and martial arts instructors, he was taken by elevator to a computer laboratory deep below a barnlike structure. It contained large rooms packed with so many devices that he thought they could have constituted the cybernetic stronghold of the country.

A salt-and-pepper-haired NSA official greeted him without using his own name, and then introduced him to a tall, attractive woman with black hair.

"This is Lana Elkins. She's one of the world's foremost experts on encryption and, to use the vernacular, hacking."

Absolutely beautiful, Ruhi could not avoid thinking as Elkins shook his hand firmly. Her clear dark eyes were dazzling. Older than him by almost five years, he guessed, and every bit as striking in her own way as Candace. It made him wonder what it was about the spy trade that seemed to attract such appealing women. He knew that they couldn't all be so alluring, not any more than all the men could resemble James Bond.

You sure don't, he told himself.

A moment later Candace joined them as Ruhi's tutorial began on his new MacBook. Candace had her own laptop and took copious notes. Elkins sent both of them material every few seconds for the first ten minutes.

"I guess it's got a ton of memory," Ruhi said to her.

"You're guessing right," Elkins replied without looking up. "Agent Anders is your immediate backup," the computer expert went on, "but I'll also be based in Riyadh for the time being."

"Where?"

She shook her head as if he should have known better than to ask.

"You're going to stand out in my home country," he said.

"Conveniently enough, I'll be doing some agency contract work."

Probably for the Mabahith, he thought. The Saudi secret police. Ruhi wouldn't want to be grabbed by them. They had a well-deserved reputation for ruthlessness. But they were also reputed to work closely with U.S. intelligence services.

"'Conveniently enough'? What isn't planned for?" Ruhi asked rhetorically.

"An attack on our country," Elkins responded flatly.

Both Ruhi and Candace nodded.

While his computer skills were reasonably sophisticated, by the time he finished with Elkins later in the afternoon, he realized that she'd primed him for an entirely new universe of knowledge.

"You're a quick study," she complimented him. "But you still might need me in a jam. That's why I'll be there."

"And if I leave?"

"There are all kinds of ways for me to follow you," she said, letting her long slender fingers drift over her keyboard.

• • •

At nine that night, Ruhi sat at a window seat on Saudi Arabian Airlines. Coach. Nothing fancy. Nothing to draw attention to him. Not many people were flying, not with the threat of planes dropping out of the air with the next cyberattack. He made an effort to put that fear aside. Foreign carriers were permitted in and out of a few key points on the Eastern Seaboard. Dulles was a principal hub. The Saudi airline was permitted one flight a day. Ruhi—and no doubt other passengers as well—hoped that the airlines had rejiggered their electronics to prevent penetration by cyberattackers. But who really knew? The lack of an answer probably explained the scores of empty seats.

He wore dark glasses and an oversize ball cap. He also had that dog "bite" in his right thigh. A doctor had dressed and then covered it with a white bandage. Thirteen stitches. Ruhi tried not to be superstitious about the number of sutures.

His testes had also taken a hit—of electricity—and were similarly bandaged. Thankfully they were still anaesthetized. Lying on his back, all Ruhi had seen of the "procedure," as the doctor put it, were two perturbing tendrils of smoke rising from his crotch. The doc had given him a bottle of Tylenol 3, saying, "It's not as bad as it looks or smells, and you won't feel any pain in a couple of days."

Doctor?

He had his doubts as he looked out the plane's window. Ruhi had assumed that the white-coated man was a physician, but now realized that he could just as easily have been a veteran torturer. He'd certainly wielded those electrodes with alarming enthusiasm.

Ruhi's fellow passengers gave no note of his presence. Most appeared studiously preoccupied with their tablets, smartphones, and laptops. He wondered how many of them were CIA agents keeping an eye on him—and other passengers.

Ruhi also wondered if his window seat had also been planned. All he noticed as the wide-bodied jet rose over the Washington area were fires. He quit counting when he reached twenty. Too depressing. One of the more recent ones occurred only this morning when a natural gas pipeline exploded in Alexandria, consuming most of the downtown.

The invasion by the cyberattackers might have been invisible, but it had brought all the brutal signs of real battle fully into view.

Death, fire, rage, and fear. All of them boiled below. But even that grisly toll—horrendous as it was—paled before the realization that control of the country's own nuclear missiles now lay in the hands of its most vicious enemy ever.

CHAPTER 13

LANA LOOKED AT EMMA, slouched on the couch watching TV, and wished more than anything that she could have evacuated her daughter from the Washington area. Their little burg of Kressinger lay well within the capital's kill zone for nuclear missiles—or a cyberattack that could target the wickedly cruel stores of chemical and biological agents left over from the Cold War. Those nightmares included chimera viruses like Veepox, which combined smallpox and Venezuelan equine encephalitis, and could wipe out entire populations.

Horrific scenarios seemed never-ending, when Lana let herself consider the worst outcomes—and how could she not, when her only child could fall prey to them? Such was the unprecedented threat of a cyberattack: It could turn any or all of a country's arsenals on itself. The stronger the nation, the more susceptible it became. Paradox had become the dominant paradigm. That was particularly true for the U.S., which had been the mightiest country on Earth less than a week ago. Now its very strength could turn it to cinders, or leave vast reaches rife with the dead and dying.

Lana and everyone in the intelligence services were in a race against time. How much time? Only unknown hands on unknown computers knew the answer to that question, leaving her and everyone else in the intelligence community acutely aware that the next second could be the last they lived.

She sat next to Emma and tried to hold her. Emma squirmed away. "When is she showing up?"

"She" had turned out to be the surprise caregiver. Bereft of options, Lana had decided to leave Emma at home, but that had necessitated finding a new person to keep watch on the girl. Irene was headed off to get help, if any drug and alcohol rehab centers actually remained open.

As part of Lana's networking, which entailed calling and texting virtually everyone she knew, she had contacted Tanesa Weir yesterday afternoon. Tanesa was the young choir member who, along with others on her big blue bus, had saved Lana's life, along with the lives of so many others during the first minutes of the cyberattack. She'd even been featured in the NPR report. Tanesa was such a responsible person, Lana thought she might know an older woman of like mind and spirit.

After a rushed, fifteen-minute discussion about the duties and compensation, though, Tanesa herself offered to take the job.

Lana was stunned. "How old are you?"

"Seventeen," Tanesa replied.

Only three years older than Emma. But she seemed a lot more mature emotionally.

Lana had been in a supertight spot, expected to depart for Saudi Arabia ASAP, and everyone she knew was dealing with personal and professional emergencies, so she told Tanesa that she had the job, which had outraged Emma:

"I can't believe you're bringing someone that young in to take care of me."

"Would you rather I find another fifty-six-year-old like Irene?" Lana had retorted.

"You don't have to bring in anybody. *I* can do the job."

"I don't think so, Emma. Just last weekend you came home tipsy from drinking Palm Bays. Then you left the house in the middle of a crisis when I told you not to and almost got yourself killed. Those aren't signs of someone who is ready to take care of herself. And Tanesa is very responsible. *I've* seen her in action."

Glowering, Emma had stormed into her bedroom.

Lana had arranged to have Audrey, Jeff's executive assistant, check in with Tanesa daily to make sure she had whatever she needed.

The young woman could take the position because, as a homeschooler, she had a highly flexible schedule. She had never sat in a classroom, yet had excelled on all the standardized tests administered by the school district. She seemed a fine choice, given the circumstances. Lana's main regret was that she had no time to set up a meeting between Emma and Tanesa first. Technically speaking, they had met—at the hospital. But Emma had been so drugged at the time that she had no memory of the bright-eyed choir member.

The doorbell chimed. Both mother and daughter jumped up.

"Do you want to get it?" Lana asked.

Emma shook her head. She looked startled, or maybe it was sudden shyness. It still happened, though rarely.

When Lana opened the door, Tanesa stood there smiling. Behind her, an NSA driver waited in an unmarked car to whisk Lana to Andrews Air Force Base, about thirty minutes away.

Lana welcomed the young woman, who rolled her modest-size suitcase into the entryway, turned, and then hugged her as naturally as if she had known Lana all her life. It made Lana feel good about her decision.

She led Tanesa into the living room, where Emma was still standing, stiffly, Lana thought.

But Emma brightened when she saw Tanesa, who reached out and took Emma's hand in both of hers.

"You are some kind of beautiful, girl. You take after your mom, don't you?"

Emma blushed. Lana hadn't seen that in a while, either. The two young women started talking right away.

Sensing that everything was as settled as it could be, Lana said good-bye, kissed Emma, and ducked out.

She handed her carry-on bag to the driver and climbed into the backseat, looking at the pair still chatting away near the window. Then Emma signaled Tanesa to the stairs, presumably for a tour of the house.

If Lana could read Emma at all, which was a challenge these days, to be sure, she thought her daughter liked the idea of having a young African American living with her. In fact, Lana would have bet that Emma found the idea pretty damn cool, especially compared to the starchy Irene.

The NSA car ferried Lana directly to Andrews for a military flight to Riyadh. Deputy Director Holmes did not want Lana or Agent Candace Anders on the same plane with each other, or on the flight with Ruhi Mancur; other agents were seeing to his safety en route. Both women would be traveling with diplomatic cover to the emirate of all emirates.

Lana looked out as they drove past the big blue chevron-shaped sign for the air base. In minutes, they were approaching the terminal from which she would depart. She imagined that she'd be issued a onesie flight suit, walk up a wide cargo ramp at the rear of the plane, and strap herself into a bare-bones military cargo carrier, as she had once done for an unscheduled trip to

Colombia. Instead, they passed through a guarded gate and drove up to a Bombardier Global Express jet.

An airman loaded Lana's bag while she thanked her driver. She stepped aboard, looked around, and smiled: There would be no funky onesie this time. With its pale blue carpeting and buttery, cocoa-colored leather seats, the interior of the Bombardier might have been luxurious enough to satisfy the Saudi royal family. Clearly, the military's top brass knew how to fly in comfort. Then again, she reminded herself, the Pentagon was the last bastion of loose money.

Seating was arranged much like a series of living rooms. Directly in front of her, a long couch was fixed to one wall, and a set of what appeared to be plush recliners sat in an arc facing the couch. A male flight attendant led Lana to one of them and explained the controls; it converted into a bed.

The U.S. ambassador to Yemen, sporting hair transplants that looked like they'd been implanted by a drunken cosmetologist, looked up from his perch on the couch and smiled, before promptly returning to his laptop.

What's he *doing on this flight?*

She knew better than to ask.

Lana opened her own device, pleased to find Internet service so readily available. The envoy might have noticed her smile. He cleared his throat. "You don't have to worry about cyberattackers messing around with the controls in here. This thing usually carries around four-star generals. *Nothing* can penetrate it."

Nothing? You think so? If virtual hands had commandeered nuclear missiles, then *nothing* was impenetrable, least of all a military jet.

Lana indulged him with an appreciative nod, taking comfort in knowing that her own cover was secure, for surely the envoy would never have served up such techno-tripe if he knew to whom he was speaking.

The flight attendant asked if she wanted a drink. Lana ordered a glass of red wine, a good merlot, if they had it, and wondered about the attendant's real role. He looked much too rugged to play the waiter.

She used an elaborate code, committed to memory, to log on to her computer and access the files that had occupied her of late—an online Islamist magazine that had defied her best efforts to hack it open so she could hack it to pieces. She and Holmes and others in the intelligence community strongly suspected that deep beneath the online magazine's cover, the site was a center for terrorist command and communications.

Not that they weren't producing articles for open consumption. On her screen at that very moment was a headline for the issue's lead story: "How to Make a Bomb in the Kitchen of Your Mom." The English was stilted, but the step-by-step instructions appeared painfully precise and accurate.

Intelligence analysts credited the late Anwar al-Awlaki, the American-born-and-educated promoter of Islamist terrorism, with having encouraged Yemeni Al Qaeda to publish the magazine. It was called *Inspire*, of all things. Building a bomb in your mother's kitchen? Inspiring? To some, it appeared: The Boston Marathon bombers might well have used that very "recipe."

Lana took solace in knowing that al-Awlaki would never oversee the writing of another headline, or the delivery of another inflammatory speech for unbalanced believers everywhere.

• • •

Ruhi felt the landing gear clunk into place and looked down at the King Khalid International Airport. The desert glare made him squint. Even so, he couldn't miss the dome of the massive mosque at the heart of the facility. He recalled a prior visit when a cousin—not Ahmed, thankfully—dragged him to the prayer center that could hold five thousand worshippers inside, and another five thousand in the plaza outside. On that occasion, there had been fewer than fifty people in the mosque.

"But you should see it during Ramadan," his cousin had said, eyes growing large as the dome. "So many people that you're scared for them. For yourself."

"Why?" Ruhi had asked.

"Terrorists. Bombs. The perfect place to kill so many loyal Saudis."

That had been another stark reminder that all was not well in the House of Saud. Ruhi stared out the window now, wondering how much longer the royal family would be able to rule this fiefdom.

He saw the plane near the runway, spotted the shadow of the wing on the tarmac, and felt the slightest bump. The passengers clapped. It sounded dutiful to him. He didn't bother. Neither did he thank Allah; but he saw enough lips moving under enough head scarves to know that many of his fellow passengers were offering their gratitude to God. It appeared no less obligatory than the applause.

Off in the distance he spotted the Royal Terminal, where heads of state and some seven thousand Saudi princes planted their feet first upon coming back to the kingdom. Just seeing those perks riled Ruhi up all over again. How long did the royal members of the lucky sperm club who passed through that luxurious terminal think they could withstand the pressures of the Arab Spring? A country with a king who actually ruled his subjects? Bad enough the Brits and other Europeans had royal families for ceremonial purposes, facile reminders of colonial power now as shuttered as the eyes of the dead. But Saudi Arabia, his homeland, remained rooted in a world that should have been shelved centuries ago. Only the most downtrodden believers could accept the theological rot necessary to support such a system.

Better chill, he advised himself as he headed toward the plane's exit. *You don't want to be trudging into passport control with the proverbial chip on your shoulder. You've already got a cousin the Saudi secret police would love to club to death.* The last Ruhi heard, Ahmed had fled to Yemen, on the emirate's southern and most porous border. Yemen was the destination for scores of Saudi Islamists who wanted more, not less, fundamentalism in their faith.

Ruhi handed his filled-out entry forms to a flight attendant. The man scarcely glanced at him. Ruhi thought his ball cap and beard were ample disguise—at least to the casual observer. A little scruffy today, a little scruffier tomorrow.

He trudged behind the other passengers into a wide, brightly lit terminal, thinking the immigration service would probably give him a good going-over.

Ruhi wished that the intelligence agents who had recruited him had given him a phony passport. He hadn't even thought of that till now. But perhaps U.S. intelligence knew that he could never pass himself off as someone else—not entering a country where his family had close associations with terrorists even more disgusted with royal rule than the expatriate now arriving home.

Within minutes, he queued up in the cavernous entry area. Nothing unusual. Not yet. His imaginings of Saudi secret police descending on him right away had not materialized.

He shuffled forward with his lone bag, obedient as a dog. He knew better than to draw attention to himself at a Middle Eastern border crossing, especially not in Saudi Arabia, where the officials held the keys to a *bona fide* kingdom.

Even the word "kingdom" spoke of a bygone era that still thrived in his homeland. Women were not permitted to drive or vote, but the Saudi king had recently decreed that they could have a seat on the Shura Council, an assembly that considered laws and offered counsel to the king. But the Shura had no real power, certainly not to legislate, and the women would not be permitted to mingle with the men.

Big whoop.

He knew from one of his six sisters that the nascent feminist movement in the emirate was gaining steam. But the great majority of women were subject to strict religious guidelines about the clothing they were permitted to wear, just like Ruhi's cousin, Ahmed, wanted for every woman in the world. Forced conversions and hijabs for all.

A Saudi immigration officer in a long-sleeve white one-piece thawb and a keffiyeh signaled Ruhi to come to a table. While the officer looked from Ruhi's passport to a computer terminal and entered data on a keyboard, another similarly attired officer combed through Ruhi's carry-on.

Ruhi realized that he was holding his breath. *You're such a spy,* he chided himself. *Try breathing.*

"Purpose of your visit, Mr. Mancur?"

"I'm visiting my family."

"It appears that your parents haven't been back in many years. When will we have the pleasure of a visit from them? Or don't they care about the country that succored their souls?"

"They care very much. But my father is working so hard."

"Yes, you do have to work like a slave in the great United States of America. It's all work, work, work. And now it is a disaster there. So is that the reason you have come back? Because it's so unbearable to be in your America now?"

"I won't deny that Saudi Arabia is in much better shape. I—"

"And you," he interrupted, "are you in much better shape after what you have been through?"

"I am okay."

"Okay? Really? I would think what you went through was all but unbearable."

Play hard to get, the Middle East expert at the Farm had counseled Ruhi. *Make it appear that you're too traumatized to talk about the torture.*

"I am very happy to be in Saudi Arabia," Ruhi said carefully.

"Of course you are. But look at what you were doing in your America. You were making fossil fuels out to be a tool of the devil. At the Natural Resources Defense Council you were smearing the emirate. The source of our wealth, our financial lifeline, and you were doing all you could to demonize it." He shook his head. "They say you are a terrorist. Maybe that is true?"

"No, they admit it was a mistake."

"But they let you leave. They wanted to get rid of you. And they did torture you. It says so right here." He looked at his computer screen, hidden from Ruhi. "Do you hate them?" He leaned so close to Ruhi that he could see a lone gray hair in the man's beard. "What did they do to you?"

"It hurt," Ruhi said, hoping to leave it at that.

"And is there any *evidence* that it hurt?"

Ruhi nodded, filled with revulsion at the man's manner, his eagerness, but he also realized that his reaction might be seen by the officer as appropriate for someone who had been severely violated, who had suffered a dog bite and burns from electrodes.

"How long do you plan to visit your family?" the officer asked, changing the subject abruptly.

"A few weeks, maybe a month or two."

"Why not stay here? What do you owe a country that tortured you?" He wasn't interested in an answer. "I will tell you, Mr. Mancur. Not a thing. You owe those devils nothing. Millions of good Muslims can't wait to get to the land of Mecca and Medina. But you?" He shook his head again. "You come just to visit. After what they did to you? But maybe they didn't do anything. Maybe that explains why you're here and why you plan to go back. Maybe there are secrets about your 'torture,' beginning with the fact that there was no torture."

"There was," Ruhi said fiercely. "I can show you."

"Maybe in time you will," he said, sending a chill through Ruhi.

"And I might stay. I miss my country. My family."

"And you would leave your parents in that hellhole over there? Is that what a loyal son does now in America?"

I can't win to lose with this guy.

"No, I would bring them back home, too."

"That is the right word, Mr. Mancur. The magic word: 'home.' Use it wisely. Do not abuse it. Think about it."

The officer slapped Ruhi's passport closed and, for the first time, spoke without feeling: "Welcome to Saudi Arabia. Enjoy your visit."

• • •

Granted, Tanesa was black, and that was cool. Granted, she'd saved her mom's life, and that was cool, too. And, granted, she was a massive improvement over Mrs. J . . . Then again, a stone effigy of Kermit the Frog could have carried that load. But Emma was starting to have her doubts about Tanesa. They'd just checked out the upstairs bathroom and stepped into her room. Up till now, the new caregiver had *oohed* and *ahhed* every few seconds.

But now she was raising her eyebrows. Okay, the room was a mess, but that's not what drew the new caregiver's attention. It was a can of strawberry-pineapple Palm Bay, a purple thong, and the picture of Emma with her skirt up in the ambulance. Skateboarder Boy, whose name was Shane, had left them for her in their mailbox, and Emma had failed to hide them very well after hurrying them upstairs.

"Where'd that garbage come from?" Tanesa demanded, holding up the panties. Then she picked up the Palm Bay. "And you've got no business drinking this stuff."

Emma tried to strike a casual tone, explaining that she'd met Shane in the ambulance. "He gave them to me. They're like a get-well gift."

"Get-well gift? They're a disgrace is what they are. And taking a nasty picture of you when you're hurt and can't do anything about it? That's just wrong."

"It's no big deal. You can't see much. And look at my face. I look good."

"He's not looking at your face, I'll tell you that. And yes, it is a big deal, and if he's bringing you alcohol and a thong, he's going to want pictures of you in that too. He's definitely not welcome when I'm around."

"We'll see about that."

But Emma felt less sure than she might have sounded. She checked her watch and saw that things could come to a head very quickly: Shane had texted that he was coming over with another "surprise."

"Yes, we will," Tanesa vowed.

Now, as Emma headed downstairs, the doorbell, indeed, rang. She raced to open it. Shane, arm in a sling, held out a little bag with his other hand.

"I got you another pair in pink."

But before Emma could take it, Tanesa appeared and reached past her, snatching the bag. She took one look inside and crunched the bag closed.

"You are not welcome here," she said to Shane, "bringing this kind of trash around. And you"—she pointed her long finger at Emma—"and I are going to have a talk."

Nobody had *ever* spoken to Emma like that. She was so stunned she reeled into the living room as the door closed on Shane's shocked face.

"Emma, sit down."

Emma dropped onto the couch.

"Let me tell you something about boys and this stuff." She held up the Palm Bay and the purple thong as if they were diseased. "There is no free lunch with guys. And when they start giving you this kind of stuff, they want the whole buffet. You hear what I'm saying?"

"Yeah, but maybe I want the whole buffet, too," Emma said, making another stab at defiance. But she felt more tentative than she sounded.

"You may think you do, but you don't. What's important to you? Really important. Can you tell me that?"

Emma looked like she'd hit her personal mute button.

"What are you good at, girl? Come on, tell me, please. You play an instrument? Swim fast? Do you like art? Soccer? Science?"

"No, I suck at science. I'm not really good at anything."

"I don't believe that. What do you want to be?"

"A movie star." Emma loved telling adults that, even a young one like Tanesa, just to see whether they'd be honest or say something completely stupid, like, "You could do that."

"Are you working at it?" Tanesa said. "You do any plays at school, that sort of stuff? Or do you just dream about it?"

Emma felt boxed into a corner, but she knew one sure way to shift the subject fast: "Boys like me."

"I believe that. But if they're coming around like that loser, they're only liking one thing about you."

"So what?"

"So once they get it, they're gone."

"Not always."

"Mostly. Hey, I know."

"I doubt that. My mom says you're in a Baptist choir."

"Yes, that's right. But do you think I was born in that choir? Uh-uh. I was not. I've only been in the choir for two years. Before that I spent most of my time striking the wrong notes with the wrong guys, and I paid for it."

"What do you mean?"

"I mean I got pregnant and had an abortion."

Shocked, Emma had to look away. When she turned back, Tanesa's steady gaze met her own.

"Has anybody talked to you about birth control?" asked Tanesa.

"My mom. I know everything. I don't want to talk about it."

"That's good. I'm glad you know everything. Where do you keep your condoms? And are you on the pill, or getting a monthly shot?"

"It's none of your business."

"I'm your *care*giver. That means I am going to take care of you, and if you're so sure that the only thing you're good for is having sex with the first guy who throws some panties at you, then I am going to make doubly sure you have those condoms and birth control pills. I am not kidding. And we are also going over the ABCs of the STDs. Those things and a whole lot more. You hear what I'm saying?"

Emma looked out the window. Shane was gone. She turned back to Tanesa and sighed. "There is something else I like."

Tanesa waited, one foot tapping the carpet. "What's that?"

"I like to sing."

• • •

Ruhi's uncle Malik waited for him at the end of the terminal, where his nephew passed through the airport's tightest security zone. Bearded, Malik still wore plain black glasses with tinted lenses, and dressed as traditionally as the Saudi immigration officers.

Malik was the father of eight children, with two wives. "One wife was enough," he often said in the presence of his spouses, "and two were twice as bad." But he called his children "the great consolation for the curse of matrimony."

"It is really good to see you, Uncle Malik."

His uncle hugged him and held him by both shoulders. "I'll bet it is also great to stand on Saudi soil after the way they treated you in that disgusting country that you call home. You are a hero to us here, Ruhi."

He certainly hadn't received a hero's welcome in passport control, but the Saudi street was often at odds with Saudi officials, which was why the royal family had to keep a tight lid on the populace—and tossed their subjects an occasional bone from the skeleton of democracy.

But Ruhi mentioned nothing about the immigration officer who had questioned him, saying only that it was always good to see family.

Uncle Malik led him to the exit. "You return an older and wiser man, Ruhi. Are you thinking of staying this time, now that the U.S. is the world's biggest disaster zone?"

It irked Ruhi to hear his uncle take such pleasure in America's pain, but he responded evenly. "That is possible. I am considering it."

"I had to laugh when I saw pickup sites for Saudis to donate clothes and food for Americans. I donated one of Shabina's old hijab. I tell you, that made me laugh even harder. Oh, how the mighty America has fallen. And good riddance, right? So tell me, what did they do to you?"

Hard to get, Ruhi reminded himself again.

"They did what you would expect," Ruhi said as they approached Malik's luxurious Mercedes, one of the perks of being an executive of the Saudi Arabian Oil Company.

Ruhi stretched his long legs, appreciating the cool air in the idling car.

The driver, who had been with Malik's family for forty years, merged the full-size sedan into traffic.

"But what could you tell them, right? You know no secrets. Not like Ahmed."

Malik had always been so proud of his firstborn boy, even after years of Ahmed's radicalism.

"I know nothing."

"Not really. You know Ahmed. I'll bet they wanted you to tell them everything you could about him."

What Ruhi wanted to tell Malik was that his uncle's firstborn was an asshole and the reason he himself was caught up in this mess. But again, he refrained, confining himself to a nod.

"I expect my boy will be a martyr one day." Malik shook his head. "That is so sad. I share so much of his faith, but not his methods. Saudi Arabia is a great society. We do not want to undermine the great spiritual wealth we have by seeing our best and brightest kill themselves."

Ahmed? Best and brightest? Ruhi shuddered, he hoped not visibly.

"You will see that you are in the best place in the world to find your faith again, Ruhi. I hope you do. You look like a lost sheep to me." Malik shook his head again.

"No, the first step to finding my faith again came when they threw me into a dark cell with a big dog. That was the first time I prayed in many years."

Malik took Ruhi's hand in both of his. "I'm so sorry they did that, but I am so grateful to Allah that you have found your faith.

You remember the Prophet's words: 'A sincere repenter of faults is like him who hath committed none.'"

Not another proverb. Uncle Malik had always been a great one for quoting the Prophet. Ruhi forced himself to nod, then looked out the car window.

As far as he could see, the Saudi Arabian desert rose and fell in wind-sculpted dunes. Riyadh lay in the direction they were speeding.

Malik leaned so close that Ruhi could smell his breakfast of eggs and onions. It didn't smell good. "Did they put that dog on you? I have seen the pictures from Abu Ghraib."

Ruhi nodded.

"They are beasts!"

"Worse than beasts," Ruhi said. "They are cornered beasts. They will do anything to try to save themselves. I know that now."

Ruhi withdrew his hand and turned away, filled with disgust. It wasn't directed at Malik's curiosity, and it wasn't a performance. It was real. He acted on the anger and fear and even the frailty that he had known during his torture—and the resentment that he harbored for all of that. And it had worked. He could tell that his uncle sensed the genuineness of his hurt and fury.

Ruhi wondered whether it was the right time to ask if Ahmed had slipped back across the border to come home, or was still in some Islamist redoubt in Yemen. No, he told himself. *You don't want to push too hard too fast, even with Uncle Malik.*

• • •

A feast was prepared that night in Ruhi's honor. A sheep was ceremoniously slaughtered and butchered and roasted in a great stone pit in the wide courtyard of Malik's huge home. Oranges and limes and lemons, papayas, dates, and pomegranates—tropical fruits of all kinds—adorned a sideboard, along with breads and rolls, vegetables, and scented olive oils. It astonished Ruhi to see such wealth, such unbridled abundance, after leaving the U.S. in such a decimated, desperate state.

Many toasts were made in Ruhi's honor, all with nonalcoholic beverages, of course. His siblings and extended family avoided asking about his detention. Perhaps Malik had told them to be respectful, that his nephew was a wounded man. Not a word came up about Ahmed in any of the necessarily fleeting conversations that Ruhi had in the course of so many greetings. He was surprised and pleased that he could remember all the names of his relatives. Family was sacred in Saudi Arabia, and no matter what America had to offer an immigrant such as himself, close family ties were not as common there, even among the native born.

The celebration was such a whirlwind—and filled with such singular good cheer—that by the time Ruhi settled in a guest room, he had forgotten about Ahmed. He lay in a large bed, dozing off, when the bedroom door to the courtyard creaked open. He bolted upright and saw a torch burning behind a gowned and hooded man.

"Ahmed?" Ruhi whispered.

The shape moved closer. "Why would you think it was me?"

• • •

Agent Candace Anders sat alongside a senior Saudi intelligence official. They were only a few miles from Ruhi, glimpsing him from a camera drone the size of a hummingbird.

"That's him. That's Ahmed Mancur," said the official, who'd told Candace that his own name was Omar, never offering a family name. "And that's your man, the one inside?"

"Yes, that's Ruhi, his cousin. Look," Candace said quickly, "we want to work with you. That's why we tipped you off that Ahmed Mancur might come home. But it's critical that you not grab him now."

"That is asking a lot. We have been searching for him for a long time."

"If you can wait a little longer, your country's biggest customer would appreciate it." Candace smiled as she spoke. "And one of your biggest benefactors," she added, a not-so-subtle nod to U.S. military largesse to the emirate.

"You think Ahmed Mancur will lead you to your prey?" Omar asked.

"We don't know, honestly. But we want to find out."

They watched Ahmed slip inside the house and close the door.

The drone pilot, sitting only feet away, brought the tiny device up to an altitude of two hundred feet.

"You have no 'ears' inside?" Candace asked.

"Not in that place," Omar acknowledged. "Malik has it swept at least once a week. He has differences with his son, but he doesn't want him taken by us. But we have never been in such a position to take him down, either." He was smiling now.

"So, what are you saying?" Candace asked bluntly. "That you're going to take Ahmed now?" she asked.

"No, we will play ball, as you say."

"How equipped are you to follow him in Yemen?" she asked.

"It depends. You?"

"We got Awlaki."

"It took forever. So your answer is no, you're not well equipped."

"We don't know yet, honestly. But we have huge resources invested in this case."

"You say 'honestly' a lot. Should I assume you're lying other-wise?"

She shook her head. Felt foolish.

They were back to waiting, as they had been before Ahmed showed up. Omar returned to briefing her about two Saudi Islamists, Abdullah and Ibrahim al-Asiri:

"Ibrahim was the explosives expert, supposedly. His brother, Abdullah, stuffed one of Ibrahim's bombs up his anus. Please excuse my scatological reference, but it is essential to understanding how grim it is getting down by the Yemeni border."

"That's fine," she said and shrugged. She almost added "honestly," but choked it down.

"Abdullah was posing as an Islamist defector when he met with my boss, the chief of our counterinsurgency agency. He is a prince, you should know. Abdullah made it into the prince's study in his home not far from the border. He even hugged him. Then Abdullah's phone rang and set off the bomb."

Candace winced.

"I am so sorry. I should stop."

"No, you should not. I've seen worse." Unfortunately, that was true—in Kabul. Moreover, Candace could not let herself be seen as a weak woman. Not in Saudi culture.

"The prince survived in good shape because the force of the bomb went straight up, taking Abdullah's head off. It blasted clear through the roof."

"Somebody was looking out for the prince," Candace said, fully aware that she was setting herself up for a display of piety.

"Yes, may the blessings and peace of Mohammed be upon him." Omar paused for several seconds before going on. "So the border keeps us busy with bombs and spies, defectors, men of no faith and men of great faith, and they are all at war with one another."

"And that's where we're going, it looks like?" Candace asked.

"Yes, I am certain of it now."

"It's your own Casablanca."

"That is true, but there is no Rick's Café Américain for us."

"Drinking and gambling? There wasn't supposed to be then, either," Candace said.

"I know, but times have changed."

Have they ever.

Candace shrugged and nodded, acknowledging his point. She could not have been happier to hear that they'd be heading for the Yemeni border. It was extremely difficult, diplomatically speaking, for U.S. intelligence agents to operate in Saudi Arabia without alerting their counterparts in the emirate. That was a problem because they didn't always know the loyalties of individual Saudi agents. Yemen, however, had been most cooperative with the United States, even covering up U.S. drone attacks on its own people. In other words, Yemen wasn't Pakistan, which had become openly outraged over American assassinations on its soil, after bin Laden and Abbottabad.

But large regions of Yemen had been reduced to anarchy, which provided the most compelling reason of all for heading to the southern Saudi border: The lawlessness made Yemen a possible center for the cyberattackers. Their tools were sophisticated; nobody, including Lana Elkins, had been able to hack below the "cover" of the online magazine, *Inspire,* to what Candace and other intelligence agents thought might be the command center for Al Qaeda in Yemen. Whoever was doing the website's dirty work clearly had extensive cybertools, knew how to use them, and were all but taunting Western intelligence by affiliating themselves with an Islamist site brazenly urging the faithful to make bombs.

Yemen also had many anarchic tribal regions, much as Waziristan did, but Yemen shared a highly penetrable border with the technologically advanced Saudis. The emirate's most radical Islamists had a well-earned reputation for traveling the world to spill the blood of infidels, which they had demonstrated most brutally on 9/11. That the faithful might simply hop their country's southern border—to carry out cyberbutchery—appeared painfully plausible.

"Here he comes," Omar said, interrupting Candace's thoughts.

In the spare light of the courtyard's torch, they spied a tall thin man with a long beard standing, once more, by the open door to Ruhi's room.

Bin Laden incarnate, thought Candace.

The small drone descended. They heard Ahmed offer a Muslim blessing to his wayward cousin. Then they picked up Ruhi, saying, "I will see you then."

What's that mean? When? Where?

Candace glanced at Omar, who spoke as if he could read her thoughts:

"I doubt they're talking about the food court at the Riyadh Gallery."

"It definitely sounds like a meeting."

Omar allowed that this was true. "But Ruhi won't know where. Ahmed would never give up that information this far in advance, I can assure you of that. What he's saying is that Ruhi should be ready to move at any time. They have plans for him. That is good."

"What kind of plans?" Candace wondered aloud.

"They'll be testing him," Omar said, "even though he's Ahmed's cousin."

"Testing? You mean torture?"

Omar nodded. "When you think about it, they have to. He shows up right now?"

"But it's not a coincidence. He was tortured."

"And now he works for you."

"But they don't know that," Candace said.

"They are going to try to find out. I can tell you that much."

• • •

But nothing went as planned, not for Ruhi and Ahmed, not even for those who had been spying on them.

The call came to Candace in her hotel room at five the next morning. The Mabahith, Saudi Arabia's notorious secret police, had just burst into Ruhi's room and hauled him to a windowless black van. According to Omar, Uncle Malik looked stunned, his protests muted by the attending Mabahith officer.

Candace sat up in her hotel bed, still absorbing the shock. "But Omar, these are *your* people! What's going on?"

"No, they are their own people. They are very secret."

"What do they want from him?" Candace asked.

"I suppose they want to test him too." Omar sighed, then hung up.

Candace dropped her head back to her pillow and stared at the ceiling, whispering, "Don't fail, Ruhi. Remember, you're tougher than you think."

But her whole country was going to have to be a lot tougher, she realized moments later when she received a text message from Holmes's office: URGENT: THREAT LEVEL RISES.

It contained a link to an Islamist website.

Candace's fingers flew over her keyboard. The following words appeared in simple white letters on a black background:

"The great jihad tells America the Defeated that martyrs are now in your homeland. They will take control of a very special group of children. There is nothing you can do to protect them.

They will be in our hands soon. When our martyrs slay them, you will know that even children who defy our plans will suffer the worst retribution. They will die at the location of a great symbol of American power. At that moment you will witness what you have done to us for so many years. That is how our final attack will begin, America. With your hope for the future. With your children.

"Then we will launch your own missiles at you because we have taken control of your most powerful weapons. Your leaders know this. They are hiding those facts from you. We are telling you the truth. We will leave you destroyed forever."

CHAPTER 14

RUHI WAS SPRAWLED ON the floor of the large, swiftly moving van, surrounded by four bulky, bearded men. None was masked. Neither did they blindfold him. They might as well have announced that they would never be accountable to him for what they had done—or were about to do. They had Flex-Cuffed his hands and ankles, closed the doors, and shut off the world.

Not one of them spoke. After Ruhi's initial outcry—"What are you doing?"—he quieted, too. What was the point? They were field operatives, doing what they did best: abduction, subduing targets.

The seconds ticked away. He felt the miles adding up. The men leaned against the walls, he presumed. He could not, of course, see them in the complete blackness. But he sensed their breath and body heat receding.

His worst suspicion was that the men hailed from the Mabahith. No sane Saudi wanted to trouble the nation's secret police. But he, Ruhi Mancur, American *and* Saudi citizen, had traveled 6,750 miles to put himself into this painful predicament.

You're a real wunderkind, Ruhi. He shook his head in the darkness. *What was I thinking?*

He told himself that he'd been caught between a rock and a hard spot, and that he'd experienced the rock, right? In America. Well, this was the hard spot.

They must have Ahmed, too, he thought. *First, the son-of-a-bitch cousin leads American intelligence services to my doorstep. Now he's brought in the Mabahith.* Ruhi was no expert on the Saudi secret police, but just about every reasonably educated Saudi knew the Mabahith held people at Úlaysha Prison, or Al-Ha'ir Prison, both within a few dozen miles of Riyadh.

Mabahith . . . The very word made him shrink inside. In the furthest reaches of memory, he recalled Deputy Director Holmes saying that he was tougher than he thought. But Ruhi knew better. That dog had scared him nearly senseless back in the States. But now—

The van turned a corner so sharply that Ruhi's thoughts rolled away as he pressed against one of the men's legs. Then the vehicle went airborne—or so it seemed—as it started down a steep decline. A hill? Possibly. Riyadh certainly had some. But Ruhi concluded from the smoothness of the descent that they were now speeding into an underground facility.

Moments later, the van slowed and came to a stop. The men stirred. One pressed the flat of his hand on Ruhi's shoulder, the universal language of "Don't move."

The door flew open. Ruhi blinked. The sudden glare of artificial light almost blinded him. In Arabic, a man asked simply if he was Ruhi Mancur.

"It is him," said the man whose hand had not shifted from Ruhi's shoulder.

The next thing Ruhi knew, two men grabbed his feet and dragged him across the floor of the van. No one reached to support his upper body. He saw the fall coming, which did nothing to ease the drop to the concrete floor. He managed to cushion the blow partly with his right elbow. But his head crashed hard, and the bright lights above darkened in an instant.

● ● ●

WE'RE TRYING, Holmes texted Lana at the U.S. embassy in Riyadh. Encrypted, without question. BUT WE HAVE TO GO THROUGH CHANNELS. IF WE GO DIRECTLY TO THE MABAHITH, THEY'LL KNOW HE'S WORKING FOR US. AND THEN THEY'LL KNOW WE'RE, ONCE AGAIN, VIOLATING ALL KINDS OF AGREEMENTS NOT TO OPERATE IN THE KINGDOM WITHOUT THEIR APPROVAL. THAT WILL MEAN . . .

Lana tuned out even as her eyes scanned the rest of the message. She knew what it meant when one of your own fell into the hands of another country's secret police.

She quickly replied: AGENT ANDERS IS WORKING WITH THEIR MILITARY INTELLIGENCE. CAN SHE FIND A WAY?

It wasn't as if they weren't prepared for this kind of contingency. The problem was that in the delicate dance of the spy trade, every situation was unique. There were no formulaic solutions.

Lana walked down to one of the washrooms. She splashed water on her face, wondering what the hell they were doing to Mancur right now. She admired him. Yes, she knew he'd been boxed into a corner by the one-two punch of the NSA and the FBI, but he still could have refused, or been so fearful that they wouldn't have dared use him. He was a young man for such a weighty mission, and deeply inexperienced. *Which is probably the only reason he agreed to take it on.*

She stared at her face in the mirror above the basin. Then she shook her head and turned away.

As she exited the fully tiled washroom, replete with mosaics of orchids, she spotted the ambassador, Rick Arpen, coming out of the men's.

"My office," he said to her, pointing down the hall. "We need you right now. My aide was just texting you."

"I was—"

"Right," he cut her off. "Let's go."

Something wasn't right. By the ambassador's urgency, it seemed he was clued into the Mancur disaster. But Arpen wasn't supposed to be in the loop. He needed deniability when he met with the king or any of the royal's closest advisers.

But Ruhi wasn't the reason he'd summoned her. She understood that the moment he led her into his private conference room. All of the embassy's top staff had assembled—and none of them was supposed to know anything about Mancur, either. All looked as tense as guy wires attached to a leaning structure. In a manner of speaking, that's what they were.

"There's not a single train running in the United States as of fifteen minutes ago," Ambassador Arpen told them, taking off his wire-rimmed glasses. He held them out as he spoke. "Our enemy has announced what they call 'The Final Countdown to Our Total Destruction.'"

"But if it's just the trains," a redheaded woman said, "maybe their 'invisible invasion' is actually failing."

"That's just for today," the ambassador replied. "They made that clear minutes before the trains stopped. Not even the diesel-powered ones can run with switches and signals down. The enemy says that every day they will execute another catastrophe, each one worse than the day before."

"Didn't they say they were going to take down the whole grid at once, like last time?"

"Are you complaining?" Arpen said sharply. He put his glasses back on and glared at the redhead. "They said the panic in our country has been so 'entertaining' and so 'instructive' to the rest of the world, what with the widespread rioting, shooting, and so forth, that they want to 'bleed us to death slowly.' Today, trains. Tomorrow? We don't know, but the FAA has canceled all flights immediately, not that there're many takers. The CIA estimates that if the enemy focuses on taking down the major sectors sequentially, our nation could be completely shut down in seventy-two hours. But that's not the worse news." Arpen took a deep breath. "The president has just confirmed this to his top staff and communicated it to our embassies around the world. Here it is."

He held up a sheet of paper. It looked, in that moment, archaic to Lana. Like a diplomatic cable of old. But also more real, more eerie an item than anything in the world of screens and cursors.

"This is top secret. You will not breathe a word of this to anyone. The terrorists have secured access to more than a thousand of our nuclear missiles. That means they have taken control of the warheads and launchpads. And they are, even as I'm talking to you, targeting *our* cities and those of our closest allies. Our most skilled experts have not found a means to override their commands."

A gasp came from the redheaded woman. Others showed their horror less demonstrably, with silent shakes of the head or by looking away.

A man with a Santa Claus beard and shocked demeanor spoke up from the other end of the table: "They've got control of the circuitry, the computers. I get that. But can't those missiles be monkey-wrenched, if everything else fails?"

Ambassador Arpen nodded. "Right. Except you have to gain access to them through the most sophisticated control panels in the world. Or what we *thought* were the most sophisticated control panels in the world. And it's not like we can bomb those missiles with impunity. Even monkey-wrenching them has to be done with the greatest care. If we can't get our nuclear engineers inside those silos and other installations, all bets are off in that regard."

He turned to the rest of his staff around the table. "Look, I also have to tell you that the president has just confirmed that the enemy has taken control of vital U.S. stores of Veepox."

Lana suppressed a gasp.

"I didn't even know we *had* Veepox," a young man said.

"Of course we have it," Arpen retorted. "Because we can't trust others *not* to have it." The parity of pain. "There's no good news here, people. This is asymmetrical warfare, and all the weapons are pointed at us."

"Even the Veepox?" Lana asked.

"I don't have confirmation of this, so I hesitate to say, but the enemy claims they are releasing it right now in an unspecified location."

"This is madness," the bearded man said.

A stillness followed his words. It was the most frightening silence Lana had ever heard.

The ambassador cleared his throat. "The CDC is, as you might imagine, doing everything it can to detect outbreaks and plans to confine them, but there's no antidote for Veepox, and the CDC's travel and communications are terribly hampered."

Hampered? Lana thought bitterly. *Try shattered.*

"What about the threat to the children?" asked a young translator with a husband and two young twins in Alexandria, Virginia.

"Despite their threat to do so, there has been no word about any action directly targeting our kids," the ambassador answered. "So that's the one bit of good news."

"But they haven't been making empty threats," the translator said. Arpen merely shook his head.

What else can he do? Lana asked herself.

"This is unbelievable," said a middle-aged woman in a navy pantsuit.

"It's all too believable. It's happening right now," the ambassador replied.

He urged them to return to their desks. "Keep working. Do what you do best. It's all we can do."

• • •

Agent Candace Anders sat in her hotel room staring at her computer screen. Her orders were clear enough—and deeply disturbing: Go to Yemen immediately.

WHAT ABOUT RUHI? she texted back.

HE'S NOT GOING ANYWHERE.

SHOULDN'T I STAY IN RIYADH THEN?

NO, IF HE GIVES YOU UP, YOU NEED TO BE OUT OF THE COUNTRY.

The irony stunned her: Candace's intelligence boss was saying that Yemen, with its widespread lawlessness, would be safer than Saudi Arabia. He was probably right. But what about Ruhi's safety? She hated leaving him at such a moment. It felt like abandonment of the worst sort.

The communication from the Farm continued: FLY TO NAJRAN. YOU'LL BE MET BY AL JUHANI. Fahim Al Juhani was an operative long active in the region. HE'LL PROVIDE

Flight time was in about an hour.

Move.

• • •

Emma looked out her window, wondering aloud if the big blue bus would really come. She'd heard the cyberattackers had shut down the trains and that "More is in store," according to the excited news anchor she'd been watching.

"They're coming. Don't you worry, girl," Tanesa said. "When William Senior says there's choir practice, it's going to take more than some terrorists to stop him."

"Well, you got to wonder, with everything going—"

Right then Emma stopped talking because the bus rolled up in front of her house.

Despite trying to keep a cool demeanor, Emma was excited. She did love to sing but had always thought choirs were not for girls as hip as her. She had fantasized plenty about standing at a mic singing (well, *screaming*) obscene angry lyrics at kids dancing (well, *bashing* into one another) in a seedy nightclub.

But Tanesa had challenged her, saying, "You probably can't hit the high notes anyway."

So Emma had let go with a soprano range that visibly startled her caregiver. She'd hit those upper Cs as if she'd minted them.

Which, to be fair, Tanesa had matched without any difficulty at all, then moved down the range with equal aplomb. Emma hadn't even attempted the lower register.

Tanesa then said, "Emma, your voice has a really pure quality, even if your mind is on your underpants too much."

That had thrilled Emma. Not the underpants part, but hearing that she had a "pure quality." It was the first time she didn't feel bullshitted by a compliment. Tanesa was tough. So when she said Emma could try out for the choir, actually audition for William Sr., some kind of religious man or preacher or pastor, or whatever they called themselves, Emma felt genuinely excited.

"You sure I have to go to church to do this?" she asked Tanesa as they headed out the door to the bus, suddenly nervous about meeting a whole new group of kids, especially the older ones.

"Yes, I'm sure. You want to sing about the Lord Almighty, you don't get to try out in a shower. You go to His house, and then you thank Him for your God-given talent, because that is what you have."

"How do you know it's a Him?"

"I don't. It's just what we say. But you can think whatever you want." Tanesa smiled as they approached the sidewalk.

Emma followed suit, thinking, *Wait till Mom hears I'm going to church.*

The door to the bus swung open, and they hurried up the steps. Not until it closed did Emma see the gunmen and a big black man tied up and gagged.

"Pastor William!" Tanesa cried out.

Emma looked around, panicked. Men with guns and head scarves stood on both sides of the bus. At least four of them. But the one closest wore a heavy canvas backpack that had a tube with what looked like a trigger sticking out the end.

• • •

Crossing the Yemeni border proved painless. Fahim Al Juhani bribed the border guard, as customary as praising Allah, while Candace—in hijab and veil—kept her head down like a good subservient woman.

They passed through an opening in the ten-foot sandbagged barrier that divided the two nations and headed south.

Fifteen miles later, in the burning sunlight of the unforgiving desert, they passed several Bedouins on camels. One of them watched their small sedan speed by. He did not take his eyes from the vehicle. It was as if he'd never before seen an automobile.

Moments later, Fahim slowed. Candace looked up. Another Bedouin was crossing the two-lane road with his camel. The animal stopped in the middle of the road. The Bedouin climbed down and took the reins, pulling on them—to no avail.

Fahim looked tense. Candace saw his eyes searching for a way around either side of the big beast, but a culvert ran under the highway right there.

Of all places.

"This doesn't look good," Fahim said, wiping his brow.

She saw sweat spots on his keffiyeh. Then she glanced at her watch. "We're fine, Fahim." They were headed to Sana, the Yemeni capital and the country's largest city. "We have time."

"That's not what I mean. Why would they be crossing here?"

He slowed to a crawl. The camel driver stopped pulling on the reins, like he was giving up. Then he turned to them with a semiautomatic handgun and started shooting.

Candace watched the horror unfold in what seemed like slow motion. The man was not shooting at them. He was aiming at the tires—and hitting them on the driver's side. That's when she realized they were in serious trouble. He must have known the car was bulletproof, so that meant he also knew who they were and why they were wanted. They'd been targeted.

She raised her own semiautomatic and tried to lower the window. Fahim yelled, "No! Keep them up. This is a trap. There'll be more."

Fahim tried to speed away on the flat tires. He bumped the camel hard enough to make it bolt, opening up the road. But they were going no more than ten miles an hour.

Off to the right, Candace saw a dual sport motorcycle race from behind a dune. A second appeared on its tail.

They overtook them in seconds, shooting out the tires on the passenger side. Not one of the shooters wasted a bullet on the windows. They were disciplined, which scared her even more.

Fahim rode on rims until a Hummer with camouflage paint pulled across the road a hundred yards ahead of them, blocking any possible path. A man raced around the back of the vehicle, shouldering a rocket launcher. He aimed at the windshield. Another man raised his hand for them to stop.

Fahim braked. Neither of them said a word.

"Get out," one of the motorcyclists yelled in accented English. "Out! No guns! Hands up!"

Candace was hoping a car or plane, *something*, would come along. Someone who could stop this. But no one appeared. She guessed that all the traffic on the road had been blocked.

She opened her door, and eased out with her hands up. The heat alone was an assault.

Fahim climbed out from behind the wheel. Both of them were thrown against the car. They faced each other over the hood.

More men poured out of the Hummer. Two of them pulled her belongings from the car. Two more stripped off her hijab and took her gun. She was in jeans and a T-shirt.

No one spoke as they went about their work, plundering the trunk, tearing through their luggage.

She watched a man walk up to Fahim, followed by a guy with a camera. The first one placed his pistol to Fahim's temple and fired twice.

He crumpled to the pavement, out of Candace's view. The man with the camera tilted it down, then raised it and pointed the lens at her. She stared into it numbly.

A loud engine approached from her blind side, drawing closer until it stopped. Candace prayed it brought help—a last-minute rescue from friendly forces. But when she turned, her blood ran cold: It was an old truck with an open cargo area crowded with armed jihadists. They jumped to the road and rushed toward her.

CHAPTER 15

THE BACK OF RUHI'S head throbbed. Blood trickled down below his hairline. He'd been dragged by his feet across the concrete parking area into an elevator—or so he gathered by the grim evidence: His shirt was bunched up around his armpits, and his shoulder blades were scraped and burning, and bleeding as well.

"Get up!" yelled a man he didn't recognize.

But Ruhi was so dazed the man's face could have been Uncle Malik's and he wouldn't have known for sure. All the men in his blurred vision had beards.

He heard the elevator doors clank close behind him. Someone pushed a button. Each movement, each sound, registered slowly. The elevator jerked and started upward.

"Now get up!" the same man yelled.

Ruhi could tell it was the same man, more by his voice than his shifting features.

Before he could try to stand, two other men jerked him upright. With his ankles still cuffed, he was wobbly on his legs and spilled into a fourth man, who shoved him away. Then he was pushed from one to the other like a 160-pound hacky sack. That was when he realized that his abasement also was planned. Just as he wondered when all the pushing and shoving and snarling would end, a punch plowed into his stomach. It came with the hardness of an anvil and left him doubled over, unable to take a breath.

He sank to his knees, then onto his side, the men watching as he curled protectively into a fetal position and tried to gulp air.

The elevator shuddered as it stopped. The doors clanked open, and he was once again dragged to his feet. He could not straighten up.

Someone behind him reached down between his ankles and cut apart the Flex-Cuf binding his feet together. He was able to walk, though not well, still doubled over in pain. A man on each side of him supported most of his weight, effortlessly, it seemed. Ruhi noticed for the first time that they all wore dark pants and short-sleeved white shirts. *Odd attire for thugs*, he thought.

They hauled him into a room the size of a basketball court, with an assortment of cables hanging from pulleys cinched to the ceiling at the far end. That's where he was headed.

As they drew closer, he saw that the end of each cable held a shackle. But rather than string him up, the men forced him onto one of several white vinyl chairs with shiny metal legs. A heavy-looking wooden cabinet, the approximate length and width of a man's body, lay on the floor a few feet away. He wondered if it was a coffin—or simply another means of providing slow death. His eyes returned to the other chairs, each of which had bloodstains. He thought it likely that white had been chosen to better expose the streaks and splatters. It amped up his anxiety, which had been redlining since he'd been roused from Uncle Malik's guest room.

Only two of the men remained with him. He heard retreating footsteps very clearly, and he couldn't help but envy those who made them.

One of the men standing in front of him wore round glasses, reminding him of John Lennon, of all people. The other, who had facial scruff much like Ruhi's, circled behind him. Then he bent Ruhi forward, yanked up his cuffed hands, and jammed his arms over the back of the seat. A sharp pain wracked Ruhi's shoulders.

His heart pounded. As a long-distance runner, he was acutely aware of his pulse and savvy enough to know that it wasn't only his anxiety that was redlining; he estimated his heart was beating in the 180s, astoundingly high for a man in his fit condition. The man in the Lennon glasses picked up a chair and held it by two legs, like a bat. He appeared to be weighing the pros and cons of whacking Ruhi's head off.

Ruhi felt himself flinching, or maybe he'd developed a tic. He wasn't sure, and felt strangely aloof, almost clinically detached. But he wasn't kidding himself: Any sense of distance from his circumstances would surely end with the first strong hint of pain.

Lennon, as Ruhi now thought of him, was large, but it wasn't his broad chest or thick neck that drew his attention. It was the man's forearms. They were bigger than Ruhi's biceps, and each thick vein rose in relief and appeared shrink-wrapped in skin.

Lennon flipped the chair, catching the opening in the back with his index finger. With what had to have been a well-practiced twirl, he brought it upright and set it down in front of Ruhi. He stepped over the back and perched on it, less than a foot from him, so close that his boulder-like knees pressed against Ruhi's considerably narrower ones.

"Bring it in," Lennon shouted.

Two men entered. One carried a plywood board about six and a half feet long and two feet wide. A two-by-four had been secured by its narrow side on one end of the plywood, creating a tilt when the man laid the board on the floor.

Ruhi had a sick feeling about this. Lennon stared at him as he watched the second man set down a large white plastic bucket of water and a roll of plastic wrap, the kind usually reserved for food preservation. But Ruhi knew he was about to be waterboarded, and the only thing the plastic wrap would preserve was the extraordinary pain he was about to endure.

"So tell me, Mr. Ruhi Mancur," Lennon said, speaking in accented English, "whom do you work for?"

"Work for?" Ruhi managed.

"I will tell you, Mr. Ruhi Mancur, that when I engage in dialogue with one of our distinguished clients, when I practice the art of conversation with him or, on those rare occasions, her, I expect an answer, not a question. So that's the one break you're ever going to get from me." He nodded, as if this were fully agreed upon. "We know the games you play. We know they held you in the States, 'questioned' you. *Tortured* you. Yes, we know that, too." He patted Ruhi's face. "And we know they said that they were sorry and let you go. They said you were innocent."

"It's true," Ruhi volunteered. "I was innocent. I am."

Lennon sat back, shaking his head at Ruhi. "Yes, innocent. But then you jumped on a plane to Riyadh, like you could not get to your homeland soon enough. And we welcomed you, didn't we? We didn't stop you at the airport. We didn't humiliate you with a full-body search. We didn't drag you into a van and crack your head on concrete. No, we didn't do anything but show you respect. We said, 'Welcome to Saudi Arabia.' Those very words. We thought, '*Mr. Ruhi Mancur is coming home. He knows who his real friends are.*'"

As Lennon spoke, he cast an occasional glance at the board. And that made Ruhi look at it, despite his fear that even a glimpse would encourage Lennon to begin the infamous torture. The two other men stood by, as if awaiting Lennon's next instruction.

"But we did watch you, Mr. Ruhi Mancur. Just to be sure. And what did we see? Ahmed Mancur going to his father's house on your very first night to talk to you." He leaned into Ruhi's face. "We heard every word. We could scarcely believe our ears. A good son of Saudi Arabia, who has every reason to hate America, comes to his homeland to support the worst elements in the kingdom." He shook his head in what might have passed for sorrow under different circumstances. "Every word."

Lennon nodded at the larger of the two men. "Get the straps." Then he turned back to Ruhi. "So I'm going to ask you again, and if you are smart, Mr. Ruhi Mancur, and we think you are very, very smart, you will not ask another question. You will give only answers. So, whom do you work for?"

Ruhi looked up as the large men returned with black leather straps at least two inches wide.

"I'm not working for anyone," Ruhi said, sickened by the sound of his own lies, for all they would soon mean.

· · ·

Emma was grabbed by a man who smelled like old sweat and stale deodorant and shoved onto a bench seat near the middle of the blue bus.

"What's your name?" another man yelled.

"Emma."

"Emma what?"

"Emma Elkins."

He looked at a small notebook. "You're new." It sounded like an accusation.

She nodded.

"Spell it."

She did. The man wrote it down.

A girl sat next to Emma by the window, staring straight ahead. Her lip quivered. She was older and looked just as scared, which frightened Emma even more.

The man who shoved her onto the seat waved a gun in her face and shouted, "Don't move!" with such a heavy accent that she guessed right away that the command was probably among the few words of English that he actually knew. The man with the notebook now demanded Tanesa's name. He appeared to check it off on a list. Then he headed to the back of the bus, putting away his pen and taking out a gun.

Emma looked around as much as she dared without shifting her head. All the kids were at least fifteen or sixteen, and some looked older than that. The girl across the aisle caught her eye and held it. Emma noticed that her hands were folded in prayer, then saw that the girl right next to her also had her hands clasped. Maybe that was a prayer on her lips, not fear. Or both.

She took several studied breaths, like her mom had always told her to do *before* Emma lost her temper. It kind of worked. She didn't feel so shaky.

The bus rumbled down the end of her street. The big guy in a head scarf with his gun to William Sr.'s head forced the pastor to sit while he remained upright in the aisle.

"Now that we have all of you aboard, give me your attention."

He spoke impeccable English without any accent. Emma thought he was one of those terrorists who grew up in the U.S. and then went crazy. But there was a silly, cunning quality to the way he talked, as if he'd patterned his speech after some old movie character, like Dr. Evil, whom she'd seen on cable. Not that ridiculous, but kind of. He drew out his words as if he enjoyed their torment as much as she and the others feared their intent.

"A week ago you tried to defy our plans. You saved people from the train crash on the first day of our jihad. So many Americans think you are heroes." He smiled, shook his head. "You probably think so too because you had your pictures in the newspapers and on the Internet. Now people will see what happens to their 'heroes' when they defy us, because we are taking you on a long trip." He glanced at his three compatriots, then back at them. "Some of you will make the journey alive." He paused, as if to let the implication sink in. "And some of you will die because you will do things to try to show that you are brave, or that your Jesus will protect you. But he won't, and we will kill you."

He looked them over, making eye contact with Emma, the only white kid on the bus. Maybe he just realized that. *Duh!* She stared back, thinking over and over, *I hate your guts. I hate your guts*, hoping to burn his brain with her anger. He didn't even flinch.

The man's dark eyes moved from child to child as he talked until they settled on Tanesa. "I should also tell you that our patience is very thin, and that the first person who tries to stop us will get to see something very special before dying." He thrust his pistol in William Sr.'s face. "You make a mistake, and you will make us shoot him. That's why he's right here in the front of the bus, so we can kick his body off. Then"—he smiled, displaying perfectly straight white teeth—"we'll shoot the offender and kick him—or her—off, too. Two for the price of one. That's how we'll get started."

Emma looked over at Tanesa, who was seated in the row ahead on the other side of the aisle. She was staring at the man. Emma realized that she liked Tanesa a lot. No, it was more than just liking. She admired her. Tanesa was strong, the way she looked right at that guy. Maybe, Emma realized, she wanted to *be* like Tanesa.

Emma moved her head just enough to look at the thug who'd forced her onto the seat. He crouched in the aisle three rows ahead, so his leader could stare down all the kids. He held an assault rifle, like the model used every week or so in a massacre. But he also had a handgun jammed into his waist. One of the old-fashioned ones, as Emma thought of it, with a cylinder for the bullets that spun around.

When she was six, Emma got an Annie Oakley outfit for Christmas, fringe skirt and vest, with a pair of six-shooters and a holster for each hip.

Emma sure had killed a lot of bad guys back then.

The leader's glare now returned to Tanesa. Emma could tell by the tension in the caregiver's jaw that she was seriously pissed off. And then Emma thought Tanesa was exactly the kind of person who would stand up to those guys.

Don't do it, Tanesa. Whatever you're thinking.

● ● ●

The jihadists surrounded Candace, raising their Kalashnikovs and semiautomatic handguns in the air. One even wielded a scimitar, which made her fear a public beheading. It didn't escape her notice that the cameraman kept focusing on the sword-bearer.

They were chanting in Arabic. Something about the Great Satan. She rued her woeful language skills, then felt spittle on her face as they pressed closer, jostling and groping her.

Not the truck, she thought. *Don't put me in there with them.*

The men appeared to have claimed her. But a commander of some sort—he wore the semblance of a uniform—bulled his way through the teeming crowd. The cameraman instantly turned his lens on him. The commander, wider than any two of the mal-nourished-looking mujahedeen, grabbed her arm, wrapping it in his meaty grip. At almost the same moment, a man who could have been his brother came up on her blind side and took her left arm. They pushed her through the shouting mob.

In seconds, she was in the Hummer, an air-conditioned vehicle more lushly appointed than any of the ones she'd driven during her Afghanistan service.

The two beefy men sat on either side of her. Neither had relinquished his grip. Next to the driver was a man in full head scarf. She could not see any of his features until he turned to look at her. Even then his eyes were hidden behind dark lenses. His face was skeletally thin with a beaky nose. His thin lips barely moved when he spoke:

"Agent Candace Anders."

Although it wasn't a question, he stared as if he expected a response. She did not answer.

He shook his head and turned back around.

The Hummer headed down the highway. So did the truck with the jihadists, their weapons still waving victoriously in the air, the scimitar catching blinding beams of sunlight.

They turned several miles later onto a desert road. She knew they weren't going to Sana any longer. They were headed to hell.

● ● ●

Ruhi wished he *would* die, and he'd never before been that desperate. But he'd never known pain that could compare to waterboarding. Lennon's men had strapped him down, cinching the leather so hard across his forehead that he thought they'd drive the back of his head through the lower part of the board. Then they bound his mouth with the plastic wrap and poured water down his nostrils. In less than fifteen seconds he was out of air from trying to expel the water. They let him gag for another twenty seconds before Lennon pulled the plastic wrap off his mouth.

Ruhi took four huge breaths, and then saw the big man scoop up another jarful of water. Lennon pulled the plastic back over Ruhi's mouth and ordered the torturer to give the glass to him.

He took over, pouring it slowly, deliberately, into Ruhi's nose. Worse this time, because he knew the deadly agony was imminent. As soon as his trachea and larynx filled with water, instinctive raging panic lit up his brain.

He passed out in the grip of horrific pain, certain that he was dying. When he awakened, he was still bound to the board. Lennon's face hovered right over him. He had jerked the plastic wrap down to Ruhi's chin.

"Are you here for Al Qaeda?"

"No. That's Ahmed," he pleaded. "Not me."

"We don't have Ahmed. We have you, Mr. Ruhi Mancur."

They don't have him. How the hell—

But Ruhi's tormented thoughts stopped for yet another scream— "No, no, no"—as Lennon spread the wrap back over his lips.

"No? Did you say 'no,' Mr. Ruhi Mancur? But that's not what we want to hear. We want to hear 'Yes, I have names.' We know about your cousin. We want to know more about you and your friends."

Lennon leaned forward. Ruhi wished he could head-butt the bastard. He imagined Candace would do that. But the only thing he could move were his eyes, and all they saw was Lennon moving that jar of water from the bucket toward him once more. He tried to talk, but couldn't with the plastic.

"What, Ruhi?" Lennon pulled the wrap down again.

"I don't know anyone in Al Qaeda in Yemen or anywhere else. I swear I don't. I just got here. I'd tell you. I hate those people."

"And do you know who we hate, Mr. Ruhi Mancur? We hate liars, especially the ones who leave our country, and then come back and try to turn it into an American garbage pit. We really hate them." He leaned even closer. "Names, Mancur."

It was the first time he dropped the "Mr. Ruhi Mancur" business. Ruhi wondered if the sudden depersonalization was a prelude to the worst waterboarding could offer, a psychological distancing that would allow Lennon to actually kill him.

"Names, Mancur," he repeated.

Ruhi had to give up someone. He yelled out the name of the one person he thought might be protected.

"Lana Elkins."

"Who is she?"

Ruhi told him. "I don't know anybody in Al Qaeda but Ahmed. But she's CIA, I think."

Slowly, the straps came off. Slowly, he was allowed to sit in the white vinyl chair again.

Lana Elkins's name traveled quickly, however. Within minutes it was heard on a blue bus almost seven thousand miles away.

CHAPTER 16

DEPUTY DIRECTOR HOLMES WAS enduring more crises at one time than he'd ever known—and that was before Lana Elkins was ordered out of Saudi Arabia by the kingdom's top cop. The king now knew that the U.S. was actively inserting operatives into his domain without prior approval, which violated a host of written and unwritten agreements.

But Holmes couldn't simply pluck her out of the emirate, because planes were literally falling out of the sky. Not the commercial airliners—they were already grounded by the FAA—but two private jets had dropped like stones, killing all aboard. Both were owned by corporate titans who did not wish to be inconvenienced by a national catastrophe, and who had been assured by their cybersecurity teams that their onboard computer systems had not been tinkered with.

Holmes wasn't even confident of the military's aircraft. Though few knew it outside the upper echelons of the intelligence services, routine monitoring flights conducted by the U.S. around the world had been halted. Those surveillance sorties were the first line of defense.

No, not the first, Holmes corrected himself. The first line of defense was the one people never saw—cybersecurity—a word that he felt no U.S. official should use for the foreseeable future.

Defense of what? If the cyberterrorists weren't stopped, there wouldn't be a country left to defend.

With the countdown under way, panic had, once again, taken over much of the nation. The raw, unbridled reactions were like a volcano that had regained its force and now threatened to rain death and destruction on everyone. Rumors of a Chinese invasion spread with the speed of instant messaging—where ISPs were back up and running, that is. The rumors were false, but countering them with a fragmented national communications system proved extremely difficult. What really perplexed Holmes was how the rumors reached regions of the country that were essentially incommunicado because they still hadn't recovered from the initial cyberattack. But the "news" spread there, too. *What were those rumormongers using?* Holmes wondered. *Smoke signals?*

Thankfully, no one outside security circles had learned that U.S. missiles were now targeting U.S. cities. But word about a potential Veepox epidemic was starting to leak, talk that appeared as difficult to contain as the disease itself.

The only "positive" development, in his view, was that it seemed a handful of America's largest urban areas were all "rioted out," as one of his aides put it.

Terrific, so a great mass of citizens were hiding in their homes and rationing their last few scraps of food because vast numbers of supermarkets had been plundered. And just when supply chains had started functioning again, the incremental destruction of the grid had begun anew, which immediately set off more madness in the streets. Police in New York, Philadelphia, Dallas, Minneapolis, Phoenix, Tacoma, Miami, and Cheyenne had walked off the job. The cops were reportedly terminally weary, understaffed, overworked, and, increasingly, the targets of armed and angry residents. For them, community service had become tantamount to suicide.

To make matters even worse, the end-of-summer weather was the hottest since record keeping began in the U.S. in 1895. The scorching heat had not helped the already sketchy national disposition. The wildfires in the West, set off by those natural gas explosions during the first cyberattack, were now raging out of control. Parts of Denver had been incinerated. Not that many miles away in the forest, smoke jumpers had become smoke hikers because there were no planes to ferry the men and women to the front lines. No aerial water tankers, either, to douse flames.

And now we've got to get Lana out of the kingdom.

But right then the news got grimmer: Holmes received an encrypted text message that Agent Fahim Al Juhani had been murdered on camera by AQAP—Al Qaeda in the Arabian Peninsula. Al Juhani was an operative whom Holmes had personally commended for outstanding bravery. The same crew had abducted Agent Candace Anders, also recorded for viewing by the faithful. Holmes's text said the Islamists were bragging about the killing; apparently the entire abduction and murder was airing, at that very moment, on several Islamist websites. The terrorists even had it up on YouTube. Holmes watched it and felt sickened by what he saw. He found solace only in Anders's stoicism. She remained composed throughout the ordeal. But that didn't leave her any less abducted.

Holmes feared AQAP's next video would feature Anders herself getting—

Teresa McGivern walked in, interrupting his dismal thoughts. The veteran analyst was trailed by Donna Warnes, his executive assistant. The latter looked flummoxed. McGivern? Unflappable.

"It's not Donna's fault," she said, pushing her gray bob behind her ears. "I couldn't stand on formality, so I barged in. We *have* to make a decision on Elkins. I just found out that thousands of Saudis are screaming for her head outside our embassy. Ambassador Arpen says he fears they'll occupy it at any second. If they get their hands on Elkins, there's no telling where she'll end up, or whom they'll hand her over to."

"That would be a massive violation of international law."

"A mob is a mob," McGivern responded curtly, "and there are elements of the Saudi street who would love to curry favor with Al Qaeda by handing her over. As for the government, you might have already guessed that they're saying *we're* the ones who violated international law. The painful truth is—"

"We did. I know."

McGivern went on: "The ambassador says it looks as bad as Tehran, 1979."

"How would he know? He was in grade school," Holmes growled. "You say there are *thousands* in the streets now?"

"More as we speak."

"You're right, we've got to get Elkins out of there, but we also need to keep her within easy reach of Mancur."

"Why?" McGivern asked. "He may disappear down the Saudi shithole."

"Not likely," Holmes said with more assurance than he actually felt.

"You're not thinking Yemen, are you?" McGivern asked.

"Show me a border that's less porous," Holmes responded.

"If we lose two people to that goddamn backwater, we're going to end up spending the next twenty years in front of oversight committees. You know that, don't you?"

Holmes eyed her steadily. "The sad truth is that we should have such problems."

"Where in Yemen are we going to stick her? And how can you be so sure Mancur's getting out, or the condition he'll be in if he does get out? He could be a basket case. We could be risking Elkins on a hope and a prayer."

"A hope and a prayer?" Holmes shook his head. "I've had to bank on less lately. If he gets out, he'll be useless without Elkins. We have no way to resupply him with *our* sophisticated systems that are now in the hands of the Mabahith. Rest assured, the Saudis aren't going to give him back his toys. They'll have already started reverse-engineering everything Elkins put in them. And if they succeed, they'll be generous in sharing their booty with all of our 'friends' in the Middle East."

"Maybe the president should make a call."

"No. That would make it clear that Mancur is working for us."

"So the fact that he may well be critical to us means we can do that much less to help him?" McGivern shook her head ruefully. "But wait, they must know he's doing something for us. He gave up Elkins's name."

"That's right. But what do the Saudis know about her? What does Mancur, for that matter? That she's a computer expert. Big deal, right? The Saudis are letting an uproar develop over Elkins to show their militants that they, too, can stand up to the Great Satan. But for all they really know, she could be a low-level embassy employee. Bring in the president, and we confirm their worst suspicions about her and Mancur. The way I see it, if the Saudis suspect Mancur is just part of a smaller effort to destroy AQAP, then they're likely to see it as in their interest to let him proceed. They're more threatened by AQAP than we are. But if the president begs on his behalf, they'll know Mancur is a major player who's privy to a great deal, and they'll think that he's someone we've been grooming for years. They'll want to know everything he knows, and they won't stop until they find out."

"So what's the cover story for Elkins?" McGivern asked.

"Like I said, low-level embassy employee. We're getting her out for her safety and to please the king."

"Scrape and bow?"

"Indeed," Holmes replied. "But we need to provide a security detail for her. *She* absolutely can't be taken by some Islamist extremists. If that happens, we'll be lucky if they shoot her. More likely, they'll extract the most advanced encryption systems in the world, then put her to work for them."

"I'm assuming a SEAL team is already trying to find Anders."

Holmes confirmed that. "Now I'd like you to make sure they send in another detachment for Elkins. Let's get everybody to Sana. The lawlessness in Yemen works in our favor right now. The CIA already has a safe house."

McGivern and Warnes left. Holmes leaned back and stared at the ceiling, knowing that Lana's life was now in play as well as Mancur's. But the choices were terrible. Sometimes you had to give up a great operative for the greater good. Sometimes you didn't know if losing a life did any good at all. No matter what the outcome, you remained haunted by the death forever.

• • •

Ambassador Arpen called Lana into his lavishly appointed office, took her elbow, and led her to a wide window.

"Look at *that*," he ordered, as he used a pair of binoculars.

"I know. I've seen it." Thousands of Saudi protestors massing outside the embassy gates.

"The kingdom has lodged an official complaint with Washington." He put the binoculars on the windowsill. "Seems one of our spies they've been 'debriefing' has identified you as a computer specialist of some kind. They're saying that you're a spy. If they come over that wall, your little charade here will have cost us deeply."

"Have you been in touch with the king's—"

"Of course I've been in touch with them," he said dismissively. "However, I'm not sure all the king's men are in touch with the Saudi street. But it's safe to say that everyone beyond those walls is playing games with us because you played games with them."

Lana had had enough: "Are you so thick that you thought the secretary of state really had sent over new technical support for the embassy at a time when every one of us is needed in the States to try to fight cyberterrorists who are systematically destroying the country? Grow up!"

He backed away, as if struck.

"You have just violated all kinds of protocol, Ms. Elkins, and you will pay for it."

"You have no idea to whom you're speaking, so don't ever threaten me again. And stop playing the blame game. This isn't a school yard, Rick." She dropped his honorific as if it were a communicable disease. "I did not orchestrate my own targeting."

The ambassador cleared his throat. "I was a little testy just then. I apologize."

"Apology accepted. Look, I'm less than thrilled about leaving with that happening in the streets. Could you contact the palace and see if they'll at least provide aircraft for us?" She looked at the teeming protestors. "A helicopter would be nice for starters, as soon as possible."

"They're not in the mood to grant favors, Ms. Elkins. They're in the mood to extract teeth, if need be, to find out what we're really up to. I'd like to know, too."

She ignored his entreaty. "We did some huge favors for them on 9/11," flying Saudi royalty out of the U.S. after all commercial flights were canceled. "Maybe it's time to collect a chit or two."

"If the king really wanted to help us, he could make those people down there go away with a snap of his finger."

"I'm not so sure. You said yourself that his staff isn't exactly attuned to the Saudi street."

The ambassador turned his attention back to the demonstration. She knew what he feared. She worried about it herself. A replay of the Iranian hostage crisis. The protestors outside the embassy gates right now looked furious enough to do just about anything. Then her attention was grabbed by a huge poster starting to burn. She snatched up the binoculars, shocked by what they revealed: a close-up of *her* face on fire. *Jesus Christ. Where the hell did they get it?*

Lana had always been far removed from the blood and mud of actual struggle. To see that kind of hate, directed so personally at her from only a few hundred feet away, was alarming.

"I feel that they know something about you that I don't know." Arpen looked at her. "But I do know this: You're going to Yemen."

"Yemen? Nobody's told me that."

"That's my job at the moment."

"You've got to be kidding. They just snatched Agent Anders down there."

"It's not my decision. Take it up with Deputy Director Holmes. He's ordering it. We have to get you out of here quickly. A SEAL team is on the way."

She nodded, thinking that Holmes and his staff would have thought through the decision to move her south. But still, *Yemen?*

"You won't be going through a formal border crossing. When you get down there, you'll be working from a CIA outpost. Mancur will be heading to a safe house in Sana, if he's released."

"Do you know what they've done to him?"

"Everything, I gather."

"What kind of shape is he in?" she asked.

"Ms. Elkins, I've never met the man. Have you?"

She lied, shook her head. Clearly Ruhi Mancur wouldn't be in very good shape, if and when she ever saw him again.

"He gave you up. Maybe Anders, too," the ambassador said.

"We all give up someone. He was smart to name me. At least I have some security." Though another glance at the demonstration showed the streets leading to the embassy clogged with angry shouting men, possibly belying her hopes.

"What if they come over the fence?" she asked the ambassador. "How are you going to stop them?"

"We are not going to start shooting Saudi citizens, I can tell you that much. The preferred approach here is restraint, and getting you out of here so they can have their little victory over your expulsion."

She looked at the swelling crowd, spotting a Saudi demonstrator atop the wall. "It had better be fast," she said as the man jumped onto embassy grounds.

He was quickly caught by guards. But he was just the first drop in a powerful storm.

• • •

Giving up Elkins had bought Ruhi a reprieve. Not the name of an AQAP Islamist terrorist, to be sure, but Elkins represented everything that Saudi intelligence loathed about the manner in which the U.S. operated—with utter disregard for the kingdom's borders and sovereignty. The kingdom's power and control violated by a woman, no less.

Beyond her name, though, Ruhi could offer them little. "She worked on my computer. I don't know what she did."

He must have said some variation of that a hundred times.

Lennon had eased up a bit. He'd ordered an aide to pat him dry with a towel. While they swabbed Ruhi down, Lennon sipped from a water bottle.

Getting dry had eliminated Ruhi's fear of being waterboarded again. He was still trying to recover his senses when a video screen was rolled in front of him.

Oh, no. What's next? Ruhi wondered.

Lennon dismissed the men who brought the monitor in, then turned to Ruhi, seated across from him on the vinyl chair. "So tell me, who else is operating out of your kingdom without our express consent? You see, I'm beginning to think that you're not Al Qaeda because no one in Al Qaeda would have known about Elkins. So that was good, Ruhi. Very good. But not good enough. Nobody would send a new guy like you out on your own. Even the U.S. isn't that stupid. And if you are not new, if you've been working on your 'game moves' for a long time, then you have a long list of names inside your head. It's one or the other, Ruhi. Either the list, or who's helping you?"

"I don't know anybody else," Ruhi said. "I've told you everything I know."

Lennon crossed his arms and said, "Okay, you told me a little something, so I'll tell you something. We just got a report that an American was taken by AQAP a couple of hours ago. Do you know her?"

He used a remote. The screen came alive. Ruhi warned himself not to react, to silence even his body language. Even so, he shuddered when he saw a group of armed men rip a hijab off Candace. Then he startled when the dark-haired man taken with her was executed on camera. The lens followed his fall before tilting back up. Lennon worked the remote, and the screen froze on Candace's face.

"Who is she?"

"I don't know."

"You're lying."

Ruhi was so beaten down that he almost nodded in agreement. He couldn't even brace himself for more waterboarding. But Lennon didn't call his thugs back in. Once more, he pressed the remote. Once more, the video played. Once more, Candace's face filled much of the screen. But this time, behind her, a man pulled back a curved Arabian sword. He looked like a batter getting ready to smash one out of the park.

At the last second, Candace must have caught a reflection in the lens, because she tried to look back. The same instant the blade sliced through her neck and her head toppled out of frame. Not for long.

The camera tilted down one final time, and her face filled the screen.

Ruhi stiffened, stifling a groan, but he was too late. Lennon had been watching him closely and nodding.

"Thank you for your honesty."

• • •

Emma and Tanesa exchanged a quick look. Emma imagined what Tanesa would say, if she could: "You hang in there, girl. You're doing great."

Why had she *ever* given Tanesa a hard time? She wished she could just say she was sorry.

She wasn't the only one sending looks Tanesa's way. Other girls were eyeing her, too, as if to take their cues from their natural-born leader. Some of the boys were doing the same thing. Even the older ones. The terrorists, meantime, had been working their walkie-talkies, bragging to their listeners, whoever they were, wherever they were stationed. They couldn't be too far away, at least based on what Emma had learned using walkie-talkies in summer camp.

But maybe theirs are more powerful.

The leader suddenly put the walkie-talkie closer to his ear, adjusting the volume so others could not hear. Then he stormed down the aisle and dragged Emma from her seat.

She thought he'd taken offense at her glance toward Tanesa. Emma was sure she was about to watch William Sr. get killed, and that she would die as well.

But once the leader hauled her to the front of the bus, he yelled to his compatriots, "Her mother is a spy. Our brothers checked the names. They say the Elkins woman at the embassy is the mother of this girl."

"My mom's not a spy," Emma said. "She's a—"

He smacked her face hard enough to draw blood from the corner of her mouth.

Emma wanted to kill him. *Right now!* She glared at him. Her mouth ached. William Sr. was shaking his head at her. It looked like he was trying to tell her *no, don't do anything.* Trying to calm her down, despite the gag in his mouth.

She knew she had to stay cool.

"Yes, a *spy.* Our brothers have checked. They are sure. The Elkins woman has a computer company in Bethesda. That is her cover. They say she has a fourteen-year-old daughter. This is the girl."

He grabbed Emma's hair and shook her so hard that her roots felt like they would explode. Tears ran down her face.

"They are calling for her mother's head in Riyadh. We have her daughter right here, praise be to the Prophet Mohammed, peace be upon him." He said that as if he were announcing a celebration. Then he yelled right in Emma's face, "Outside the embassy, my brothers are holding pictures of your mother. They are *burning* them. But we have you. And now we will tell the world."

He forced Emma to the floor. Her head was bowed, roots still throbbing from the thrashing. He told someone on the walkie-talkie, who must have been relaying messages to and from the men on the bus, that they would murder Emma if their demands weren't met.

What demands? Emma wondered hopelessly.

The answer came when the man shouted into his mouthpiece, "Tell them we want safe passage to Times Square. If anybody tries to stop us, we will shoot her first. And if they keep trying to stop God's will, we will *all* be martyrs."

Now he exchanged a look of his own—to the man with the backpack bomb. He was in the last row all by himself. The leader had confirmed that the pack could kill them all in less than a second, and that the trigger was at the end of the long tube, just like she'd thought.

Emma saw the bomber nod. His eyes looked glazed. She wondered if he was high.

Sure he is, she said to herself. High at the thought of blowing them all to bits so he could go to heaven and have sex with a bunch of virgins and eat a lot of fruit.

That's so crazy.

But Emma didn't dare give evidence of her thoughts. Without realizing it, she folded her hands like the other kids on the bus. She wasn't praying, not exactly, but she was certainly hoping harder than at any other time in her life.

CHAPTER 17

LANA WAS SHOCKED BY the fury of the Saudis pouring over the tall, dun-colored wall. They rose up along the entire length of it. Many shook their fists in triumph and screamed before jumping onto the embassy grounds. Behind them, tall lush palms moved languidly in a mild breeze, their calm appearance an eerie backdrop to the mob's rage.

She watched a man crumple to the ground upon landing, then grab his lower leg as if he had snapped his ankle. She might have been the only person to notice his agony. The other demonstrators—even those who almost fell on him—raced right by the prone, pained figure.

An explosion turned her attention to a steel reinforced gate at the south end of the compound. In the attack on the U.S. embassy in Tehran, the angry Shiites had only needed to use bolt cutters to open a gate. Here, their bitter and longtime rivals, Sunni Muslims, needed a great deal more—and had just demonstrated their powers of procurement.

In the next few seconds, dozens of demonstrators raced through the bombed gate—and hundreds more pressed forward, forming a great, seemingly endless flood of men.

Ambassador Arpen paled. His hand rose to his throat, as if he already feared the nature of his death.

"Call someone," he yelled at his executive assistant the moment the stately, middle-age woman poked her head in the door. "We need protection. Where are the Saudi police? This is U.S. soil. Call them!" he bellowed at her.

You can call till your fingers go numb, Lana thought, *but the cork is out of a very unsettled bottle.* She didn't think any police force was likely to jam it back in, certainly not in the minutes—maybe just seconds—that embassy personnel had before the wrath of so many Saudis closed down around them.

She was sure the entire compound was in lockdown, but the mob had already blown open a steel gate. Doors would be the proverbial putty after that. The fact that there were bombs showed that this was hardly a spontaneous demonstration, at least by those equipped with the hardware to penetrate sophisticated U.S. security. Lana had no doubt about the backbone of this operation: AQAP.

One protestor carried a large American flag that was almost fully engulfed in flames. Pieces of the Stars and Stripes broke off as he ran. The flaming swatches had to be burning others in the densely packed horde, but no one dared to put the fire out.

A crude figure of Uncle Sam bobbed above the sea of heads, but other than the posters of Lana and a handful of signs proclaiming the U.S. to be the demon incarnate, there were few other displays of printed animus. Maybe AQAP had made it clear that this would not be a polite protest, but a siege. It sure looked like one.

They hate us.

Lana knew there was no mistaking the depth of ill will. And there would be no escaping the anger. On a government-to-government level, there might be friendship, or at least a relationship of convenience. *But the Saudi street wants us dead.* That last thought had her shaking her head.

She kept her eye on the ambassador, guessing that whatever security could be spared would try to protect him.

He had taken control of the phone himself, screaming into the mouthpiece the same question he'd yelled at his assistant: "Where are the Saudi police?"

Not here, and not likely to show up anytime soon, was all Lana could think as he slammed down the receiver.

The cyberattacks had shifted the balance of world power with precipitous speed. Former friends—or frenemies, more accurately—were backing away from the U.S. as fast as picnickers from a park skunk. It looked like frenemy number one, Saudi Arabia, was even willing to let Americans . . .

No, she barked at herself. *Don't even think it.* But the stubborn impulse to acknowledge a brutal possibility would not ebb, so she finished her sentence with the succinctness of death itself: . . . be slaughtered.

Three uniformed men rushed in. "You have to leave," the first said to the ambassador. "Now!" Not that the ambassador showed any reluctance to flee.

Embassy staff and other security officers also crowded into the office, then proceeded to smash the computers, even the ones on the ambassador's desk, until the hard drives lay in pieces. They used cudgels that might have been kept on hand for precisely that purpose.

Paper files—no doubt just as damning—were hauled from file cabinets and thrown into shiny metal carts. Documents marked "Secret" fluttered to the floor. No one bothered to scoop them up. It looked like a drill they might have rehearsed many times, but terror had taken over.

"Burn them! Burn them!" a senior embassy official yelled. She looked rattled, wet-eyed, but not as shook up as the ambassador. As the three-man security detail escorted him from his office, he shouted at them, "Don't let them take me. Whatever you do, don't let them near me."

None of the officers responded to him.

"Where are we going?" Arpen now shouted, his voice high-pitched with panic.

"Just keep moving, sir," was the only response.

The ambassador sounded pathetic to Lana, but she trailed his security team closely. She knew she could not, under any circumstances, fall into the hands of AQAP. Only minutes ago a poster of her had been burned, to the cheering approval of the throng now invading the embassy grounds.

The officers moved the ambassador quickly down the hall. He looked back, spotted her, and yelled, "Go away. Burn files! Do something useful. You're not coming with me."

A scant second later, she wished she'd followed his order—instead of him: Five scruffy men with beards burst out of the stairwell and headed straight for them.

"Oh, God," the ambassador cried, echoing Lana's thoughts for the first time.

The men had their weapons drawn and overwhelmed the three security officers before they could even draw their guns. The five shoved them aside, along with the ambassador, and grabbed Lana.

"U.S. Navy. We're taking Elkins," one of the SEALs announced in a deep Texas drawl. "Out of our way."

A large man gripped her left arm and hauled her down the hall. The commander caught up and took her right. Two of the SEALs worked the point; one covered them from behind.

"SEALs?" Lana asked the new guy on her right. He seemed to be the commander. "Really?"

"We've been called a lot worse," he responded calmly.

"What about me?" yelled the ambassador, running after them.

"Go away," the SEAL covering their rear yelled at him.

Lana glanced back as the ambassador tried to push past the officer. Bad move. In a flash he was pinned against the wall.

"I mean it, Ambassador Arpen. This isn't your show."

The diplomatic food chain had never been clearer.

"We don't use elevators unless we have to," said the commander as they swept her into the stairwell. He was as square-jawed as Superman. He even had a cleft in his chin. "Power goes out, and we have to break out of the damn box."

They were two floors above ground level. Embassy personnel rushed past them, going up the stairs. A woman shouted, "They're breaking down the front door."

When Lana paused to look at her, the commander growled, "Don't stop!"

As they hit the ground floor, one of the two SEALs on point peered into a lobby with a lavishly tiled blue fountain. Before he could close the door, a dozen Saudis ran into view. They spotted him—perhaps the others too—and sprinted toward them. The SEAL coming up the rear released three tear gas canisters. The rest resumed their downward flight.

She heard the gas hissing above the screams and the thunder of pounding footsteps.

"Go, go, go!" the commander growled.

The two men in the lead threw open the door to an underground area that was bigger than any big-box store in Bethesda. It looked like it had been built for parking, but there were no cars that Lana could see, only evenly spaced concrete pillars.

Now they were running. She was lifted off her feet repeatedly. She knew she had never moved this fast and was unlikely to ever again.

That was when the lights went out. She guessed a main power source had been compromised—by a bomb or a malicious pair of hands. Darkness descended quickly as a clamp. But in startlingly fast fashion the SEALs had headlamps lighting their way.

"We're big bright targets now, men," the commander drawled, "so go—go—go!"

"Shit! You hear that?" the man on her left muttered in a thick New York accent.

Hear what? Lana couldn't hear anything—at first. Then, above the SEALs' heavy footsteps she heard the shouts of men chasing them, countless shoes pummeling concrete.

The SEALs veered left. In seconds, Lana saw that they were headed toward an older Japanese four-wheel-drive van with a notable amount of ground clearance.

"This oughta be fun," the New Yorker said.

They were fifty feet away from the vehicle. She looked back over her shoulder. She couldn't see their pursuers in the darkness, but it was definitely an unruly crowd that sounded like it was growing by the second.

They can't know it's me. How could they?

But the unwanted answer came to Lana the next moment when she realized that the mob would be looking at five men racing away with a lone woman.

Who else is it going to be?

The van doors were unlocked. One of the SEALs pushed her into the middle row. A hijab was thrown over her. Two SEALs garbed her so fast she wondered if they'd rehearsed those moves, too.

At the same time, the driver started speeding backward. She turned, frightened to find the van hurtling into blackness. But she saw why when the headlights revealed a thick stream of men—more than a hundred, easily—racing at them. They were so close the driver couldn't have turned around right away without moving the van within easy striking distance of them.

But he can't keep this up, she thought with another glance back, expecting at any moment to crash into a concrete column or wall.

She reached for her seat belt, but the New Yorker grabbed her hand.

"Uh-uh," he said. "We don't get caught in elevators *or* cars."

Right then the driver whipped the wheel around. The tires squealed, and the van did a 180-degree turn, rising up—*Oh, shit!*—on two wheels and barely missing a formidable-looking post.

For a nanosecond she felt suspended in space. Then all of their weight shifted with the momentum, and the van smacked back down on all fours. With another squeal they were off, speeding through the cavernous realm with the headlights on.

The sound of the mob softened. But less than twenty seconds later a solid metal garage door, wide and high enough for a semi-truck, appeared in the headlights in front of them. The commander, riding shotgun—and never had that term resonated more starkly for her—pointed a remote and clicked.

The door rose—*slowly.*

The driver braked till they rolled toward it at five miles per hour.

"They're still coming," announced the officer who covered the rear action. "Forty meters."

The door clanked as it opened, creaky as an old man.

"Who designs these things?" she asked, anguished.

"This isn't an emergency exit," the commander replied. She read the tension in his jaw. "This is purely a service entrance, so we'd better hope the caterers, or whatever you people use this thing for, aren't on the way down."

"Twenty meters," the officer in back yelled. "Getting closer. Fifteen."

"Go, go, go!" the commander said again. "It'll clear."

"*Ten* meters!"

The driver hesitated.

"That was an order. Go, goddamn it!"

The driver shook his head, but floored it. When the van bumped over a raised metal plate, the clearance was so slight that the roof hit the bottom of the rising door. Lana looked up and saw a crease three inches above her head.

Even before they cleared the exit, the commander hit the remote again.

Without an order, the SEALs on either side of her tossed tear gas canisters out of the old vehicle. They rolled toward streams of men slipping under the door.

"They're picking those things up and throwing them back at us," reported the officer in the rear seat.

He no sooner spoke than one of the canisters banged down on the roof and bounced noisily off. Enough profanities followed to paint a prison blue.

"How many are there?" asked the commander.

"A helluva lot. That damn door didn't go down any faster than it went up."

"Ain't democracy great," the New Yorker cracked.

"They're *still* slipping through there," the SEAL behind them added.

"What's ahead?" Lana asked.

"You tell me," the commander said to her, gripping his handsome jaw. "Just joking. We hope pure fucking chaos. That's our favorite medium."

"You'd love the States right about now, then," Lana said.

"Been there, done that," he replied. "And now we're getting a taste of it right here, aren't we?"

Lana nodded as daylight opened up ahead.

"Head scarfs, glasses," the commander ordered.

The SEALs had them on in seconds. The commander and the men on either side of her had prayer beads out, in a fair imitation of piety.

"You are not to say a word, no matter what," the commander said to her. "Play the meek Muslim woman all the way."

She nodded again, this time with her head down, assuming the part.

"That's a good start," he said. "As of now, you have five brothers."

In arms, she thought.

They burst into the brilliant Saudi sunlight. Lana suddenly realized that she was perspiring profusely.

It was about to get a lot hotter: A sea of men and boys pounded on the windows, engulfing them in flailing fists. The driver was forced to slow down. The crowd shouted imprecations. She didn't know the language, but there was no mistaking the mood.

"What are they saying?" she asked, keeping her head bowed.

"That we work for the Americans," the commander said. "That we're turncoats."

"What do they want?"

"They want us to stop, and that's the one thing we never do in a situation like this."

The mob pressed in on all sides. The driver now slowed to the speed of a brisk walk: fast enough to display a sense of purpose, but not so fast that he'd run over anyone.

She wondered, though, how long before a cell phone delivered the daunting news: Those are Americans in the van.

• • •

Ruhi harbored a faint hope that Candace's murder had been staged somehow, or rendered through the magic of digital production. He was staring at the darkened screen when Lennon spoke up:

"My men will take you to a shower. You will have clean clothes. Then we will talk. You may eat at that time, too. Do you like coffee?"

What? Ruhi was confused, still not as lucid as he would have liked. Finally, the question registered. "Yeah, sure." But he didn't believe a word of what he'd just heard.

The shower was cold, bracing, perhaps by design. It focused his thoughts quickly.

She can't be dead. Never a religious man, he now found himself pleading to an Almighty as nebulous to him as dark matter itself: *Please let her be alive.* He remembered her brutal death and thought, *Anything but that.*

Ruhi turned his attention to his naked body. Lennon's waterboarding had been far more punishing than the Americans' torture. Even his dog bite throbbed almost as badly as it had when the local anesthetic wore off at the Farm. He didn't remember them touching it, but he'd blacked out. Had they probed it, studied the ragged flesh to see if the bite was real?

"Get out of there," ordered one of the guards outside the stall.

After dressing, the men led him to a cubicle in the same large room in which he'd been tortured, but at the other end—far from the board and bucket.

A plate of falafel and hummus, along with strips of roasted lamb, awaited him at a card table. So did Lennon.

"Go ahead, eat," he told him. "You will need your strength."

For what? Ruhi looked back at the board. *More of that?*

But he said nothing. He didn't even pause when he thought the food might be poisoned. As long as death came fast.

"You are a mystery to me," Lennon said after watching Ruhi eat the last of the lamb. "You gave up the name of Elkins, but you never did give up the name of the agent. Your heart made you strong, didn't it?"

Ruhi didn't answer, but looked up from his plate, asking, "Was she really killed? Could they have faked it?"

"Believe me, Ruhi, they do not have a little Hollywood studio to fake that kind of crime. But we do. I did not want you dead, so I had my men use video of them threatening her with the sword that they put up on the Web. I wanted you to talk, and you did, in a manner of speaking. I can tell that she means a great deal to you."

Ruhi filled with the biggest breath of his life. Immensely relieved, he asked if Lennon knew where the jihadists had taken her.

"We're working on that. Your adopted country is trying to find her, too."

My adopted country. The barbs were back. But Ruhi didn't care. People were looking for Candace. There was hope.

"Eat," Lennon said. "I'm telling you again, you really will need your strength."

Ruhi helped himself to more hummus as Lennon went on:

"We are on the same side, in the bigger picture. Look, I do not like the way your country operates here, but I am a realist. So is the king. We were not nearly as concerned about Lana Elkins or Candace Anders as we are about AQAP, but if we do not stop them they *will* cut off her head. They have cut off many heads. On the other hand, we now know that you are not Al Qaeda."

"I told you that right away."

"Every suspect does. It means nothing. But I started believing you when you gave us Elkins. As I said, AQAP would not be likely to know that. But I was sure you were not with them when I saw your reaction."

Ruhi looked over to where he had been shackled, but said nothing.

"AQAP has been getting all the rabble into the streets," Lennon continued. "They want to take over our country."

"That's no secret. I'd know that from reading the *Washington Post*."

"But they are very emboldened now, Ruhi. Since the U.S. went down, a lot of bad people are getting bolder, and a lot of us are not happy about that. There has always been an element of Saudi society that, let us say, is a bit unsettled, misguided, if you will. They are . . . susceptible."

"Like the ones who attacked us on 9/11?" Ruhi couldn't resist.

"'Us.' So America is truly more your country now than your homeland?"

Ruhi nodded. Lennon shook his head, went on:

"So, yes, then, like the men who attacked *your* country on 9/11. But do you think they would have spared the palace or our king if they had had a similar chance? They want to destroy the monarchy. I doubt you are a monarchist, though, are you, Ruhi?"

He didn't respond. What he felt about the Saudi royal family would never help him here.

"It does not matter. I know your type. You are too American, too 'us' now. You cannot understand your birth country any longer. But I am sure you understand that the devil you know is better than the devil you do not know. That is an Americanism I have always treasured. It is not a simple world, but the monarchy is much better than Al Qaeda or any of the ayatollahs in Tehran. So we are going to let you continue with your mission with one huge condition."

Here it comes. "Okay, what is it?"

"Every bit of intelligence that you gather will be shared with me—without exception. And you will not divulge any of our agreement to—"

"What agreement?" Ruhi interrupted. "I haven't agreed to a damn thing."

"But you will. Let me go on. You will continue to track down those cyberattackers who are destroying your country. We do not want to see America so weak. We get one billion dollars a year in arms from your generous taxpayers just for military aid. We need those fighter jets and tanks, and then there are all those American dollars for our oil. So go save your country. But you, Mr. Ruhi Mancur, are now working for your other country, the one that claimed you first. Or else you will have a very difficult time in the next few days."

"Are you trying to turn me into a double agent?"

"Strictly speaking, the answer is yes. But you are not, in this case, playing one side against the other. Let me put it this way. Saudi Arabia and the U.S. have a strong common interest at the moment."

"You're joking, right? You expect me to report to you? And how come you didn't grab Ahmed?"

"We tried. We are holding your Uncle Malik for questioning. But your cousin was gone when we arrived, while you were sleeping. Ahmed is a slippery man. We are looking for him everywhere. Your uncle Malik is helping us. We are all Saudi Arabians. We are your family, first and foremost. That is my point. Do not ever forget that."

Ruhi stared at Lennon, knowing that he himself had passed another test.

"Now I want to ask you about the tools of your trade," the Mabahith man said. "We have our best people working on your computer at this very moment, and they are so frustrated that they want to beat it with hammers because they cannot get past the firewalls. They say you have the most sophisticated encryption system that they have ever seen. I am not going to ask who did that for you, though I have my suspicions. I am not even going to ask if you do that kind of encryption work yourself, but I think I know that answer, too. We will have ample time later, if you survive, to chat about your computer. But I will tell you that we think it is vital for us to leak information to certain quarters about the superb software that we have discovered in your possession. We think that might help you on your great quest and serve our needs as well."

"How's that going to help? You'd be turning me into a target."

"That is right," Lennon said, smiling broadly for the first time. "When we let it be known that you have these extraordinary skills, maybe strong enough to save your country from final destruction, they will come looking for you. They would be fools not to, and they are not fools, Ruhi."

"Hold on. You're not trying to turn me into a target. You're trying to turn me into a piece of bait."

"We already have, Ruhi." Lennon's eyes fell to Ruhi's thigh, the one bearing the dog bite. "We embedded a tracking chip deep in your muscle. Only a highly skilled surgeon can remove it without doing crippling nerve damage and possibly even cutting the femoral artery. The chip is so close to it that you couldn't pass a blood cell between them."

"I don't remember anything like that." But he did recall staring at the wound in the shower, wondering if it had been tampered with.

"Of course you don't. You were blacked out long enough for the surgeon to inject a drug to keep you under while he performed the operation. The painkiller will be wearing off soon. You will want these." He handed Ruhi a bottle of Tylenol 3, just as

Ruhi's minder at the Farm had. "Don't take too much. You need a clear head more than you need pain relief. Besides, from what I have seen, you handle pain very well."

Lennon leaned forward and offered a paternal pat to Ruhi's knee, then added, "We have our computer skills, too. Maybe a little crude at times, but they serve our purposes well. And now, Ruhi, so will you."

CHAPTER 18

THE CHOIR'S BIG BLUE bus encountered no traffic on I-295 north. The ringleader, the young man who sounded like he'd grown up in America, forced Emma to remain on the floor of the aisle right by his feet. With her back to him, all she caught were receding glimpses of the towering steel girders of the Delaware Bridge as they headed into New Jersey. But even if she'd been up on a seat facing forward, she would have seen only a police escort a few hundreds yards ahead of them and another cruiser trailing an equal distance behind. Law enforcement was giving the terrorists plenty of space. Emma worried that the cops were sure that the bus—and everyone inside it—was going to blow up at any second.

"My name is Hamza," the leader announced as they drove past a rest stop. He scratched his cheesy beard and added, "It means 'the lion.'"

He paused after issuing those words, as if the real meaning of his proclamation needed time to be fully absorbed and appreciated by his captives. It was long enough for Emma to bet dollars to donuts with herself that his name had been Josh or Andy or Lucas just a few years ago.

"Okay, Hamza," the driver said, breaking what the leader might have thought was a reverent silence, "maybe you should get your lion self up here and check out the gas, because this gazelle is going to run out of gas."

Hamza kneed Emma in the back of the head and ordered her not to move, then swaggered up to the driver and cracked his head with the butt of his gun, knocking the man's cap off. Emma turned just enough to see a thin stream of blood run down the back of his neck.

"Do not insult me again, infidel, or I will shoot you."

"Roger that," the driver said.

Emma stiffened, fearing Hamza would shoot him right then. Instead, he leaned into the driver's face.

"You think you are playing a game with me, don't you?" Hamza smacked the man's skull again. Now she saw two streams of blood running down his neck.

"It's not a game," the driver said, sounding chastened. "I can't control that thing. It's not like we've been able to get any gas in the last few days. So I'm guessing we've got fifty miles to fill up. Then it's going to stop no matter what I do."

Hamza jabbered into his walkie-talkie, saying that fuel would have to be made available to them or they would start killing kids one by one and tossing their bodies off the moving bus, adding, "We will start with the spy's daughter."

He walked back to Emma as he said that and tapped the barrel against her cheek. Emma stiffened. He looked like he'd enjoy putting a bullet in her brain.

Then he stopped, and she dared to glance up. Hamza was staring at Tanesa, and Emma thought, *No, not* her. *Jesus Christ.*

"So tell the president to get us gas," he shouted into his device.

"Diesel," the driver said. "Gas isn't going to help."

"Tell him to get diesel," Hamza said, but Emma could tell that he did not like being corrected.

As if to confirm this, he walked back up front. The driver tried to turtle his head this time, but to no avail. A third line of blood darkened his skin.

"Inshallah, I should kill you now," Hamza shouted at the cowering man.

Emma shook her head without realizing it, and then worried Hamza had seen her and would pistol-whip her, too. But he was just now turning away from the driver.

"This"—he held up his walkie-talkie—"lets me speak to the world. Even the president must listen to me. Do you know why? Because we have you."

That's not the only reason, Emma thought. It was because they had him, too, the mad bomber sitting straight down the aisle from her in the middle of the wide backseat, all by himself. He had never moved an inch away from the backpack bomb beside him. He looked goony-eyed with glory, like he couldn't wait to blow them all to kingdom come.

She heard a helicopter, then Hamza barking into his mouthpiece: "Tell them not to come any closer or I will kill her."

Her?

"But," Hamza quickly said, "they can use their spy in the sky to see this."

He grabbed a fistful of Emma's dark hair and dragged her to her feet. The sharp pain pooled her eyes again, but that instant burst of agony was quickly eclipsed by his next, far more frightening move: roping his arm under her chin and jerking her head up. With her neck fully exposed, he forced her to turn toward the window, then pressed the edge of a long filleting knife, the kind she'd seen fisherman use, against her bare skin.

She saw the copter keeping pace with the bus, guessing they could see what he was doing to her. Now Hamza pressed the blade against her skin.

"Stop, oh, Jesus," she cried.

"She prays to her worthless God," Hamza yelled into the walkie-talkie, which he'd clipped to his shirt, "because of a little blood on my knife. I will bleed her like a pig if they don't leave."

Emma closed her eyes. Her world was no bigger that that blade, her fears as large as the whole of humankind.

• • •

Lana was still in the middle seat of the van, wedged between the commander, the Texan named Travis, and the New Yorker. She did not dare look up, lest one of the men or boys pounding on the windows spot eyes that betrayed a less than pious woman. Travis still worked his prayer beads, subvocalizing as if he knew what he was doing.

With all the pounding on the van, she feared the glass would shatter any second. Then, despite the brisk walking pace that the driver maintained, the mob started rocking the vehicle.

"That's a bad idea, folks," Travis drawled under his breath, still working those beads. "Very bad. Prepare to execute our exit, men."

"Our exit?" she asked.

He didn't explain. He didn't have to. The answer came with the metallic clinks of weapons surreptitiously readied.

The van, with its high clearance, felt terribly unstable, like it might tip over any second, as it almost had in the huge open area below the embassy.

"Go, go, go!" Travis growled.

All around her, the SEALs began to shoot, a furious fusillade that blasted out the windows, sparing only the driver's window and the windshield. Though the shots were aimed above the heads of the screaming, chanting mob, chunks of safety glass showered the crowd.

The deafening sound numbed her ears. She couldn't even hear the engine when the driver started to accelerate. But she heard the horn when he leaned on it and never let up.

Thump, thump, thump.

She also heard men screaming as bodies bounced off the front of the van and others scrambled to get out of the way.

The van ran over at least one person, maybe two, while the guns continued to blaze. To her knowledge there was no return fire, though that would have been hard to tell with the horn and the nearly nonstop volley that surrounded her.

How long could this go on? she wondered. Were there endless blocks of humanity still ahead of them?

There might have been, but the driver hung a sharp left, scattering a thinner crowd on a narrower street. The SEAL riding shotgun shouted directions. He wore dark glasses. She glimpsed a color-coded street map, presumably of Riyadh, on the inside of his lenses. The map—what she could see of it—changed as they moved. The driver, she now saw, had donned a pair of identical dark glasses.

"Where now?" she asked Travis, looking past him to see the shocked looks on the faces of the people they were passing. Shards of glass still protruded from the black rubber molding in most of the windows, and the onlookers undoubtedly had heard the gunshots.

It looked like the van could be pinned in easily on this street. Lana no sooner thought that than the driver wheeled right, turning onto a thoroughfare with huge homes on both sides. Now the only obstacles were cars, but the SEAL at the wheel darted around them easily.

Just as Lana started to breathe, a convoy of police vehicles pulled into view, blocking an intersection. Uniformed officers rushed to get into position behind the SUVs and cars. They aimed their weapons at the van. The driver took cover by keeping them behind a car in the right lane.

"This is gonna be rich," the New Yorker said.

"Are we going to stop?" Lana asked.

"Like I said before," Travis replied, "that's the one thing we do not do at a time like this."

As he finished speaking, the first blasts of gunfire hit the van.

• • •

Candace sat roasting in a cage made from rusty rebar. Tent fabric was draped over the top and three sides, providing shade, but the heat was unrelenting. At least 130 degrees. She was sure they were covering the cage to hide her from aerial surveillance.

It looked like a Bedouin camp, now that most of the mujahedeen had left. There were two tents, the Humvee in which she'd been driven, which was also covered up, and three camels, presumably for verisimilitude.

She guessed U.S. intelligence knew by now that she had been taken. She couldn't imagine that her captors had resisted putting up video of Al Juhani's murder and her abduction. Bragging rights counted for much in that violent realm.

Candace looked at the sky, praying for a drone, even if it meant her own death. What scared her more than dying was what awaited her in the closest tent. She'd seen them carry in two car batteries with wires and alligator clips, plus a toolbox and camp stove. Simple instruments of savagery.

She was so scared she felt sick, but she also felt for her parents. Tim killed in Afghanistan, and their only other child about to be murdered in Yemen.

One of the jihadists opened the tent flap and stared at her. They didn't bother guarding her. They didn't have to. The rebar was unyielding, and even if she got out, where could she go? Nothing but endless miles of open desert surrounded them. No one who cared would hear her screams.

Now the man by the tent nodded and smiled. She turned away, knowing that he was already taking pleasure in her pain.

• • •

Emma felt the blade slide across her skin, right to the tip, and drop away. He didn't dig in deep, just enough to make her bleed and scare her almost senseless. Hamza shoved her onto a seat in front of him. She saw a narrow red streak on the knife, right along the razory edge. As if that weren't enough scary enough, the Islamist grabbed her and wiped the blood off on her skinny jeans. Then he pointed the knife to the suicide bomber in the back of the bus.

She turned and looked obediently.

"They know about you," Hamza yelled back to him.

Even without looking, Emma knew Hamza was smiling.

"They know you are a special man for special times."

She didn't notice the helicopter suddenly veer away, but the leader did. He shouted in Arabic and flashed the blade in the air.

"Yes, a special bomb for a special time."

Emma made the mistake of looking back at him. He lifted her chin with the tip of the blade.

"You will have a lot of company in hell."

• • •

Lana ducked as the police blocking the intersection continued to shoot at the van. None of the SEALs took cover.

"They're not going to do any damage by hitting us from the front," Travis said.

She inched back up, ashen-faced. The commander went on:

"U.S. taxpayers can afford a bulletproof windshield and metal plating all around. It might not look like much, but it's got a lot of ponies under the hood and an extra-large fuel tank."

A big bump interrupted him as the four-wheel-drive van jumped up onto a sprawling home's front yard.

The navigator in the shotgun seat shouted instructions that took them across a lush lawn and down the side of what looked like a mansion, then into a service alley. The sound of sirens rose behind them. But their luck—or skill—ran out seconds later: The service alley was blocked by a police car, and a big Hummer was rolling toward them from behind.

"What the hell?" Lana said.

"My thoughts exactly," Travis replied. But he didn't sound overly concerned.

The driver put the old Delica van into reverse, spinning tires so hard and fast that black smoke rose on both sides of them.

He twisted his upper body around so he was staring straight back. Lana followed his intense gaze. The van, which appeared as crushable as a Coke can, and the Hummer, which did not, were speeding right at each other in an alley that allowed no passage.

She grabbed the seat belt, but once again the New Yorker stilled her hand.

When they were less than twenty feet apart—a breath from a vicious collision—the SEAL at the wheel cut hard to the left, so fast that as the backward-racing van cornered sharply into another service alley, it rose up on the left wheels, and this time she knew they were going over.

Indeed, they were. But as the Hummer's brakes screeched— and its momentum forced the hulking vehicle past the alley claimed by the careening Delica—the left side of the van bounced off a stone wall, which banged the right side against the narrow alley's other wall.

With a few more vicious wobbles, the driver righted the van and kept the now-battered vehicle in reverse, tires *still* smoking.

He backed onto a street and jammed it into drive as a chopper headed toward them, swooping so low that the SEAL had to brake.

"Bye-bye, sweetheart," the driver said, jumping out.

Lana thought he was talking to her, but he meant the van. Travis hauled her out, and the five of them ran to the hovering gunship, run by a U.S. military crew. Cars all around them came to screeching stops. Men jumped out—but only to stare in astonishment. Once more, Lana was pushed on board.

With her legs still hanging out, the chopper rose so rapidly and turned so sharply that she would have fallen hundreds of feet if the New Yorker hadn't had both of her arms firmly in hand.

She looked over her shoulder, shuddering at the fall she would have taken, stomach rolling for all kinds of reasons.

"Don't worry, darlin'," the New Yorker said, launching into an old Springsteen song with a big smile, "'I came for you, for you, I came for you, but you did not need my urgency.'" Now he was joined in by the whole SEAL team: "'I came for you, for you, I came for you, but your life was one long emergency.'"

• • •

Lennon helped Ruhi don a white head scarf, much like his own, with a black band around the crown. Then he escorted him, along with three similarly attired officers, into an underground garage.

The five of them piled into a Ford Expedition. Lennon placed him in the middle row between himself and a taciturn man. "Think about getting some sleep, or you may enjoy watching the endless Arabian Desert fly by."

"How far are you taking me?"

"All the way, Ruhi. Don't you know that by now? We're with you all the way."

"My people are sure going to suspect something," he said.

Lennon shook his head. "No, your people have been pleading for your release, begging lower-level staff at the palace to intervene. We knew the game they were playing, not wanting to let on how important you were to them. We've let them know that you are back in business. American arrogance will assume that your release came from the power of their persuasion, and we will not disavow that. They can have their little victory—for now. We will hand you over to your American minders in Sana."

"And you're not worried about Al Qaeda."

"I would like them to try something. Believe me, I would."

Ruhi took an obvious look around, taking inventory of the "troops." Four of them, plus himself.

"It is always the enemy you do not see that you should worry about," Lennon said. "And if you are Al Qaeda looking to stop us, that is what you should be thinking about. Your minders let your Candace down. They gave her poor cover and one operative. We do not underestimate our enemy, but perhaps that is because we live much closer to him than you do."

What Ruhi drew from Lennon's last remark was that they would not be traveling alone when they crossed the Yemeni border.

Ruhi was right.

● ● ●

Deputy Director Holmes was conferring with Teresa McGivern about Ruhi Mancur's release when his executive assistant, Donna

Warnes, entered his office and handed him a file. Warnes exited immediately, as if she knew both the urgency and secrecy of the information.

Holmes opened the large envelope and slipped out a document. Within moments, he shook his head and lifted his eyes to McGivern. "That chopper got close to the bus, but they couldn't get any radiation readings. None of that stuff is working anymore. They thought they had it up and running, but when push came to shove, nothing registered."

Military computers and those running the entire U.S. intelligence system had been disabled in the past few hours by viruses that had been "seeded" many months ago, even before the first cyberattack, according to an NSA forensics team feverishly trying to find the source of the shutdown.

"So we have no idea what's in there?" McGivern asked.

"Just that there's a man in the back of the bus with what appears to be a backpack bomb."

Holmes reached into the envelope and pulled out several photos. "They had to use an old film camera to get these. It was just run over here, and I mean that literally—by a Marine marathoner. Can you believe that, Teresa?"

Even Holmes wasn't sure what begged credulity more: photos that had to be developed in a mothballed darkroom, or their means of delivery. Fuel allotments were so small that any messages and parcels that could be carried by a runner were immediately dispatched in that manner, often with a phalanx of equally fleet-footed armed guards to ensure the safe delivery of top-secret documents.

As Holmes had waited to hear about the radiation readings, he felt like a magistrate in ancient Greece anxious for word of victory or defeat from the prototypical courier, Pheidippides. The renowned herald ran from the city of Marathon to Athens to announce a Greek victory over Persia. "Joy to you, we've won," he supposedly said. But the absence of radiation readings was hardly good news in present-day Maryland, and the photos in Holmes's hand were even worse. He passed the first one to McGivern, saying, "It shows the guy next to the backpack bomb."

"That's a hell of a surveillance shot," she said. It showed a triggering device at the end of a tube that ran out of the pack. "What do we make of it?"

"Not much," Holmes replied. "Could be a nuke, could be plastique, could be a red herring to keep us preoccupied while their real intentions are in play somewhere else. I don't think we can underestimate their canniness."

"That's a nice way to put it."

"I'm doing all I can to keep my profanities in check," he replied, passing her two more photos of the presumed bomber.

"Can't the techs tell anything by the trigger? Its width, length, that sort of thing?"

"They're looking at these photos even as we speak, but I'm guessing not, based on my own experience." He pulled out the last photograph. "Then there's this." He handed it to McGivern, adding, "That's Lana Elkins's girl."

"Oh, shit," McGivern said, looking at a black-and-white of Emma Elkins staring bug-eyed into a telephoto lens with a knife at her neck. There was an unmistakable line of blood on the blade.

"Where's her mother?" Holmes asked Teresa.

"Somewhere in Saudi airspace. We don't know where." She shook her head. "We're not in touch."

"Is the king going to let her go?" Holmes asked.

"That's what we hear via carrier pigeon."

Holmes knew she was kidding. What McGivern didn't know was that he'd already investigated the possibility of using homing pigeons. The military, not surprisingly, didn't have them anymore.

Rest assured, Holmes vowed, they would in the future. At least birds that could fly to and from the White House and all major intelligence centers.

"How bad is the Veepox outbreak?" he asked her.

"Minneapolis–St. Paul is totally closed down. No traffic is moving in or out. The only good news is the outbreak came after air travel ended, so that might slow it down."

"How many cases?"

"More than a thousand, but that information is fourteen hours old."

"So we have no trains, no planes, and—"

"They've knocked out all the computers at the CDC. That's the latest."

The cyberattackers had been as good as their word. Day by day they'd been taking the U.S. apart. In addition to knocking out all military and intelligence communications, they'd disabled GPS and other satellite-based directional capabilities. Holmes believed that the only reason the attackers allowed electric power for many civilian areas was to spread the panic even faster—and to make it clear to the American people that U.S. defense capabilities had been rendered almost useless. From a psychological warfare standpoint, it was a shrewd move.

Highway transportation was also a mess, but the agency's analysts weren't so sure those breakdowns would have made much difference, because the Strategic Petroleum Reserve in salt-dome caverns in Louisiana and Texas was no longer functioning. It had been subject to a cyberblitzkrieg that made the Iranian attack on Aramco, which derailed thirty thousand computers at the world's largest corporation, look like a stalled vehicle in rush hour traffic.

But worse than all the breakdowns in America, in Holmes's view, was what was to come. He had no doubt that the cyberattackers' coup de grâce would arrive when they targeted 350 million Americans with the country's own nuclear missiles. Considering the growing misery of the American people, he suspected that a fair number of the nation's terrorized population might welcome a quick deathblow.

"We're not there yet," Holmes said.

"What?" McGivern asked him.

Holmes hadn't realized that he'd spoken aloud. "Nothing. Just weighing the worst outcomes, and we're not there yet. That's all."

Teresa nodded, but probably didn't believe him. They were old hands and had been through a lot of crises together, so she would know something deeply disturbing must be bothering him. She would also know better than to press him.

"What about the embassy?" Holmes asked her.

"They've got Ambassador Arpen and more than a hundred and ten embassy personnel. No one has been killed. Some beatings, we understand, but nothing life-threatening."

"I just wish I knew what was on that bus, Teresa. We can't let that thing go up into New York. Do we have anything that can get a reading?"

"Yes, we're already looking into that. We're resurrecting some old-school Geiger counters."

"And they're stopping for diesel, right?"

She nodded. "You want one of our guys pumping it."

"I do, but make it a woman, someone rough around the edges. Believable. Play to their prejudices. They're not going to think a woman's going to be much of a threat."

"And if the readings are high?"

"We have to find a way to keep them from moving. How many hours away from New York are they likely to be when they stop for fuel?"

"Three, at best. But no matter where it goes off, if they've got a nuke, we're looking at a huge death toll. They're in southern Jersey now. It's not exactly the Bonneville Salt Flats."

Holmes nodded, implicitly acknowledging the brute facts before him. "But the greater metro area has eighteen million people." He almost said "souls." It was like he could see them all rising, instantly incinerated. "What do our tactical folks say?"

"That the bus has a range no greater than two hundred and sixty miles on a full tank, and that it had made three runs around the Washington area since the cyberattack, so it probably had between two-thirds and three-quarters of a tank when they started out, but a lot less now. So I'm guessing that we knew even before they did that they were going to have to stop. But the governor of New Jersey is already screaming, as you can imagine, that he wants that bus out of his state."

Holmes rested his chin on fists. He could not stop thinking that wherever that bomb went off, whether it was plastique or a backpack nuke, those kids would be at ground zero.

• • •

Hamza pointed to the police car in front of them as it pulled off the interstate.

"See, those police are cowards. Nobody wants to challenge us because we are such powerful martyrs."

Hamza's words appeared to cheer his compatriots. All four of them shouted in victory and shook their fists when the vehicle behind them also exited. The man wearing the backpack bomb was especially vocal.

"We will go wherever we want, and take millions with us," Hamza announced.

Millions? What is he talking about?

Emma's mom had a word for creeps like him who thought they were so important that they could kill or control "millions" of people. She wished she could remember it now. Then she did: "megalomaniacs."

"Do you know what we have?" Hamza asked her, flashing his knife before her face, and then turning his eyes to the rest of the kids on the bus. "Has anyone been able to guess?"

No one volunteered an answer.

"A nuclear bomb! Yes, that's what it is. Stand up," he shouted to the man with the backpack.

He stood, beaming.

Hamza nodded at him. Then his gaze swept over all the children. "You will die with great martyrs. But that won't save your souls." He shook his head, but Emma saw no sadness in his eyes. "You are all damned anyway."

Emma watched him flick his knife inches from her eyes. In those seconds, the brutal magnitude of the bomb didn't register as clearly as the sharp threat of the blade that had already cut her throat and left bloodstains on her collar. She watched him slip it back into a leather sheath that hung from his belt, inches from his gun.

Then she glanced at Tanesa and saw her caregiver's eyes staring at the knife, too. Tanesa nodded at Emma ever so slightly.

She knew exactly what Tanesa was saying. And if she could do it, she would. But just to be sure, she looked at Pastor William Sr., still gagged. He did not move his head, not even a little, but his eyes opened wide on her and looked up and down three times.

Yes, yes, yes.

He wasn't trying to stop her. This was no time for caution.

CHAPTER 19

DEPUTY DIRECTOR HOLMES FOUND himself flying in the copilot's seat of a hurriedly revamped Boeing B-29 Super-fortress that the agency had borrowed from a Smithsonian facility at Dulles. And not just any World War II–era B-29, either, but the *Enola Gay*, which had dropped the atomic bomb on Hiroshima. Ironically enough, the NSA, the cybernetic heart of the intelligence services, needed a pre–computer age aircraft to fly Holmes safely over the latest disaster triggered by the escalating attacks of the invisible enemy. The White House had also plundered the Smithsonian, taking a Stinson L-5 Sentinel for the president's use.

Holmes was headed into the heart of Dixie for an overflight that he already dreaded. Computer programs that controlled nine dams on the Tennessee River, all run by the Tennessee Valley Authority, had long been zealously guarded against terrorist bombs. But months ago—long before their first cyberattack—the unseen enemy had infiltrated the TVA's extensive computer network with "bomblets" that thirty-six hours ago had stopped turbines from moving and closed off spillways and sluice gates. The buildup behind the dams had created crushing pressure until the great walls burst, one after another, like a series of deadly dominoes.

From Knoxville, Tennessee, all the way down to Paducah, Kentucky—more than 650 miles—walls of water had ripped through millions of tons of concrete and earth. The dream of providing electric power for much of the South in President Franklin Delano Roosevelt's day became another means of sending furious torrents of terror through the heartland of the country in the second decade of the twenty-first century.

And there it is.

The damage filled his window. Sickening, like Hurricane Katrina or Superstorm Sandy, but far worse, because in river-valley towns the force of cascading water—not steadily rising seas—had torn houses and schools and hospitals from their firm foundations and sent the bodies of thousands of men, women, and children tumbling downriver in a viciously engineered maelstrom. Few survived the tsunami-force waters. Limp bodies were strewn like seaweed wherever he looked.

Souls.

Holmes, never much of a believer, once more heard the word repeating in his thoughts as he looked down at the devastation.

Hours after the dams had broken, another message arrived on the screens of the NSA. Nothing else worked on those computers, but someone, somewhere, had somehow executed a series of keystrokes that produced the same video of a burning American flag that had appeared on tens of thousands of Aramco's screens. This time the flames were accompanied by the deep, unaccented voice of a man saying, "You are destined for a new kind of D-Day. We call it Death Day, when your country is obliterated, when your flag will look like this." The burning Stars and Stripes turned to cinders with an audible *whoosh,* followed by the sound of a powerful bomb exploding. The voice had continued:

"You should keep your eyes on Appalachia. We are not done with your most-exploited citizens yet. So do not count your dead, because more will die. There is nothing you can do to stop us. You must see that by now. But you may wish to watch what we can do with the worst of your poisonous policies."

"Rhetoric," Teresa McGivern had spit as she turned to him in his office hours ago. She, along with other top members of his team, advised him to disregard the additional warning about Appalachia, telling him bluntly, if coldly, "It's coal-mining country. Hitting that area would be the domestic equivalent of bombing Afghanistan, turning rubble into more rubble."

But Holmes had insisted on seeing the region before flying back. Maybe he'd spot something. Maybe he could actually take action to prevent yet another catastrophe.

Given the threat to the region—and the invitation for it to be observed—Holmes did agree to have two World War II P-51 Mustangs join the *Enola Gay* for this leg of the journey. More than seventy years ago, the Mustangs had driven the Luftwaffe from the skies and been hailed as the greatest dogfighters of the European Theater. But when Holmes spotted them off the wings of the Superfortress, he experienced a powerful sense of displacement, a feeling that he'd stepped into a time capsule that had swept him back to an earlier era, even as he was observing the wretched results of the most advanced warfare in human history.

And here I am in a museum piece.

His eyes lowered to coal country. By any reasonable measure, there was not much to see, mostly a region ravaged by the brute claws of the coal industry. Holmes considered himself a forthright defender of his nation, but he couldn't abide the greed of a young generation of corporate titans. Below him was reason number one:

mountaintop removal. Everywhere he looked he saw moonscapes looming, the once picturesque region so damaged that it was inconceivable conditions could be worsened by a hacker sitting at a distant computer. The despoilment was so extensive that it could be seen from space. He wondered if the enemy just wanted a Washington official to eyeball the destruction.

What are they, environmentalists?

In minutes, he would learn that the answer was just the opposite. As the *Enola Gay* banked north—as it had once turned, high above its Hiroshima target—he watched a sludge pond filled with millions of gallons of toxic runoff burst the earthen walls that contained its liquid death.

"Circle back!" he ordered.

As the pilots complied, Holmes watched the black waters race down a chewed-up mountain and swallow entire towns. He beat his knees in frustration, realizing that the enemy had given him clues to their deadly plan that he'd never made sense of. First the TVA dams. Now this. He should have seen it coming.

But he knew, despite his roiling anger and regret, that even if he'd been able to imagine such grotesque disregard of human life, there was no way for anyone to have warned those poor people. Rural electric power throughout most of the South had failed when the TVA dams collapsed.

The sequence, Holmes knew at once, was part of the plan. The countdown was getting crueler. And the best scientists in the country had not been able to penetrate the firewalls thrown up by the enemy that had taken control of the nation's nuclear arms.

The day's damage was hardly done. Unknown to Holmes, the Palo Verde Nuclear Plant, two thousand miles away, to the west of Phoenix, went into full-scale meltdown. The exodus from the city—already suffering from temperatures approaching 130 degrees, the highest in its broiling-hot history—had proved riotous and furiously violent. People with four-wheel-drive cars and SUVs tried to blast their way across open desert. Road rage took on new, even more lethal dimensions as racing gun battles ensued among carloads of men *and* families trying to shoot their way free of radiation sickness and death.

Palo Verde, with its containment buildings rising above the desert floor, was the first nuclear power plant to go into meltdown, but operators of other plants were also facing record-low river and lake levels—and doing all they could to try to keep their reactors cool enough to prevent catastrophes that could take thousands of years to recover from.

• • •

The helicopter with Lana and the SEALs landed in another desert half a world away. No landing strip, only three unmarked concrete helicopter pads. Two were occupied by Sikorsky UH-60 Black Hawks clad in radar-absorbent materials. In short, they were stealth birds, exactly like the one used on the raid on Osama bin Laden's compound. Lana wondered if they were the same Sikorskys.

A Quonset hut hangar was the only structure at the "base," and she understood, as she walked across the searing Arabian Desert sand, that the hut could probably be dismantled and carted away in hours. The desert would have no difficulty burying the concrete pads on its own.

The hangar provided shade, but little relief from the scorching daytime heat.

She spotted unnerving evidence that the hangar had been a black site: Wall and ceiling-mounted pulleys lay on the floor; discarded steel cables and shackles collected dust nearby; and buckets and ragged towels that could have been used—*No, they were. Don't kid yourself*—for waterboarding were jammed into a corner.

That was when she knew the hangar had been out there for some time, for who would have left behind a grisly display of evidence like that? It would never be a stop on a congressional junket that included U.S. military bases. The only people who would ever see the hangar were prisoners, those who minded them, and the intelligence personnel like her who used the hangar in emergencies.

She also realized that in all likelihood, they had landed in Yemen. The Saudis permitted U.S. drone bases on their desert, but their imperial pride never would have countenanced such a brazen display of antiterror tools—not evidence that could undermine the moral authority of the royal family.

A propane camp stove sat on a rudimentary counter.

"Coffee?" asked Gabe, the New Yorker who had held her life in his hands as they roared out of Riyadh. "Or do you wanna get some shut-eye?"

He nodded at cots with blindingly white sheets. *Odd*, she thought, *for such an otherwise grungy redoubt.*

Lana answered with her feet, trudging to the nearest cot to lie down, fully clothed. She might have fallen asleep before her head hit the pillow.

"You think she liked our song?" Gabe asked Travis.

"I sure hope so," the commander replied. "Because there's no encore. Sun goes down, and our bird goes up. And we're not singing a single note on our way to Sana."

Travis set up a computer with a satellite link. In minutes he clicked onto a European website and began to update his team on the embassy takeover: "They say they're going to put the ambassador on trial."

"Good; I hope they convict him of being a pussy," said the SEAL who'd pushed Arpen against a wall to keep him from following the team assigned to rescue Lana.

The officer who'd driven the Delica carried over half a dozen folding chairs and doled them out.

"Nothing from the palace yet," Travis went on, "so they're letting all the action at the embassy play out."

"Kissing some militant ass," said the driver. "Anybody killed yet?"

"No reported deaths. Hey, that's a good sign," Travis offered.

"Only if you like Arpen," Gabe volleyed. "I hate those Yalies."

"He went to Harvard," Travis replied. "Just like you. Christ, you make a lousy good ol' boy, and I know my good ol' boys."

"Well, you make a lousy Aggie, and Arpen makes a lousy ambassador."

"Okay, guys, here's a German news report with video." Travis pointed to the screen.

"What the fuck is that?" Gabe demanded, pointing to the screen, where it looked like thousands were rioting at Chicago O'Hare Airport.

"Veepox has hit the Windy City," Travis said, back to watching the news scroll. "It's under quarantine, and—"

"Those people are totally out of control," Gabe finished Travis's comment without looking away from the monitor. "And that's Santa Monica," he added when video appeared of an Army tank rolling down Highway 1.

"Right," the driver said. "You know your cities."

"And my beach towns. Tell you something else I know. I'll never lose money by underestimating the intelligence of the American people," Gabe shot back.

"And even an Aggie knows you ripped that line off from a guy named Mencken," Travis said.

"It's weird being where the action isn't," Gabe replied, ignoring the plagiarism charge.

"Don't worry about that," Travis told him. "We'll be heading into the darkest night soon enough."

• • •

A couple of hundred miles away, Ruhi still sat between two Maba-hith agents in the Ford Expedition. Lennon, in the passenger seat, controlled the playlist, so Ruhi had been forced to listen to an end-less stream of Arabic music, which he loathed. He was more of a Simon and Garfunkel fan, or just Simon would do. Maybe some John Denver. A girlfriend once told him that he had "atavistic taste." He readily agreed. A loop of "Country Roads" might have played in his head if the racket from Lennon's iPod could have been silenced.

He'd complained, of course, but Lennon had looked at him like he was a bug badly in need of insecticide.

But hard as Ruhi tried, he could not drive out the grating sounds of buzzes, dafs, tablahs, and the other screechy Arabic instruments ripping at his ears.

Signs for the Yemeni border appeared, now only a few kilome-ters away. Given its import, Ruhi would have liked a little more warning.

For what? He shrugged to himself. *To get ready, I guess.*

But as they pulled up to the border crossing, with its high walls and thick metal gate, he saw very quickly that there was little he could have done, except remain quiet—Lennon's sole warning to him.

His minder handed documents and cash to one of the Yemeni guards. They were all dressed in desert camos and bore assault rifles and pistols.

The guard pocketed the cash, offered a cursory glance at the passports, and sent them on their way.

Ruhi dozed, escaping the grating music. When Lennon roused him an hour later, the iPod had been shut off. But whatever relief that might have provided was instantly supplanted by Lennon pointing out where the jihadists had abducted Candace. He explained what took place in some detail, and then finished by saying, "Everything happened in minutes."

Not everything, Ruhi thought. *What are they doing to her now? How many fingernails does she have left? How many ways are they violating her?*

Then he asked himself one last unavoidable question: *How many people did she give up?*

As Ruhi closed his eyes, Lennon spoke up:

"Do not worry, Ruhi. We have ample protection. Yemen is a lawless nation, so we make sure we bring the law with us. Do you know what the law is down here?"

"Guns?"

Lennon laughed. "Yes, many, many guns and the men we pay to carry them for us."

Ruhi glanced out the windows and saw yellowish mountains that looked incapable of supporting life of any kind, save the microbes that he thought would outlive all humanity.

Their destination, Sana, was already on the verge of perishing. Not from internal strife, of which Yemen had plenty, but from a simple lack of water. The World Bank said it was likely to become the first global capital to run completely dry, a terrifying prognostication for the city's two million inhabitants.

It was already drained of law and order. Al Qaeda members routinely benefited from not-so-mysterious prison breaks on a nearly regular basis, and jihadists almost took armed control of Aden, the capital, in 2012. Aden was also the site of a 2000 suicide bombing against the U.S.S. *Cole* that claimed the lives of seventeen sailors and injured thirty-one others, for which Al Qaeda was quick to claim credit. It was the most lethal attack against a U.S. Navy vessel in the previous twenty-five years.

Yemen was now number one in U.S. concerns about terrorism. So it came as no surprise when Lennon casually informed Ruhi that the failing state was bin Laden's ancestral home.

More recently, it had become the principal target for U.S. drone attacks, which the complacent government, such as it was, had tried to cover up by claiming that its own military was targeting its citizens. The ruse—promulgated in exchange for considerable U.S. military hardware—had failed miserably, and the government that offered the hapless lie was reputed to be hanging on by its fingernails.

Hardly a shock, then, when Lennon told him that Iran was also getting involved in Yemen, sending weapons, especially for the Huthis in the north, the very region they were traversing. That ragged crew took their inspiration from Hezbollah. The Saudis had fought the Huthis in the late 1990s but failed to defeat them.

"How much longer?" was Ruhi's response, feeling like a kid again in the back of his parents' minivan.

"Go back to sleep, Ruhi. Let him have the back row," Lennon ordered the Mabahith officers on either side of him.

Ruhi climbed past the men and curled into a fetal position, the only way to accommodate his long legs.

Lennon returned his gaze to the road, searching. Always searching.

● ● ●

Hamza "the lion" held his pistol to the bus driver's head as they rolled off I-295. The fuel tank was almost empty. The hijacker looked jumpy to Emma, which worried her because he was the one in charge.

His walkie-talkie had squawked an hour ago with news that diesel would be delivered to the Paulsboro Travel Center, a truck stop. Hamza had demanded that the entire lot be cleared of vehicles before they arrived. But as they pulled in, Emma spotted a tow truck racing away with an old Buick.

At a glance, the truck stop looked like a ghost town. Then, as they drew closer, she saw that the station's big plate-glass windows were shattered, and realized that the store had been looted. Even the pumps looked vandalized.

But Hamza's remote contact had assured him that the fuel would be available. Still, there were no signs of anyone. There were, however, a trailer sitting unhitched at the back of the lot and a cattle truck closer to the fuel island.

"I said I wanted everything out of here," Hamza shouted into his mouthpiece. He looked scared—and that frightened Emma, too. It was like everything was out of control and getting crazier by the moment.

He looked at the ceiling of the bus. His lips moved rapidly. His walkie-talkie came alive with a screech that made him jump. She did, too.

His contact person said the "authorities," whoever they were, had told him that they had just now located a tanker to carry the diesel he wanted.

"That's a lie," Hamza yelled. "A lie! Tell them I'll take a life for every lie, starting now. Do you hear? A life for a lie."

"Hamza." A distinctly new voice came on. "We have your fuel. We also have your friend in custody. Listen to me carefully. If we wanted to do something stupid, we could have sent a team to move that tanker and cattle truck. But we're guessing you don't want us anywhere near there. If we had cell phone service, we could send you satellite photos of the lot before the first cyberattack and after, so you could see that those two trucks have been there for almost a week. The cattle truck won't start, and we don't have a tractor to drive away with that trailer. That's why they haven't moved. So please listen carefully. We have a diesel delivery lined up. But it's coming down from Long Island. It's at least four hours away. If you've followed any news at all, you know pumps are dry everywhere. But we got fuel from a New York State armory, okay?"

"No, it is not okay. I said I wanted fuel when we stopped. I said if it wasn't here, I would start killing. Now you listen to me because I'm going to let you hear that I mean what I say."

He switched the mouthpiece to "transmit," clipped it to his shirt, and stormed down the aisle.

Emma started crying. She knew Hamza was going to murder someone. She could see it in his eyes. They were strangely blank and unblinking, yet intensely dark, like pools deeper than death.

He grabbed Pastor William Sr., using his filleting knife to slice the gag from his mouth with no regard for the man's swollen cheeks. Blood spilled onto his black suit, white shirt, and splattered his shiny blue tie. Then Hamza dragged the bound man to the front of the bus. Pastor William Sr. stumbled but stayed on his feet. Two of Hamza's cohorts kept their weapons trained on everyone, including the driver. The bomber had his hand on the bomb trigger, as if ready to blow them all up at any second.

"Open the door!" Hamza screamed.

The driver obeyed immediately.

Hamza shoved the pastor down the stairs. William Sr. fell hard. He couldn't break his fall with his hands cuffed behind his back. His face hit the pavement, bloodying his nose and lips.

Hamza pounced on him like a jackal, dragging him upright, keeping the pastor in front of him.

"Tell them what I am doing," Hamza demanded as he jammed the muzzle of his pistol into the back of Pastor William Sr.'s head.

Everybody in the bus stared out the window. Most of the kids prayed. Emma was on her feet, along with all the other choir members on the far side of the aisle. She didn't want to watch, but she did. She could hear Pastor William Sr. clearly:

"He has a gun to my head." The pastor's words were shaky, but then he spoke quickly and decisively: "Don't worry about me. Just do whatever you have to save these—"

Silenced by a gunshot.

Emma watched the pastor's body slump to the ground.

Hamza jumped up the steps of the bus, as if fearful now that he had lost his human shield. He unclipped his mouthpiece.

"Did you hear? Did you?" he shouted. "The pastor is dead. We killed your first 'hero.' We'll kill them all if you don't listen."

No answer came from the walkie-talkie.

Hamza's eyes roved over every one of the choir members. Emma knew what he was doing—picking out his next victim. And then she was sure of it when his eyes landed on hers, and he nodded.

He came closer to her. "They know I am not kidding," he said to her. "You and your friend"—he glared fiercely at Tanesa—"started this journey together, and if they don't bring the diesel soon, you will end it together, too. Sit next to her," he told Emma.

When she stood, shaking visibly, Hamza grabbed her arm and dragged her up to the next row. He jerked the girl sitting next to Tanesa from her seat and pushed her toward the one Emma had just vacated.

Emma sat with her shoulders curled forward, cowering. But when she looked over, Tanesa wasn't slumping at all. She sat erect and kept her eyes staring straight ahead, not once glancing at Hamza, who still hovered over them in the aisle.

Then he moved toward the front of the bus.

Emma felt Tanesa's hand rub against her back, and then she heard her caregiver's faint whisper: "He's not getting away with this."

Tanesa nodded, so subtly that Emma scarcely noticed. But she did, and then Emma nodded in return.

Not getting away with it. No way.

• • •

Candace's mouth had never felt so dry. Three hours without water. *What are they waiting for?*

To make me even weaker, she said to herself. *What else?*

Two of them walked out from the tent and started toward her. She stood and backed up, quickly hitting the limits of the small metal cage.

Each of their steps buried their boots in the fine soft sand. They moved only a few feet from their tent when the first rocket flew down from the sky. In a blazing flash, it incinerated them and their portable torture chamber, sending a storm of sand and debris over Candace and her cage.

A second rocket obliterated the other tent.

I'm next.

That was Candace's fully justified fear. With her eyes on the sky, she screamed above the roaring flames and a man's agonized cries.

But help did not descend from above. It rolled up in a battered old Jeep. Three men who looked more like office workers than operatives climbed out with an acetylene torch and wire cutters, freeing her in minutes.

"Who are you?"

"Can't say exactly," said the one with the torch.

"Just tell me this much: Are you Americans?"

He nodded.

Good enough for her.

CHAPTER 20

WHEN LANA AWOKE, SHE was so groggy that it took several anxious seconds for her to remember where she was: a hangar in the desert. *With them.* She blinked the blurriness from her eyes and saw the SEALs gathered around a computer screen.

One of them walked over to her. The New Yorker. What was his name? "Gabe" came to her as he asked if she'd like coffee.

"Yes, thanks."

Always affirmative on that score. She needed to wipe the sleep from her entire system.

He returned with a travel mug. Black. That would do just fine.

She stood, no more steady than a weather vane in a storm, wondering how long she'd slept. A glance at her watch told her almost three hours. More than enough to bring her around for quite a while.

Travis, the commander, threw her a quick smile, then pulled a jacket off a folding chair and told her to have a seat.

"What's that?" she asked, looking at what appeared to be satellite video of a large crowd surging against a tall cyclone fence.

Not the greatest resolution, but she made out heavily armed troops standing by on the other side.

That's America, she realized before anyone answered. She wondered how she knew so instinctively.

You recognize your own tribe, she told herself. *Sometimes as easily as you recognize your own face.*

Travis was saying something to her.

"Sorry, I missed that."

"That's O'Hare in Chicago," he repeated. "All flights are canceled, but something like twenty thousand people are down at the airport trying to get out."

Veepox, she remembered. Deadly. Agonizing. Fiercely contagious. The plague that had been carefully engineered by both the Soviets and her own government must have made it down to Chicago from Minneapolis. The Mall of America had been ground zero for the contagion. What was it about terrorists with all their symbolic targets: World Trade Center? Mall of America?

"They can't contain that," she said, thinking it might make it down to Maryland in days. To Emma. She thought better of her words: "Can they?"

"If they hold firm in Chicago, they might be able to stop it," Travis replied. "They're saying they can, and that they'll shoot anyone who breaks through that fence. They actually shot out the tires of an old prop plane that was trying to sneak away. It was rolling down the runway, seconds from liftoff. They've got to hold the line there, Lana. Hold the line," Travis said once again, as if for the benefit of the soldiers on screen.

"How bad is it in Chicago?" she asked him.

"Spreading like crazy. The only thing they can do right now to stop it, so there's a huge military presence. Army, Marines, National Guard, Coast Guard, and Navy have Lake Michigan. The Air Force has pulled more old fighters from the mothballs and has orders to shoot down anything that flies. They actually took out a hot-air balloon twenty minutes ago."

Hot-air balloons? About as low-tech as flight got. But about par for the course now.

She thought of her friends in the Windy City. Good times on Rush Street long ago. She wondered if any of them were part of the mob raging at the fence. If her Emma's life were at stake, she would have been trying to get the hell out of Dodge, too.

Travis clicked on the touch pad, shifting to another satellite view. She wondered what country's links the SEALs were poaching from. Not the U.S's, that was for sure.

The new video was sharper. It showed a truck stop. Empty lot except for a couple of semis and a bus she recognized at once. She'd seen the choir bus only on the day of the first cyberattack, but its rounded shape and blue paint were unmistakable.

"What's happening to them? Why are you showing me this?"

Travis took her arm. "Holmes says you should know."

"Know what?" she exploded. "Emma?"

When he didn't answer immediately, she knew the answer. "What's she doing there?"

"She joined the choir. She's okay, Lana."

"Don't tell me that. There's a satellite staring at it for a reason. What is it?"

He explained what had happened. Highlights only.

Oh, God. "Why the hell didn't someone tell me right away?"

"When, Lana? During the siege at the embassy? Your rescue? Flying out of Riyadh with you hanging out of the chopper? We wanted to make sure you got some sleep. We need you thinking clearly. Now you know everything we know."

Not everything. He hadn't told her what kind of bomb was on the bus. She took a breath, and then asked.

"We're not sure," Travis replied.

"What are *they* saying it is?" Those pigs always told you.

"They claim it's a nuclear bomb. Backpack bomb. We're trying to confirm that. They're trying to get it to Times Square." Travis shook his head. "It's not going to happen. They're never getting out of that truck stop."

Never getting out alive. That's what you mean.

"So they'll set it off there." Lana rose, kicking the chair aside. "Jesus Christ. I should be there."

Travis jumped up, held her arms, stared right in her eyes. "No, you should be here. I'm going to tell you what Holmes told me. The only way we're going to shut these fuckers down is by penetrating their codes, by hacking them to death. Do you hear me, Lana? Hack. Them. To. Death."

"It won't stop some suicide bomber with a nuke."

"No, it won't, but what you don't know is that they have taken control of the country's nuclear arsenal. All land-based missiles are now aimed at more than a hundred American cities."

Lana backed up, almost fell.

"That's what's at stake. And we're pretty damn sure we're moving you right into the heart of it."

"How do you know that?"

"We have Mancur waiting. He's the bait. There's strong Saudi intelligence."

"The Saudis!" Lana felt like tearing out her own hair when she realized whom they were depending on.

"Yes. Don't dismiss it. You'll be working with Mancur. You think it's a coincidence that he was picked up and ended up here? Don't you know Holmes better than that? Once you're in Sana, it's you and Mancur. He gets in there, you'll be twenty-four-seven on your link to him."

"If they grab Ruhi, they're going to drag him off and squeeze every last drop of intelligence out of him. How am I supposed to take care of him with a computer link?"

"Because every last drop of intelligence is in the computer code you designed for him. You'll take control of his computer. Plus, you'll have your eavesdropping program. You'll listen. You'll have an Arabic interpreter, if you need him. Look, Ruhi will be with them, if this plays out. Let them penetrate your firewalls. Let them think they're smarter. Then spend every second you can looking to penetrate theirs."

"And if I have to just shut them down, if I can't finesse it, then Ruhi's dead."

"That's right, he's dead, and the country survives."

She nodded somberly, knowing she'd do it to Ruhi. She'd do it to herself. "Look, even getting Ruhi in there is a long shot."

Travis shook his head, his neck so thick it looked like it could handle the weight of five men. "Mabahith let it leak that Mancur's firewalls can't be broken. Whoever's working this madness will want him. Hell, *I'd* want him. They'll want any bit of protection so they can cover every contingency as their countdown finishes. They're looking at the total annihilation of America. They're not going to take any chances, and that, Lana, gives us our only chance."

"But those kids are finished," she said, gazing at the screen. "There's nothing I can do to stop them. Why do they even want to blow up New York if they've got nukes fastened on every single city?"

"All they've done since the start is crank up the hysteria. They want to blow up New York so the rest of the country gets a real clear picture of what they're in for. They want complete madness in America before they destroy it. Lana, take them down over here and there's no telling how the crazies on that bus will react. Right now they're set on having their own Armageddon. They think they have the most powerful force in the universe on their side—God. Show them something different, and maybe they'll back down. But even if they don't, there are tens of millions of Emmas whose lives are riding on everything we're doing."

Travis let go of her arms. She felt boneless, like she could melt into the floor. He led her back to the chair she'd kicked aside, sat her down.

"How sure are you that we're moving in on them?" she asked. At that moment, she wanted nothing more than to smash the invisible enemy into the farthest reaches of the universe.

"We're close enough to smell them. In twenty minutes we'll be cleared to fly to Yemen. We need you there. All of you, Lana. Your heart, soul, and that incredible intelligence of yours. You want to stop *them*?" He jabbed his finger at the screen. "Then you have to stop the bastards down in Yemen."

She stared at the bus. The pictures showed only hints of color, but enough to make a small red spot glow. That's when she noticed that it was blood on a body. "Who's that?" She hoped like hell it was one of them.

"The choirmaster. Pastor William Sr. is what all the kids called him. One of the best in the country."

"I've heard of him. You know those kids saved my life."

"I do know that."

"So they killed Pastor William?" She shook her head, thinking sorrow never stops.

"Horribly. To make a point."

About violence, death, the unbending willingness to kill. She understood all that because she felt it too. Wanted it right now as much as she'd ever wanted life itself.

"What do they know about Emma?" she asked.

"They know," Travis said. "So they'll keep her alive. They say you're a spy, so she's the best chit they have."

"Don't ever call my kid a chit again."

"Sorry. All I'm saying is Emma won't be the first one to die. That's just a cold fact."

• • •

Deputy Director Holmes had a series of monitors in his office, all solar powered. One showed Times Square, its big electronic billboards dark for days. No flashy ads for music, software, Broadway shows, or blockbuster movies. Nothing but black screens at the heart of the nation's entertainment center.

Holmes turned to McGivern and several lesser aides as the Sony screen blazed to life with a crescent moon and star that made New York's inveterate wanderers look up and take heed. Holmes, too. On the screen and on the street. Those suddenly glimmering lights looked clean and bright and maybe even beautiful—until a voice, deep, resonant, and male, spilled out of unseen speakers used only for emergencies.

"Not again," Holmes groaned, sitting forward.

"Worshippers of the fallen God, of infidel passions and satanic verses, listen to what we have to say."

Times Square was not crowded but the booming words drew people running down Broadway to stand in swelling groups, staring upward at the symbol, as if it alone had become animate, the voice they heard so well.

"We are bringing a great gift to your city, to the seat of all sin, to the heart of your foul exports. A gift that will burn you alive. We will make 9/11 look like a child's game. Nothing that lives will be spared. Not your babies, your children, or your sick."

News crews raced into the street, working with reserve batteries to shoot the stunned reactions of the growing crowds. *Where did all those people come from?* Holmes wondered. And they were still coming. It was as if they had been cued for the next stage of the national tragedy, and yet he knew better. He knew that they were desperate for news—good news—and had been waiting days for the lives they had once known to come back to them. Most assuredly, they had not been waiting for this:

"You can try to run now, but your cars have no gas, your buses and trains no fuel. You will never run far enough to escape the flames that will chase you down. And after you burn to ash, you will know the eternal fires of hell. But you will show the rest of the country what awaits them—Judgment Day on earth."

Those words suddenly lit up the giant billboard. Holmes saw people taking pictures. *For what?* he wondered. *Why in God's name are they doing that?*

"When we are done, every American will be dead; your country will be as much a wasteland as your unforgiven souls."

People yelled defiant curses at the crescent moon and star once more blazing on the billboard. Then the screen went black, as if heeding their fate, but the voice carried on:

"We have warned you repeatedly. We warn you no more."

A mushroom cloud burst into brilliant blooming reds and oranges on the giant screen, casting shades of the promised flames on the street and buildings.

"This is good," Holmes said.

McGivern agreed.

There was no need to spell it out. They all understood: The bus hijackers were still determined—or under orders—to get their bomb to Times Square. The ominous display, the wretched words, meant that rescue teams still had a few hours left to try to stop those children and millions of others from dying.

But the message also meant that the terrorists' claim of a nuclear bomb on the bus was unlikely to be a bluff.

• • •

Ruhi woke up from his nap in the back row of the SUV and saw Sana in the morning's earliest hours. It loomed before him as they drove across the desert, a pauper's city with so few lights in the bleak darkness that it might have been abandoned by all who could flee. And perhaps they had, but more than two million people remained, living amid frequent and often long-lasting power outages.

The country was on its knees, running out of oil and water, the two substances that made life in a desert land bearable. Yemen was the mendicant of the Middle East. Little wonder that Al Qaeda drew young men so easily from the ranks of the nation's disaffected. Yemen had become the chief focus of American anti-terrorism efforts, which only served to enflame so many Yemeni: Three different bomb plots against the U.S. had been hatched there, including the infamous—and painfully ineffective— "underwear" bomber. It was as if in the midst of so little, at least some had achieved a desired notoriety by becoming the bête noire of the world's mightiest nation.

Ruhi would have wagered that out there more plots were unfolding, for how could they not in a country that could manufacture so little else? It was certainly the consensus of two intelligence agencies that the biggest plot in world history had come to life in those desert sands and mountain redoubts. And who was he to question the men who had so ruthlessly taken over his life?

In little more than a week he had gone from director of research for the Natural Resources Defense Council to bait for the CIA, thanks to his supposed computer skills, which had withstood the test of the Mabahith.

"How do you even know that they've heard of my so-called skills?" he asked Lennon, seated once more in the front-row passenger seat.

And what was he supposed to do when they abducted him and demanded that he display the power of his knowledge? Die, that's what. Or worse, *not* die, he thought immediately. *Become, instead, the object of their undying hate.*

"We are riddled with Al Qaeda supporters," Lennon answered him. "We are sure they know you are on a mission for your country, and what other mission would it be at this point? What other mission matters?"

"So your secret organization is banking on your inability to actually keep secrets?" The irony astounded Ruhi.

"Yes, in a word," Lennon said.

They entered the center of the squalid city, driving through a labyrinth of streets where he imagined men hiding in the darkness, staring at the big SUV with eyes dark as demitasse. They certainly could not roll down these streets unnoticed, even at this hour. Neighborhood Watch had nothing on the surveillance skills of people desperate for life's necessities—and able to earn them only by diligent observation.

"We're here," Lennon announced as the SUV rolled to a stop.

The officers in the middle seat, who had flanked Ruhi for the first part of the journey, climbed out.

Ruhi sensed their reluctance, saw their wary eyes scanning darkness so thick that it might have hidden the sun.

"Now you, let's go," Lennon said to him.

Ruhi crawled over the seat and stepped out into the cool air, the desert having exhaled the last of its vast heat.

He saw that the officers, including Lennon, had their guns out but held to their sides discreetly, black barrels against black slacks, no more visible than white shells on blinding beaches. But no one would surprise and take them as easily as Candace had been claimed.

Lennon drew Ruhi into an old building with a dimly lit outer arcade with arabesques carved into the columns he passed. They walked past an elevator that looked eerily like a cage. Five flights of stairs later, Ruhi wondered what had become of his fitness. Had he succumbed to terminal fatigue? He barely kept up with Lennon.

Down a narrow hallway he toiled, catching his breath as he passed under a single bulb, yellow as the mountains they had passed, the ones that had looked so completely lifeless.

Lennon knocked twice on a door. Raising his gun, he turned a brass handle and stepped into a candlelit room. Three men sat on a sofa. One was hooded, but Ruhi would have known his cousin Ahmed anywhere.

• • •

The stealth helicopter flew without lights. This time Lana was belted in, not held by Gabe or serenaded by a Springsteen song.

The SEALs were quiet. No joking around. No hard-ass humor. Mission bound. For Lana, that would soon mean sitting in a room linked to a satellite and working on her computer. And if she were extremely lucky—or the shattered intelligence services of the U.S. extraordinarily adept at adjusting to the most extenuating circumstances—she would be in touch with Ruhi Mancur, aka the "bait." His future looked no brighter than her daughter's, whose likely fate she could not put aside for more than seconds.

After the blow of learning about Emma, Lana had received her computer from Travis. Shockingly, she had lost track of it during the frantic escape from Riyadh. Even more startling, she'd fallen asleep in the hangar without realizing her loss. But a separate team of SEALs had been assigned to the computer's rescue. Those three men had traced an electronic locator deep inside the device's densely constructed core to find the laptop in the hands of a young woman in a head scarf.

"Give it to me," said a bearded man who resembled the hundreds of other Saudi males taking control of the corridors and offices that been in American hands only minutes before.

Tearfully, the young woman had handed it over.

Lana knew nothing of this, just that her computer was back in her possession, while her only child's life depended on other men like the SEALs almost seven thousand miles away.

● ● ●

Not only men.

Kalisa Harris drove the tanker truck off I-295. She wore faded Carhartt jeans, Red Wing boots as scuffed as a bootblack's hands, and a plaid flannel shirt that had been purchased originally at an Eddie Bauer's in Chicago, then picked up in a Goodwill by the FBI in Atlantic City three months ago. She'd chopped off the sleeves, exposing arms that were toned and tattooed.

A Geiger counter had been installed under her seat. The FBI special agent in charge, the SAC, had instructed her to leave her door open and pull as close to the bus as possible.

"And if they hear the damn thing?" she'd asked, already in character with a female trucker's seductive CB drawl.

"Appeal to their manhood," said the SAC in his $2,000 Armani suit. "If they've got a nuclear bomb, they should be happy to have it confirmed. Tell them that now we know they're not bluffing."

"That's assuming I get a word in edgewise before they shoot me. How many am I going to be dealing with?" Kalisa had asked, wanting to cut to the chase.

"Four. They're all in head scarfs playing the macho jihadist, from what we've seen and heard. The leader's been on the radio speaking perfect English, so we're almost certain he grew up here. Then there's the guy with the backpack bomb. He's on the rear seat. Two other gunmen are on board too."

What did Kalisa Harris have? Her .45 and the go-ahead to use it—if she saw an opening. She'd been field-tested plenty and found to be superb in critical situations. She'd already played out a deadly gamble in a hostage rescue in Cleveland two years ago. Four dead. Not the kids.

"You're gold-plated," the director himself once told her.

She preferred Kevlar, for all the good it would do if those boys on the bus decided to end the world as they knew it. Her weapon of choice was strapped to her calf under the billowy Carhartts, chosen for that very reason. She was a crack shot. Turned down a spot on the Olympic team to serve her country in the aftermath of 9/11. No regrets.

But Kalisa Harris was sweating. It was "a hot New Jersey night." She knew that line from some song somewhere. Plenty humid, too, which wasn't part of any verse that she'd ever heard. The drive had taken much longer than she'd expected, even with a tow truck clearing away abandoned cars that would have stopped her rig. The added pressure of running late bore down on her like a pile driver.

She used the signal code for a guy named Hamza.

"I'm the driver. I'm about to pull in. This Hamza?" *The lion.* Which made her think that he'd watched one too many Disney movies growing up.

"This is he."

"Please tell me if you want me to put the diesel in the underground tank or deliver it directly to the bus."

If he wanted it pumped from an underground tank, because he feared having the tanker truck close enough for a direct fill, then the Geiger counter in the truck wouldn't work.

"Pump directly from your truck. It will be quicker," Hamza replied.

Relieved, she said, "Okay, will do. Can you see me?"

"Are you a woman?"

"That would be a big ten-four. Last time I checked, anyway."

When he didn't respond, she clicked again. "Yes, I'm a woman."

She would have bet that gave him a moment of relief.

"How long is the hose?" he asked.

"I've got fifteen feet of it."

"Use all of it. Get no closer. Whom do you work for?"

Whom? This is he? Son of a bitch speaks without an accent and uses perfect English. Not just brought up here, but probably went to a pricey private school. *And this is his payback?* His manner would have incensed her, if she'd let it. But of course she nipped that dark bud before it could bloom.

She rolled to a stop, answering him, "Richfield Oil. Garden City, Long Island."

"I don't believe you. Stay as far away as you can, or I will shoot two girls. The one who could be your sister, and the white one who's the daughter of the spy."

Kill either one and I'm going to want to drop a load of hate on your sorry head.

Kalisa left the engine running and opened the door, pausing when she saw that her headlights were shining on the faces of frightened children on the bus. She had no difficulty reading the rich full lips of a young girl pleading, "Help. Please help."

I'm here for you, little sister. I'm here.

A second later the first *click-click* from the Geiger counter sounded, loud as a cathedral bell in the silence of that station.

CHAPTER 21

LANA AND THE SEALS sighted little more than glimmers of light as they neared Sana in the Black Hawk, hinting that the capital might be suffering one of its chronic power outages. No more equipped for final hours of night than a medieval city.

The chopper was the quietest bird Lana had ever flown in. Specially designed blades reduced the *whup-whup-whup* to a mere whisper. They were to sound what the dark, radar-absorbent material that coated the copter was to electronic detection.

Not that Yemen had a military of note, much less an air force or sophisticated antiaircraft weaponry, though the lack of arms or service personnel trained to use them was not for want of U.S. funding. The last time Lana had checked, the Department of Defense had channeled hundreds of millions of dollars into the dying desert kingdom—for all the good it had done.

Look at us, she said to herself. Trying to chase down the worst attack on the U.S. ever—*here*. So counterintuitive that she felt certain it would flummox historians for generations to come. *Of all places.* It was almost as if the Pentagon's millions for Yemen had actually produced the enemy, rather than softened or eliminated it.

"We're not going into the city," Travis reminded her over the headset. He had made no effort to hide his relief at avoiding what he called the "Sana cesspool."

She nodded, but also gazed out the windows as the high-tech helicopter carved a wide arc of airspace and headed west of Sana's sprawl. She saw the day's first light on the ocher-colored mountains and terraced farms, doubting the latter would survive much longer with Sana sucking up the last drops of groundwater.

The Black Hawk eased toward a landing zone far from any dwellings. The pilot set the bird down so softly he might have been laying a newborn in a bassinet. Maternal memories for a mother who could do nothing to save her child.

No, not nothing, she forced herself to remember. *Just nothing that you can do directly.*

When the dust cleared, she saw another hangar and assumed that she was at a second black site, undoubtedly where some of those millions had ended up. But they had no plans for a stopover, no time for a nap or a satellite hookup to view video of the bus on which her daughter was held captive.

Travis led a quick exit from the chopper into a desert camo–painted Humvee. They were joined by almost half the team, including Gabe from New York. The rest rode in the hulking vehicle's twin.

The drivers raced side by side, low beams blazing across the flatlands, never taking a road.

"We're heading for an underground bunker," Travis informed her. "Without GPS, you could drive right over it and never know it was there. But it has electronics. Crude stuff compared to what you're used to, but by Yemeni standards, they're absolutely deluxe."

"What about Mancur? Where is he?"

"He's in the city at another location. You'll be linked up in minutes."

• • •

Ruhi turned on his computer, satisfied when it fired up properly. That gave him great hope in the dim confines of the small room he shared with Lennon, the other four Mabahith officers, and his cousin Ahmed.

Ruhi nodded approvingly as documents appeared on the desktop and opened readily. He looked up as a candle fluttered on the lone windowsill, marveling over the strange juxtaposition: perhaps the world's most sophisticated laptop, powered by the building's generator, but a lone candle because the light fixture didn't work and sunrise was only beginning to brighten the horizon.

But now he found himself waiting . . . and waiting . . . and waiting to link to the network established for Lana and him. He clicked on it again . . . and again . . . and again, to no avail.

He scratched his head. A familiar impatience overcame him, as it often did whenever a computer failed at what it was supposed to do.

"What's wrong?" Lennon asked.

"It's not connecting." Ruhi had to unclench his jaw to respond.

"She might not be in Yemen yet."

"This should work if she's anywhere outside the U.S." He didn't need to say why: the decimated grid. "I should be able to reach her, even if she were at Amundsen-Scott."

"Amundsen what?" Lennon asked.

"The U.S. camp in Antarctica. Look, it doesn't matter. It's not working *here*. Did your people sabotage this?" Then he looked at Ahmed, sitting on the couch across from him, pious in his head scarf. *Or you?*

Lennon, so confident on his own soil, turned away for the first time. Ruhi wondered if his most recent torturer just realized that

294

Al Qaeda's penetration of his agency might have gone deeper than he'd thought. It was one thing to leak information that a U.S. spy in your custody had a computer so powerful that both the man and his weapon might be worth scooping up—if you were launching cyberattacks to murder America. But it was quite another matter if Al Qaeda operatives or sympathizers in your agency had sabotaged the network program most critical to the mission's success.

"They wouldn't have to be super techs to just screw it up," Ruhi said. "Did you get anywhere near this?" he asked Ahmed.

"Ruhi, how can you accuse me of such a crime?" Ahmed spoke soothingly, in such a practiced voice that Ruhi knew his cousin had used it many times before to try to deflect suspicion. "I would—"

"How can I accuse *you*?" Ruhi fired back. "I'm *here* because of you."

Ahmed shook his head, looking offended. "No, Ruhi, we were both moved like chess pieces. I assure you, this is the first time I have ever seen your computer."

Lennon nodded. But of course he would agree if the two were in cahoots.

What a hall of mirrors.

What could he possibly make of his cousin's double-agent claims? Though they might explain why Ahmed escaped from his family's home on the night Lennon nabbed Ruhi—and then turned *him* into a double agent.

But if Ahmed really was working both sides of the battle, he was playing a much more treacherous game than Ruhi, if that were even possible. That's because Ahmed was answering to Al Qaeda and the Mabahith, two bitterly opposed forces—notwithstanding the latter's traitors—while Ruhi was providing information to U.S. intelligence and the Saudis, who shared a common interest in stopping the cyberattacks.

"Your master technicians," Ruhi said to Lennon in a lacerating voice, "probably fucked it up when they were trying to get past the firewalls. So if I'm grabbed now, do you know what that means? This thing"—he almost pounded the laptop—"won't perform, but they won't believe me, so they'll torture me to try to get me to do the impossible. And then there'll be no way to stop the destruction of my country."

•　•　•

Lana walked down narrow concrete-block stairs lit by bluish light, entering an extensive bunker nestled below the drifting sands of the Arabian Desert. It was carved out of the denser earth below. She found the walls, tinted gold and orange, almost beautiful, but crumbly to the touch.

Before she could take more than a breath, the CIA station chief, a squat man so pale that he might never have emerged from the underground labyrinth that he called home for weeks at a time, handed her a document. He did the same for all the SEALs.

"Just sign them. 'Sheep-dipping' time."

Turning each of them into CIA functionaries. That would be to abide, on paper at least, with both U.S. and foreign covenants. Thus, with the stroke of a pen the SEALs and Lana became employees of the agency.

Lana signed under shadowy light, hearing the low hum of generators.

My God, she thought as she settled at a desk with her computer, *there's even an espresso maker.* But as she turned on her laptop, she realized that what the bunker did not provide, most assuredly, was any connection to Ruhi Mancur's device, a veritable clone of her own computer. She scrambled for another minute to try to find a link, looking up at the chief in exasperation.

"I can link to ISPs in five European countries. What I can't do is link to Mancur. Do we even know whether he's in Sana?"

The chief, laying the signed documents on a cabinet, affirmed that Mancur was in the city.

"How far away is he?" Lana had little sense of distance down there. From the bird, Sana had appeared large, mushrooming into the surrounding sands with what looked like a dense maze of arteries radiating from the city's heart.

"Forty-five, fifty minutes at this time of day."

"Either you move him here or you move me there, but we have to get his computer in my hands so I can work on it." All along the plan had been for her to take control of his laptop, even if she were hundreds of miles from him. But her inability to link to it made that impossible, so now she'd have to get her hands on it to enable her to have remote access later.

The station chief wiped his lower face so forcefully that he peeled his lower lip open. Then, in an even more unflattering move, he tugged on his ample wattle, repeating the tug twice more. "There are huge risks in taking you into Sana." He worked his wattle again, adding, "But it's an even bigger roll of the dice to extract him. We don't want to do that until he's taken."

Bizarre, she thought: The plan to bait the attackers might be too successful too soon.

"You've got them," the chief said to her, glancing at the SEALs. "So you get moving."

She and the SEALs dashed back up the stairs into the dawn.

"We're not going into the city," Travis had reminded her with evident relief on the chopper.

Yes, we are, Lana said to herself now. *Right into the Sana cesspool.*

• • •

Emma could see most of the kids in the bus, plus the hijackers, now that the tanker truck's headlights were pouring through the windows. She'd seen Hamza's animated face and heard his back-and-forth with the female driver. Why would they send a woman? All Emma could figure was that whoever was trying to save them didn't want the terrorists to freak out by having some macho guy show up. But for that very reason, she wished a dude like Daniel Craig's 007 had come to the rescue. Her mom's big crush, though she'd never admit it. But Emma had caught her watching that movie for the *third* time the day before the first cyberattack.

She wondered what her mom was doing right now. Probably scared to death, if she knew her daughter was on this bus. But her mother had always been trying to get her to join some kind of activity.

So I did, she thought. *Great timing, huh, Mom? Sorry.*

Emma meant it, too, stripped down now to longing and love and a deep desire to throw her arms around her mother again.

Whatever her mom was doing had to be better than this, right? Sitting on a bus with a suicide bomber holding a frickin' nuke.

Emma looked back at the guy with the backpack and trigger in his hand. He'd fallen asleep. *Thank God.* His head hung forward, chin to chest, and his hands—

Jesus H. Christ. His finger was resting on the trigger.

"Hamza," she said as respectfully as possible.

He'd moved down the bus steps and poked his head out an inch or two, staring intently as the truck driver set up to fill the tank.

"Hamza, sir?" she called out louder.

His eyes turned to her, *feasted* on her. A wide, dark, murderous gaze. He hauled himself up into the bus proper and headed toward her, pulling out the filleting knife.

"Trying to distract me? What kind of plan do you have, spy's daughter?" He raised the knife. He'd already cut her neck.

"No plan," she pleaded. "Look!" She pointed to the bomber.

Hamza yelped. Emma heard the panic catch in his throat. He rushed past her.

• • •

Kalisa Harris saw Hamza, the Lion King, or whatever the hell he called himself, running toward the back of the bus. She'd been waiting for some kind of ruckus, and his pounding feet would do. She clamped a magnetic bomb with a locator to the chassis. Once she'd heard that Geiger counter click, she knew she would have to set the plastique as soon as possible, because the bus couldn't go anywhere with a nuclear bomb aboard. Computers had firewalls, but so did an operation like this, except the backup security that she'd just put in place was as basic as mud pudding—by the standards of contemporary computer wizardry. Old-style war versus cyberterror.

She grabbed the fuel hose to try to make up for lost seconds, but the commotion inside froze her in place. She placed her hand on the bus. The pounding had stopped, but there were still vibrations. Some kind of tussle in the back, where the bomber was. She saw her life, those kids, and most of central New Jersey vaporized.

Get a grip, she warned herself. *If it goes, it goes.*

• • •

Travis did not like the latest turn of events. Lana could tell, even before he spoke up.

"We did not plan on taking you in there. That place has more random elements than the Hadron Collider."

He sounded disgusted and looked away as their driver veered sharply right, angling across the desert toward Sana, blanketed by haze.

The Humvees were leaving the safety and relative anonymity of the sands behind. She stared ahead, their destination somewhere in that vast urban maze. With so few towers and smokestacks, it looked wide and flat, like a magic carpet of myth, but deeply soiled by all the ill effects of modernity.

"So what are you saying?" she asked Travis. *That we're about to get caught in a crossfire from hell?*

"He's saying it's going to get *interesting*," Gabe said in the voice of some silly Russian antagonist.

She wasn't up for humor in any guise. Neither was Travis, apparently:

"Not now," he said brusquely. After the briefest pause, he went on: "It's not so much a physical security issue. We'll get you there. It's just that we're going to be noticed. There's no slipping in and out on such short notice."

"Just get me close, and I can walk in on my own."

"And not be noticed? You? No," Travis said. "You may have been sheep-dipped, but you're no spy. Not for the streets, anyway." He poked her shoulder. She winced. "We're going to stay as close to you as blood to bone."

A dune suddenly reared up before them. She hadn't noticed it. At the last moment, their driver swerved left.

"What's he doing? Playing chicken with the desert?" she asked.

"Diversionary driving," Gabe advised. "Staying unpredictable, wherever he can. Like this assignment of ours. It's improv all the way."

"I'll bet they've got drones watching every step," she replied. Yemen was now the epicenter for Predator activity, although Africa was catching up fast.

"No doubt," Travis said. "But they can't use them on Sana. The collateral would have the rest of the world swearing bloody murder."

For good reason. But she kept that comment to herself, considering the company and the exigencies of the moment.

Lana saw the poor making their trek to the city from shantytowns and tents or, for the most miserable, berths on bare sand.

Most looked too weary to even note the Humvees. Lana understood that kind of profound tiredness. She'd felt plenty of it herself of late. But now she was as alert as she'd ever been, endowed with what felt like preternatural awareness seeded into every pore of her skin.

Even with the absence of traffic, it took the full fifty minutes to make their destination. In the sharply angled morning light, the building they pulled up to looked beautiful, with its ornate arcade and inlaid Arabic designs. But the pleasure of that glimpse passed quickly.

Travis readied his gun. So did the others.

"Gabe's going to be by your side at all times," the commander said. "You stick with him. This is all catch-as-catch-can. We have to take them by surprise."

"The Mabahith?"

"We hope it's only them," Travis answered. "Our people have tracked them, but it's not like we could tell them we were stopping by. They're not exactly trustworthy, and every agency has its own proprietary interests. Theirs is to run Ruhi, even if they think we don't know that. But they're about to find out."

They rushed through the arcade, past wooden doors, and started up the stairs, SEALs in front of her, SEALs in back of her, SEALs, including Gabe, to her sides.

They stayed in formation till they reached the top floor, the fifth by her count.

Travis led two of his men to the end of the hallway. A single bulb burned in the ceiling. The building was far more attractive from outside. Crouched as she was in the hallway, it felt claustrophobic with secrets and threats.

Bam.

Travis kicked open a door. The sound of shocked breaths was so sharp it raised the hair on Lana's neck fifty feet away.

Gabe escorted her to the doorway. Holding her back with one hand, he peered into the room. Gently, he tugged her forward.

It was crowded with men; she guessed some hailed from the Mabahith. Only the SEALs, though, had their guns drawn. They'd gotten the jump on everyone.

They kept their aim as a tall thin man, hands raised to show he was unarmed, slowly stood.

"I'm Ruhi," he said, looking into Lana's eyes. "Ruhi Mancur."

● ● ●

Hamza jerked the trigger from the bomber's hand. Close, so close. *Thank you, Allah.*

"Ibrahim, this is not New York," he told the bomber in the next breath. The fool didn't hear him. He was *still* sleeping. "Not New York, Ibrahim. You idiot. Not New York," Hamza kept repeating.

"What? What?" Ibrahim mumbled in Arabic.

"You had the trigger on your lap. It could have gone off accidentally."

To think an infidel spy's daughter had saved the whole mission, made it possible to go on to New York City and blow up that den of iniquity. That was the final proof—if any were even needed—that this was a plan born in the Prophet Mohammed's own sweet bosom. *Peace and blessings be upon Him. Thank you, oh blessed one, for making this miracle possible for such a worthy martyr as I.*

"But I must be ready at all times," Ibrahim said, holding the trigger back up in front of him.

"Stay awake," Hamza ordered.

Ibrahim nodded.

"Sleep again and *I* will kill you."

"Coffee," Ibrahim said. "I have been awake for two nights now."

"No, you have not been awake. That is the problem. That is why I am here. That is why Allah has granted us the miracle of the infidel spy's daughter."

That last befuddled Ibrahim the bomber, but his next words hinted that he wanted more than just threats and reminders from Hamza. "How are you staying awake?"

"By the power of my great belief."

Ibrahim shook his head. "By Red Bull. I know you. Give me Red Bull. I am the supreme martyr here. Red Bull."

Hamza still had the knife in his hand. All along, he'd been planning to use it on the white girl, but now he had to fight an urge to stab Ibrahim in the heart. *Saying he's the supreme martyr of them all. What heresy. Who made the plans? Who handed him the bomb? Is the grantor of such an honor the honoree supreme, or the one who sits there dumb as a stump and takes it? Any fool knows the answer.*

"I'll be back," Hamza said so angrily he could have spit.

He brushed by the miracle of the infidel spy's daughter, who had been watching the whole time, probably planning to beg him for mercy now, but mercy for infidels was definitely not in Mohammed's sweet bosom.

Hamza grabbed a Red Bull from his pack and walked back to Ibrahim.

"Here, drink Red Bull. Fall asleep, and you will never wake up to kill yourself and so many others. And keep your finger off the trigger until I say so."

Ibrahim glared at him.

• • •

Emma turned away before Hamza started back to the front of the bus again. His hand was on the hilt of his knife.

Turning away didn't save Emma from his attention. He stopped by her side and placed the tip of the blade under her chin, just like last time. He raised it up until she was staring at the ceiling, headlights streaking on the gray surface. Then he nicked her skin.

"Thank you," he said to her. "You saved our mission. Allah has worked his will through Godless filth. As smart as I am, sometimes I do not understand His wisdom. How does it feel to be the savior of such divine intentions?"

She tried to speak, but moving her mouth made her feel the blade, which hurt horribly. Blood was already running down her neck again, warm as sweat.

"Speak."

"Good. Good." It was all she could think to say.

Tanesa was staring at Hamza's back. Emma could just glimpse her caretaker out of the corner of her eye. But the other two "martyrs" were watching as well. Droopy-eyed, though. They looked like they could use some Red Bull.

Hamza backed away from Emma. "I'm saving you," he said. "I'm saving you so I can offer you up to Allah at the right time. You will pay for the sins of your mother even as she is butchered alive."

Emma had her hand on her chin. Her fingers were wet and sticky. She hated him so much it made her feel crazy. She'd never known hate like this. She could hardly sit still for it.

Tanesa also looked ready to leap.

A noise sounded outside by the fuel tank.

Hamza rushed to the door. "Fill it up!" he yelled. "You're taking too long."

The woman truck driver said something to him. Emma didn't catch it, but she heard Hamza's reply:

"Do it faster, or I will throw another body out there."

• • •

The plan had been for Kalisa Harris to delay as much as might seem reasonable with the fuel delivery, but morning was still a few hours off. So now she would keep her headlights on the bus as long as she could to help the snipers with their night scopes. And she'd milk another minute or two topping off the tank with a blend containing just enough diesel to make it smell real. The rest was water—the bus would never move.

That was Washington's decision: to make absolutely sure the bus never left the truck stop. First the bomb, and now the "fuel." Kalisa had no quarrel with the call, but it made every moment that she could stall all the more precious, because who could say what Hamza and the others would do when the driver couldn't get the bus started again?

She reached down to scratch her leg, a motion to cover the reassuring touch of her .45 semiautomatic.

Kalisa said a prayer. Not one prescribed by any church that she'd ever heard of, but the only one she could offer at that moment. She'd said it once before—in Cleveland.

Sweet Jesus, let me kill the bastards and save those kids. After that, You can do what You want with me.

With her heart and soul on the line, she didn't stop to wonder how many times an agent could put herself in this kind of jeopardy and survive.

• • •

Seconds after Ruhi introduced himself, an explosion rocked the hallway. Six SEALs went down in a blinding instant. One of them lay bleeding from the neck, legs jerking. An assailant shot him in the head as she watched.

The detonation blew Lana into Ruhi, tumbling them both onto the couch. Lana, stunned, wasn't sure she was alive until she heard shouting in Arabic. Gunfire filled the fifth floor.

Travis was at the doorway, shooting back with two of his men. *Thank God.*

Then Travis and the man to his right were hit by a fusillade.

It sounded like an army out there. A thousand rounds a second. Lana looked around frantically for a way out. Only the window—shattered by gunfire—looked like a possibility.

The top floor.

She crawled to it anyway and peered out, expecting to be shot in the back any second. She saw a rusty six-inch pipe running up the length of the building.

When she turned to signal Ruhi, only Gabe was still standing; none of the other SEALs or Mabahith officers had survived. One of the latter had died with his handgun by his side. She grabbed it.

"Go!" Gabe yelled.

"Mancur, move!" she said.

Lana poured herself out the opening, grabbed the pipe, and pressed herself against the brick, fully expecting the bolts, also rusty, to rip loose. She heard a loud *creak*, but the pipe didn't pull away.

She had thought she would climb down, but saw she was only about six feet from the flat roof and would likely be killed or taken prisoner if she dared a descent.

Jamming her knees into the brick, she clawed inches upward, making enough room for Ruhi.

He pressed up below her. "Use my head," he gasped.

She did, pressing her foot down. Seized by strength and fear, she climbed toward the edge of the roof.

More gunfire, a harsh spate of it, and then heavy steps sounded in the room. Shouts. None in English. Gabe, she knew, was dead.

She reached up and grabbed the chiseled edge. Again, she stepped on Ruhi's head, gaining inches more precious than air. She was up and over.

Immediately, she reached for him, grabbing his underarms to get him up.

As he rolled over the edge, she pulled the gun from her pants—a Browning Hi Power—and racked the slide. The Mabahith officer had never gotten off a shot.

Without a word, they crept away. Then, when she judged they were no longer above the room, she started running. So did Ruhi.

For their lives.

CHAPTER 22

LANA AND RUHI RACED to the edge of the flat roof, which was bordered by a two-foot wall. Beyond it loomed a six-foot gap to the roof of the next building—and a five-story drop to the alley below.

"Can you make that?" she asked Ruhi, aiming her Browning back at the spot where they'd climbed up on the roof—exactly where she expected those killers to show up any second.

"I think so. What about you?" Like her, he sounded breathless.

She just nodded. It felt like all she could do, so shaken by witnessing the death squad slaughter of the men who had rescued her in Riyadh and protected her ever since.

They knew we were there. How? Who set us up?

No time for questions without immediate answers. "Go!" she urged Ruhi.

She sighted down the black barrel of her pistol at that spot on the roof, saw the gun shaking, and told herself to get a grip—in every sense.

• • •

Ruhi stood on the short wall. The tile felt firm beneath his feet, the distance doable. All this registered in an instant.

A standing long jump, he told himself. Six feet. *You can do it.* "Use your arms," he remembered a gym teacher telling him. Sixth Grade Olympics. An intracity event. In the 1,500-meter run, Ruhi had won a silver.

No medal for the long jump.

He crouched and sprang out over the gap, thrusting his arms forward, driving himself as hard as he could.

He felt the bite of gravity in less than a second.

• • •

Out of the corner of her eye, Lana saw Ruhi's legs go airborne, but most of her attention was back on where they'd hauled themselves up onto the roof. She was trying so hard to see into the sun that she was shocked when a door to what looked like a rooftop shed flew open forty feet away and a man in a turban peered out. She saw his rifle and knew she had but one chance to kill him. It lasted less than a blink—scarcely long enough for her to get off two shots. The second round tore into his head, killing him.

She turned. Ruhi hadn't made it.

Oh, God.

But then she spotted him pulling himself up onto the roof on the other side of the chasm. He'd managed to grab the edge. He stood, shouting, "Come on."

"Catch," she called softly, throwing him the gun. He'd need it—if she didn't make it across.

But as soon as she tossed the Browning, *she* needed it.

A clamor arose in the shed. She looked back and saw a mujahideen stumble over his comrade's body.

She climbed onto the top of the short wall from which Ruhi

had launched himself seconds ago. Riddled with adrenaline, she crouched to leap as a bullet buzzed the very spot where her head had been an instant before. She jumped.

A second shot followed, missed, but she knew it wouldn't make any difference: She wasn't going to clear the gap. Felt it as soon as her feet left terra firma—or what passed for it up on the roof.

She pumped her legs, as if they might prolong her flight and defy death, reaching for Ruhi's outstretched hand.

He seized her wrist as she fell, her weight almost pulling him down, too.

He dug his knees into the wall, dropped the gun by his side, and gripped her with his other hand. In a mighty move, he dragged her up, eyes widening as he glanced across the narrow divide.

Lana picked up the Browning, turned, and aimed, keeping her profile low. The dim outlines of three men were racing toward the edge of the other roof.

Bam. Bam. Bam.

She hit one of them.

"Get down!"

Using the roof wall for cover, they crawled toward the street side of the building, hoping none of the mujahideen would risk the leap. Shouts rose from across the divide. Then nothing.

"See that?" Ruhi said, pointing to what appeared to be another shed roof about forty feet away.

She nodded. "Let's try it."

What other chance did they have? A whole series of buildings lined the street. How many more jumps could they possibly survive? The distances might be even greater.

But a sprint to the shed door would leave them in the open.

"You first," she said. "I'll give you cover. Then I'll go. Dodge and dart."

She pushed him—she hadn't pushed anyone since childhood.

Almost immediately, two gunshots rang out. They missed Ruhi. She rose from behind the short wall and fired, missing her targets. But she forced the gunmen to duck.

Ruhi threw his shoulder into the door. It didn't open. He worked the handle frantically, an easy target. She opened fire again, emptying her weapon, but the bullets kept the shooter down. Then Ruhi kicked it in a fury and disappeared into the darkness.

"Go, go, go!" Lana told herself, the only push she would get from anyone. One last look behind, and she was off. She saw the turban, spotted the other man raising a rifle, and dived through the doorway bruised but otherwise unharmed.

"You're good," Ruhi said.

"I'm trained, but I'm also out of ammo."

They found themselves inside a flimsy shed that she doubted could stop a .22. She saw the top of a wooden ladder poking up from a dark opening in the floor and started down without a word. Ruhi followed.

They lowered themselves into an attic. Spiderwebs wrapped around her face as she stumbled over old wooden boxes. She spied light streaming through a crack in a door and made her way forward, Ruhi only steps behind.

Her nerves felt like they were frying. The pair burst out of the attic onto the top floor of an apartment building, spotted the stairwell, and started down, clearing three, four steps at a time.

They encountered no one, only the odor of piss and sickness. Moments later, they burst out of the stairwell onto the ground floor—and were taken down by at least four men.

Bones in her gun hand felt snapped by a vicious blow. The Browning skittered across the floor. She heard its clatter stop abruptly, and then they were bagged in the most literal sense: dark burlap sacks dragged down over their heads, jammed into the back of a windowless van, hands and feet Flex-Cuffed with frightening efficiency.

"Let me see his face," she heard a man say. Then: "Cousin, it is good to see you again."

"I will kill you, Ahmed, I swear," she heard Ruhi reply from the darkness that still surrounded her.

"It is not I who should fear the reaper," Ahmed said in a soothing—tormenting—voice.

• • •

Holmes didn't know how bad it had gotten in Yemen. He knew only how grim conditions had become in the States. Pure misery.

In the jury-rigged manner that was the only means available, he sat in his office reading bulletins typed out on old Royals, using the last of their ribbons. They detailed what might be the final hours of the failing republic.

Phoenix, with a runaway reactor core, had descended into bedlam, in the original meaning of that word. The Valley of the Sun more closely approximated an eighteenth-century insane asylum than a series of contemporary communities linked by highways, freeways, cloverleafs, and surface streets, all of which were littered with evidence of panic: dead bodies, smashed cars, weeping survivors, and the invisible death rays of radiation that were seeping into every corner of the city.

Radiation plumes were ravaging much of the Pacific Northwest as well, rising from the Hanford Nuclear Reservation about a hundred miles east of Portland, Oregon. Driven by winds, the invisible poison, like the invisible enemy, was sweeping over the land.

Chicago had not been annihilated by Veepox yet, but the chimera virus was arguably crueler than a melting reactor core. Even the uninfected inhabitants were behaving like the countless extras in *Night of the Living Dead.* The military still had the city, suburbs, and lakefront surrounded, but soldiers and National Guard troops were frequently forced to fire on throngs of citizens too desperate to care about death. Or perhaps they preferred mass execution by machine-gun fire to the microbes that would make slow madness of their lives.

Swift death was also coming to those caught in raging wildfires set off by pipeline explosions in the first cyberattack. Those fires now scorched millions of acres, turning the West into a Hades of previously unknown proportions.

And the South, still reeling from the collapsing TVA dams, faced a Category 5 hurricane as the tropical storm season moved into overdrive. Hurricane Becca, extending more than six hundred miles, was expected to pile into the east coast of Florida in the next twelve hours, and then churn northward—with no way to warn tens of millions of residents in the direct path of the storm. Holmes knew of the danger only because of emergency ham radio communications.

Was Becca a coincidence? Holmes's rational side said yes, of course, but he could not help but wonder if the invisible enemy had cooked up the Category 5 somehow. Who would have imagined, for instance, the devastating extent of a cyberattack? Well, Holmes reminded himself, he had, in fact, conjured up just such a grim scenario, along with colleagues in government and the administration. But they were called prophets of doom and roundly ignored.

His own people at NSA, who had been laboring so hard to try to make cyberdefense a priority, were now tasked with trying to retake control of the country's own nuclear arsenal. The only good news on that front was that three of the Navy's nuclear-armed submarines had been able to reprogram software to regain control of their nuclear firing mechanisms. Unfortunately, the advance had no direct application to the land-based missiles aimed at American cities, though the Navy's success did mean that revenge would be in the offing—if the enemy could ever be identified.

Holmes had his suspicions about the culprit, but without proof he kept that speculation to a tight inner circle. All he allowed beyond his closest colleagues was that the enemy "wasn't as obvious as people might think."

The only target Holmes could see clearly right now, besides the NSA building in which he sat, was the blue choir bus in that New Jersey truck stop. It was still lit up by Kalisa Harris's fuel truck. German satellites provided video to him through a link in Greenland. It was ad hoc and hardly as reliable as the networks to which he had long been accustomed; but Holmes was grateful, nonetheless, for the chance to monitor the slowly building insanity a couple of hundred miles north of him.

He hoped Harris and everyone else there would see a way to save those kids. But he also knew that so much more than their lives was at stake if that backpack bomb blew up.

As he looked away from the screen, McGivern hurried in to tell him that Agent Anders had been rescued.

"That's great news. Was it the encryptors?" he asked. Desk jockeys in Riyadh who'd been pressed into service, the ultimate nerds were directed step-by-step by the CIA station chief. Everybody else who could be mobilized in the kingdom and Yemen had been tracking the takeover of the embassy or searching for the cyberattackers.

"Yes, they managed to pull it off," McGivern said.

"Those three will be dining out on that for the rest of their lives."

"Let's hope so. But there's more. After the rescue the Saudis intercepted them in the desert, and, well, I don't have a final word on this yet, but I guess our geeks were seriously outgunned and turned her over. Without further incident," she added.

Holmes's joy fled like a fugitive.

"But she's back with Omar at least." The senior Saudi intelligence official.

Holmes nodded, relieved. He knew Omar. Trustworthy. And Anders was a lot better off with him than she'd been with those thugs out there in the desert. Besides, Omar was doing exactly what Holmes would have done: going for the debrief as soon as he could.

"At least she can keep her head down now," Holmes said to McGivern. "She's been through enough."

• • •

Emma had fallen asleep. Even abject fear couldn't keep her awake forever. Other kids had nodded off, too, including Tanesa, slouched against the window. Emma had been dreaming of a day on the Maryland shore with her mother when she was a little kid, maybe five or six. She was chasing a big colorful beach ball on the sand. Every time she tried to grab it, the ball slipped away. Finally, it rolled into the water and floated away, leaving her with the deepest sorrow she had ever known.

She awoke sad, but only for a moment. Then she was scared. She checked Ibrahim the bomber first. The trigger was lying on his lap, his hand nowhere near it. His eyes looked glazed, but open. The Red Bull can lay empty by his feet.

Emma thought she'd been asleep for hours—the dream seemed to go on and on—but it might have just been minutes; the lady truck driver was pulling the nozzle from the bus, from the sounds of it. And Hamza kept poking his head out to watch her.

The other two jihadists were at their posts, fore and aft. They looked exhausted too. The one up behind the driver slipped down into a seat periodically, a motion that appeared to jar him awake. He had an assault rifle and a pistol. They all had pistols. She wished that *she* had a pistol. The guy a few rows behind her, near Ibrahim, had the same weapons. Only Hamza also had a knife. The cuts on Emma's neck and chin proved his eagerness to use it.

A huge explosion made her scream and jump. She thought the bus had been blown up. Looking around, panicking wildly, she saw windows on both ends were ripped apart by gunfire. The rounds kept coming. She saw the head of the jihadist up by the driver cut up in a blink, leaving little that was recognizable when he crumpled onto the aisle floor. Blood gushed from what was left of his brain stem.

She glimpsed all that gore in an instant. Then she looked back at the shot-out window behind her and saw the jihadist a row away from Ibrahim slumped over the seat in front of him with a head wound of his own. Though less devastating at a glance, it had left him just as dead.

Ibrahim was shocked out of his open-eyed slumber. Kids were screaming. The bomber looked at them. He appeared confused, as if he didn't know what was happening. Hamza bellowed, "Blow it up! Blow it up, Ibrahim!"

That was the only reason Emma knew Hamza had survived the initial assault.

Ibrahim reached for the trigger on his lap—but never took it in hand. Quicker than a heartbeat, bullets slammed into his head from the left and right, as if timed by snipers to the hundredth of a second.

Hamza howled, crouched, and started barreling down the aisle. Emma saw his eyes fix on the backpack bomb.

Stop him.

The voice in her head was harrowing. Tanesa was already hurling herself past Emma and launching herself up the aisle at Hamza. He pushed her viciously to the side, with his eyes still fixed on Ibrahim. Tanesa whipped back around and jumped onto his back, reaching around to scratch his face. Hamza raised his pistol to try to shoot Tanesa over his shoulder.

Emma, sick with fear, legs like jelly, grabbed his wrist, falling in front of him in the process, but he never let go of that gun.

Hamza, with Tanesa still on his back, toppled onto Emma, the barrel grinding into her gut.

• • •

Hamza had not been spared in the initial barrage. He had simply gotten lucky at a horrible price: With the first shot, Kalisa Harris bolted for the front of the bus, .45 drawn from her calf holster. As she rose up onto the steps, she intercepted a round aimed at Hamza. She couldn't have known who fired the bullet that cost her life—or whose worthless existence it had spared.

• • •

Lana felt the van's leisurely motion. No sign of panic driving. In a voice that reflected that ease, she heard Ahmed speak in Arabic. A moment later the burlap sack was pulled off her head. A dome light burned in the back of the windowless van.

She could have picked out Ahmed easily. His physical resemblance to Ruhi was unmistakable.

"Hello, Lana Elkins. It is so good to have your company."

"You set us up. You ambushed us." *And killed a lot of good men.* But she wouldn't give him the satisfaction of hearing that from her lips.

"People die every day," Ahmed replied airily. "Your country kills them; mine does, too." He waved his hand as if her concerns were a trifle. "Now, we are taking you where we all want to go."

That smile again.

"Where's that?"

"Oh, you know where. So do you, cousin. Maybe not the exact address, but you know what you'll be doing when you get there, don't you? Making sure the attack on your country is not stopped in the final hours." That comment was directed at Lana. "We know you are the brains of the operation. America is almost history now. But this attack has other targets and far greater goals. So you will cooperate. You will join forces with us. And if you don't?" He shook his head. "That would be sad. But even if you think you can accept a painful death for yourself, rather than give us every last secret of your encryption and hacking experience, I doubt very much that you'll be able to watch your daughter dismembered on streaming video. Our martyr has a special knife that he's already used on her, I am told."

Lana, though bound, tried to lunge at him. A man seized her.

"He hasn't done anything serious to her," Ahmed went on, "not yet. She even has her fingers and nose still. Just a cut on her neck and chin. But he's a young man, our butcher, and a real animal. So get ready to share your expertise with us. You were always the one we wanted. My cousin?" Ahmed shrugged. "He has served his purpose, but blood runs thick, doesn't it, Ruhi?"

Ahmed pointed a gun at his cousin's face. Lana thought he was going to shoot him right then. But he didn't.

Now, we are taking you where we all want to go.

When Ahmed had said that, did he mean it ironically? she wondered.

What difference does it make?

But then she realized that it could make all the difference in the world.

CHAPTER 23

THE THROBBING IN LANA'S hand awakened her fully. She'd been napping in the back of the van through most of the drive. But pain now overcame weariness. She tested herself, flexing her fingers. She could make a fist. It was her only weapon as the driver wheeled into a dingy garage whose lone window bore spidery cracks. *A fist.* She shook her head at the pathos. What good could it do in the company of such heavily armed enemies?

A skinny bald man rolled down the garage door.

The jihadists jumped out of the vehicle and dragged Lana and Ruhi from the back. Two men forced a keffiyeh on Ruhi, while another unbound Lana's wrists, which befuddled her. Not for long. Ahmed thrust a dark hijab into her hands and ordered her to put it on. She found it odd, after their murderous actions, that several men turned away when she slipped it over her clothes. But not Ahmed. He kept a gun on her the whole time. Once she was fully veiled, her hands were quickly bound again.

Immediately, they loaded her and Ruhi into another van, similar to the one the SEALs had used to rescue her from the embassy in Riyadh.

She was seated, as she had been then, with armed men on both sides of her. But the jihadists pressed their weapons against her—knives lodged so tightly to her ribs that she feared a sneeze, cough, or sudden turn would leave her bleeding.

Ruhi was forced against a boarded window. A bony-cheeked man jammed a pistol under his chin. Ruhi's life, she realized, was cheaper now because of her presence. They didn't need him. She thought they must know that, and couldn't comprehend why he was still alive. Ahmed had certainly shown a complete absence of compassion, so it wasn't a blood link keeping Ruhi among the living. Maybe it was nothing more than an oversight, or Ahmed's desire to lord as much power as possible over his expatriate cousin.

Death would come to both of them soon enough, as well as to Emma. *To the whole of her country.* But she focused—how could she not?—on the unbidden tragedy of her only child. *I'm sorry, dear heart,* she said to Emma in the silence of her thoughts. *I'm so sorry.* She had no hope of ever being heard, but in the only way she could, she sought Emma's forgiveness for dragging her into this horror. *Your pain is all on me.*

The turban-headed driver navigated desert roads without pause, but just as Lana nodded off again, she was jarred awake by a small crater.

"IEDs," Ahmed said with evident pleasure from the front passenger seat. He turned to bestow his smile on her. Even as she noticed how much it resembled Ruhi's, she felt her stomach sour. She would have ripped out his eyeballs, if she could have. "Just a carful of NGOs," he explained. Nongovernmental organizations. "Good-bye, kafirs."

The jihadist on her left must have spoken English, because he laughed at the insult and nodded enthusiastically at Ahmed.

"Do you want to say where you're taking us?" Lana asked Ahmed.

He nodded, but not at her, to the English speaker. She turned to the man, puzzled. He punched her hard enough that her lips and nose exploded with pain. It felt like he'd bashed her face with a lead weight.

"Never speak to any of us," Ahmed said calmly, "unless you are spoken to. I did not ask you a question."

She swallowed blood, rage, and tears that wanted to run from the sudden crack of bone on bone—the involuntary response that comes from any blow that catches the tender spot between the upper lip and nose. It's the way a woman can reduce even the strongest man to tears. The way she wanted to begin an attack not on her assailant, but on Ahmed—and then work her way to all points south.

They passed ancient cliff dwellings, shadowed by the harsh light. She guessed the rudimentary homes had been carved out of the mountains thousands of years ago, yet might well be occupied now. Her suspicion was confirmed with the flash of a child's face, a little boy. Already poisoned by hate and intolerance? She could not muster enough hope to think otherwise.

The canyon widened, and they drove around an outcropping as wide and tall as a building. She glimpsed a floodplain miles ahead and a small town, and the pale green glimmer of fields in the distance.

Ahmed tapped the driver on the shoulder and pointed for him to keep going straight. "Hurry."

• • •

A mujahideen stood guard in the doorway of a broad, flat-roofed building with mud-colored walls, the brightly striped red, white, and black Yemeni flag flying before it. He squinted in the blanketing glare of the sun. A village woman in a black hijab was plodding toward him. A beggar, no doubt. Make that *another* beggar. Yemen was a nation of beggars. She'd want food, maybe water; she wouldn't dare ask for coin. He sighed and looked away from her. *Go back to your fields. Great matters are at hand. Leave us to do our work here. Soon you'll hail from the proudest nation on earth, and you will have mujahideen to thank for that honor.*

He glanced back. She was nearing him now. He waved her off.

Submissively, she kept her head down. But she raised her hand above her waist, the wide black arms of her chador drooping. *Yes, food, that's what she wants.*

"I have no food for you," he shouted. He made a gesture for her to go away.

Still, she came toward him. Past the children playing soccer. She placed her hand on the head of a boy who looked eight or nine. He looked up and grinned at her. *So she's borne a son. Fine. I'll talk to her. Tell her the world changes soon. Be patient. Always the women are impatient.*

As his body language softened, she nodded at him. She might have smiled. It was hard to tell with the veil. You see only the eyes, and she mostly kept her gaze toward the ground out of respect. She seemed to have difficulty breathing. So that was it. *She's sick.*

"What is it?" From behind, his fellow guards converged quickly at his side. Eight of them. They had been covering the other exits and entrances. They must have heard him yell at the woman.

"A beggar," he told them. "Sick. Not breathing well."

She turned to regard the children, no more than thirty feet away, as their soccer ball rolled toward the group. The commander stepped out and kicked it back to the little ones.

They cheered him.

As they turned their attention back to the beggar woman, she slipped a thick canister out from beneath her chador and blasted a weapons-grade blend of pepper and tear gas at them in a swift arc.

After another blast from the canister had them retching and kneeling, she tore off her veil, revealing a form-fitting gas mask and blond hair.

• • •

Candace took a step back to protect her eyes, the only exposed part of her face. She looked behind her, willing her companions to hurry. Far beneath this structure lay the nerve center for the cyberterrorists, according to information gathered by Saudi intelligence in the last few hours. The nature of the site seemed confirmed by the route taken by the mujahideen who'd abducted Ruhi Mancur and Lana Elkins, to judge by the Mabahith's locator chip in Ruhi's thigh.

Within seconds, Omar and officers of the Mabahith—all in gas masks—converged on the disabled guards as the children ran toward their parents in the distant fields. Candace wasn't worried about the villagers; Saudi intelligence said they were farmers, not fighters, and many were angry that their hamlet had been overtaken by jihadists.

With chilling efficiency, the Saudis slit the throats of the guards and swiftly dragged the blood-soaked bodies deep inside the building.

Omar, who had secured Candace's capture from the American computer jockeys in the desert, studied a smartphone and said, "They are close."

He had been tracking the chip in Ruhi's leg on their chopper flight here. The Black Hawk helicopter had put down behind a low range of hills a mile from town. Running in the heat had been grueling for Candace in her chador. Now, with the mask stripped away, she forced herself to breathe evenly, despite her urge to gulp air. While the parents of the soccer-playing children did not pose a threat, Ruhi Mancur and Lana Elkins would be arriving shortly with the heavily armed jihadists who had killed the SEALs and Saudi officers in Sana.

● ● ●

As the van drove closer to what appeared to be a community center, Lana guessed they had arrived at their destination.

The end is coming.

She felt flushed with fear, as if it might seep from her pores as easily as sweat.

The driver braked. Dust rose from the wheels and floated away. They had stopped by a flagpole, about fifty feet from the center's open doorway.

"You will walk from here," Ahmed announced to Ruhi.

Ruhi's guard placed the muzzle of his gun back to the soft spot under his jaw, where a thin beard had sprouted since the first cyberattack.

Ahmed snapped at the gunman in Arabic. The man lowered his weapon. Lana did not know what Ahmed had said, but it possessed the cadence of "Not in here. Not yet."

Maybe the gunman appeared too eager, even for Ahmed's taste.

"Cousin," he said to Ruhi, "I want you to go first."

The side door of the van swung open, and they all climbed out. Lana kept her eye on Ruhi, subtly adjusting the veil to keep him in view. She worried that each second might provide her last glimpse of him alive. In an unspoken way, she felt she was honoring a man who had suddenly found himself immersed in a violent realm that he'd never sought.

"Walk to the door, cousin," Ahmed said, racking the slide on his semiautomatic pistol.

Lana heard the rush of metal and remembered the way the chamber accepted the small brass cylinder of death.

"You will die for this, Ahmed," Ruhi replied with surprising equanimity. He shook his head and went on: "Maybe not today or tomorrow, but you will die. They will hunt you down like al-Awlaki, and they will destroy you."

Ahmed pointed his pistol at Ruhi's face. "She was struck for speaking out. See what happens to you. Go!"

The jihadists with Lana lined up on both sides of her. There would be no escape.

Up ahead Ruhi walked closer to the entrance with his shoulders pulled back, his head held defiantly high. She adored him for that, for the spit it offered to Ahmed's eye.

Ahmed lowered his gun, but called to Ruhi, "Keep going, cousin. You're getting closer to your destination."

• • •

Holmes turned to one of the screens with a German news report. That country's communications systems were now the most dependable for the few people capable of receiving signals in the U.S.

He'd studied German at the Defense Language Institute in Monterey, California, and had used it daily in Berlin, where he was stationed until the collapse of the Soviet Union. A lifetime ago. But he didn't need all that background to translate the word now blazoned across the screen: "Cybergeddon."

It appeared as the German announcer enunciated it with great care. Satellite video of the U.S. then showed thousands gathered in half a dozen city centers in spontaneous prayer vigils. Rumors of imminent nuclear devastation had spread. The faithful were no doubt praying for deliverance. For forgiveness. For the Lord's will to be done. But mostly, Holmes thought, they were praying for the most human desire of all: to survive.

He felt deeply for them. He believed that he had failed them all. But the most heart-sickening news that he'd received this morning came from a Russian operative in Sana who had passed along news that two SEAL units had been wiped out in an ambush. What an ignominious end for such gallant young men, killed without a country that could even grieve them properly, that might perish as readily in the coming hours.

The array of screens kept Holmes, McGivern, and others abreast of developments throughout the nation. They saw throngs trudging north through New England, Michigan, Wisconsin, North Dakota, Montana, and Washington State, trying to escape to Canada.

The Canadians were accepting all comers, but so much of their grid had gone down when the U.S's was attacked that they were poorly prepared to save their American friends. Fuel distribution had ceased in the U.S. and throughout much of southern Canada. Only that country's most northern regions remained wholly viable—remote villages and a handful of smaller cities. Radiation would eventually eat them alive as well, if the worst came to pass.

As for Chicago, the only good Holmes could muster about the Veepox epidemic was that over the past decades the city had lost more than a million residents for lack of jobs and other opportunities. The next Detroit, it had often been called. But where had all those former Chicagoans gone? Somewhere safer? Not likely. Not with the whole country now a target.

But the most repulsive display he saw on those screens was the joyful response of Iranian leaders, and their Shiite brethren now ruling Iraq, over an America brought to its knees—the Great Satan of their theology about to be reduced to rubble. He knew those fanatics had thoroughly penetrated Yemen's Political Security Organization, leaving it riddled with terrorist sympathizers, some of whom likely had the blood of those SEALs on their hands.

Tehran's long shadow fell over much of Yemen, and Holmes found himself suspecting more and more that Iran had played a role in the cyberattacks on the U.S. Those zealots wanted nothing but the complete collapse of Western power. Was there a deal they wouldn't make for that outcome? It had Holmes thinking about where the Iranians might have turned for help.

Holmes had never loathed even the most ruthless Muslim leaders on sight. He had an understanding of the long history of Middle Eastern colonization and its attendant crimes. He could quote Edward Said as readily as Noam Chomsky or Norman Podhoretz. But now he and his countrymen had their backs to the wall, and he could not bear the sanctimony coming from Tehran and Baghdad, much less the murder of those brave young men in Yemen.

There could be no room now for the nuances of reason, for the values of philosophy alone or the redemptive worth of forgiveness. It was far too early for any of that. There was only winning the race to stop the wholesale murder of his people: Americans of every stripe.

His eyes returned to one screen in particular, where a satellite lens was trained on a truck stop in New Jersey.

• • •

Hamza straddled Emma in the aisle, looming over her face. His gun barrel felt as if it were drilling into her stomach, his murderous gaze boring just as deeply into her eyes. She was certain he would kill her right now. Instead, he seized her hair with his free hand and pounded her head onto the floor, oblivious in his rage to Tanesa still clawing his face. But Tanesa's fingernails, though leaving bloody trails across his chin and neck, didn't register nearly as much as the nail file of a twelve-year-old choir member. The girl pulled it from her purse and stabbed him in the cheek. Only the tortoiseshell handle stuck out.

Emma glimpsed the length of the file in Hamza's mouth, which dripped blood onto her shirt. His teeth pinkened as they chomped down on the metal, like a pirate with a knife, but this blade had plunged into his mouth *through* his face.

He turned to the young girl, raised his pistol from Emma's belly, and shot the child in the neck. Blood pulsed out like a garden hose rapidly kinked and unkinked. The girl grabbed her mortal wound and reeled into the arms of her seatmate.

They all froze: Emma, dazed from the pounding of her head; Tanesa, mouth agape at her friend's imminent death, the victim's eyes still open as her life closed down; and Hamza, who still had the nail file sticking out of his cheek.

But he recovered first, yanking it out. He raised the bloody length, and in a rage tried to plunge it into Emma's chest. She rolled furiously to the side, catching the file in her upper arm, where it stuck like a dagger.

She shrieked with pain as Tanesa tried to rip Hamza's eyes out. He delivered a powerful elbow into Tanesa's side. Even in her own agony, Emma heard her friend's rib crack and saw tears race down Tanesa's face.

Hamza dragged Emma to her feet, breathing deeply, as if to get a grip on his fury. The file stuck out of her arm just below her shoulder. She thought to pull it out, as he had from his face, but couldn't bring herself to do it.

He thrust his gun to Tanesa's head, ordering her to stand, then grabbed the backpack bomb and demanded the two girls move to the front of the bus with him.

Staying low, he forced them onto the front seat and yelled at the bus driver to go.

The older man cranked the ignition, put the bus in gear, but the watered-down diesel fouled the engine immediately.

Hamza told him to get off the bus. He obeyed, moving around the dead woman who had pumped the fuel, whose body lay below the vehicle's steps. Hamza then shot the driver twice in the back. The man staggered several feet toward the fuel truck's headlights and fell, showing no further signs of life.

Crouching, keeping his gun on the girls, Hamza pulled keys from the slain woman's pocket. Emma watched his eyes land on the backpack bomb, which he'd left by the driver's seat. She thought to throw herself on it, as she'd once seen a soldier hurl himself on a hand grenade in a war movie. But there would be no absorbing the impact of the weapon hiding inside that pack.

Hamza jumped back onto the bus and grabbed the pack, then stared at them and said, "They're not stopping Hamza the Lion." He sounded solemn, like he was repeating a vow.

He yelled at Tanesa and Emma to move to the rear and open the emergency exit. Still crouching, he tailed them. The two injured girls struggled mightily to dislodge the lever holding the door in place. With the exit open, Hamza grabbed the bomb trigger.

"We're going out to the truck. You two stay right with me the whole time. If you run, I'll set off the bomb. Millions will die. It will be your fault."

Emma knew whose fault it would be—the person who pulled the trigger. But she also knew she would not run off, and doubted Tanesa would, either. There was no hope for them or anyone else if he set off the bomb.

"You in front of me," he said to Tanesa. "And you stay behind me," he ordered Emma. "Stay very close. If they hit me, I'll pull the trigger."

Emma thought all three of them would be shot the second they stepped out. But he crouched and kept them bunched up in front and behind him.

An unearthly silence greeted them, so still Emma heard the odd shuffle of their shoes as they moved, a six-legged cluster. Still, she wondered who would be killed first.

In the next instant, two sniper shots rang out. One hit Tanesa in the leg with such force it spun her around and spilled her onto the parking lot. She rolled over, screaming, clutching her thigh. The other shot sailed over Hamza's shoulder. Emma wondered if he even noticed.

He rushed her toward the truck as another bullet sailed right over their heads. The door was open, the dome light on. He threw his upper body across the driver's seat, pushing the backpack bomb ahead of him with one hand, and dragging Emma up behind him with the other.

She saw the filleting knife in its sheath as another shot hit the outside of the cab just inches from her head. She slipped the blade from its sheath as Hamza frantically forced the backpack onto the passenger seat.

Emma drove the long thin blade into his lower back, guessing she stabbed a kidney.

Hamza groaned horrifically, and tried to pull himself all the way into the cab. Emma threw herself onto his back, slowing him down. But she also prevented the snipers from having a clear shot at their target.

Then Hamza tried to turn toward her with his gun. She felt the knife handle against her belly and squeezed herself against him. A low howl arose from him.

He gave up trying to shoot her, putting all his effort into try-ing to pull himself onto the driver's seat. Maybe he recognized that the surest way to end his agony and complete his diminished mission was to reach the bomb trigger.

She heard his howl turn into a rhythmic gasp that sounded like a prayer in another language. He was but a hand's length from the trigger, bellowing now, still fierce in trying to claw his way forward.

Emma braced her feet against the truck's big wheel, using her legs to pull on him as hard as she could. A horrible pain rose from her shoulder, and she saw the nail file brushing against the open door, jabbing it deeper into her flesh. Grinding her teeth, she jerked the file out and—in a spasm of fury—sank it into the middle of his back. It struck bone and lodged deeply in his flesh. She regained her grip with both hands, pulling with all the strength left in her arms and legs—weeping, screaming, holding on to him for all the world.

CHAPTER 24

RUHI ENTERED THE THICKENING shadows of the
community center, wary of the first few steps that drew him into
the darkness. He expected a knifing—violence teeming with ven-
detta—so he was not surprised when hands reached from the
engulfing blackness and seized him so hard that he thought his
bones were being crushed.

"Quiet, Mancur," murmured a man as he pressed a heavy
hand over Ruhi's mouth. "We are on your side. If you yell, we die."

"It's true, Ruhi," he heard Candace whisper, offering so many
reassurances in so few words that his joy and gratitude might
have lifted monuments.

Ruhi nodded. The man's hand dropped away. Ruhi stared at
Candace.

"You're here—how?" he murmured.

"Later. No time now," she replied.

Candace guided Ruhi against an interior wall. Her touch felt
magically restoring, all the more so for the bloodshed that he
spied as his eyes adjusted to the darkness. The slain bodies of
nine mujahideen sprawled across the floor told the story of a

successful ambush, while the armed men he now saw crouching on both sides of the doorway—Mabahith, he guessed—spoke of the imminence of another surprise attack.

He sensed increasing tension in the shadows as Ahmed neared the entrance. His cousin held Lana's arm with one hand, her computer in the other. Fighters moved alongside them. The armed escorts didn't appear on guard, and why should they have been? The community center belonged to them; their brothers-in-arms should have been waiting inside, hidden from the prying eyes of Predator drones.

Without warning, the Saudi agents crouching in the shadows opened fire on the jihadists, a disciplined and muffled fusillade that lasted no more than two or three seconds. Their targets never had a chance to fire their weapons.

Only Ahmed and Lana were spared. Ruhi's cousin huddled close to the ground, still gripping his prisoner's arm. That Ahmed survived seemed like the greatest crime of all to Ruhi.

Why?

Because he held Lana *and* her computer. They were his shield. That was the only fathomable reason. Ruhi vowed to kill Ahmed quickly, now that all of his cousin's protectors were dead.

Ruhi launched himself straight at Ahmed, who simply raised his hand and looked Ruhi in the eye. "I am on your side. I always have been. Time is absolutely essential now. We're down to less than an hour to stop them."

Incredibly, Ahmed's words were not challenged by anyone, not even Candace. In fact, a man named Omar put his arm on Ahmed's shoulder and said, "It is true."

"What about the murder of the SEALs?" Ruhi demanded. "And the Mabahith?"

"That was the price we had to pay to get her here," Ahmed replied calmly, glancing at Lana, who had pulled away from him and was the only other person who looked horrified by what she was hearing.

• • •

More than horrified, Lana could scarcely make sense of Ahmed's words: that he'd casually traded off the lives of all those good men to bring her to the nerve center of the cyberattack. It seemed the cruelest equation of all. But as she stood there, sickened by the brutal logic of Ahmed's plotting, she also recognized the implacable understanding of war at the heart of his plan.

"Did you get them all?" Ahmed asked a man who stood foremost in the doorway.

"Nobody got away," he answered.

"Then let's get her down there quickly." Ahmed turned back to Lana.

"What about the noise?" she asked him, looking behind her.

"They can't hear. They're in a cavern deep underground, and then steel doors have to open when you're lowered down. Only one person gets in there at a time. That's part of their security. You'll be handcuffed, just like they would have done. We'll try to come in through a ventilation shaft on the far side of the cavern."

"What do they want from me?" she asked. "And what am I supposed to do? It's not like they're going to let me hack their computers."

"They don't want anything from you today," said Omar, speaking rapidly. "They just want you under their control until they launch those missiles. Once they heard you were in Riyadh, they knew you'd been sent to try to stop them. So when Ruhi's computer ended up in our hands, someone in my agency sabotaged it." Omar stated that as if it happened every other day. "That's how they forced your rendezvous with him."

"So I'm basically dead once they get those missiles launched."

"No. Just the opposite," Ahmed replied. "From what I understand, they have plans that go beyond destroying the States. I've never been down there, but I know they really want you. So until we can get through that ventilation shaft, listen to what they have to say, but whatever you do, don't make them want to kill you. We're going to need you."

"If we can take control down there," Omar explained, "we want you to get on their computers and shut them down for good, if that's at all possible."

Lana remembered Travis's words: *Hack. Them. To. Death.*

Omar looked at his watch. "We've got to move."

All but two of the men rushed deeper into the community center. The pair stayed behind to lead Lana across the floor. They stopped by the edge of a wide hole that she couldn't see. They warned her not to move. One of them slipped a rock-climbing harness around her. She wondered if it had been scavenged from Westerners scaling peaks in Pakistan or elsewhere in the Himalayas. It was not the kind of gear you'd normally find on a floodplain in the Yemeni desert.

Then the man with the climbing gear clipped a carabiner to the harness and another one to a rope that had hung hidden in the darkness only feet away. He drew her hands around the length, Flex-Cuffing her wrists together.

She didn't understand the need. It's not like she was going to let go when they suspended her over the deep emptiness that she sensed below. But then she understood that a real prisoner, knowing she was about to be delivered to torturers and murderers, might undo the harness and hurl herself into the hole. Men steeped in a culture of suicide bombings would be sharply attuned to the self-destructive potential of others.

The pair eased her off the edge. For several seconds she swung over what seemed like a bottomless abyss. She heard the creak of a pulley above her. As the pendulum-like swinging slowed, she felt herself beginning to descend.

Twenty, thirty seconds passed. She counted them out carefully: *One-one-thousand, two-one-thousand, three-one-thousand* . . .

When she looked up, only the dimmest outlines of the two men appeared, and she heard nothing but the protest of the pulley. If it suddenly snapped from its bearings, she had no idea how far she would fall.

Fifty seconds passed, then a full minute. Always descending.

Without conscious thought, she began to count anew. *One-one-thousand.* Perhaps numbers, with their illusion of precision, were the only way she could endure so many unknowns, which included the viability of her life as well as her daughter's.

The next second her feet touched a metal surface that she could not see, contact that triggered the opening of panels directly beneath her. They parted to what appeared, after so much blackness, to be a blaze of light rising from a cavern at least two acres in size, with rows and rows of computer equipment and what looked like ten thousand miles of wires and cables. She figured every last diode had to be powered by the sun, because nothing less than a powerful array of solar panels could ever generate the juice for such a remote operation.

And there were scores of people. Men in dress shirts, others in ragged jihadist garb. And not just men. Women, too, some wearing slacks, most chadors. An odd mix. They worked at computer stations at least three stories below her. Rows of them. Most paid strict attention to their screens, ignoring her. Or perhaps they'd been ordered to pay no heed to whatever the ceiling revealed.

She scanned the entire space, looking for the ventilation shaft or a means of escape. She saw only the floor, and curved walls and ceiling. It was an arena-size hole in the ground.

Then she saw the man she guessed she would be answering to. He wore no turban, unlike the men waiting for her on the floor below. Nor did he deign to turn to look at her. Large computer screens engulfed him on three sides, and plush chairs and a settee distinguished his large work area from any other.

She looked back at the men waiting right under her, wondering in the final seconds of her descent whether she had been taken captive by Shiites, Sunnis, or Wahhabis, certain only that fundamentalists had her in their grip. Silently, she cursed them all, the fanatics that plagued Islam, Christianity, Judaism, Buddhism—every conceivable faith. Why couldn't they all just pray or chant in peace and leave the less crazed elements of humanity alone?

With that thought she was delivered to their hands. To free her, they cut away the cuffs, then stripped off the harness so efficiently it was as if they had spent their lives bagging peaks instead of people. Another guard kept a gun inches from her head.

Only then did the man at the large computer console turn to Lana, shocking her. He was unmistakably Korean, with bristly black hair, a rectangular face, and almond eyes.

As soon as she saw him, she thought he was probably from the North, and if that were true—and North Koreans were among the real fanatics of cyberterrorism—then she was undoubtedly looking at a veteran of Unit 121, the infamous North Korean cyberwarfare unit. Three thousand strong at last count, which was more than three times the number of cybercounterterror agents in the entire United States.

And we wonder why we're dropping like flies.

Guards on each side of her, including the one with the gun at her head, guided Lana toward him. The Korean smiled, gesturing to a chair that would force her to face him. Even as she approached—scanning the man's computers, trying to familiarize herself with them—she could not make immediate sense of this strange alliance. What could jihadists possibly have in common with godless North Koreans? What perverted confluence of desire and ambition could they conceivably share?

"I welcome our esteemed guest, Lana Elkins," the man said with a brightening of his otherwise dark eyes. He spoke with no discernible accent—Western-educated, she guessed. "I can see that you are shocked to meet me. I, on the other hand, am only pleased to finally have your alluring company."

Don't flirt with me, she thought, staring him down.

"And I trust that you will remain comfortable in the coming days."

"Days? You mean even after my country is destroyed?"

"Please, do not think of it as destruction. Think of it as salvation. A new world is coming, and the U.S. has brought so much destruction and terror, not just to Asia but to the whole world, that Earth will be a much better place without its predatory ways. You will see that this is true."

Where are they? Ruhi, Ahmed, the man named Omar, and Agent Anders, whom she hadn't even had a chance to meet. And all the others. There were armed guards down here, too. She tried to count them casually. At least fifteen, maybe twenty.

"And North Korea is going to usher in the grand millennium?" She wanted to see if he would deny his nationality. It could help to know. She'd hacked North Korean codes numerous times and monitored them as a matter of course.

"Not North Korea." He shook his head, as if he pitied her inability to grasp his real plans. "I have no sympathy for my brother's kingdom."

Kang-dee Rang, she realized, the brother of the Supreme Leader of North Korea. Only three years ago, Kang-dee, though older, had been passed over by his father for the leadership of that bizarre country, leading to a scathing sibling rivalry after the aging dictator's death.

Giving us this catastrophe.

"The 'Supreme Leader,'"—Kang-dee's voice dripped with sarcasm—"is already defeated. We shut down his pathetic rule a few hours ago. But the kingdom's infrastructure is so poor it might take days for the rest of the world to recognize that even its elementary level of functioning has stopped. Our kingdom is here, and soon it will be everywhere."

Lana wanted to hurl herself at him, but restrained herself, for the tang of real terror hung in the air, and she had no choice but to play a waiting game. Still, she could not keep from shaking her head, appalled to understand the brute mechanics behind his presence and all that it explained and portended: After being snubbed, Kang-dee had decided to grab a much greater prize than the ruined state of North Korea. He had gone after the entire planet.

"I don't think Yemen is going to love hosting you and the plans you're hatching down here," Lana challenged, mostly to keep him talking but also to garner any bit of information that might prove helpful if she ever got her hands on his console.

"Yemen, at the end of the day, as you Americans like to say, is an arm of Iran, even more than Iraq has turned out to be. And the Iranians and I have provided for each other in vital ways. Through their control of Yemen's highly effective Political Security Organization, my Shiite friends have strong influence in the Ministry of the Interior, which has accorded me great assistance and freedom in building my army. Look at them." He gestured at the rows of cyberwarriors. "I took only my country's and Iran's most elite fighters. They have promised me their allegiance, and I have promised them the world."

"And what did you promise Tehran?" Though Lana had no doubt about the answer to her question. She questioned only whether he felt cocky enough down there to respond honestly. He did not keep her in suspense:

"We have promised them nothing. We have *given* them all they need to build their nuclear weapons. It is ironic, isn't it? Your country and Israel attacked the Iranians with the computer virus Stuxnet to destroy their centrifuges, which were so vital to their nuclear ambitions. But that made them ever so willing to work with us. I saw the opportunity and took it. I will forever be grateful to the short-term thinking of the United States."

He glanced at his watch. "The last of the nuclear silos is opening. In less than fifteen minutes the U.S. will be destroyed. There is already much wailing in the streets. Show her."

One of the three large screens came alive. It was only feet from where the would-be emperor sat. What Lana noticed on the video, even more than the prayer vigils and people weeping on their knees or screaming imprecations at the sky, was the trash scattered everywhere. That was the one constant as the big screen changed with video from city after city, disaster after disaster. Each clip showed a country defeated militarily, economically, and socially—but the endless mounds of uncollected, uncontained garbage spoke most revealingly of the deepening desperation of her homeland.

The last clip showed the opening of a nuclear missile silo somewhere in the American desert. She heard a humming sound from the screen, like an idling dentist's drill.

"You should be grateful," Kang-dee said to her. "You are alive, and you will remain alive. The world belongs to the likes of us."

She looked around. The mujahideen appeared grim. She wondered whether that was because those jihadists wanted to kill the only Western woman in their midst. Or had they recognized that they were also expendable to Kang-dee, that real victory might accrue only to this creature with his sickly smile and those who plied cyberwar on his behalf? His minions would never include her, she vowed silently, solemnly. *No matter what happens.*

He glanced at the screen with the missile silo and resumed his work as if she were not present. With the absence of talk, she again heard the hum of the silo opening.

At any other time, Kang-dee would have been considered delusional, and rightly so. But she knew this was not any other time. This was a new age with the most lethal means of warfare ever devised, one that could bend even nuclear arsenals, fighter jets, and long-range bombers to its own designs. And she had the grinding misfortune of finding herself perched on the very precipice of its wholesale slaughter.

• • •

Holmes hadn't slept in thirty hours, and for days before that had only catnapped, yet he remained intensely alert and fully engaged as the minutes ticked away, his thoughts always circling back to words that played in his mind like a song you can't shake:

Ruhi Mancur, lost somewhere in Yemen.

Lana Elkins, lost somewhere in Yemen.

Fourteen SEALs, lost forever in Yemen.

And now, in a curious twist, the last of the mighty weapon silos of his own country was opening on a screen only a few feet from him. He thought about how he and his fellows in the intelligence service—and a number of women as well, back in the day—had faced down the Russians, the growing threat from "Red" China, then terrorists of all stripes with their plastic explosives and box cutter conspiracies; but the computer, which arose largely from the most creative minds of his country, had turned war upside down and, in a purely demonic sense, democratized it to the point where an invisible enemy could bring Holmes's powerful nation to its knees. Just as the terrorists had claimed in one of their communications to the American people.

He had strong suspicions about the attackers, of course, and would have chiseled those thoughts into stone if he thought they would have survived the imminent nuclear blasts.

Teresa McGivern looked at him. "What do you think? Do we have any hope?"

"The only hope is that we haven't heard from them."

• • •

Emma screamed for help. Hamza was still trying to pull himself across the driver's seat to grab the backpack nuclear bomb. Despite her intense shoulder pain, she clung to his back, with her hands now wrapped around his throat, trying to choke him. Then she remembered Tanesa tearing at his eyes and scratched as hard as she could. But he squeezed them shut and kept inching away, so she jammed her legs against the big tire, once more trying to drag him out of the truck.

In seconds, she heard boots on pavement. Looking back, she spied soldiers about fifty yards away racing toward her. But here, in the midst of violent struggle, she watched Hamza snag a strap on the backpack nuclear bomb and start to pull it toward him.

She drove her knees into the truck wheel so hard that she might have bent steel. With a shriek, she dragged him out. But the backpack bomb came with him.

Hamza fell on her—with the bomb. She searched frantically for the trigger and saw that it had fallen aside like a loose belt. They both lunged for it. Hamza grabbed the tubular conduit that contained the wiring. But before he could pull the actual trigger to himself and set off the explosion, she threw herself on the device, then curled her body around it—like the soldier in the old war movie who saved his buddies by hurling himself onto a hand grenade.

She felt Hamza claw her arms as he tried to tear them loose. And then the son of a bitch bit her shoulder, right where he'd stabbed her with the nail file. She screamed, wanting nothing more than to unpeel her body to try to stop the pain, but she knew she could not do that, no matter what. *Hold on*, she pleaded with herself, but the agony was so intense that she didn't know if she could stand another second.

And then she felt Hamza torn away from her by the soldiers. She looked up and saw his eyes on her, her own blood dripping from his mouth.

One of the soldiers yelled, "Don't move, Emma. Not a muscle."

Her shoulder throbbed. Blood ran down her arm. But more than anything else, she felt the trigger lodged in her hand.

"Emma, if you can hear me, just wiggle a foot," the soldier said in a calmer voice.

She did.

"That's good. Stay super still. We need to disarm the bomb. Can you stay still for us?"

Crying, she wiggled her foot once more.

• • •

Ahmed handed Ruhi a semiautomatic pistol. Not a Glock, like he'd trained with on the Farm, but when Ruhi racked the slide the motion felt familiar. Ahmed now had Lana's computer strapped across his chest, bandolier style.

Ruhi was the last to head down the three-foot-high ventilation shaft that his cousin had identified as the only means of access to the cyberattack center. There was no way they could enter from the ceiling, not as an invasion force, and no tactical advantage in doing so.

The shaft angled downward, but not sharply, prompting whispered speculation from Candace that it might also have been intended as an emergency exit. She was directly in front of him in the black chador. If she spied chadors when they entered, she would keep it on.

From that point on the two remained silent, moving behind the combined forces of Saudi intelligence and the Mabahith. They were the officers who could be spared with a full-scale takeover of the U.S. embassy in Riyadh still under way—and a possible insurrection by the Saudi "street."

Ruhi heard only the brush of clothing and shoes on the metal floor. To make sure he didn't spill forward as he crawled, he pressed his back against the roof of the shaft, as did the others. It offered a degree of control as they continued their descent.

What worried him most was the absence of a plan beyond Omar's parting words: "Go in firing at anyone who's armed or resisting. We have no idea how many people are down there. Just don't shoot Lana Elkins, and try not to damage their computers. That's not how we're going to shut them down."

Then he'd eyed each of them in the shadows of the community center and added, "No matter how many of us die, we must get Elkins on their network as fast as possible. At that point, our job is done and hers begins."

When Omar had spoken, Candace squeezed Ruhi's hand. Not to ease his fear, he thought, but to encourage him. He'd never been in battle. Never served in any branch of the military. He supposed what she'd done was called camaraderie. He'd squeezed her back, nodding. For him a far greater feeling was in play.

Now he spotted light at the end of the shaft and noticed air sweeping over him for the first time. It came alive on the beads of sweat that dotted his forehead.

The man at the front of their column quietly set a small explosive on the ventilation shaft cover. Seconds later, the device blew up, and they surged into a brightly lit room. The men in front of Candace and Ruhi threw flash grenades, blinding those nearby for several seconds. His own ears felt rocked, stunned senseless, but he heard the overpowering rage of gunfire erupt immediately.

Momentum alone swept Ruhi forward. He felt himself shaking and saw that Candace still wore the chador.

As soon as he exited the shaft, he had to crawl over one of the first men to have braved the cavern. He lay on the floor, eyes open on the ceiling but lifeless. Then, as Ruhi crawled along—guns firing all around him—he passed a wounded man groaning loudly.

Candace, still in front of him, was shooting an M4 carbine that she'd been issued by Omar. Ruhi watched her kill three mujahedeen, then two unarmed Asian computer operators who proved foolish enough to rush her. The chador would disguise her no longer in that part of the cavern.

She and the others were fanning out, targeting shooters who had hunkered down around the cavern, as if digging in for a long firefight.

Ruhi knew there was no time for that. He saw Candace brashly force her way past several more Asian men and women who were cowering under their desks. None threatened her. Maybe they had seen what she had done moments ago. But Ruhi watched them closely as he sneaked up on them. And good that he did: One of the men stood and raised a pistol to shoot Candace from behind. Ruhi gunned him down. Then, without having to think he kept his weapon raised, aiming left and right at the group as he had at the life-size targets at the Farm.

None of the others attempted to retrieve the dead man's gun. Ruhi grabbed it and forced them facedown on the floor. They didn't resist. He knew he should probably kill them—one had already tried to shoot Candace in the back—but couldn't.

Around him, the gunfire continued unabated, and more flash grenades turned the nerve center into a thunderous sky. Then Ruhi spied a man in a turban squirming along the floor toward tall screens in the middle of the cavern.

Ruhi crawled no more than five feet before the jihadist spotted him and raised his rifle. Ruhi fired twice, missing him. Fired again. Missed again, though the bullet might have hit someone, because he heard a man scream the very next instant.

Bullets from the jihadist's rifle flew right by him, so close they sounded like bees buzzing around his head. He threw himself onto his elbows and aimed. As another bullet seemed to part his hair, he fired three more times. The man slumped. With the shadows and screaming, Ruhi had no way of knowing if he'd hit his target or if someone else had shot him.

Now he heard more cries and flash grenades. The uproar was deafening. He looked around. Omar and Ahmed's men were on the move. Ruhi saw clusters of cyberwarriors clinging to one another or hiding abjectly. They might have been stone-cold killers with a keyboard, but few appeared ready for this kind of combat.

● ● ●

Candace spotted a jihadist crawling under desks, dragging Lana toward a Korean man who was protected by two guards. Their leader, she presumed. Candace couldn't imagine that Lana Elkins's life would be spared if these cyberwarriors thought they were about to be defeated.

Still in chador and veil, Candace belly-crawled toward the turban-headed man who had Lana, whose face looked bloody and stunned.

Another flash grenade exploded, and Candace spied them all heading to a trapdoor in the floor, including Lana and the Korean. The guard in the lead opened it, climbing into it quickly. Then he guided the legs of the second guard, who kept his weapon up, covering their retreat.

Candace had only seconds. She waved her left hand, weaponless, at the man in the turban who was dragging Lana behind him. He looked over, saw the chador, and acknowledged her with a nod, as he might a comrade. But that was a feint. He quickly pointed his weapon at her, but before he could shoot, she fired three times, hitting him in the throat twice. But the third bullet hit Lana in the arm. Candace saw her roll away in grievous pain. The agent, though, never paused.

The second guard at the trapdoor scrambled into what must have been an escape tunnel, then helped the leader down into it. Candace lunged forward as the trapdoor started to close. She reached in, felt an arm, and seized it. It had to be the leader's; he had been the last one to climb down.

He tried to jerk free of her grasp and almost succeeded. She knew from his frantic movements that she'd never be able to hold on. Then he bit her savagely. Squeezing his wrist as hard as she could, Candace used her free hand to pull out the gas canister. Gasping from pain—his teeth were grinding into the bones in back of her hand—she maneuvered the nozzle toward her trapped hand and let loose a long blast. The bite ended immediately, and she had no trouble dragging the Korean out from under the door into breathable air. The two guards in the tunnel must have fled as far from the gas as they could, for there was no further resistance from down there.

The Korean now lay in a fetal position, gulping air.

Lana, kneeling and bleeding profusely from the bullet wound in her arm, had found a weapon and trained it on the gassed man.

"Who is he?" Candace asked her.

"Kang-dee Rang," she told her.

"Cease fire," Omar bellowed, drawing their attention.

Candace looked around. Huddles of the dead and barely breathing appeared with each glance. Other members of the assault team rose carefully from all corners of the cavern, pointing their weapons at everyone at once.

• • •

Lana also stood, looking at her arm. A Mabahith medic ran up with a length of tubing and applied a tourniquet. The gunshot wound was so painful she barely noticed the enormous pressure, or the pain from where she'd been punched in the nose and knocked almost unconscious by the man who'd dragged her across the floor.

In her fury, she kicked Kang-dee. "Get him on his feet," she shouted.

The Korean didn't move. His knees were still pressed to his face. Not hard to understand why: Even the little bit of gas that had escaped into the cavern continued to irritate Lana's eyes.

Omar rushed over. "What do you need?" he said to Lana.

"I need to get to his console," she said, already striding to Kang-dee's computer.

Ahmed joined her.

"Hook mine up," she told Ruhi's cousin.

Ahmed ran a cable from her port in seconds.

She checked his work and settled where Kang-dee had held forth only minutes ago. With a groan, she used her right hand to lift up her wounded left arm to the keyboard. But she quickly saw the problem: She couldn't even log on because access was biometrically controlled.

"I need his eye," she said to Omar.

"You want me to take it out?" Omar asked.

"God, no." Lana cringed much as she had when watching that ploy in bad movies. "He's got to actually look into the scanner."

"No problem."

In a moment, Omar, with the help of three beefy officers, had Kang-dee hunched over his computer.

"Look at it," Omar demanded.

Kang-dee refused. Omar seized his wrist and studied a chronograph on the Korean's watch. "Is that right?" he shouted at him. "Less than three minutes?"

Again, Kang-dee offered no reply.

Candace stepped over, jammed the canister nozzle between Kang-dee's lips, and released a tiny amount of the fiery gas. The shock of the gas forced his eyes wide open involuntarily, swollen as they were. Just long enough to gain Lana access to the console.

The equipment was familiar to her, the most advanced in her field. She knew it the way a baseball player knows the basics of any bat. What worried her were all the curveballs hiding inside.

"Do you need anything?" Ahmed asked her, staring at the blood dripping from her left arm.

"Nothing," she replied tersely. Then added, "I'm just getting through the simple stuff right now. This will take a minute. How much time do we have?" she asked as her fingers continued to fly.

"If this is right"—Omar had Kang-dee's wrist again—"less than two minutes."

Kang-dee's swollen eyes opened once more. He nodded and smiled, perhaps finding pleasure in a final measure of torment.

Ahmed shoved a pistol into Kang-dee's mouth. "Shut it down!" Kang-dee refused.

Omar shook his head at Ahmed. The Saudis wanted Kang-dee alive.

So do we, Lana thought. *But less than two minutes?*

Even as she envisioned her next moves, she remembered the nurse handing Emma to her, the first glimpse of her only child. *Don't let me lose her.*

Willing away the pain in her crippled arm, she typed furiously, working to penetrate levels of security not unlike the ones that she had so artfully constructed for her own computer.

It took maybe thirty seconds. Without pause, Lana began releasing malware of every order: worms that she hoped were racing through the heart of each program in Kang-dee's networks, ideally taking the entire system to the verge of collapse. Viruses, too, that she'd tried to adapt to the invisible enemy's possible weaknesses after her brief flurry of forensics following the first cyberattack.

Included in her assault was a distributed denial of service attack, instantly turning thousands of computers around the world into robots working for her, assailing the system in her sights exponentially more quickly in an effort to overwhelm it.

Next, with a few strokes, she released logic bombs to try to erase all the data and software on the cavern's systems.

"One minute," Ahmed said softly.

She winced, unsure what would work—if anything *could*—so she began unleashing every technological trick in her arsenal without pause.

"Thirty-three, thirty-two, thirty-one." Ahmed stopped, perhaps knowing she was fully aware that overwhelming peril was impending.

She was so close to the final keystrokes, so close to executing the reason she had made the long, perilous journey here. So close to firing all the bomblets into his elaborate network.

Don't slow.

Her fingers flew. The only sounds in the entire cavern were the clicks on the keyboard—and the low hum of that nuclear missile silo opening on the screen a few feet away.

Lana had always been a strong typist. Now she was accessing code burned into her brain as it was into the hard drive of so many intelligence agency computers in the U.S.

And then she neared the last keystroke, which could cripple his computers as he had crippled her country—or leave them with no recourse but to witness, from afar, the final destruction of America. She hit it.

Nothing?

She could scarcely believe it.

"Eight, seven . . ." Ahmed said.

And that's when Lana noticed a word in the corner of the screen directly in front of her: "Ahn Yeong." Korean for "good-bye."

She was desperate. Nothing had stopped the cyberattack. The silo was still opening on the screen a few feet away.

Do it!

She hit "Ahn Yeong."

The first thing she noticed was the disappearance of the low hum of the missile silo. She looked up; the shield was frozen. Then she looked down. Her screen was blank. All the screens were blank. Only the lights in the cavern still burned.

Still, she wasn't sure until she looked at Kang-dee. His smile had disappeared, replaced by a look of utter defeat.

Final confirmation came moments later when Omar rushed up, phone in hand:

"You did it," he said to Lana. "Everything has shut down."

• • •

Teresa McGivern and Holmes watched the ICBM shield stop moving. Seconds later one of her aides rushed in. "Pentagon reports say the attack has ended."

Holmes bowed his head to his desk, out of fatigue or a renewed sense of faith, even he didn't know.

Then he turned right back to another screen as two technicians finished disarming the nuclear trigger that Emma Elkins had held for so long to her chest. An Army medic picked her up and carried her away in his arms. The photograph of the young woman, pale and bloody in the dawn, with her arms wrapped around the young man's dark neck, would become emblematic of the hope and pain that now defined America.

The good news didn't stop there. By noon, Eastern Standard Time, Holmes received word from the Russian operative in Sana that Lana Elkins and Ruhi Mancur were in a safe house, having survived the assault on the stronghold of the cyberattack.

A SEAL team from Afghanistan was already in flight. They had been deployed to reclaim the bodies of their brothers. Now they would take home the living heroes as well.

EPILOGUE

SIX MONTHS LATER

A SUNDAY MORNING IN mid-February. Lana glanced at the kitchen clock and called upstairs to Emma, reminding her that they needed to leave in five minutes. After countless funerals and other somber services, they would be driving to D.C. for a joyous celebration at a very special Baptist church.

Emma bounded down the stairs, her National Intelligence Distinguished Service Medal already pinned to her blue robe. She and Tanesa had become the nation's youngest recipients of the honor, awarded in the Oval Office last week. Lana, Ruhi, and Candace had also received the medal, as did Pastor William Sr. and Agent Kalisa Harris posthumously.

When Lana and Emma parked near the big white church with its stately Georgian columns, they saw streams of well-dressed worshippers walking up the stone steps. Greeting them on an easel was a poster-size photograph of the man who had led their Sunday services for more than five decades. Garlanded with flowers, the face of Pastor William Sr. still smiled at each of them.

Emma spotted Tanesa at about the same time as her former caregiver—and now close friend—saw her. They rushed to each other and hugged. Lana didn't always join Emma for the Sunday service, but she would not have missed this one if she'd had to walk all the way from Kressinger. Her daughter and Tanesa were to be feted for their bravery during the worst crisis in the country's history.

Lana's eyes pooled when she saw Tanesa walking for the first time without a limp. Her recovery from the bullet wound to her thigh had been grueling, but then again, she was a gutsy kid. Well-wishers had raised funds for plastic surgery for Tanesa—the scar was five inches long—but she'd refused to accept the help until medical care had been provided to the many others in much greater need.

Lana had postponed cosmetic surgery on her arm for the same reason: The nation was still in a state of triage. And when Candace had apologized for her errant shot, Lana had spoken from the heart, saying, "You saved my life and a whole lot of others. We can leave the small stuff to the doctors."

• • •

The national emergency might not end for quite some time, as Deputy Director Holmes knew all too well. He sat at his desk at the NSA after reviewing a report for the president that summarized the devastation of "Web War I," as the media had dubbed the catastrophe.

The death count stood at a staggering 1.6 million Americans, more than U.S. losses in all of the country's previous wars combined—and the number of dead was still climbing. They had been claimed by explosions, fire, train wrecks, airplane crashes, starvation, widespread panic and rioting, accidents of all kinds, and disease. Before Veepox finally burned itself out, the engineered virus alone killed 540,000 people in the Twin Cities and Chicago.

Forest fires in Colorado, New Mexico, northern California, Oregon, and Washington also burned out, but not before incinerating thousands of houses, many in urban areas. Denver, Colorado Springs, Taos, Eureka, Eugene, Portland, and Spokane were among the cities where large numbers of homes and business turned into cinders. But no area suffered as horribly as Atlanta. The pipeline explosion there burned down half of the Big Peach before the blaze was finally quelled, making Sherman's efforts appear paltry by comparison.

In Phoenix, the meltdown of the Palo Verde Nuclear Generating Station claimed ninety thousand lives. Almost a quarter of them perished during the chaotic and violent flight from the Valley of the Sun as vehicles tore across the desert desperately trying to outrun the radiation. The terror led to shocking slaughter in ring upon ring of suburbs as residents—including heavily armed street gangs—battled furiously over scarce food, water, and gasoline. Then the melting core quietly claimed a much greater toll. The entire region had become America's Chernobyl. People were still blistered and dying from radiation sickness, nudging the numbers upward.

Holmes was to present the report to the president tomorrow morning. He'd be joined by the director of the CIA. Holmes's colleagues in Langley had done their damnedest to recruit Ruhi Mancur for the agency, but the Saudi-born hero would have none of it. He was back at NRDC, which had its hands full trying to keep an environmental agenda alive at a time when immediate survival trumped the nation's long-term health, in the view of Washington officialdom.

Holmes privately cheered Ruhi's decision to stay at NRDC. He didn't think any family should have to pony up more than one agent, and Candace Anders had surely proved that she could carry that load for the new Mancur-Anders clan. They had married last month, and in a private moment at the reception Candace confided to him that they planned to have children soon.

And who knew, maybe by staying with NRDC Ruhi could find a way to shut down the coal companies that had made such a mess with their mountaintop removal. A day didn't go by when Holmes didn't recall the horror of that sludge pond breaking loose far below him—or his feelings of helplessness as hundreds of houses and thousands of lives were swept away.

Holmes also made a point every day of reading a quotation engraved in marble that he'd placed on his desk a few weeks after the attacks. The lines were from Cormac McCarthy's *The Road*: "All things of grace and beauty such that one holds them to one's heart have a common provenance in pain. Their birth in grief and ashes."

Grief and ashes. The country had endured more than its share of both. Holmes was determined to never let that happen again, and he'd been putting in seven-day weeks to try to make certain that the nation's defense was rebuilt as soon as possible. For too many years the most critical first step of fully funding a cybercorps had been thwarted by White House and Capitol Hill indifference. That task had finally been accomplished—in the grimmest possible way—by a renegade North Korean in a hole in the ground in one of the poorest nations on earth.

In the end, Holmes considered that the most telling message of all.

But right now he put aside his official duties to race over to the District. A couple of young heroes were to be honored in a church service, and that pleased him greatly. It also gave him immeasurable faith in the country's future when he thought of what those young women had done in New Jersey. "Can America Bounce Back?" a national news program had asked last week. *How could it not?* Holmes thought, with young people like Tanesa Weir and Emma Elkins coming of age.

ACKNOWLEDGMENTS

I'd like to thank my literary agent, Howard Morhaim, who represents me well and provides valuable feedback on my writing. Thanks also to his assistant, Kim-Mei Kirtland, who ensures that no detail is overlooked.

I wish to also thank David Pomerico and Jason Kirk at 47North for their enthusiasm for my work and helpful advice reviewing my manuscript. I would also like to thank the rest of the 47North team, particularly Britt Rogers and Ben Smith. Thanks also to my editor, Fleetwood Robbins, whose comments encouraged me to rework sections of my novel for the better.

I also want to thank my readers for their encouragement and their word-of-mouth support.

I owe special thanks to two experts in the field of cyber warfare. The first is Richard A. Clarke, who served in the White House for Presidents Ronald Reagan, George H.W. Bush, George W. Bush, and Bill Clinton, who appointed him as the National Coordinator for Security, Infrastructure Protection, and Counterterrorism.

The second is Leon E. Panetta, who served in the Barack Obama administration as Director of the Central Intelligence Agency from 2009 to 2011, and as Secretary of Defense from 2011 to 2013. Among his many accomplishments, he oversaw the U.S. military operation that led to Osama bin Laden's death.

ABOUT THE AUTHOR

Thomas Waite was born in Ipswich, Massachusetts. His debut novel, *Terminal Value*, was critically praised and reached #1 in Contemporary Fiction, #1 in Contemporary Books, #1 Paid in the Kindle Store, and #1 in Kindle Store Suspense at Amazon. *Lethal Code* is his first in a series of cyberthrillers.

Waite is the board director of, and an adviser to, technology companies in online security, media, data analytics, cloud computing, mobile, social intelligence, and information technology businesses. His nonfiction work has been published in a number of publications, including the *New York Times* and *Harvard Business Review*.

Waite received his bachelor's degree in English from the University of Wisconsin–Madison and was selected by the English Department to participate in an international study program at the University of Oxford. He now lives in Boston.